PRAISE FOR M

The Faye Longchamp

WRECKED
The Thirteenth Faye Longchamp Archaeological Mystery

"Absorbing and erudite, *Wrecked* is a powerful new edition to this long-standing, often-awarded series."

—Claire Matturro, *Southern Literary Review*

"…the vivid description of post-hurricane events—the misery, the destruction and despair, the hopelessness of losing so much to nature and to looters—all are graphically and realistically portrayed and lend a sense of reality that is incredibly gripping."

—Bill Gresens, Mississippi Valley Archaeological Center

CATACOMBS
The Twelfth Faye Longchamp Archaeological Mystery

2020—Oklahoma Book Award Winner
2020—Will Rogers Medallion Award Winner

"Fast-paced, well-plotted… Those who like richly textured, character-driven mysteries will be rewarded."

—*Publishers Weekly*

"Overall, a solid entry—based in part on an actual Oklahoma bombing—in a popular series."

—*Booklist*

UNDERCURRENTS
The Eleventh Faye Longchamp Archaeological Mystery

2019—Oklahoma Book Award Finalist

"The Longchamp mysteries combine history and mystery in a gritty way that makes them feel different from most amateur-sleuth fare—dark-edged rather than cozy. Faye, too, is not your traditional amateur sleuth; she could just as easily anchor a gritty thriller series and give some of the giants in that genre a run for their money."

—*Booklist*

"Evans expertly juggles a host of likely suspects, all the while breathing life into the city of Memphis, from its tourist-filled center to its marginal neighborhoods and the spectacular wilderness of the state park."

—*Publishers Weekly*

BURIALS
The Tenth Faye Longchamp Archaeological Mystery

2018—Willa Literary Award Finalist, Contemporary Fiction
2018—Will Rogers Medallion Award
Bronze Medalist, Western Fiction
2018—Oklahoma Book Award Finalist, Fiction
2017—*Strand* Magazine Top 12 Mystery Novels
2017—*True West* Magazine Best Western Mysteries

"This is a highly successful murder mystery by an author who has mastered the magic and craft of popular genre fiction. Her work embodies the truism that character is destiny."

—*Naples Florida Weekly*

"Evans's signature archaeological lore adds even more interest to this tale of love, hate, and greed."

—*Kirkus Reviews*

"Evans sensitively explores the issue of how to balance respecting cultural heritage and gaining knowledge of the past through scientific research."

—*Publishers Weekly*

ISOLATION
The Ninth Faye Longchamp Archaeological Mystery

2016—Oklahoma Book Award Finalist

"Evans skillfully uses excerpts from the fictional oral history of Cally Stanton, recorded by the Federal Writers' Project in 1935, to dramatize the past."

—*Publishers Weekly*

"A worthwhile addition to Faye's long-running series that weaves history, mystery, and psychology into a satisfying tale of greed and passion."

—*Kirkus Reviews*

"Well-drawn characters and setting, and historical and archaeological detail, add to the absorbing story."

—*Booklist*

"Working in Louisiana, archaeologist Faye Longchamp doesn't expect a double murder and pirate plunder, but by now she's used to the unexpected."

—*Library Journal*

"The explosion of the Deepwater Horizon rig in the Gulf of Mexico provides the backdrop for Evans's engaging, character-driven seventh mystery featuring archaeologist Faye Longchamp."

—*Publishers Weekly*

"Details of archaeology, pirate lore, and voodoo complement the strong, sympathetic characters, especially Amande, and the appealing portrait of Faye's family life."

—*Booklist*

STRANGERS
The Sixth Faye Longchamp Archaeological Mystery

"Mary Anna Evans's sixth Faye Longchamp novel continues her string of elegant mysteries that features one of contemporary fiction's most appealing heroines. The author also continues to seek out and to describe settings and locations that would whet the excavating appetite of any practicing or armchair archaeologist. Mary Anna Evans then commences to weave an almost mystical tapestry of mystery throughout her novel."

—Bill Gresens, Mississippi Valley Archaeology Center

"Evans explores themes of protection, love, and loss in her absorbing sixth Faye Longchamp Mystery... Compelling extracts from a sixteenth-century Spanish priest's manuscript diary that Faye begins translating lend historical ballast."

—*Publishers Weekly*

"Evans's excellent series continues to combine solid mysteries and satisfying historical detail."

—Kirkus Reviews

"This contemporary mystery is drenched with Florida history and with gothic elements that should appeal to a broad range of readers."

—Booklist

FLOODGATES
The Fifth Faye Longchamp Archaeological Mystery

2011—Mississippi Author Award Winner

"Mary Anna Evans gets New Orleans: the tainted light, the murk and the shadows, and the sweet and sad echoes, and the bloody dramas that reveal a city's eternal longing for what's been lost and its never-ending hopes for redemption."

—David Fulmer, author of Shamus Award–
winner Chasing the Devil's Tail

"Evans has written a fascinating tale linking the history of New Orleans's levee system to the present and weaving into the story aspects of the city's widely diverse cultures."

—Booklist, Starred Review

"Evans's fifth is an exciting brew of mystery and romance with a touch of New Orleans charm."

—Kirkus Reviews

"Evans's fifth series mystery...reveals her skill in handling the details of a crime story enhanced by historical facts and scientific discussions on the physical properties of water. Along with further insights into Faye's personal life, the reader ends up with a thoroughly good mystery."

—Library Journal

FINDINGS
The Fourth Faye Longchamp Archaeological Mystery

"Evans always incorporates detailed research that adds depth and authenticity to her mysteries, and she beautifully conjures up the Micco County, Florida, setting. This is a series that deserves more attention than it garners."

—Library Journal, Starred Review

"Faye's capable fourth is a charming mixture of history, mystery and romance."

—Kirkus Reviews

"In Evans's fine fourth archaeological mystery...the story settles into a comfortable pace that allows the reader to savor the characters."

—Publishers Weekly

EFFIGIES
The Third Faye Longchamp Archaeological Mystery

2007—Florida Book Award Bronze Medal Winner
for Popular Fiction

"As an archaeological tour alone the book would be worth reading, but it's the fascinating and complex characters that give the story life and vibrancy."

—Rhys Bowen, author of the Constable Evans mysteries

"The best one yet… A fascinating read."
　　　　　—Tony Hillerman, *New York Times* bestselling author

"Though Evans has been compared to Tony Hillerman, her sympathetic characters and fascinating archaeological lore add up to a style all her own."
　　　　　—*Publishers Weekly*

"Starting with racial tension between blacks and whites, Evans adds Native Americans into the mix and comes up with a thought-provoking tale about people trying to live together."
　　　　　—*Library Journal*

"A captivating combination of archeology, Native American tales, romance, and detection. A must-read for those so inclined."
　　　　　—*Kirkus Reviews*

"Like Randy Wayne White in his Doc Ford novels, Evans adds an extra layer of substance to her series by drawing readers into the fascinating history of ancient American civilizations."
　　　　　—*Booklist*

RELICS
The Second Faye Longchamp Archaeological Mystery

"An intriguing, multi-layered tale. Not only was I completely stumped by the mystery, I was enchanted by the characters Evans created with such respect."
　　　　　—Claire Matturro, author of *Wildcat Wine*

"The remote setting engenders an eerie sense of isolation and otherness that gives the story an extra dimension. Recommend this steadily improving series to female-sleuth fans or those who enjoy archaeology-based thrillers like Beverly Connor's Lindsay Chamberlain novels."

—Booklist

"Evans delivers a convincing read with life-size, unique characters, not the least of whom is Faye's Indian sidekick, Joe. The archaeological adventures are somewhat reminiscent of Tony Hillerman's Jim Chee mysteries. While the story is complex, *Relics* will engage the imagination of readers attracted to unearthing the secrets of lost cultures."

—School Library Journal

"A fascinating look at contemporary archaeology but also a twisted story of greed and its effects."

—Dallas Morning News

ARTIFACTS
The First Faye Longchamp Archaeological Mystery

2004—Benjamin Franklin Award for Mystery/Suspense
2004—Patrick D. Smith Florida Literature Award

"A haunting, atmospheric story."

—P. J. Parrish, New York Times bestselling author

"The shifting little isles along the Florida Panhandle—hurricane-wracked bits of land filled with plenty of human history—serve as the effective backdrop for Evans's debut, a tale of greed, archeology, romance, and murder."

—Publishers Weekly

The
PHYSICISTS' DAUGHTER

—··—·—··—·— A Novel —··—·—··—·—

MARY ANNA EVANS

Poisoned Pen
PRESS

Published by Poisoned Pen Press, an imprint of Sourcebooks
P.O. Box 4410, Naperville, Illinois 60567-4410
(630) 961-3900
sourcebooks.com

Library of Congress Cataloging-in-Publication Data

Names: Evans, Mary Anna, author.
Title: The Physicists' daughter / Mary Anna Evans.
Description: Naperville, Illinois : Poisoned Pen Press, [2022]
Identifiers: LCCN 2021056220 (print) | LCCN 2021056221
(ebook) | (trade paperback) | (epub)
Subjects: GSAFD: Mystery fiction.
Classification: LCC PS3605.V369 P49 2022 (print) | LCC PS3605.V369
    (ebook) | DDC 813/.6--dc23
LC record available at https://lccn.loc.gov/2021056220
LC ebook record available at https://lccn.loc.gov/2021056221

Printed and bound in Canada.
MBP 10 9 8 7 6 5 4 3 2 1

*Sameera Moussa, the Egyptian nuclear physicist
who was the first foreign national to be granted
permission to visit secret U.S. atomic facilities*

*Katherine Johnson, recipient of the Presidential Medal of
Freedom for her contributions to space exploration*

*Rosalind Franklin, who used X-ray diffraction to create an
image of DNA that changed our understanding of biology*

Mildred Dresselhaus, the "queen of carbon science"

*Tu Youyou, who won a Nobel Prize for her discovery
of a treatment for malaria based on traditional
Chinese medicine, saving millions of lives*

*Maryam Mirzakhani, the first woman and
the first Iranian to receive the most prestigious
award in mathematics, the Fields Medal*

*Wanda Díaz-Merced, the Puerto Rican astronomer who
discovered "sonification," a means of using audible sound to
detect patterns in huge data sets, after losing her sight*

*This list is admittedly incomplete and idiosyncratic, as there
are far more women I'd like to honor than I can include here.
It is arranged in order of birth date, when available. The
women featured were chosen from a longer list compiled by
the Beyond Curie project (beyondcurie.com), which celebrates
female scientists, mathematicians, and engineers with the aim
of shedding light on their often overlooked accomplishments.*

Chapter 1

Justine Byrne liked taking out the trash. It was her favorite part of the workday.

Her factory work was monotonous by design. She understood that, and she was more or less resigned to it. The whole point of an assembly line was efficiency, and efficiency apparently required a whole lot of people to do the same thing, over and over, all day and every day. Monotony got the job done.

Since the world was at war, and her job was to build war machines that would fly and float the Allied troops to victory, Justine was happy to stand at her station all day and every day, plucking parts off an endlessly moving conveyor belt and bolting them together. Well, mostly happy. Daydreams of romance and faraway places helped the long days pass.

She didn't even know exactly what she was building. It wasn't her job to know, and she had sworn not to tell anybody about it anyway. She just did what she was told, and she did it well. One of the things she was told to do was to take out the trash every afternoon.

On this particular afternoon, Justine carried a wooden crate loaded with soiled packing material and flattened cardboard boxes that were past reusing. Her destination was a lowly trash pen, a square area enclosed by tall wooden fencing that stood behind Higgins Industries' huge Michaud plant. In the Carbon Division, the part of the factory where Justine worked, there was no exterior door other than the big, open loading dock where trucks made pickups and deliveries. This meant she had to go through the main part of the plant to get to a door when she needed to get her trash outside.

Passing through that back door took her away from the cacophony of an industrial plant where boats and ships and airplanes were taking shape. It took her to a swath of pavement bounded by low vegetation, green and shrubby, that stretched all the way to the bank of the industrial canal where barges brought raw materials and carried away finished products.

People who had lived in New Orleans for a good long while called this area east of the city *Prairie Tremblante*, and Justine thought there was a sweetness in the way the French words described the land's understated beauty. She was looking at grassland, yes, but the scene had an only-for-now feeling. If she stepped into the waving grass, she might sink or she might just feel the earth tremble, vibrating at a frequency peculiar to this time and this place. It was a beautiful place to be outside on an afternoon that was cool for late September.

She passed through the trash pen's gate, emptied her crate into a bin, and walked back to the factory door, but she did these things slowly. Fresh breezes and silence were hard to come by for the workers at the Michaud plant, and Justine liked to make the most of them. She used her slow stroll to admire the afternoon sunshine and the smell of damp earth. Then she opened the factory's heavy door, bracing herself for clanging metal and whining machinery. Walking through that door was always like falling into an ocean of sound, but Justine was used to it. She was new to the Michaud plant, but she'd worked at one Higgins factory or another for three years, since she was eighteen.

She guessed she'd never get over her awe at walking past the long lines where Navy boats were built. Those boats, Higgins Industries' original product and still the pride of the company, took shape as they moved across the factory floor, one after another. An entire flotilla of watercraft hung overhead, some of them belly up and some of them belly down, while workers welded and riveted and bolted them together. Beyond them was a row of half-built airplanes getting ready to fly. Their tremendous bulk made the carbon and metal assemblies that she bolted together look piddly and small.

Hanging over those flashy war machines, a banner proclaimed that "THE GUY WHO RELAXES IS HELPING THE AXIS!" Justine could vouch for the fact that Higgins workers had precious few chances to relax.

She knew the sounds of a manufacturing plant so well that she felt something was wrong before she'd traveled ten steps down the boat manufacturing line. Far above the shrieking of saws, she heard shrieking human voices. Accompanying the thunder of sledgehammers, she heard the pattering sound of human feet on the concrete floor. And high overhead, she heard a rhythmic clanging that just wasn't right.

Looking up, she saw a tremendous wooden assembly, probably part of the hull of a PT boat, dangling from the hoist of a gantry crane. The metal beams supporting the crane were supposed to stand still, vertical and strong, but they weren't doing that. They were swaying so hard that their load swung like a pendulum, and Justine knew that this couldn't go on for long. The crane wasn't made to move like that. Justine knew that even steel will fail when stressed beyond its design limits.

She let the empty wooden crate fall from her hands. Her instincts said to run toward the failing equipment and help, but she had taken just a step toward the swaying crane when it collapsed, taking its load to the factory floor where a cluster of three workers stood. Justine saw it take them down.

Trying to walk upstream through the crowd of people fleeing a disaster that had already happened, she raised her voice, hoping someone would hear her over the din. "Somebody get a floor crane. We'll need it to get those people free of the wreckage."

She couldn't tell if anybody heard her, so she kept pushing against the crowd, one step at a time. She knew where to find a portable floor crane, mounted on wheels and stored in a nearby corner. If she got to it, maybe she could get someone to help her move it to the scene of the accident. Through a gap in the throng, she could see it dead ahead. Its blue-painted steel beam called out to her. After a few more struggling steps, she had her hand on it, ready to roll it to people who needed help.

Then a voice sounded over the loudspeaker that Sam-the-Timekeeper used to make announcements.

Sam's voice was calm but insistent. He might be only a time-keeper, but he had an air of command about him. "Everybody to their stations—unless your station is in the immediate vicinity of the accident, in which case we're gonna need you to gather outside the east entrance. We've got a rescue crew on its way."

Justine was absolutely in the vicinity of the accident, and her station was nowhere near where she stood. She needed to do what Sam said and get moving, but still she lingered, one hand on the blue floor crane.

Justine couldn't see two of the injured workers. That was a bad thing, since it meant they were probably under the pile of debris. The third worker had pulled herself to a sitting position, but her leg was trapped under the collapsed crane's steel beam.

Five men ran toward the pile of splintered wood and mangled metal. One of them carried a first aid kit and the others carried hand tools, but she could see that they were going to need much more than that to get the three workers free. She could also see that the first aid kit was woefully inadequate.

Justine knew one of the men slightly, a burly red-haired custodian named Martin, and she waved both hands to flag him down. Gripping the floor crane's supporting beam, she called out, "You'll need this."

Martin skidded to a stop and grabbed one of his companions by the arm. "Help me move this." He directed a tense nod at Justine, saying simply, "Thanks. You saved us the time we would've spent looking for this," then he turned his back on her and got to work.

As they wheeled the crane away, Justine walked toward the door to the Carbon Division section of the plant where she worked. Her legs went unexpectedly wobbly beneath her, so she paused to watch the rescuers at work. They were getting the blue crane into position to lift wreckage off the sitting woman's leg. From this angle, Justine could see the other two workers, and bile rose in her throat at the sight of their still bodies pinned to the floor. There was almost no blood, just a few crimson drips and spatters on the smooth gray concrete beneath them. Justine almost wished for a more obvious marker of calamity to mark the spot.

Broken bodies and death were the very thing Justine and the other factory workers were working to avoid. Everyone on the home front wanted to bring the soldiers home whole and in one piece. Nobody wanted their young, strong bodies to lie limp and still on beaches or in jungles or at the bottom of the sea. Justine saw her job as a real, palpable thing that she could do to end the war. She knew it was dangerous. She knew that there had been industrial accidents at Higgins plants before. She knew that there would be more because entropy dogged all human endeavors, but this was the first time that her day-to-day danger had been rubbed in her face.

Justine ordered her wobbly legs to take her back to her station. She was needed there. She was needed to help stop a war that was consuming the whole world.

Chapter 2

Justine's parents couldn't have known that World War II was waiting like a lion licking its chops outside a nursery school door. Or maybe they did know. They'd lived through the first worldwide war, and they could surely see that humanity hadn't changed very much in the years since the Treaty of Versailles.

They were teachers at heart, so Justine spent her first eighteen years learning things, then she spent the rest of her life being grateful she knew them. By the time she was eighteen, she could cook and sew. She could read German, and she could speak it, too. She could mow the grass with a push mower that ran like a top, because she knew how to grease it and sharpen its blades. Best of all, she could weld.

Girls didn't weld when Justine was growing up in 1930s New Orleans, but her father was never much for rules. He showed her how to stick weld, then he backed off and watched his undersized, freckle-faced daughter make an unholy mess with a rod and a torch. All the while, he whispered things she needed to know if she hoped to make a better mess the next time.

"Justine, honey, watch the puddle," he said as her yellow-orange curls escaped from her tight braids. "And soften your wrist. If you tense up, your weld will show it."

And her welds did show it, until they didn't. But how's a girl supposed to learn, unless somebody's willing to step back and let her try?

Justine's mother was willing to step way back. She stayed busy during those welding sessions, planning lessons that taught Justine things like differential equations and quantum mechanics, things that other people thought girls didn't need to know. Even after she lost her sight, Justine's mother had continued those lessons, carefully explaining the most exacting subjects without a book or notes. If a person is going to do something so stupid as to be born a girl in 1923, she could do worse than to be born to two physicists, even if it did mean that every dinner conversation was a Socratic dialogue and every playtime activity was a demonstration of the mechanical advantages of simple machines.

Justine's parents died before the bombs fell on Pearl Harbor, thanks to a flooded Louisiana back road that hadn't offered enough friction to keep their car from skidding into bayou water so dark that a day passed before they were found. When the war came, the only good thing about it was that it gave Justine a chance to weld for real. She burned to weld her heart out, so that the Axis powers would take a well-deserved fall.

———

Sonny, the Carbon Division's daytime foreman, had gathered everyone on his shift in the open area around the loading dock, the only place inside that part of the factory where hundreds of people could stand together. All those bodies made the air so hot that Justine could barely breathe.

Sonny always wore his braggadocio like an ill-fitting sport coat, but knowing that all of his workers' eyes were on him only made it worse. He preened under the unaccustomed attention. Justine found his grand stance appalling, since he had almost certainly gathered everyone to give them tragic news.

He cleared his throat loudly to quiet the crowd. "I'm sorry to inform you that one of our fellow Higgins employees has died. Her name was—"

He checked a crumpled piece of paper in his hand. "It was Cora Becker. Al Haskins is in the hospital, but they say he's doing good after his back surgery."

He checked the paper again. "Yolanda Bergeron's gonna make it, but they're doing an operation on her leg right now, so say some prayers. Say some prayers for all of 'em."

He paused, mouth agape like a man who has forgotten what he meant to say. Justine could see it on his face when the words came back to him. "Mr. Higgins has been in touch with their families. And…um…he says that he's coming to the plant a week from Sunday. He wants to say some things to y'all about how grateful he is for what you do here every day. And I'm sure he wants to say nice things about Cora, Al, and…Yolanda. Yeah, Yolanda."

A tall woman next to Justine bent her head as if to send up a prayer for Cora, Al, and Yolanda. Then she raised her eyes to look at Sonny again, and their expression gave no doubt as to what she thought of their boss. Justine noticed an elegantly coiled chignon at the nape of the woman's long, tanned neck. She'd seen that hairdo before. This was Georgette Broussard. Justine didn't know her, but she automatically liked her because of the irritated way she looked at their foreman.

Sonny stood before them, obviously pleased that he'd remembered all three victims' names this time. He closed his speech by saying, "So get back to your stations, but know that Mr. Higgins himself is proud of you. Me, too. I'm proud of you, too. Now go build some stuff."

So they did—except for Justine, because Sonny walked over and grabbed her by the elbow.

"I need you to weld something. I don't know what's going on with the lateral guides, but this is the third one I've needed you to fix for me this month."

————

Ships and planes and mysterious assemblages that are probably still classified or should be…the time came when Justine welded them all together. But in late 1944, the only welding jobs she got from Sonny were quick patch jobs that the real welders were too busy to bother with. Justine wanted to be one of the real welders, so she took Sonny's patch jobs with a smile. She was theatrical about it, too, making a big fuss about doing her safety checks and donning her goggles, hoping that somebody might notice that she could be dropped into a high-paid job in aircraft assembly without needing to spend six weeks in welding school.

Justine occasionally fantasized that she would get one of those jobs and her supervisors would be so happy about the way her flawless welds always held—always!—that they would keep her on after the war was over, but she was a realist. Higgins Industries was well-known around wartime New Orleans as a place that hired women to do work that they usually weren't allowed to do. Black people, too. But everybody knew what would happen when the soldiers came home.

She, along with a lot of other people working themselves to the bone for an Allied victory, would be back to slinging hash and mopping floors, with the best possible outcome for Justine being that she was slinging hash and mopping floors for a husband who paid the bills. Or so everyone wanted her to believe. Maybe Justine would believe them when she met the right man, but she'd never met one yet who made her burn to start her day by scrambling his eggs.

By the time Justine welded that third lateral guide, donning her welding goggles with a look-at-me-I've-got-valuable-skills flourish was automatic. This left her mind free to chew on an interesting problem.

Why did the same part keep breaking?

Not the exact same part. Her first weld of a broken lateral guide had been solid, and it had held. So had the second one. It was just that one lateral guide after another was failing. She pondered this problem as she laid down her usual beautiful bead.

Was the problem poor design? That seemed unlikely, since Higgins Industries had been using the same brand and model of conveyor belt for years

Metal prices had skyrocketed as soon as the war broke out. Maybe the parts manufacturer was cutting corners. This was possible, even likely.

It seemed far-fetched, but she supposed that somebody could be deliberately tampering with the equipment. Mr. Higgins employed thousands and thousands of people, and sometimes people got mad at the boss. But would anybody really take their anger out on the manufacturing machinery when there was a war on? People's lives depended on the things Higgins Industries built.

The constantly broken conveyor belt served just one line at one factory among hundreds of wartime factories across the country, but it was hers. Justine's cousin Fred was in the South Pacific, and last she heard, her childhood playmate Harold was somewhere in Africa. She couldn't go help them. All she could do was work her monotonous assembly job, fastening two pieces of bright, shiny metal together and making them ready to be joined to pieces of meticulously machined carbon.

Justine coveted the machinists' jobs almost as much as she coveted a welding job. The Carbon Division was just two weeks old, but the division's handpicked machinists were quickly acquiring legendary status. There they stood, long lines of workers, mostly women, using their drills and grinders and lathes and saws to shape pure carbon to exacting specifications.

And in return for that detailed work? Each and every one of them pulled down good wages. A man's wages. A skilled man's wages.

The machinists generated tons of coal-black dust. Or at least it seemed like tons of coal-black dust. There was always an unholy cloud of carbon over their heads, as black as a Louisiana thundercloud. As a result, the Carbon Division was tucked into a back corner of Higgins's Michaud plant, surrounded by a wall built to contain all that dust.

After her first day on the job, Justine had run to the bathroom to rinse her face before getting on the bus, but she'd quickly found that nothing short of a full bath with soap and hot water would get all the carbon dust off. The black powder was a badge of honor, showing everyone that she'd been chosen to work on something special. It clung to her face, her neck, even her ears, making her oddly proud of being dirty at the end of the day as she hustled through a cavernous factory building to make it to the bus on time.

The carbon dust found its way inside the navy blue canvas coveralls that were supposed to protect her street clothes. It penetrated those street clothes. It was an all-pervasive nuisance. Still, the dust said, "I'm doing my part to bring our soldiers home."

She couldn't imagine how the machinists ever scrubbed the dust off after standing right at the source of it for a full shift. At quitting time, they looked like they'd been painted with the stuff.

Maybe it was permanent. Maybe, over time, it would soak into their skin like a tattoo.

Justine wanted to look like that. She wanted it to be obvious at the sight of her that she, a woman, had skills that were needed. She also wanted to fatten up her nest egg as a defense against the day when she was once again stuck supporting herself on a store clerk's paycheck.

Justine didn't just envy the carbon machinists' paychecks. She envied them for their specialized knowledge of whatever-in-the-heck she and her friends were making. They'd been told they were making radio parts, and maybe they were, but they were the weirdest-looking radio parts she'd ever seen. The company had been supremely close-lipped about its brand-new Carbon Division, even while focusing its attention on big things that flew and floated. Justine had been sworn to secrecy when she took the new job, which seemed strange for radio parts, but that was the nature of military contracting. Everything she'd ever done for Higgins had been secret. The only thing that had been different about this job was that the man training her for it had been *really* serious about the oath of secrecy. Maybe three years at war had just made everybody jumpy. These days, the Army probably made everybody in its vicinity take an undying oath of silence, even if they were just building latrine seats.

All that secrecy probably made the broken lateral guides seem more serious than they were. Still, any disgruntled employee targeting this assembly line was targeting her livelihood. Worse than that, the sabotage targeted Fred, Harold, and millions of soldiers, airmen, and sailors. She looked around at her coworkers. Some of them she liked and some of them she didn't, but she couldn't imagine any of them doing such a thing. It was far more likely that the repetitive stresses and strains of long hours of service were simply snapping the metal at a vulnerable point.

In any case, she had to make it whole so that the assembly line could keep running. Jerry, the Carbon Division's maintenance chief, did the best he could, but metal parts were hard to come by after years of war. He had no spare parts to speak of.

She vowed that she would do whatever it took to keep the line running, no matter what. Probably, that vow just meant that she would weld anything that broke. If somebody was breaking things on purpose, though, then she would find them, and she would find a way to put a stop to it.

Justine kept her wrist soft and watched her puddle while she plotted a betrayer's downfall.

Chapter 3

Mudcat pondered his options. He didn't have many eyes inside Higgins Industries' Michaud plant, other than his own. And he needed more eyes.

There was only one place in the plant that he himself couldn't go, but it was the most important place of all. He'd been able to put just one person behind the doors hiding the Carbon Division from him. His operative had valuable skills, but there was only so much snooping around that one person could do without being obvious about it. One person couldn't pass through every closed door or chat up every worker making classified gadgets, not without getting caught. One operative simply wasn't enough support to accomplish Mudcat's mission. He needed somebody else. So far, he had failed to secure that person.

This was an unprecedented failure. Mudcat had amassed considerable expertise in identifying people with potential. His superiors had noticed, and this had kept him in their good graces.

It all came down to finding each target's soft spots. Then, when the time was right, he poked them. A love of money was the most obvious soft spot—and, in the end, doesn't everybody love money and want more of what it can buy?—but his targets also needed the ability to deceive everybody around them. Precious few people had the wits to do that. Most of all, his targets needed a sense of adventure that drove them to take risks, just for thrills.

When faced with the right recruit, Mudcat could smell an adventurous soul. At the moment, he had his eye on an orange-haired woman whose eyes were full of thoughts she didn't share. He sensed that she had the wits to be a great agent if he could find the right words to make her say yes.

Mudcat patrolled New Orleans like a bottom feeder patrolling a muddy river, ready to gulp down any information that served his cause. He had liked the image of the bottom feeder so much that he'd gone to the waterfront and chatted up fishermen, asking the names of the fish that lurked at the bottom of the broad, brown river that carried cargo from the Port of New Orleans to a world at war.

Their tales of the mudcat, a carnivorous fish that grew to the size of a full-grown human being, had intrigued him. He'd listened to the fishers talk until he could say "mudcat" with the varied vowel sounds of speakers from all around southern Louisiana, from Irish Channel neighborhoods to rural Cajun towns to the Ninth Ward. He'd even heard a soft Uptown accent that had made him wonder what twists of fate had led the man from a patrician home to a life of grinding work on docks smeared with fish guts. For a moment, he'd considered recruiting the misplaced man—as an informant, at least—because people who have had money and lost it will often do anything to get it back. And then the smell of last night's rum had penetrated the odor of fish entrails and explained the man's hard fall. Mudcat couldn't risk taking on an operative who wasn't fully in control of himself, so he'd shoved the idea aside and just listened to the man talk. His dialect was easy on the ear, but not nearly so interesting as the harsh tones of the hardworking people around him.

Mudcat had chatted with the fishers and dockworkers for hours, crouching on a wet dock watching wet men do wet work. The full size and power of the river came home to him there, as he stood at the waterline and looked up at oceangoing vessels. Trees uprooted by an upriver flood floated past the spot where he stood. They dwarfed him, and the ships dwarfed them.

He'd enjoyed his day on the docks. Even better, it had helped him firm up his grasp of the local dialect in both English and French. Losing the last traces of his German accent was going to be a lifelong challenge. Perhaps it was better to say that he would be spending his life learning to submerge his mother tongue, pushing it into the depths of his brain. The German language would always be there at the riverbed of his innermost self, where his subconscious mind would feed on it like a broad, silent mudcat, but hard work and close listening would hammer its sounds and idioms into something that sounded like America.

To be a truly great bottom feeder, a spy needed the improvisational ear of a jazz musician. Self-preservation demanded it.

———

While Mudcat was crouching by the Mississippi River, a man who sometimes called himself Fritz walked through Higgins Industries' cave-like Michaud plant. He was pretending to work as he gazed up at half-built boats and planes. It was almost unbelievable what people could do when properly motivated. And, by proper motivation, he meant fear. Fear of attack, fear of destruction, fear of violent death—these were the driving forces behind the orgy of construction that had resulted in all of these war machines. Soon, they would roll out of the plant, fully built and ready for battle, and the next crop of war machines would be sown.

Day by day, Fritz watched them come together, memorizing every detail that his superiors would want to know, so that he could go home and commit them to paper, but a stout wall stood between him and the workers of the Carbon Division. He couldn't breach it. He had placed a single half-witted agent behind those doors, but two eyes were not enough to see all of the things that Fritz needed to know. He needed more eyes, and he needed those eyes to be set into a skull that also housed a functioning brain.

So far, Fritz had failed to secure the agent he needed—eyes, brain, and all—but perhaps his luck was about to turn. There was a woman with a sharp-eyed face that called to him. She kept to herself, which was an excellent quality in an agent, but her silent presence was not sullen. She watched. She considered. Her lively eyes missed nothing. He was aware of her whenever she was near because the flame-colored cloud of her hair drew his eye. Her glorious hair meant nothing in terms of her value as an agent, but if Fritz had a soft spot, it was his deep-seated appreciation for beauty.

Soon the whistle would blow to signal quitting time. Fritz would see her exit the restricted area of the Carbon Division and enter the main part of the plant. He would watch her walk past him, crowned with a golden-red cloud, and he would meditate on how he might convince her to do the things he wanted her to do.

Chapter 4

"Got a problem, sugar?"

Justine liked having a job, so she didn't turn to the lecherous Sonny and say, "I have a problem with you calling me 'sugar.'" Instead, she just stared at him and let him read her mind. Some of her female coworkers had given her private attagirls when she failed to kowtow to Sonny and his ilk, but others had taken a "Who does she think she is?" view of the matter. Those other women were not Justine's friends, but then Justine didn't have many friends.

"Got a problem, *Justine*?" Sonny made a face like her name tasted bad.

Sonny called men by their last names, so she wanted to insist that Sonny call her "Byrne," but she decided it was wiser to stay quiet and savor her victory over his attempt to label her his "sugar." In the two short weeks since she had transferred to the Michaud plant and started working under Sonny, she'd already learned that nothing good came of poking too hard at his vindictive streak.

Sonny carried a chip on his shoulder the size of Lake Pontchartrain. Children can be cruel, and Sonny's clubfoot had probably earned him years of playground insults when he was a little boy, so maybe he'd always nursed a long list of grudges. Now that his foot was keeping him out of the military, he was an easy target for folks who resented any man under forty who wasn't in uniform. It wasn't fair, but if people were always fair, maybe there wouldn't be wars at all.

There was a reason Justine was talking to Sonny, and she couldn't let the fact that he was an unpleasant person get in her way. She needed to tell him that somebody might be fouling up the works. If she brushed elbows every day with a coworker who was upset with the company, her boss should know it. She opened her mouth to tell him what she was thinking, then she closed it again.

"Got something to say, Justine? You look like a catfish on the hook when you flap your lips open and shut like that."

She didn't like Sonny looking at her lips—nor talking about them—but she opened and closed them a few more times, hoping to distract him from the fact that she was thinking hard. What if Sonny was the worker who was upset about how the company was treating him? Maybe he wanted a raise and didn't get it. Maybe he didn't like his job in the Carbon Division, supervising a crew that was mostly women. Maybe he wanted to be out in the main part of the plant, bossing around the people building flashy things like airplanes, and maybe the plant manager had turned him down. Maybe the plant manager had told him to get comfortable in this job, because he was going to be working it for the rest of his life. Somebody like Sonny would want to strike back at anyone who told him no.

It would have been so easy for Sonny to tamper with the conveyor belt and its lateral guides. She supposed he might even have found a way to tamper with the crane that had killed Cora Becker. Any time Sonny got in the mood to do something that he didn't want anybody to see, he could just assign the people working nearby to another part of plant, out of his way. He could even tell them to clock out early, which he had done three times in two weeks and which Justine and her pocketbook deeply resented.

The gossips among Sonny's crew thought that he was sneaking a few minutes with a girlfriend when he did that, and Justine thought that they were probably right. But why should she miss a quarter-hour's pay because Sonny wanted to run around on his wife? Now, though, she wondered whether he might be using that time to hurt a lot more people than Mrs. Sonny and their kids.

She dropped any idea of telling Sonny about her suspicions. He was still looking at her, waiting to find out why she'd walked up to talk to him.

"Um...I need to go to the bathroom."

"You just went an hour ago. Mr. Higgins ain't paying you to shit, and he especially ain't paying you to pretend like you're shittin' while you sneak a cigarette."

Justine stammered, "It's not that. It's..." She let her voice trail off while she moved her hands slightly, as if to cradle a cramping belly. Then she stood there and let him imagine menstrual blood.

Sonny flushed to his hairline and barked, "Why, oh, why do they gotta make me work with women?" Turning his back on her, he pointed to the big clock on the wall, the one everybody watched as its hands inched closer to quitting time. "Go, but be quick about it, because I'll be watching the time. And if you smell like cigarettes when you come back, you're fired."

Justine didn't smoke, because her parents had convinced her that pulling hot vapor and particulate matter into her lungs wasn't smart, but she wasn't all that quick about coming back from the bathroom, either. She wanted a few quiet minutes to think. If she couldn't go to her boss and say something simple, like, "I think somebody's sabotaging our equipment," then what were her options?

The security guards, at least the ones she'd met, would listen half-heartedly and then say, "Don't you worry, little lady. We'll take care of things."

Justine knew this, because that was exactly what they'd said when somebody filched five bucks out of the pocket of her coworker, Candace. A week had passed, and Candace was still short five dollars. If somebody had told Justine that one of the guards had picked Candace's pocket himself, she would have believed it.

She knew most of the guards. She really liked one of them—Charles, a quiet, bookish man who spent a lot of time flirting with her without actually asking her out. She just wasn't sure Charles or any of his fellow security guards cared much about...well, about security. They clearly weren't worried about the security of the Carbon Division's work because they could never be found in that part of Higgins's vast Michaud plant. They spent their time patrolling the areas where the big, flashy war machines got made.

If Higgins Industries didn't see the Carbon Division as important enough to give it any security guards of its own, then Justine was going to have trouble getting anybody's attention with a few broken conveyor belt parts that truthfully weren't very hard to repair. It wasn't like she and her coworkers were building aircraft to top-secret designs. They were just assembling radio parts that probably weren't critically important to anybody but them.

Taking her fears all the way up the ladder to the plant manager crossed Justine's mind, but she wouldn't have known him if he'd walked up and bit her. It would have made as much sense to try to get face-to-face with Andrew Higgins himself as to get face-to-face with the Carbon Division's plant manager, who was his son Frank. She'd at least *seen* Andrew Higgins (from a long, long distance), and she would know him if she saw him again because he had the stocky shape and overstated swagger of a robber baron.

His son had been one of those little men trailing along in the big man's shadow, and she had no recollection of what he looked like.

She'd even heard Andrew Higgins's voice, which she supposed made her feel like she knew him, when she most certainly did not. Mr. Higgins liked to get on the plant's loudspeaker and deliver his own version of FDR's fireside chats. He sounded almost fatherly, if a voice with the hucksterish bravado of a master salesman could be fatherly.

Andrew Higgins had a habit of inventing things that moved Allied troops where they needed to go, even when getting there seemed impossible. This was why the war had exploded his seventy-five-person boatbuilding business into a military con-tracting outfit that employed twenty thousand souls at plants spread across New Orleans and into the Louisiana countryside. He had better things to do than worry about one conveyor belt that wouldn't stay fixed. The truth of the matter was that Justine didn't know how to get the attention of anybody she trusted to help her.

What to do?

For about thirty seconds, Justine thought about paying her godmother a visit. Gloria was a physicist, and Justine held a deep-seated belief that physicists knew everything, probably because it had always seemed to her that her parents did. As did Gloria.

Unfortunately, the big problem with the idea of talking to Gloria was the fact that Justine hadn't seen her in the three years since she'd buried her parents. While they'd lived, she had breathed in air that vibrated with talk of rockets and radio waves and the endless potential of the atom. Gloria was just one of the geniuses who had surrounded little Justine. Now, the chances that Justine could ever be part of that world were slim to none.

Paying her godmother a visit would mean a morning spent talking about how much Justine was going to enjoy college. It would mean a morning spent reminiscing about the days before most of Gloria's scientist friends had moved to Chicago and San Francisco and New York, with so many others now unreachable in Germany. It would mean a morning spent talking about her parents, and every word would carve a hole in Justine's heart.

Talking to Gloria was a last resort, and Justine wasn't desperate. She just didn't have a plan yet, and now was not the time to make one. She needed to vacate the bathroom and get back to work before she gave Sonny an actual reason to sack her.

———

Sonny greeted her with a glare and an unoriginal but hostile phrase.

"Nice of you to join us."

She didn't return the sarcasm with a retort of her own like she wanted to, but she didn't flash him a kiss-up grin, either. The truth was that Justine didn't know how to handle Sonny. Her parents had done an excellent job of teaching her Newtonian mechanics, before moving on to more up-to-date topics, but they had neglected more practical matters.

Justine didn't know how to flirt. She'd had no idea how to fit in with the daughters of socialites who had been her classmates at a girls' school that had probably lived up to its reputation of being the best in the city, but which had felt more like a finishing school for future wives. She still had no idea how to deal with handsy men or clique-ish women. Justine was more comfortable with books than people, but this didn't mean that she liked it that way. She just hadn't figured out how to attack this problem yet.

———

The rest of Justine's shift passed without her line shutting down again due to broken equipment. When the whistle blew, she mumbled, "I want to see how that weld's holding," in case anybody was wondering why she was pulling a light and a stool up close to the conveyor belt. Sonny was nowhere to be seen, so perhaps he really was sneaking around on Mrs. Sonny.

Everybody else was in going-home mode. Nobody gave a hoot when she donned a headband-mounted magnifier and studied one of the lateral guides that she'd welded back together. In a few minutes, the next shift of workers would be in place, but it wouldn't take her long to look for signs of tampering.

Or to be more accurate, almost nobody gave a hoot. Justine nearly jumped out of her skin when she felt warm breath on her cheek and heard the words, "Who ya think done it?"

She fumbled with the magnifier strapped to her head, which had tried to fly off when she flinched away from the lips approaching her ear. They didn't try to kiss her on the neck while they were in the neighborhood, so they must not be Sonny's lips. The voice was low, but by the time Justine had jerked her head away from it, she'd realized that the speaker was a woman. This didn't tell her much, because all the workers on her line were women, and none of them were in love with Standard English. Any of them could be asking her this loaded and ungrammatical question.

She turned her head, and there at her elbow stood Georgette Broussard. A tall and broad-shouldered woman about Justine's age, Georgette had hazel eyes set in a striking oval face, with tanned and freckled skin stretched over a chiseled bone structure. Her customary brunette chignon seemed overly elegant for a manual laborer, but Justine knew that it served the same purpose as her own frizzy ponytail, which was to keep her hair out of her work. Georgette talked like she'd moved to New Orleans from bayou country, slow and hoarse with a faint Cajun accent. Sh lived at Justine's rooming house. And this was precisely all that Justine knew about her. Caught off guard, she didn't know how to answer the woman, so she just sat there on her stool like a possum playing dead.

Seeing that Justine wasn't going to respond, Georgette spoke again, quietly. "Gumming up the works, I mean. Who ya think keeps breaking things and shutting down the line? Can you tell by looking at it with that magnifying glass thing you got strapped to your head?"

Justine didn't think that feigning ignorance was going to get this woman to back off, but she didn't know what else to do, so she tried it. "I'm not sure what you mean."

Georgette reached out a hand and tapped the close-cut nail of one calloused forefinger on the scar where Justine had mended the piece of metal. Still whispering, she asked, "Somebody's done that on purpose, no? This is the third time one of them things have got broke. That ain't normal wear-and-tear. No, ma'am."

Still feeling that she should be noncommittal, Justine said, "I certainly hope it's not normal wear-and-tear. We can't be sending our boys off in boats made out of parts that break every time they turn around."

Not that they'd be riding in boats made out of conveyor belts that needed lateral guides. And not that the Carbon Division made boats, or even boat parts. But the boats that were built in the rest of the Michaud plant would need radios, and Justine and Georgette had been told that they were building radio parts, so Justine thought her point was still valid. Or at least it was valid enough.

They eyeballed each other for a long moment. If one of her colleagues actually was vengeful enough to be sabotaging their work, Justine wasn't anxious for that person to know she suspected something. She and Georgette had already said quite enough while standing on the factory floor where they could be overheard, so she raised her voice and said something that was safe enough for anybody's ears.

"You live in my rooming house, don't you? On the first floor, right? I'm on the second floor, just at the top of the stairs. I'll be cooking myself a late supper tonight. I've got a can of tuna and enough macaroni to feed two. Want to join me?"

"You got tuna fish? Oh, yeah. I'll be there. I got a can of evaporated milk and a tea bag. Let's make ourselves a feast."

Chapter 5

Justine and Georgette were nearly out the door that shut the Carbon Division off from the rest of the plant when Sonny called out, "Justine, honey, can you come here a minute?"

Justine said to Georgette, "You go on home without me," and turned back. She was already running late for the bus, and now Sonny was going to make her miss it.

Justine hadn't blinked at the long bus ride when the company offered her a transfer to work at the new Carbon Division. At least Mr. Higgins had figured out that it would be hard for his workers to get home, so he was running buses to get them back and forth from New Orleans to the Michaud plant, way east of the city. If Sonny made her miss the bus, she'd be in a pickle.

Sonny led her into his tiny "office," which was really more like a freestanding shed with walls that stopped far short of the roof of the hangar-like factory. Now that she was inside, she could look up and see the flat ceiling sitting on top of those walls. It kept out some of the ever-present sound of machinery, and it kept out some of the inescapable black dust, so it wasn't completely useless.

Sonny's office held two straight-backed chairs, a desk with

a black phone, and a black typewriter. It also held the black filing cabinet that he needed to keep up with his employees' pay records. And that was about it. Sonny was not high enough on the management ladder to get anything luxurious like a swivel desk chair or, God forbid, a couch where he could try to get close to his mostly female employees.

Justine didn't like the idea of being behind a closed door with Sonny, but she didn't know what to do about it. She'd heard stories about how he behaved with women when he thought nobody was looking, and his behavior was quite frankly bad enough when people were around. If the stories were true, Sonny didn't need a couch to misbehave. She took her seat in the chair across the desk from him and leaned hard against its back, putting every possible molecule of air between them.

He flopped into his chair, then leaned so far across the desk that his chest was almost resting on it. His hair grease had let go sometime during the long, hot workday. Now, his straight brown hair hung over his forehead, which seemed to be sweaty all the time. Carbon dust clung to the sweat on his pasty forehead, and it clung to his greasy hair. Looking at Sonny made Justine realize that she, too, was covered in grime. She wanted a bath so very badly.

Sonny wiped his unkempt mane back with a meaty hand while he stared at Justine. She crossed her arms over her chest, trying to look strong but thinking she probably looked defensive and small. Heck. She *was* small. She wished for her welding torch or even a red-hot rod.

"Where'd you learn to weld, anyway?"

"Papa taught me." She was careful not to mention that her father was dead. Men like Sonny kept an ear out for evidence that a woman had no male protector.

"Well, you look mighty cute holding that rod. And that flaming torch."

Justine had some thoughts about where she might like to put that flaming torch.

"Papa taught me to be really careful with a torch and rod. He said that the minute you forget you're holding something deadly in both hands is the minute you hurt yourself bad. Or somebody else."

"I bet your mama was real scared when she found out he was teaching you to do something that dangerous."

"Mama had her own torch, but she used it for glassblowing. She made all the vacuum tubes for Papa's lab because nobody else's work met their standards."

Well, now she'd spoken of her mother in the past tense, which was one step from admitting that she was dead, but Justine couldn't see that this information made her any more vulnerable to Sonny than she already was. For all he knew, her father was alive and huge.

Sonny's face said that the words "Mama" and "vacuum tubes" didn't belong in the same sentence. He changed the subject.

"Why d'you think the conveyor line keeps going down? Did somebody do a shit job of putting it together? You're doing a right fine job of patching things up, but why do them parts need so much patching, anyhow? Is somebody sending us trash for parts? Is that crazy deadline Mr. Higgins gave us too much for the machines?"

Listening to Sonny list possible reasons for the malfunctioning equipment, she realized that there was one reason he hadn't mentioned. It was so far-fetched—so very unlikely—that it hadn't occurred to her when she'd been thinking through possibilities on her own. In wartime, however, it was very real.

Espionage.

Sonny was stupid, but he wasn't so stupid that he'd never watched a spy movie or a newsreel. Besides, they'd all been thoroughly trained to keep an eye out for enemy agents trying to get their hands on military secrets. Justine had thought at the time that her trainer was being unnecessarily melodramatic, but perhaps not.

Maybe Sonny had thought he was being real smooth by not mentioning that somebody might be sabotaging their line. But, somehow, leaving something so obvious off his list called attention to its absence. She'd lay odds that Sonny was wondering the same thing she was, and he was trying to pick her brain without admitting it. Maybe he was smarter than he looked.

Should she tell him what she'd seen through the magnifying lens? The scratches on the broken lateral guide had been lined up in an orderly row, and nature wasn't orderly. The scratches had also been deep. If scratches like that had been caused by faulty machinery banging against itself, the racket would have been deafening. Those scratches had looked to Justine like the result of human activity, which was why she'd wondered whether a disgruntled colleague could have been at work.

If she had to guess, she would say that somebody had been hacking away with a small rasp held underneath the moving belt, sawing blindly while trying not to let anybody around see what they were doing. The rasp wouldn't have cut all the way through the metal, but that wasn't the goal. The person using the rasp had trusted that the conveyor belt's everyday vibrations would finish the work. Even better, it would do so after the saboteur had moved away from the scene of the crime.

She opened her mouth to tell Sonny about her worries. He was her supervisor, after all. He was the person she was *supposed* to tell about problems at work. After a second's thought, she closed it, at the risk of hearing Sonny tell her again that she looked like a catfish.

Maybe he was worried, just like she was. But maybe he was

fishing for what she knew, because he was the one doing the sabotaging. If he was working for the Axis, or what was left of it since Italy fell and Normandy was invaded, knowing too much could put her in real danger. She thought of Cora Becker and decided to keep her mouth shut.

He sat there looking at her with his tiny armadillo eyes. Sometimes, a lot of times, those eyes crawled up and down her body. Right now, they were fixed on Justine's face. He wasn't thinking about her body at all, and that wasn't normal for Sonny.

He really did want to know what she thought about the broken equipment. What was she going to tell him? Justine decided that, just this once, it was a smart idea to be a brainless broad. She gave him an elaborate shrug.

"I don't know, Sonny," she said with a voice that chirped like a bird. "It's gotta be bad luck. What else could it be? Sometimes things break, y'know, and nobody knows why. Lucky for you, you've got me to weld the pieces back together. But unless you're planning to make me a full-time welder, and pay me like one, I really need to go catch the bus. It's not like I can afford to call a cab."

She rose to leave and, to her surprise, he rose with her.

"The bus has gotta be gone by now," he said, moving around his desk. "I'll take you home. Get your things and let's go."

She hurried to get out of the office and away from Sonny, but he was fast for a man whose foot was keeping him out of the Army. He was at her side in two limping steps, his heavily muscled arm brushing hers as she walked past the Carbon Division workers gathering to start the next shift. They were looking at her funny. And at Sonny, too.

Sonny was supposed to be standing with them. It was his job to brief the incoming foreman on how his shift had gone. For example, it would be really useful for him to know that the equipment kept breaking. Instead, Sonny was completely focused on getting Justine alone in his car.

She was dizzy from watching Sonny whipsaw from one personality to another. Was he a masher intent on getting his hands on her body? Was he a concerned boss? Was he a spy intent on silencing her? She didn't know, but she would rather jump off the Huey P. Long Bridge into the muddy Mississippi than spend more than half an hour alone with him in his car.

But there was something else that could be even worse than that hellish half hour. If Sonny took her home, he was going to know where she lived, and that just couldn't happen.

These thoughts bumped around in her head as Sonny frogmarched her toward the plant exit, hardly pausing long enough at the door between the Carbon Division and the main plant for her to clock out. Their footsteps echoed on the concrete floor, competing with the constant din of sledgehammers and drills. The Michaud plant was fitted with the latest of everything, from state-of-the-art cranes to safety devices like overhead sprinklers. Sitting in a shed mounted on a platform high over the factory, far more visible than the actual plant manager, Sam-the-Timekeeper monitored it all and minded the factory whistle that told everybody when to come and go.

Justine quailed at the thought of passing throngs of workers in the company of this sweaty slug of a married man. All eyes would be on her, but nobody would be thinking, "This doesn't look right. We should help that woman." They'd all be thinking, "She'll be sorry for taking up with that man. Whatever he does to her will serve her right."

Just when she thought her only escape would be to feign violent nausea, salvation appeared in the form of a tall woman with a familiar brunette chignon. Georgette had been waiting in the alcove outside the ladies' room. Even better, she knew enough about Sonny to bring reinforcements. Charles Trahan, Justine's security guard friend, and Martin Bevans, the red-haired custodian, stood on Georgette's right, and Jerry Jenkins, who ran the Carbon Division's maintenance shop, sat to her left in his wheelchair.

Justine hadn't known Jerry before she came to Michaud, but they had chatted now and then when she needed some welding equipment. She'd worked with Charles and Martin for longer, first at the St. Charles plant and now at Michaud. It was disorienting to see them with their chests puffed out and don't-cross-me expressions on their faces.

Dark-haired, pale, lanky Charles looked more like a librarian than a brawler. He was the only man Justine had ever met who wanted to talk books with her, but his interest in her seemed to begin and end with friendship. Justine's mother's marriage had been built on books and beakers, so she'd pooh-poohed the idea that men didn't like smart girls. Justine was beginning to think that her mother might have been wrong, but she hadn't been willing to smother her interests when she talked to men. Or maybe the truth was that she hadn't been able to do so.

Unlike Charles, Martin did look like a brawler. He was a little smaller than broad and stocky Sonny, but only a little. The women of the Carbon Division swooned a little when Martin walked past, but he paid them no mind. The flirty chattiness he'd directed at Justine was more attention than any of the rest of them had received. As a result, Martin's staunchest admirers didn't like her much.

Towheaded Jerry had the impressive upper body musculature of a man who used his arms to lift himself out of bed and into a wheelchair every morning. If Charles reached out a long, thin arm and grabbed Sonny, then Martin helped hold him still while Jerry sat in his chair and whaled on him, the three of them just might be able to take out her big, slimy foreman.

As it turned out, it hardly mattered whether the three men offered sufficient protection. Georgette wasn't the type to hold back and let the men take charge. She left them glowering behind her when she stepped out of the alcove, moving into Sonny's path like a linebacker executing a flawless block.

"Here ya go, Justine," Georgette said, holding out a damp cloth. "I carry a few washrags in my bag every day, so I can wipe myself down in the restroom before I get on the bus. When I got time, of course. That dang bus wouldn't wait for Mother Mary herself, so sometimes I can't stop to clean up."

"I bet the bus is long gone by now," Justine said, steadfastly refusing to look at the man beside her.

She put the wet rag to her face and it was cool. It soothed her skin and it soothed her rattled mind. God bless Georgette.

She tried to think through her next move. Georgette had deliberately missed the bus because Justine needed her, but now they were both going to be trapped in a car with Sonny. Georgette might be physically impressive enough to keep either of them from being groped or worse, but he was still going to know where they lived.

Georgette's voice penetrated the fog of Sonny-based thoughts. "Come see. You remember Mavis? She lives in Gentilly, and her husband's on a ship in the South Pacific, same as my brothers. She's taking us home."

Mavis, a plump, pale woman with coal-black hair and bright blue eyes, waved as she hurried toward them. "There you are! There's a spot in my car with your name on it. And another one with Georgette's name on it, too!"

Before Sonny had recovered enough to speak, Justine had been hustled away, Mavis holding one of her elbows and Georgette holding the other. Charles, Martin, and Jerry, strategically positioned around Sonny, wore broad smiles as they waved goodbye.

Justine reflected that the Army was a poorer place without Georgette taking care of its logistics.

"Oh, Mavis," Justine said. "I can't let you drive me all the way home."

Mavis brushed her words away like mosquitoes.

Justine tried again. "My place isn't anywhere close to yours. Even the nearest streetcar stop is too far from Gentilly for you to drive. Just get Georgette and me to a city bus stop. We can ride home together from there. We'll take care of each other, so we'll be safe."

What she meant, but did not say, was that she couldn't let Mavis burn the gasoline it would take to drive all the way to her rooming house. Justine could give her gas money to pay for the fuel, but she couldn't give Mavis a ration stamp that would let her buy more, because she didn't have one.

Mavis fluttered her tiny, dimpled hand at Justine. "Don't you worry, not one little bit. My car hardly sips any gas at all."

Considering the size of the battered Buick that Mavis was unlocking, Justine doubted that.

Mavis was still talking and her hand was still fluttering. "I've got stamps for all the fuel I'll need till I get another ration book. And if I should happen to run out of gas before I run out of month, I can ride the bus. I only bring my car because it's easier to get the kids to my mama's house so she can watch 'em while I work."

She interrupted Justine in the middle of her chorus of "No no no no, don't you worry about us! You go get your kids."

Mavis's fluty voice cut through Justine's protests. "Justine, honey, let me just say it straight. You may have to ride with a two-year-old in your lap, but I am taking you all the way home. I'd burn every drop of gas I can get for the month, and for next month, too, just for the look I saw on Sonny's face when he figured out that you weren't depending on him for a damn thing."

At the word "damn," Justine saw Georgette's head whip around toward Mavis, who apparently didn't make a habit of cursing.

Mavis giggled and said, "When Denny gets home, he's going to be surprised that I know how to say words like that. But he'll get used to it. I just hope he don't tell Father Gautier. Denny don't scare me, but Father do."

Chapter 6

Justine chatted with Georgette and Mavis all the way across New Orleans as they debated which of their would-be saviors was the most handsome. Justine thought it was Charles, which prompted Georgette to say, "Shoulda known you'd go for the bookworm type." Mavis cast a vote for Martin and his muscles.

Georgette was decidedly in favor of Jerry. "I worked with him for a while at the City Park plant. He's always smiling, and he's always got a kind word for everybody. And nobody ain't ever built a machine that Jerry couldn't make sing."

"Since Jerry hasn't given me the time of day," Justine said, "I will generously give him to you." The other women laughed at her silly joke, and all of a sudden Justine felt like a social butterfly, albeit one who was very, very tired.

She'd enjoyed her time with Georgette and Mavis, and she had thoroughly enjoyed Mavis's three giggling toddlers, but she was ready to be cocooned in her room the very instant Mavis parked in front of The Julia Ladies' Residence. Her rooming house was one in a row of old townhouses that had seen better days. Its handmade bricks were cracked and the black paint on its shutters was peeling, but it had a sound roof that Justine was happy to have over her head.

Exhaustion overwhelmed her as she stumbled out of the Buick's rusty blue passenger door. She was glad for the chance to pause on the sidewalk, waving goodbye to Mavis while Georgette crawled out of the back seat. Then she plodded up the old stone stairs and through the rooming house's front door.

Georgette looked as tired as Justine felt, but she managed a few sentences. "I don't hear no water running in the pipes. Both the downstairs and upstairs bathrooms are empty, I bet. Go upstairs and get clean, and I'll do the same down here. Then I'll come up with that can of milk. And the tea bag. I'm real excited about that tea bag." Then she vanished down the hall and left Justine alone in the rooming house's shabby parlor.

The Julia Ladies' Residence was not actually on Julia Street, but Julia Street was in its general vicinity. Justine could see it from the front steps if she tried hard. The fact that The Julia Ladies' Residence had been named as if there were any prestige still associated with Julia Street in 1944 said something about the rooming house, and it wasn't good.

The Julia provided the necessities, and only the necessities, in exchange for its modest room rent, which bought four walls, a ceiling, a floor, a bed, a chifforobe for clothes storage, a bathroom down the hall, and nothing more. No, actually, that wasn't true. There were amenities. Justine was trudging right past some of them. She moved through the parlor, where you could entertain a gentleman caller, if you didn't mind an audience and if the man was willing to be gone by nine. In front of her was the shared kitchen, which had a refrigerator where you could keep food if you never cared about seeing it again.

You could even pay for maid service, if for some reason you had extra money for such things but were still willing to live at

The Julia. A room the size of Justine's could be cleaned in ten minutes with a mop, a washrag, a bucket, and some soap, so that's what she did. The money she saved on maid service went toward getting her sheets, washrags, bath towels, and carbon-encrusted work clothes washed at the laundry down the street. She washed most of her nicer clothes and her unmentionables out herself in the bathroom sink.

As she climbed the stairs, Justine was thinking that "unmentionables" was a silly word. When a thing existed, people needed to be able to talk about it. A thing that couldn't be mentioned was a thing that flickered in and out of existence depending on whether somebody was looking at it.

This idea was so much like the paradoxes that had kept her parents and their friends up all night that it made her smile. For one instant, she could hear them yelling and laughing and talking over each other in excitement, and it felt like no time had passed at all. For as long as she managed to hang on to the idea of underwear that both did and did not exist, her parents were real and physical and alive. Pondering things like paradoxical underpants had kept Justine's mind distracted through many an hour on assembly lines, but years of rejection handed out by her less scholarly schoolmates—not to mention their hated nickname for her, "Justine Brain"—had taught her to keep thoughts of underpants in Schrödinger's boxes to herself.

One of her parents' friends—was it Gloria?—was a passionate devotee of Erwin Schrödinger's work, so Justine had a working knowledge of his imaginary cats and their deadly boxes. She had worked her way through a thought exercise where she took the cat and the vial of poison out of one of Schrödinger's boxes, then put in a pair of underpants and a cigarette lighter to keep company with the radioactive source and the Geiger counter. Could she ever know whether the underdrawers were burned to a crisp or untouched? Probably not without opening the box and collapsing their parallel realities. Pondering this question collapsed the loneliness of her own reality, at least for a while. This was why she loved physics so much.

She slid her long, old-fashioned key into the keyhole and unlocked the door to her room. Justine worked six long days a week, so she mostly just slept there, but she spent her few non-working hours combing through her parents' old books and her own. Fate had stolen her chance to go to college, but that didn't mean that she couldn't have an education. She kept her books on shelves she'd built of boards and bricks that she'd found at the dump. The makeshift shelves held all of her valuables, which mostly consisted of books and food. Food would never outweigh books for Justine, but she'd learned the hard way that it's brutally hard to feed yourself when money's short and everything worth eating is rationed. Without a refrigerator of her own, or even an icebox, she'd found that it was well-nigh impossible, but she managed.

In short, Justine lived on food that came in cans and boxes. She cooked it on a hot plate, and she usually ate it alone but not tonight. She was embarrassed to admit to herself how happy she was to have someone who wanted to share a meal with her, someone who could be a real friend. Mavis, too, could be a good friend, and she would never have met Mavis if Georgette hadn't introduced them.

She hoped she'd done the right thing when she slipped three dimes into Mavis's purse to help her pay for the gas she'd burned while driving to The Julia. For all she knew, those dimes were a slap in the face to a woman who had done her a big favor.

Great. Now she was going to worry about the dimes all night.

———

The rooming house's upstairs bathtub was old and its finish was worn, but it was deep. And the water was hot, even if it did make a preternatural racket when it ran through The Julia's ancient pipes. Justine always bought the least expensive soap she could find, because she didn't like to feel guilty about using a heckuva lot of it. The cheap soap and her cheap scratchy washrags did an excellent job of peeling off each day's carbon dust.

She hurried to dry herself and put on a clean blouse and dungarees, because she was hungry enough to smell the tuna sitting in its can behind her closed bedroom door. She hoped Georgette had been quick about her bath, too.

Once Justine was back in her room, she'd hardly had time to hang her bath towel to dry when a knock sounded. She let Georgette in and immediately got an answer to her question about the dimes. Georgette set the tea bag and evaporated milk next to Justine's hot plate, while simultaneously saying, "You done a nice thing. I saw. Good for you for helping Mavis out without making her feel embarrassed."

"She left her handbag sitting on the front seat between us," Justine said, admiring the tea bag. "It wasn't hard to sneak a few cents in the outside pocket."

"Yeah," Georgette said, "Mavis can drive me around all she wants once the war's over. Right now, her kids need milk and bread, and they can't wait for groceries till their mama gets her next paycheck. When I saw you slip her that money, I said to myself, 'I knew I liked that one.'"

"Yeah? Well, I saw you save me from a long car ride with Sonny. Not to mention that heavenly cool washrag you handed me. Thank you. I'll wash it and get it back to you."

Justine had wiped at herself with that little bit of terrycloth all the way home. After a while, she'd probably just been moving black dust around, but the damp cloth had soothed her, body and soul.

Her new friend said simply, "You're welcome. I know I like a washrag on my face at the end of a long, hot day, so I thought you'd enjoy it."

"I did," Justine said, grabbing a saucepan. "You've gotta be hungry. I'll go down the hall and get some water for the macaroni, then we can get this feast started."

———

While Justine was gone, Georgette opened the package of elbow macaroni and found a measuring cup on the shelf where Justine kept her food. She carefully measured out two servings and not an elbow more. Then she found a can opener and got the lid off the tuna without spilling a drop of its tasty oil.

She knew it would take Justine just a few minutes to fetch the water, but that left enough time for Georgette to look at her new friend's pretty books. Their covers called out for her to touch them. Wrapped in beautiful materials like burnished leather and a rainbow of linen, their spines were stamped with shiny gold titles like *The Physical Principles of the Quantum Theory* and *The Theory of Spectra and Atomic Constitution.* Georgette's encounters with books had been limited to worn-out schoolbooks, paper-back romances, and *The Holy Bible.* She'd never seen anything like Justine's library.

Georgette thought that words like "quantum" and "spectra" were beautiful, but they were as incomprehensible to her as the titles of books from foreign countries. And some of Justine's books *were* from foreign countries. Their gilt-inlaid titles said things like *Einführung in die Theorie der Elektrizität und des Magnetismus,* which she thought was probably German. Georgette knew people back home in Des Allemands whose grandparents spoke German. One of hers spoke French, two spoke English, and one spoke

Choctaw, but nobody in Georgette's family spoke German. She couldn't read a lick of Choctaw, but she could speak it. As for the written word, she would have had a shot at understanding what Justine's books were talking about if the words printed on them had been French, because her French-speaking grandfather had handed her down a few treasured picture books in that language.

She pulled *Introduction to Theoretical Physics* off the shelf, since the word "introduction" suggested that it was a place to start. Inscribed on the inside cover, she saw the name "Isabel Byrne" and she supposed that this must have been Justine's mother's name. She'd heard that Justine's parents were dead, both of them, which she thought was about the saddest thing she'd ever heard. She didn't know what she would have done without her own parents to help her get started in the world. What must it be like to have a mother who owned such books? And to lose her so young?

Georgette hurriedly slid the book back into place, afraid that Justine would come back and see her handling her mother's things.

———

The bathroom was just down the hall and around a corner, but it was in use. Justine hovered in the hall until her turn came, then she filled the saucepan and headed back to her room.

Georgette was waiting for her with a measuring cup full of macaroni.

"Have you been working at Higgins long?" Justine asked, dumping the noodles into the water and setting the pot on her hot plate.

"A coupla years. I remember seeing you at the St. Charles plant right when I started, so I'm thinking you got more seniority than me, but not much, because I'm thinking we're about the same age.

After a while, they sent me to the City Park plant. I worked there till they sent me out to Michaud to be a Carbonite, same as you."

Justine heard pride in her voice when she claimed the company nickname for Carbon Division workers. Justine felt the same way. Their jobs didn't seem like much next to building a boat or plane, but there was still something special about being hand-chosen for the Carbon Division. The long bus trips to her new job would go quicker now that she had Georgette to talk to while they rode.

And Georgette was quite a talker. Justine found her easy to be with, which was a relief. Justine hadn't been popular with her classmates, and she'd never been sure whether they'd shunned her because she was smart and gawky, or because she wasn't worth knowing.

When the macaroni was done, Justine drained the cooking water into a mixing bowl, leaving the noodles in the pot. Then she dumped in the tuna and stirred in the milk, holding back enough to give them both a splash for their tea. The fishy concoction looked horrendous, but it smelled good.

She set the pot back on the hot plate to warm everything up again, and said, "I guess you're like me—you rented a room downtown…sorta downtown…just so you could walk to work at the St. Charles plant. And now you're working as far east of the city as you can get without falling into Bayou Sauvage."

"The Julia seemed like a good place to be," Georgette said. "Back when I was working in town, it was close to work, like you say. When I first got hired, it was hard to know where I oughta live, since I ain't from around here. You can't be surprised about that, 'cause anybody can tell it by the way I talk. I ain't never ever been to a city, nor been this far from home, before the day I took this room. To tell you true, I'm from so far down the bayou that Des Allemands is a big town to me." She put her hand over her mouth. "I can't believe I told you that."

Justine shrugged, trying to make the motion say that it wasn't even worth mentioning that Georgette wasn't a big city girl.

Georgette lowered her voice and said, "Don't you tell nobody this next thing, now."

Stirring the milky tuna-and-macaroni, Justine mumbled, "Yeah, sure," not sure what kind of revelation to expect. It must be truly embarrassing, because the woman was blushing, but Georgette had already admitted that she'd never before traveled thirty miles from home. Justine didn't care that Georgette had lived her life way out in the country, but Georgette obviously did.

With her eyes on the toes of her saddle shoes, Georgette made her confession. "Don't you tell nobody, but I like the bus ride. To work, I mean."

Justine, who was heartily sick of sitting in a stuffy bus full of people after just two weeks of doing it, couldn't think why anybody would like that long ride. She blurted out, "But why?"

"I just like it. I can handle a boat—I took my pirogue to school every day, soon as I was old enough—but I never rode in many cars or buses before I moved into town."

Justine wished with her whole self, right down to the soles of her feet, that she could take back that "But why?"

Georgette didn't seem offended. Mostly, she just seemed intent on saying out loud something that she'd been keeping to herself for two weeks.

"I like the sound of the bus motor and the way the tires hum on the road. I like the feel of the warm wind coming in the window. I even like the smell that comes outta the tailpipe and the smell rising up off the hot blacktop road. I like the pretty old buildings in the French Quarter, all pink and beige and cream like flowers, and I just love it when we stop on a street corner and let people get on the bus. It gives me time to sniff the coffee smell coming outta people's windows and the fish smell coming from the docks and the sweet fruit smell coming from the markets. I like seeing the shops and the office buildings while we roll through the new part of the city. Then the countryside comes, and the bayous make me think I'm back home for a few minutes. I see the white water-birds flapping into the sky and I wonder if my mama's looking out the back door at a flock of birds just like 'em, rising up outta the switch grass behind the house. And then the bus runs around a bend, and I see the big Michaud plant straight ahead, looking so new and up to date. Working for Higgins makes me feel like I'm a part of the wide world, and the bus ride is what takes me there. You understand that feeling, don't you?"

Justine nodded.

"Taking this job woulda been worth it," Georgette said, "even if I never got paid a penny, because Papa brought Mama to come help me pick out a place to stay. That means she finally got to see the city, after a whole life of raising babies. I love my mama, and I want a husband and a family someday, but not now. I don't want to live like she lives for my whole entire life. Am I wrong to want to live in a beautiful place like this for now? What if I never get another chance to be my own boss?"

Now that she'd gotten the words out, Georgette looked embarrassed enough to run and hide, but Justine thought she was the one who should be embarrassed. Many evenings, she'd sat in her little room and remembered a childhood spent in her parents' comfortable modern home. She'd tried not to be bitter about having to live in one room in this aging Victorian heap, but most of the time, she had failed. And all the time she'd been feeling sorry for herself, Georgette had been looking at the same shabby rooming house and seeing something else entirely.

In Georgette's eyes, The Julia Ladies' Residence was beautiful.

Justine looked at the floor, time-worn but still made of mahogany. The boarded-up hand-carved fireplace and the plaster moldings on her room's soot-stained walls showed that this had once been a fine home. A mansion, even. Georgette still saw it that way. Tears of shame pricked at Justine's eyes.

"I don't think you're wrong," Justine said. "To wait to get married, I mean. If I can have what my parents had, then I want a husband and a family. But I listen to the women we work with, and they tell me that their husbands don't want to hear what they have to say. They want wives who look good and talk sweet the whole time they're putting a nice dinner on the table and cleaning up afterward. If there's nothing more than that on offer, then I'll earn my own way, thank you very much."

"Now you're talking," Georgette said.

Justine ran her hands through her damp hair, loosed from its ponytail. "Maybe life as a housewife isn't in the cards for me, anyway, since I'm not much of a cook, and I don't like to clean. And I sure as heck can't do those things while looking sleek and put-together. Look at this stuff!" Her fingers were trapped in tangles of carrot-colored curls. "It's not possible for me to look like a movie star wife. I'll just have to be happy living all by myself in one room. And I will, as long as it's mine."

"If it makes you feel any better, you got a friend downstairs."

Now the tears were really coming. Justine mumbled, "That sounds good."

As much as she liked her new friend, she wasn't willing to let Georgette see her weep openly, so she grabbed the mixing bowl where she'd dumped the water from cooking the macaroni.

"I'm gonna go get rid of this," she said, although she knew and Georgette knew that this chore could wait until after they ate.

She pointed blindly at the shelf where she stored her plates and silverware, saying, "Go ahead and dish out the casserole. I'll be right back."

And then she fled.

When Justine returned, carrying an empty mixing bowl, her manner was briskly normal. Georgette wasn't fooled. She'd seen Justine's tears, and she knew what they were. They came from a hundred different hurts that never seemed to stop piling up. Today, some of those hurts had come from spending time with the odious Sonny, but some of them had come from having to live without parents like the ones who had left those beautiful books behind.

While Justine was down the hall, dumping the macaroni water, Georgette had carefully spooned fishy mush into neat piles on two of Justine's plates. The plates matched each other, with a spray of wheat and sunflowers adorning the center of each plate, and they weren't chipped or scratched. Unless Georgette missed her guess, these plates had come from Justine's childhood home, and so had the simple and sturdy silver-plated flatware. Probably the saucepans, too.

Georgette had laid their meal out neatly on a wooden table tucked into the corner of the room. It had so many scrapes and scars beneath its green paint that Georgette couldn't imagine it in the same house as the pretty china. Justine must have walked out of her home with the things she could carry, and no more.

"That looks really nice," Justine said, surveying the table. "Oh, wait. I forgot to get us some water to drink with our dinner. We should save the tea for dessert."

Justine grabbed two amber pressed-glass tumblers and disappeared again. Georgette thought the tumblers looked like the kind of glassware that came free in flour sacks and oatmeal boxes. Her own mother treasured a set of ruby-red glasses and plates that she'd spent years plucking out of her cornmeal. Little Georgette had loved to sit in her mother's lap and listen as the neighborhood women traded glassware, each of them haggling hard to achieve the dream of an entire table set with pieces that matched. Maybe Justine's mother had done the same thing, but Georgette doubted it. More likely, Justine had eaten her way through many boxes of oatmeal to earn her amber tumblers since she moved to The Julia.

When Justine returned with the glasses full of water, they settled themselves in two folding wooden chairs, both of them as green and as battered as the table. Georgette said grace, then they dug into the hot tuna casserole as if it were a gourmet meal and neither of them had a care in the world.

Chapter 7

Justine sat across the table from a brand-new friend, sipping tea and talking about possible espionage.

"Somebody's sabotaging our work," Justine said. "Doesn't it seem that way to you?"

"That's what I think. You think somebody's mad at the company and wants to get back at Mr. Higgins? Somebody with a temper, like Sonny?"

"Maybe. But maybe it's an enemy doing the sabotage."

"To stop us from getting our work done?"

"Or maybe just to slow us down. The Allies could have the best army, the best navy, the best bullets, and the best bombs, but we'll still lose the war if the enemy beats us before we beat them. In my head, I know that all of this is true, but it's just really hard to make myself believe in something as far-fetched as Axis spies right here in my hometown."

Justine took a sip of her tea, to which she'd added a splash of milk and nothing else, since neither of them owned a granule of sugar.

"I got five brothers and two parents that ain't got ten years of schooling between them all." Georgette paused to breathe in the scent of her tea. "Four of my brothers are off fighting, and the other one's home wounded. It woulda helped my folks if one or two of 'em coulda stayed home, but the Marines wanted 'em bad. So bad they sent recruiters to the house. And they wanted to go. Taking this job means I can do my part to end the war, same as them. If somebody's trying to undo my work, then I gotta say that I take it personal."

Now that she realized how truthful her new friend had been when she called The Julia a beautiful place to live, Justine also realized how generous Georgette had been to share her milk and her tea bag.

"Sending money home to my folks to make up for my brothers not being around to help with the fishing and farming is the least I can do," Georgette said, gesturing with her teacup. "They all worked theirselves ragged to help Mama and Papa keep me in school through the eighth grade."

She eyeballed Justine, as if to see whether she thought an eighth-grade education was an accomplishment or an embarrassment. Justine tried to look impressed that Georgette had finished junior high. The more she heard of the woman's story, the more impressed she actually was.

"Mr. Higgins ain't finished high school, either," Georgette said, lifting the cup to her mouth. "Heard him say so myself. He said he got kicked out of every school in Omaha. Anyway, I've got enough schooling to know that there ain't such a word as 'ain't' or 'theirselves,' and I know how to make my subjects agree with my verbs, but talking like you talk would make it sound like I think my family and the way they talk ain't respectable enough. I save my good English for when I want a job or when I need to impress somebody. The rest of the time? I say what I want to say, and I cuss when I feel like it. I'm a grown woman who earns my own way, and I can do that if I want to."

Justine gave Georgette's statement the respectful moment of silence it deserved, and she used that time to think about the ways that people keep their loved ones close. She finally said, "I suppose I hang on to my grammar and big words, even when nobody around me gives a damn how I talk, because it keeps my parents alive when I sound like them."

Justine savored the taste of the "damn," which her mother and father would absolutely not have countenanced. Somehow, being with Georgette gave her permission to curse, and it felt good.

Georgette smiled at her in a way that made Justine think that maybe she didn't quite have the hang of casual cursing yet. She said, "My folks was raising five boys in a four-room house when I come along. The bathroom was a two-hole outhouse. Still is. All the water we needed for drinking and cooking and bathing came from a pump out back. Still does. When I outgrowed the little bed in Mama and Papa's room, they had to figure out what to do with a little girl in a house full of men."

"Did they put you in the outhouse?" Justine hoped this joke was funny.

To her relief, Georgette laughed. "Almost. They put me on the sleeping porch. It had screens to keep the bugs out. I had a paper fan to cool myself off in the summer, and I came in and slept between Mama and Papa on those few nights in the wintertime when it got bad cold. Most of the time, my porch was a nice place to be, all by myself with good-smelling air and the sound of the night animals moving around in the dark. You know...raccoons and possums and such. The night noises here in the city aren't near as pleasant."

Justine thought of the night sounds outside her window at The Julia. People were on the street at all hours, talking and laughing and sometimes arguing. Once, there had been a horrible scream, followed by the pounding sound of someone running, and the

women of The Julia had gathered in the parlor while their land-
lady, Mrs. Guidry, called the police. The next day, they had learned
that the screaming woman was dead and her husband was in jail.
By contrast, Georgette's sleeping porch sounded about as peaceful
as Justine's childhood bedroom had been, one door away from
the room where her parents had slept. The difference between
her upbringing and Georgette's, of course, was that Justine's childhood bedroom had had walls. Georgette had essentially slept
outdoors for her entire life before moving into The Julia.

Georgette reached out and brushed a gentle hand over Justine's
chenille bedspread, cheap and acid-green. "That's so pretty. You
bought it new at the store, I bet."

Justine nodded, somehow embarrassed to have had a couple of
bucks to spend at a going-out-of-business sale. Here sat somebody
who needed her job even more than Justine did, yet Georgette was
willing to risk it by talking to her about the possible saboteur at
their workplace. That willingness spoke of someone with a clear
sense of right and wrong.

The skeptical side of Justine, the part that was trained to think
by scientists, entertained the possibility that Georgette needed
money badly enough to sell out her country for it, and this made
her realize that she no longer resisted acknowledging that somebody might be doing just that. Maybe *Georgette* was the saboteur,
and maybe she'd approached Justine to see how close she was
getting to the truth.

Justine tried to think like a German spy looking for somebody
to infiltrate a munitions plant. Or maybe a Japanese spy. Would
somebody working for what was left of the Axis be able to see
Georgette's potential, or would they write her off as the product
of eight years in a rural school full of poor people like her?

In Justine's judgment, the enemy would use one of those
reasons to dismiss Georgette as worthless. Also, in Justine's

judgment, the enemy would be wrong. She decided to trust the woman in front of her.

"If my parents were here," Justine said, "they'd be able to tell me why those radio parts that we Carbonites are building are worthy of sabotage. I don't know what the answer is, but I have some ideas."

"Now that I hear you talking, I remember hearing about some strange doings in other parts of the Carbon Division. Missing hand tools. Busted cables. Things like that."

"That doesn't sound good," Justine said.

"There's a lotta things about the work we're doing that I don't understand. I mean all of it. I don't understand nothing, starting with what we're making that's so black." Georgette waved a hand at the hook where Justine had hung her carbon-stained bath towel to dry. "I ain't never seen nothing on a boat that looks like the parts we're building, *chère*. And I might as well have got born on a boat."

It was touching to see how badly Georgette wanted to understand why Justine thought that Axis spies could possibly be interested in the Carbonites and their work. Justine had so much trouble explaining her ideas that they stayed up long past Mrs. Guidry's curfew, despite the fact that they'd both worked a ten-hour day. Justine used the time to explain—well, start explaining—mid-twentieth-century theoretical physics to a junior high graduate. Her pupil was sharp and savvy, but her knowledge of the world beyond southern Louisiana was spotty. The invisible worlds of subatomic particles and electromagnetic waves might as well have been nonexistent.

"You gotta make allowances for what I don't know," Georgette said. "Now that I live in the city, I'm trying to make up for lost time. I get to read the paper most days, and never mind that I can't afford the penny to buy it with. People throw 'em away. Even if I find one in the trash that's a day old, it's still worth reading when you got lots of catching up to do."

"You've seen newsreels?"

"One time, I saved up and saw a movie. The newsreels that showed before the main feature were the best part. It was like—" Georgette paused, unable to come up with words that were big and grand enough for what she wanted to say. "It was like I was *there*. On the deck of a ship like the ones my brothers are on, watching planes flying overhead. They kept coming, one after another after another. The war's awful, and I wish they was home safe, but just think. They're seeing the world. They're seeing miracles."

"But you had heard about such things? You had radio growing up?"

"My Uncle Herb did. We'd all go over to his house to listen to the president talk. It seemed like magic to hear his voice come out of that wood box. It's amazing to me that I'm helping build parts for one of them magic boxes. Tell me something, though?"

Justine, dazed by the blizzard of words, just said, "Sure thing. What do you want to know?"

"Why're we making radio parts for the Army? Or is it the Navy? I'm never sure who we work for, not really. Maybe they think our soldiers and sailors will fight more better if they can enjoy music on the radio? That don't make a lick of sense."

Justine was glad that the conversation had wound back around to the original topic.

"Well, soldiers and sailors and pilots need to be able to talk to each other, and radios are good for that."

Georgette's jaw fell open. "You mean—" She tried again. "You mean I could talk into a radio, and the president could hear me the way I hear him? And he could talk back? Like a telephone, except without wires?"

"I mean exactly that. Well, if you had a transmitter—" Georgette looked blank, so Justine tried again. "You could talk to President Roosevelt if you had the kind of radio that would let you talk back and if you knew how to tune it to reach him. And if he was listening to that frequency when you called."

"Damn." Georgette took a sip of her pale tea, brewed with a tea bag that had already made a cup for each of them. "That would win a war."

"It would win a war if the other side didn't have it, too. Since the Axis powers do have radio, having radios just means we're keeping even with them. I can't imagine that making more radios at this stage of the war is a do-or-die proposition."

Justine paused. A lot of the things she'd heard at her parents' parties were probably still classified, but she knew that she'd seen newspapers that mentioned the word "RADAR," and describing technology that had been brand-new when her parents were talking about it with their friends. "I've heard a rumor about a new bomb sight under development. I've wondered if that's what we're building, but I think it's more likely that we're making parts for RADAR installations. The technology is new and it keeps changing, so it only makes sense that the military would keep building newer and better equipment for as long as the war lasts."

Georgette didn't even have a vague grasp of what RADAR was, answering, "Ray-what?" when Justine asked what she knew about it.

So Justine had backed up and explained it. This was harder than she would have expected. She tried several strategies for explaining radiolocation, but Georgette finally lit up when Justine explained how bats moved in the world.

"Some scientists at Harvard," she said, "have shown that bats find their way in the dark by making squeaky sounds and then listening to the way the sound bounces off things and comes back to them."

Justine thought those words seemed simple enough to do the job, and the concept wasn't all that complicated. She looked at Georgette for signs that she understood what Justine was trying to say.

"So it's like when you're outside at night and you can tell how far away the trees are by the way your voice sounds?" Georgette's wide smile said that Justine had finally found the perfect explanation for a woman who'd had to find her way in the dark every time she'd gone to the outhouse at night.

Justine grinned and nodded.

"We're building parts for a machine that can do that?"

"Yes, I think so. Well, close. RADAR—that's R-A-D-A-R, all capital letters, and it stands for Radio Detection and Ranging—uses radio waves instead of sound waves."

"I'm just close?" Georgette smacked her flattened hand on the rickety little table where Justine had spread a half dozen books. It shook on its uneven legs. "You can't just once let me be right?"

"When you're right, I'll tell you."

"Mighty nice of you. But I do get your point on how useful it is to know where your enemies are. And just think of being able to find out from a far distance, where they can't shoot at you. That could…"

As Georgette's voice trailed off, Justine could hear the rest of the sentence. *That could save my brothers' lives. That could bring them all home.*

"You're not wrong about sound. Sound waves are useful, too. Bouncing sound off things that are underwater is a good way to find submarines. It's just that I don't think we're building parts for echolocation." She didn't recall seeing anything about echolocation technology in the newspapers, so she didn't come out and say the word "SONAR," much less try to explain the acronym.

By the time Justine had shown Georgette the 1942 article in

Popular Mechanics that had almost given away the British early warning system's secrets, Georgette was fully briefed on how important it was to know where planes and ships were and how fast they were moving. And also about how important it was to keep the enemy from getting the same information about the Allies' vessels. She had also lent Georgette her old algebra book and walked her through the first few lessons. Georgette had been thrilled by Justine's offer to teach her as much math as she wanted to learn, so thrilled that she let out the kind of squeal more usually associated with the offer of a shoe-shopping spree or a weekend at the beach.

Justine was starting to understand why her parents had enjoyed teaching so much. And Gloria. Gloria lived to teach. Being a professor at a women's college meant that Gloria had moved in a constant cloud of worshipful young women who had never met anyone like her. Gloria must have enjoyed teaching Justine to read as much as Justine was enjoying the sight of Georgette struggling with a concept and then—suddenly, miraculously—grasping it.

Remembering the afternoons that she'd spent with Gloria and *The House at Pooh Corner* had brought Justine to a decision she'd been struggling all day to make. She needed to see Gloria. She needed to get her opinion about the possible sabotage of her work at the Michaud plant, but she would have to be very careful about how she did it. She had taken an oath of secrecy that weighed on her mind. The oath might make it impossible for her to get the help she needed from Gloria, but she had to try. If she could trust anybody to help her stop the sabotage without endangering herself or the war effort, it would be her godmother. Gloria's thought processes had the transparent clarity of pure mathematics, but she'd been a refugee and she'd never lost the refugee's engrained suspicion of authority.

Justine knew that she would have eventually convinced herself that it was time to face her godmother, but her conversation with Georgette had saved her weeks of fretting about it. Just her luck, she was heading into her day off. She could be face-to-face with Gloria in twelve hours, apologizing for their time apart, and she had Georgette to thank for that. Or to blame, as the case might be.

At some point in the evening, Georgette looked at Justine's little bedside alarm clock and said, "You've been explaining this stuff to me for hours. You ain't tired of talking to somebody this ignorant?"

"Don't say that. 'Ignorant' is a terrible word. Nobody knows everything there is to know. I like talking to you because you ask questions. You want to get down to the bottom of things. You'd be surprised at how rare that kind of intellectual curiosity is. I don't know how to talk to somebody who isn't curious. I don't dislike people like that. I just can't think of anything to say to them."

"Intellectual. Huh."

Georgette rose. "Would you excuse me for a minute?" Then she walked out into the hall. Justine presumed she was going to the bathroom, although the abrupt way she'd left was a little odd.

When Georgette came back moments later, she had a battered tin pail in her hand, which was also a little odd.

"It ain't nothing," Georgette said. "Just a little something we can share while you do some more explaining."

And then she held out the pail, and Justine saw that it was full of grapes, plump, velvet-skinned, fragrant, and almost black.

"My Papa comes to town on my day off every week, and he always brings me something to help me keep my grocery bill down. It's fish when it's cold enough that they don't start to smell before he can get here on the bus. This time of year, the weather's too hot for that, so he brings me something out of the garden or maybe some wild plums. This week, it was these here muscadine grapes. They grow wild by the house. Grab a handful and tell me some more about—what do you call it? Oh, yeah. Radiolocation. RADAR."

If Justine had still harbored doubts that she was right to share her fears with Georgette, she never doubted her new friend after she shared her wild grapes. They talked all night, they laughed until the sweet, sticky juice ran off their chins, and they had absolutely no idea what real danger was.

Not then. Not yet.

Chapter 8

"Yes, please come."

Justine's godmother's voice wasn't angry, but it wasn't enthusiastic, either. She supposed she deserved a cool response from Gloria after she'd avoided her for so long, but the coolness stung anyway.

"I'll be there on the next streetcar." She paused and added, "I've really missed you, Gloria. I'm sorry it's been so long."

Her godmother said, "It's so good to hear from you." Then she hung up the phone.

———

It was a quick, easy ride to Carrollton, so quick that Justine found herself wishing the streetcar would slow down. No such luck. It moved inexorably down St. Charles Avenue, taking her to face the person who loved her better than anyone alive in the world. Facing Gloria terrified her, but it was too late to turn back.

She loved looking at the old homes along St. Charles, with their shaded galleries and lush gardens, and she had her favorites. Justine had a soft spot for wrought iron, and long stretches of

St. Charles were lined with wrought-iron fences and gates and pergolas. She liked the way the hardness of the iron was softened by tendrils of green ivy and gray shadows of old live oaks. She wouldn't have minded spending a little extra time on the street-car, just to look at the iron, but that wasn't why she wanted to move slower.

She just wasn't ready to face Gloria.

Gloria had to know why it had taken her so long to make this trip. She was an exceedingly intelligent person, perhaps the most intelligent person Justine had ever met, and that was saying something. Justine had seen Gloria go toe-to-toe with her father, and her mother, too, and all of their scientist friends from all over the world. Gloria had always prevailed. Of course, it's easier to prevail if you wait quietly, marshaling your facts and arguments while you let the rage build until, at just the right moment, you let it explode all over your hapless victim.

Gloria was more than smart enough to understand that her goddaughter had been avoiding her because she couldn't face the pain of her past, and she was more than capable of building up a towering grudge anyway. Gloria's ability to wait quietly while she planned her adversary's destruction was the reason for Justine's vain hope that her streetcar would expire somewhere on St. Charles Avenue. She was about to come face-to-face with a woman whose fuse had probably been burning for a long, long time.

Her godmother's fuse would grow even shorter when she realized that Justine had come to her for help, but that she'd taken an oath of secrecy keeping her from telling Gloria much of what she'd need to know to solve Justine's problem. Gloria didn't suffer fools gladly, and Justine tried desperately to avoid being a fool in front of her. Sometimes she was even successful in that effort.

The streetcar refused to expire, and Justine wasn't cowardly enough to "miss" her stop. She walked the rest of the way to Gloria's house, moving through a neighborhood of cozy modern bungalows that looked nothing like the historic European architectural styles common to the rest of the city. These streets had been an enclave for the out-of-towners who had moved to New Orleans in the 1920s and 1930s to take posts at universities like Tulane and Xavier or, in Gloria's case, to teach at Tulane's sister school for women, Sophie Newcomb College. Most of the houses in Gloria's neighborhood were ten or fifteen years old now, so the lawns and bushes and trees had grown enough to make the bungalows look comfortable in the landscape. Or maybe that's what everybody who'd had a happy childhood saw when they came home again. Comfort.

Justine walked past the spot where she'd wrecked her bike when she was eight. She slowed a bit as she passed a patch of pavement where she'd drawn hopscotch squares with crumbly gray rocks. At the next corner, she caved in to the pain and made a small detour. She couldn't stand the thought of walking past one special house, the house where she'd lived until a rain-slicked country road took the light out of her world—not to mention taking away any hope she might ever have had for paying the mortgage on it.

She'd faced the past once, taking a single stroll past her old home. She'd survived everything else, so she had believed that she could take this blow. The sight of a strange child's face peering out the window of her parents' study had ripped her heart right out.

One day, she'd do it. She'd walk down the street and stare that house down, but she couldn't do it today, not when she was going to have to look Gloria in the eyes. She took a cowardly left turn and a right one, just so she wouldn't already be crying when she knocked on a very familiar door.

And she wasn't. She was calm as she stood on the front porch of Gloria's modern-for-New Orleans home, custom-built when Justine was a kid growing up around the corner. It was September, practically still summertime, so she felt over-warm in her cardigan and full skirt, but she'd worn them for Gloria. Gloria had always liked it when she wore green. Justine let the familiar bricks beneath her feet support her. She didn't cower, but her knees knocked a little. Then the heavy oak door opened and she was enfolded in a familiar pair of scrawny arms that had always been so different from her mother's soft, pillowy ones.

"Oh, baby. Oh, sweetie, I missed you so much."

A familiar set of long fingers wrapped themselves around Justine's upper arms and dragged her inside. Gloria Mazur hadn't changed much, but her house was unrecognizable. Justine had never seen it so clean, not since the day it was built. She stood in the entry hall and gawked at Gloria's treasured collection of blue-painted Newcomb pottery, painted by her students at Sophie Newcomb College. The various pieces had always been stuck on random shelves and tables throughout the house. Displayed together, the grouping of graceful vases and pots was stunning.

Justine let herself be dragged into the dining room where more Newcomb pottery was displayed in an oak étagère that she hardly recognized. She'd never seen it when it wasn't piled high with books, lab notebooks, and the detritus of everyday life. For little Justine, a visit to her godmother had taken on the feel of a treasure hunt or a trip to a museum or a dive into the city dump. Seeing the étagère in its orderly glory gave her a strange feeling of loss.

She could see Gloria's living room through an open archway. There, the hundreds of books that had always been piled on every horizontal surface were now neatly shelved on built-in bookcases. Justine felt a pain in her chest when she saw the copy of J. J. Thomson's *Recollections and Reflections* that her father had given Gloria from his own collection. The polished oak shelf where it sat shone. So did all the house's polished and oiled woodwork. There wasn't a speck of dust in sight, and that lack of dust was the most disorienting thing of all.

As far back as Justine could remember, her mother had worried about Gloria's tendency to alternate between frenzied, brilliant work as a physicist and periods of sad silence, neither of which was conducive to housekeeping. Justine remembered a year when Gloria had finished teaching in the spring and simply collapsed. Isabel had visited every day, holding her hand while torrents of words about anguish that little Justine couldn't understand poured out of her. By summer's end, Gloria was herself again and the darkness that her sadness had cast over Justine had lifted. She wished her mother could know that Gloria's home finally seemed like a comfortable place where a happy person lived.

Justine had never realized until that moment that she'd inherited her mother's worry for Gloria. Her godmother looked wonderful, with bright eyes and a wide smile, and Justine was grateful.

Gloria's hair was still a mass of salt-and-pepper frizz, although maybe it had become a little saltier since the last time Justine had seen her. It was still forced against its will into a coil of braids at the crown of her head, in the same spot where her mother's graying red-blond locks had always been gathered into a bun, but Gloria's head no longer drooped with overwork. Her eyes, behind bifocals framed in silver wire, were still an intense black. Justine guessed that Gloria was well into her fifties, but her pale skin was firm over her high cheekbones and angular jaw. She was still very beautiful, in the way that hurricanes and rushing floodwaters are very beautiful.

Justine wrapped her arms around her godmother and squeezed hard. Gloria squeezed her back for a long time, then she tipped Justine's head back and looked into her eyes. In her lightly accented English, she asked, "Did you eat?"

When Justine admitted that she had skipped breakfast, Gloria barked, "Sit down at the table. It will take me just one moment to scramble some eggs for you."

As Gloria hurried to the kitchen, eyes alight, Justine realized that she was a fool. If anybody understood what it was like to be a young woman on her own in the world, it was Gloria. Gloria didn't talk about the years before she was fifteen, when her Polish parents had put her on a ship alone. Justine had heard her utter a single short sentence, only once, that gave a glimpse of the reasons they sent her away.

"We were hungry."

She should have found a way to come back to her godmother sooner.

Gloria's disembodied voice boomed from the kitchen. "You called me from a phone at your rooming house, yes?"

"Mrs. Guidry lets us use it for emergencies. I told her it was an emergency."

"And so it was. Yes, it was quite the emergency. I have not seen you in…oh…well, it has been too long."

Within minutes, Gloria emerged carrying a tray bearing two cups of steaming coffee. Then she went back to fetch Justine's eggs and toast.

Justine's mother had told her the bare bones of Gloria's history. Within days of arriving in Chicago, the teenaged girl had found a job making buttonholes for a woman who sewed men's shirts. Within weeks, she was in night school, learning English and arithmetic so that her employer would never again be cheated by the men who bought her shirts.

By the time Gloria was thirty, she was working for physics professor Gerard Byrne beside his pregnant wife, Isabel, who had earned her doctorate alongside Gloria. By the time Justine was born, they were all in New Orleans, where her father had refused to accept Tulane's job offer until Gloria was offered a position at the university's coordinate school, H. Sophie Newcomb Memorial College for Women.

Isabel had stayed home to take care of the baby, helping Gerard and Gloria with their calculations while she dandled Justine on her lap. Over time, her vision had failed, but she had kept going, writing the letters, numbers, and symbols bigger and bigger until she couldn't make out even the largest and boldest markings. Then she had switched to braille. All the while, Justine was growing older and learning to spare her mother's eyes by helping her with more and more complex work. Her father's final paper had credited Justine as the fourth author, behind her parents and Gloria.

As Justine looked around the dining room at the shining woodwork and the windows free of a single bug speck, she imagined Gloria venting her uncontrollable grief over the loss of Gerard and Isabel by controlling everything else that she possibly could. All Justine had done with her grief was run away from it.

Gloria plunked a plate of moist and fluffy scrambled eggs in front of Justine. The toast was a perfect and even brown, and it was spread with butter that was soft but not melted.

"You still cook like a scientist," Justine said.

"Is that a good thing?" Gloria said, nibbling on a piece of dry toast.

"You bet. Everything's precisely the way it should be, cooked for the optimal amount of time at the optimal temperature."

Justine looked at her coffee, white with milk, and its creamy color woke her from her nostalgic dream. She hadn't had a breakfast like this since before the war, and she shouldn't be having it now.

"You put sugar in this, didn't you?"

Gloria feigned surprise at the question. "Of course."

Justine wanted to say, "I see that you didn't put any milk in yours, and probably no sugar," but they both knew why Gloria wasn't drinking her beloved *café au lait*. Milk and sugar were precious things in wartime, when they could be had at all.

Gloria couldn't afford to give away her eggs. Her milk. Her bread. Her coffee. And, dear God, certainly not her precious sugar. The administrators of Sophie Newcomb College had never appreciated having an opinionated woman, and a foreigner at that, forced on them, so Gerard Byrne's power as a renowned scientist had only gone so far. Gloria's academic position had always been precarious, only a year-to-year contract and an inadequate lab space. When Gerard died, Gloria lost the inadequate lab space and most of her course load before he was even buried.

"Have some plum preserves, dear," Gloria said, holding out a jar of store-bought preserves that might as well have held a pint of dollar bills.

Justine's heart sank. Gloria couldn't afford to pamper her like this.

Justine knew exactly how close to the edge her godmother's budget was. If she'd let Gloria do what she had wanted to do when her parents died—put a roof over Justine's head and send her to college—the house where they sat would have been gone in months.

So Justine had run. She'd sold her parents' house and everything in it before the bank could take it all, then she'd run to The Julia without saying goodbye. She'd run from Gloria's need to take care of her, even at the expense of her own future.

Remembering all of these things, Justine found that her breakfast plate offended her. Locking her eyes defiantly on Gloria's face, she took her clean coffee spoon, scooped up half of her untouched eggs, and dumped them on the saucer holding Gloria's toast. When Gloria tried to protest, she cut her off. Justine supposed that she was too gruff about it, but there's no gracious way to say, "Eat something. You're too skinny."

Then she grabbed Gloria's cup before she could even start drinking the dark, bitter brew and began sloshing coffee back and forth between their cups like a chemist pouring reagents between two beakers. When each cup held a mixture of the same shade of brown, she knew that the fraction of coffee was the same in both cups and so was the fraction of milk. And presumably, so was the fraction of sugar. The heat lost to the air while she sloshed meant that the temperature of their coffee would now be less than optimal, but she was satisfied, because there was no way in hell that she was going to slurp down a perfect cup of coffee when Gloria didn't have one.

She handed Gloria's cup back to her. Her godmother's steely gaze held hers for a long second, and Justine braced herself for the explosion. Then Gloria lifted the cup in a toast. "My little girl is all grown up now."

They both drank deeply.

Then Gloria, who had never been known for tact, sliced through the veil of politeness that had been separating them from the hard truth. "You could have grown up without running away, you know. You were cruel to go without a word."

Gloria sipped the sweet, milky coffee, holding it for a moment in her mouth to savor it. "But I knew why you did it. That's why I let you go without tracking you down and bringing you back where you belonged."

Justine imagined Gloria storming The Julia and hauling her home. She was very glad to have missed that humiliation.

Gloria continued to muse. "I did the same as you, you know. I went away so that my parents wouldn't have the burden of feeding me. And I survived. I always do. And so shall you. Let us call our scores settled. Fate dealt us hard hands and we played them."

Gloria's short nod put a period at the end of that sentence. Justine knew that this was the only time she would ever hear about Gloria's long-lost mother and father and the Polish home she would never see again. Gloria had said what she had to say. This was bad because Justine needed distracting. She just could not cry in front of Gloria. It would be unseemly.

"Eat your eggs." Gloria's crisp voice scared the tears away. "So you are working at Segram's Fabrics? Have they made you a manager yet? Well, assistant manager. Sam Segram would never put a woman in a manager's job, but he would be happy for you to do the managing for him while he paid you a woman's salary."

"I left Segram's a couple of years ago. I took a factory job at—"

She interrupted herself when she saw Gloria sit up straighter, while still glaring down at her eggs.

"—at Higgins. I'm working at Higgins Industries now."

The black eyes flicked back up at her, brilliant with pride.

"You are working in manufacturing? You are welding? If your father could only see this. So proud. He would be so proud."

"No welding yet. Well, just a little, but I'm mostly doing assembly work. You know—standing on an assembly line…screwing in screws…twisting nuts onto bolts…"

Gloria brushed aside those humble details.

"You are building boats? Aeroplanes?"

"That's why I'm here. I don't know what I'm building. I hoped you could tell me."

The shining eyes stayed on her face, but the smile faded a little. "They don't tell you what you are doing? If your work is for the war effort, they should tell you, so that you will be proud and work hard."

"We're sworn to secrecy. The penalties for giving away war secrets are…"

"Harsh? Indeed. But how can I tell you what you're building if you can say nothing about it?"

"Gloria, I think somebody's trying to sabotage our work. I don't know who it is, and I don't know why." She swallowed hard, then spit out the words she hadn't even been able to say to Georgette. Or to herself. "I'm afraid."

Gloria reached behind her without looking and pulled a cloth-bound lab notebook off an incredibly organized shelf. Justine was stupidly happy to see it. Her godmother must have bought cases of those notebooks in 1924 or so, because Justine had hardly ever seen her without one, and they all looked the same.

Gloria pulled a pencil out of the knot of braids on the top of her head. It must have been there the whole time, but Justine hadn't noticed. Gloria had always kept her writing utensils in her hair.

"What kind of sabotage do you mean? Why do you think this? Can you tell me?"

"I can tell you about the broken parts I mended. There's nothing about them that could give away anything about my work. They're just standard parts on a conveyor belt that could be used in any factory in America. Three times in the past two weeks, the assembly line apparatus where I work has broken down because a lateral guide has failed. Under magnification, I can see damage to the metal that isn't random, and it can't be explained by malfunctioning equipment."

"You think it looks intentional."

"Yes. My boss knows I can weld, so he keeps asking me to fix the broken parts, but they keep breaking."

"Your saboteur is not smart."

The word "saboteur" gave Justine chills.

Gloria jotted something in her notebook. "It would be far better to leave no pattern for someone to notice."

"That's true. But 'not smart' is not the same thing as 'not

dangerous.' I've also heard rumors about other strange happenings within my department. Missing tools. Broken cables. Things like that. Outside my department...well, there was an accident yesterday and somebody was killed, but I just can't tell whether it's connected."

Gloria nodded as she stared at the notebook page, letting her pencil hover an inch above the paper. "Your boss? I presume you haven't told him about your suspicions. Him?"

"Yes, him."

Gloria nodded. "Of course."

The pen descended to the paper and began sketching a network of straight lines and curves. Justine knew that it would grow more elaborate as they spoke. Gloria had left a lifelong trail of doodles behind her, on ink blotters, on newspapers, on tablecloths. Only her best students opened their graded papers to find them decorated with Gloria's scribbles.

Without looking up, she said, "You have not told your boss. Why? Because he is incompetent? Or because you don't trust him?"

"Yes."

This earned Justine a glance through the top half of her godmother's bifocals. Gloria's eyes squinched into a quick smile, then they darted back down to the notebook.

"Ah. Both incompetent *and* untrustworthy. Lucky you. You have considered talking to the police?"

"That oath of silence covers everybody. Everybody. Besides, I've heard things about the police that—"

"You've heard correctly. Power corrupts."

"Then what should I do?"

"You could go to the military, but it is a hierarchical organization. I do not know how you would find an individual of a sufficiently high rank to help you, instead of handing you up the chain of command. Any chain of command has weak links, and some of those weak links are traitors. Approaching the wrong person would gain you a pat on the hand and a phone call to your boss explaining your tendency to hysteria. Approaching the wrong person could even get you killed. And how would you begin? Stroll into a random recruiting office and start talking?"

"So I wasn't wrong to come here. Nobody can help me but you."

"What do you think I can do? I presume that you want me to determine what you and your fellow workers are building, so that you can get some sense of why someone would sabotage your work. That is a tall order, but it is not completely out of the question."

Despite Gloria's claim that she probably couldn't help her, Justine was already beginning to feel hopeful.

Gloria stopped speaking for a moment of silent nods and scribbling. "You cannot trust your boss with your fears, and you cannot know which of the people around you might be a saboteur, if there is one. Unfortunately, your oath of secrecy means that you can't tell me what I need to know to help you, and I do not suggest that you break your oath. Should your loyalty ever be called into question, the truth will show on your face."

Gloria's stern expression bloomed into a warm smile. "You have a very honest face, my dear."

The pen went down. "It seems we are at an impasse. Is there anything you can tell me, within the constraints of your oath?"

Justine unbuttoned her cardigan and slid it from her shoulders to reveal a simple white cotton shirt. Every square inch of it was smudged with carbon dust.

Chapter 9

Mudcat walked away from a certain Craftsman-style house in a certain residential neighborhood, head down and hat pulled low over his face. He was free to go because he'd seen what he needed to see. The air was warm and he wished for a beer, but it wasn't even noon yet. Besides, he couldn't buy real beer in this part of the world. The best he'd been able to find was a New Orleans brand called Dixie. The locals loved it because they were Americans and they confused watery lager with actual beer.

Technically, he was American, but apparently nothing more than a German mother was needed to develop a palate adapted to more potent brews. These days, he drank America's thin, pale excuses for beer because he had to drink something. The war and a long period of Prohibition had dominated his life, so drinking German beer had always required travel or influential connections or more money than he wanted to spend. Fortunately, his career provided travel and connections, and sometimes those connections had money.

With every weak, astringent mouthful of Dixie Beer, he wished for *doppelbock*. Strong and sweet, *doppelbock* was like liquid bread, and it was a quick route to the kind of happy drunkenness that might obliterate, at least for a while, the constant fear that drove him. Everyone in his line of work was driven by fear, although not so many were honest enough to admit it.

This job wasn't going well, but Mudcat reminded himself that all was not lost. He had one agent behind the doors that stood between him and the Carbon Division's secret lair, and that agent had brought him information that provided a partial understanding of what was going on behind those doors. He simply needed more. He was coming to believe that Justine Byrne was the right person for the right time and place.

Justine's face was stuck in his mildly hungover brain. She was the key, the secret weapon that could not have been anticipated. Mudcat had never failed yet. To succeed here, he knew that he needed to secure this asset or, at the least, he needed to control her.

His agent had only learned a little bit about Justine Byrne and her mysterious-for-a-woman ability to weld. He was told that her personality was best described as "intense," but he'd seen her. The word he would have used was "passionate." The women around her reportedly saw her as strange for the scholarly approach to life that she had apparently learned from her late father, a professor of some science too difficult for his contact to adequately explain.

Although Mudcat was no scientist, he was more than capable of putting two and two together. The number of colleges and universities in New Orleans was not infinite, and neither were professors of arcane sciences. The name Byrne was not particularly common. Successful scientists did not hide their tracks. Mudcat was confident that he could find out what he needed to know about Justine Byrne's father. And then he could find out what he needed to know about Justine herself.

Chapter 10

Gloria gaped at Justine's blackened shirt. "They do not pay you enough to afford laundry soap? How long has it been since you washed your blouse?"

"It was clean when I arrived at work yesterday. They don't make us change clothes when we leave, so nothing about this blouse can possibly be a secret."

Gloria made a gesture with her hand, asking Justine to stand up and spin in place. The black dust clung to the white fabric evenly, front to back and top to bottom.

"I see that you are working with carbon. Such a quantity of dust so fine floating in the air suggests that it is being machined. It also suggests that your employer is not taking proper care with your lungs, but never mind that for now. You say that you only assemble the parts?"

"Others are doing the machining, although I certainly wouldn't mind having that job. There are walls around our manufacturing lines, within the factory's outside walls. We're like a plant within a plant," Justine said, feeling reasonably sure that it was okay to describe something that was visible to the thousands of Higgins employees, not to mention the delivery people and outside contractors working outside the factory building. "They say those internal walls are meant to keep the dust off of everybody else, but…well…they keep everybody else's eyes off of us, too. My line assembles metal parts that are small and light enough for us to hold in our hands—"

She paused as she realized that this last detail was probably too much information to share.

She began again. "That's enough about what I do. Let's focus on the carbon, which you deduced without any input from me but my dirty shirt. I haven't gotten a good look at the carbon parts, but I've heard the machinists joke about the slots they're carving into them." That, too, was probably too much information to share, so she tried again. "The carbon parts and the… things…that the women on my line assemble are taken into a separate walled-off area by the loading dock that I can tell you about because it's visible from outdoors through the open loading dock where deliveries come and go all the time. I presume that's where the various parts we make are assembled into the final product. Whatever it is."

"Yes, whatever it is." Gloria doodled for a moment. "You work within a walled-off area of the plant, but the final product is assembled in a walled-off area within that one?" She doodled some more, drawing circles within circles. "The spaces are nested, like the dolls my father carved for me. The contents of the final doll must be so very precious."

Gloria reached out a hand and brushed it on Justine's collar. Then she held that hand close to her face, rubbing the pad of her thumb around on the tips of her carbon-dusted fingers. "Have they given you protective clothing? It would be heavy, made of lead."

Justine gestured at the carbon residue that permeated her shirt. "Does it look like we wear protective clothing? I had coveralls over this shirt and see how much of the dust sifted through?"

"That's actually good. Well, I think it's good. Hmmm."

Gloria's silence stretched for an uncomfortably long time, but Justine was used to that.

"Have you been told anything at all about where they're sending your handiwork? Or can you say?"

"I can't tell you what they've told me, but it's not much. However, I don't see how it could be a problem to tell you what the workers who *aren't* working for the Carbon Division are saying. It's just gossip, but it's not secret gossip."

Gloria's impatient raise of her eyebrow said, "Go on."

"Most people think we're building radio parts. Others think we're building parts for RADAR devices."

"The parts for a RADAR device would have a certain amount of overlap with parts for a radio, at least in function."

Justine nodded. "A few people have heard rumors about a new bomb sight. They think we might be working on that."

"Yes, yes, yes. These are rumors, and they are not very helpful. What do *you* think?"

"I don't know. The most persistent gossips are behind the radio parts theory, so I've had my mind set on that."

"Do you think this—" Gloria held out her blackened fingers. "Do you think this belongs in a radio?"

Justine shrugged. "I have no idea."

"Justine," Gloria said, and Justine felt her reproach, "of course you have an idea. Perhaps your friends are gullible enough to believe this rumor, but I doubt any of them had a father who liked to spend evenings tinkering with radios with his little girl. How many hours did you spend building radios with Gerard?"

"Those were just crystal sets. Are they really applicable to—"

"No, a crystal set is not the same as a modern radio used by the military, but yes, it is a radio receiver. Wouldn't any radio receiver have parts that fulfill the same functions?" Gloria counted those parts and their functions on her fingers. "An antenna to pluck the signal from the air. A resonant circuit to select the desired frequency. A means to make the captured signal audible."

"Papa and I used a capacitor and some wire coiled around an oatmeal box for our resonant circuit. Correct me if I'm wrong, but I don't think the military uses oatmeal boxes."

Gloria pulled off her glasses because they were interfering with her ability to glare at Justine. "All that may be true, but is there any reason to use carbon for a resonant circuit? Or for any function in a radio transmitter or receiver? What are the properties of carbon?"

"Um...it's insoluble in water, which makes it really hard to get the stuff out of my clothes. It combines with oxygen to form carbon dioxide and carbon monoxide, but that takes a fairly high temperature."

"If they were going to burn it, they would not be paying people to machine it into shape." She paused a moment, her brow furrowed, before continuing. "Whatever you are making, it has a function."

Justine nodded. "Carbon comes in different forms, like graphite, diamond, and...um..."

"Amorphous carbon, which is much like the coal we burn. Do you recall whether carbon is a good conductor?"

"I think it's not."

"Amorphous carbon is not. Graphite is. Both forms have their place in electrodes." She waved her blackened fingers around. "So would carbon in any form be useful as part of a resonant circuit?"

"No? I don't think so?"

"I doubt it. What else is in a crystal radio set?"

"The crystal. Papa and I used a piece of galena and a fine wire. Wait! We did use graphite once. A graphite pencil lead and a razor blade. He said it was a foxhole radio like the soldiers in the last war used."

"Very good. So maybe your carbon parts are useful in that way, but I doubt it. What were the other components of your crystal radio?"

"We needed earphones to make the sound audible. Newer sets use loudspeakers for that. Also, newer sets use vacuum tubes instead of crystals. To answer your next question, I don't know how you would use carbon to make any of those."

"Nor do I." Gloria stared at the stains on Justine's shirt. "These things you are making are very odd, considering that you work for a business famous for building boats and aeroplanes. Is this something that they've done for quite some time? Is this a secret?"

Justine shook her head. "Everybody at the plant knows when the Carbon Division started up, and so do the families who see us come home covered in black dust, so that's no secret. It hasn't been long. Mr. Higgins got a government contract, put the Carbon Division facilities behind a wall at one end of the Michaud plant, and moved two thousand of us out there a couple of weeks ago."

"Two thousand? All of a sudden? Now, at the supposed end of the war? And you think someone is sabotaging the effort?"

Gloria let herself slouch against the back of her chair, and this disturbed Justine. Gloria never slouched. "Everything you've said—the secrecy, the speed, the thousands of workers—says that our government is mounting a last-ditch effort to gain an advantage in the war...the same war that they would like us to believe is almost over. You have reason to think that the effort is being sabotaged, although you have no way to know whether it is a fellow employee with an ax to grind or whether it is an enemy saboteur. If the enemy is doing it, they have a foothold inside the factory. This is ominous. I know that asking questions is in your nature, but it is not safe."

Justine shivered, although Gloria's house was warm. She had wanted her godmother to tell her that she was worried about nothing. She hadn't wanted her to grill her within an inch of her life about the science of carbon. She certainly hadn't wanted Gloria to warn her away from a quest that she knew in her soul that she was going to have to take. Her only comfort was knowing that she would have her godmother to lean on while she did it.

"We can work together, Gloria. I can use the phone at my rooming house to call you whenever I see something interesting and—"

"No." This denial was unexpected from the person she trusted most in the world. "I cannot help you."

Justine couldn't believe the finality in her godmother's voice. "Why not? I need you."

Gloria roused from her slouch and leaned forward, elbows on the table and black eyes glittering. "They will know. There are no listening devices here inside my house at this moment, but they surely have devices on the streetcars. And at your rooming house."

"Who do you mean by 'they'? What kind of listening devices are you looking for? Radio transmitters? Gloria, they're too big to hide. You'd know if someone had put one in your house."

"Don't be such a fool. The most brilliant scientists in the world are working to make them small, smaller, always smaller. These are people you yourself know. They were your parents' friends. My friends. And now they serve governments. Our government. The governments of our allies. Of our enemies. Who can say? Consider what you know of these people. Can you honestly doubt what they can do? When they are able to build replacements for vacuum tubes that function in a solid state—oh, Justine. Listening devices will be everywhere. They will even come in our houses concealed in the mail."

Justine's beloved Gloria was afraid of her mailbox. She listened for the sound of her whole world cracking open.

"Every day, they try to catch me in a mistake. And every night, they try to plant their bugs. When I wake, I must search again." Gloria looked over her shoulder, peering into the kitchen at... what?

"You could stay here with me if you promised never to leave. I am often lonely. I see no one but the neighborhood boy who does my shopping, and I do not dare converse with him for fear that he cannot be trusted. It would make all the difference if I had you here."

"What do you mean when you say 'never to leave,' Gloria? Aren't you leaving the house? Aren't you teaching?"

"Of course not. Spies are everywhere at the college."

Now the miniscule salary that had kept Gloria housed and fed was gone. How long could she limp along like this with no income?

"Gloria. What are you doing for money?"

Gloria stared at the wall behind Justine's shoulder. She didn't answer.

Then she was in sudden motion. Her right forefinger and thumb pinched Justine's left earlobe and used it to drag her closer. Justine struggled to keep her chest from dragging across her eggy plate as Gloria yanked her close enough to hiss her fears into her goddaughter's ear.

"Keep your voice low. They are likely gathered just outside the window. They will hear us." Justine felt Gloria's grip loosen. The hand gripping her earlobe pulled away as Gloria plastered its palm over her own mouth, as if to lock in words that might be overheard.

"They are out there." The words were muffled by Gloria's hand. "It is good that my hearing is excellent, or I would not know that

they were back. I sometimes think that I can hear radio waves.
It occurs to me that they may have implanted a crystal on my
eardrum. If I could somehow fine-tune this ability, I might finally
know why they torment me so continually."

Oh, Gloria.

"They are all-pervasive," Gloria insisted, gesturing with both
hands. "They have wormed their way into my bank account,
where they taunt me."

"They're stealing money from your bank account?"

"No. They're too clever for that. They leave money behind,
so that I will know that they have been there. Sometimes—" Her
eyes darted from the window to the door to all four corners of the
room. "Sometimes, they sneak money into the bags the neighbor
boy uses to deliver my groceries."

"Gloria, that's your change."

"This is what they wish me to believe."

Justine didn't know how to respond.

"My sweet child, they have been waiting a long time for me to
make a mistake, but I am too smart. Look around you."

She held her hands out, palms up, inviting Justine to scrutinize
the room where they sat.

"I do not trust the telephone, and I will not speak a word outside these walls, but my house is safe. I inspect everything, every
book, every can in my pantry, every dress in my closet. Every day,
I do this. I clean each item and put it away. My every possession
has a home." She turned to the shelf behind her. "This book…
here. That book…there. You see? There can be no radio receivers
or transmitters in this house, no matter how miniscule. I would
know. But after I sleep, I cannot be sure, so I must do it all again.
If you came to live with me, we could take turns standing watch.
But you will not come. I know this."

Justine looked at the sparkling clean house with new eyes.

"Who, Gloria? Who would be planting radio receivers and transmitters?"

Her godmother gave an elaborate shrug. "I don't know. Them."

Speaking carefully, Justine said, "If there are no radio receivers to hear you talk, then I could call you on the phone."

Gloria leaned—no, lunged—toward her, hissing, "No no no! Don't you see? Someone would be listening on the line. What did I say to you when you called?"

"You said, 'It's so good to hear from you,' and 'Yes, please come.' That was about it, but I figured I deserved the silent treatment after staying away so long."

Gloria graced her with a beatific smile. "You see? I gave away nothing to listening ears. I risked letting you come here, just this once, because I needed to see you so much. Now that you know how things are, you understand why we must be apart. You must go." She rose. "Now."

Gloria had Justine by both elbows, and her grip was ferocious. As they walked, Gloria muttered continuously. "If you insist on learning about the sabotage, you must find a way to do it safely. If you find the saboteur, then perhaps my persecution will end. Young. He is young."

"What?" Justine asked. "Who's young?"

"Electrodes are both positive and negative. You know that, yes?"

Everybody knew that.

They reached the door and Gloria threw it open. Staring blankly out at…something? nothing?…she said quietly, "Which way? Do you know which way?" Without waiting for an answer, she shook Justine hard and hugged her.

"You must be careful," she said. "Very careful. Surely you have guessed why I say this?"

Justine didn't know what to say, but she didn't want to upset the agitated woman. "Because the voices say I should be careful."

"*No!*" Gloria bellowed, momentarily forgetting that "they" were waiting outside, listening. "You should understand the danger better than anyone. *What do you think happened to your parents?*"

Justine was incapable of absorbing what Gloria was trying to say. "What?"

"If you think your parents' deaths were an accident, then you are a fool. Now go."

She pushed her goddaughter out the door, and Justine stood trembling on the doorstep.

"What? What are you saying happened to them, Gloria?"

Gloria said, "You must be more careful than they were," and the door slammed shut between them.

Chapter 11

It had not been hard for Mudcat to follow Justine home from work on the day she fled the loathsome Sonny. He had merely followed her to her friend's Buick, and then he had followed the Buick to The Julia Ladies' Residence.

It had also not been hard to return before dawn and watch the rooming house until Justine appeared, nor to shadow her to the home of a woman who was obviously very close to her. It had then been easy to leave her there and trek to the public library where he had learned so many useful things.

For example, he had found shelves loaded with university yearbooks. The Tulane University volume from 1940 had proven particularly useful. Inside its gold-stamped cover, wrapped in leather dyed the warm red of cinnamon, the *Jambalaya* had included a photo of Gerard Byrne in his physics lab, probably taken just months before he died. This photo was worth examining later, so Mudcat had slid his trusty Minox Riga out of a pocket hidden inside his left sleeve and snapped a photograph.

With the camera safely stowed, Mudcat had continued studying the yearbook and its printed photo. Gerard Byrne's round face was a serious one, framed by a close-cropped brown beard going gray and an out-of-fashion silver pince-nez. Beneath his photo was a caption touting his publications and awards. This caption had told Mudcat enough about Byrne's publication history to make the *Readers' Guide to Periodical Literature* useful, so he had followed that research trail. There, he had learned that Dr. Byrne often listed his wife, Isabel, as a coauthor, as well as a woman named Gloria Mazur. And, once, Justine Byrne.

Mudcat might not be a physicist, but he knew enough to recognize that it wasn't the usual thing for renowned scientists to collaborate with women. The Byrnes were people one might expect to produce an unusual daughter.

Some of the scientific journals that published Byrne's work were on the library's shelves, so he'd asked the librarian to fetch them for him. The journals had appeared at his elbow as if by magic, with no need for him thank her or even to acknowledge her, but he had.

As he said, "Thank you very much," he had flashed a smile designed to secure her ongoing helpfulness. Careful to squint his eyes, forming trustworthy wrinkles at their corners, he'd shown his teeth to prove his openness. The effort was effective, because she had mirrored his smile in a way that thawed her frosty efficiency by a degree or two. The ability to artificially project charm and charisma was a valuable one for a spy. He practiced it daily.

The scholarly journals turned out to be a gold mine. The articles themselves weren't particularly meaningful—Mudcat knew next to nothing about crystallography—but each one included a brief biographical sketch of the authors. Those biographical sketches were meaningful indeed. Justine Byrne's father had studied under J. J. Thomson at Cambridge and Owen Willans Richardson at Princeton, both of them Nobel Prize laureates. Byrne had written his dissertation on positive rays and mass spectroscopy under Arthur Jeffrey Dempster at the University of Chicago.

The people with whom he'd coauthored a steady stream of papers formed a kind of scientific genealogy for Byrne. At the top was Thomson, the discoverer of the electron. Even Mudcat could see that Byrne's mentors were an impressive intellectual patrimony. How did Gloria Mazur fit into this pantheon where all the gods were fathers?

At this point in his search, the luck that came with deep research gave him a great gift. Or was it luck since people who didn't dig deep enough never received its gifts? Appended to one of Byrne's publications, Mudcat saw a biographical note for his collaborator, Dr. Gloria Mazur, and it gave her academic affiliation as H. Sophie Newcomb Memorial College.

Aha! So she was a nearby associate, not somebody like Ernest Lawrence and Enrico Fermi, who would have corresponded with Byrne from their labs in California and New York. Gloria Mazur's position at Sophie Newcomb had set Mudcat's intuition aflame, as he had just seen Justine greeted warmly by a woman who lived within a reasonable walk of that college's ornate iron gate.

A recent yearbook for Sophie Newcomb was as easily found as the Tulane yearbook had been. Within minutes, Mudcat was looking at a photo of Gloria Mazur in her lab, which looked sad and empty when compared to Byrne's forest of modern equipment. No wonder she was forced to play intellectual handmaiden to Byrne.

Mudcat knew women like Gloria. She would be willing to be Gerard Byrne's barely credited collaborator for her entire career, if that was what it took to see her work in print. And she would be bitter.

Understanding Gloria Mazur would be the key to understanding Justine Byrne, who was clearly as intelligent and driven as this woman in her inadequate lab. In thirty years, Justine would either be the contented wife of a man who had tamed her, or she would be as thwarted and bitter as Gloria Mazur. Or perhaps she would be looking back on her years traveling the world at Mudcat's side as an agent who was just as intellectually accomplished as Dr. Mazur but with far more personal autonomy.

Mudcat had been lonely, but he didn't realize how lonely he'd been until he caught his breath at the thought of life with Justine Byrne. She was attractive in her unconventional way, which was light on cosmetics and hairstyling and long on vibrant youth, but there was more to Justine than her face and form. She moved through the world like a human being with a goal and a plan. He had seen her throw her arms around Gloria Mazur like someone who didn't have to be given permission to love.

Mudcat had been content to make his way alone, but he felt something shift inside him when he thought about Justine. He wasn't sure he'd be willing to leave her behind when his work in New Orleans was done, so he'd best focus his mind on recruiting her to his cause. After that, he could focus on winning her in all the other ways.

He shoved those thoughts aside and realized that he was still staring at the small black-and-white photo of a woman who wasn't Justine. The picture of Gloria Mazur made him think that she, too, would have been an unconventional beauty in her day. He slid a magnifier out of his other sleeve to get a better look at her face. He had no doubt that she was the same woman who had wrapped Justine in her arms with such love.

He retrieved the camera and carefully snapped photos of each page of the article cowritten by Justine and Drs. Byrne, Byrne, and Mazur, then he snapped a shot of Gloria Mazur in her tiny, ill-equipped lab. The world of science had not been kind enough to Dr. Isabel Byrne to leave a photo of her in its journals for Mudcat to find.

Many hours would be spent developing the photos, which did not bother him at all. He loved the smell of the photographic chemicals in the red-lit closet that served him as a darkroom. He loved watching faces surface on the prints where they would remain trapped on paper.

He would particularly enjoy developing his first photo of the day, a long-distance shot of a flame-haired woman wrapped in an emerald cardigan who made him regret the limitations of black-and-white photography. She stood with one foot raised to step onto a streetcar that couldn't outrun her pursuer.

Chapter 12

Justine's ankle twisted under her as she hopped off the street-car, but she was light enough on her feet to stay upright, and her young ankle was limber enough to bend without breaking. These were good things, because her arms were too loaded with books to break her fall if she went down. Torn apart inside by Gloria's mental state and shaken by the thought that her parents might have been murdered, Justine had fallen back on the bed-rock belief of her family: books hold answers.

She'd never had official library privileges at Tulane. Now that her father was dead and Gloria was apparently unemployed, she couldn't even ride on the coattails of their library privileges, not officially. However, as long as Miss Hopkinton held court on weekends behind the circulation desk, Justine would have shadow privileges. From the time Justine was in elementary school, Miss Hopkinton had used her own personal library card to let her check out materials. As far back as Justine could remember, Miss Hopkinton had been the fount of all knowledge.

Miss Hopkinton knew Justine, she knew Justine's parents, and she knew Gloria. She could imagine no world in which Justine did not return the books on time and in an unchanged condition.

Librarians are not natural rule-breakers, but Miss Hopkinton had broken them for Justine.

On this most disturbing day, all Justine had needed to say was, "I'm looking for books on carbon chemistry," and Miss Hopkinton had pointed her to the exact row and shelves where organic chemistry books were kept. She'd also wished for a book on how to heal a wounded mind, but it was too risky to ask for it. Miss Hopkinton knew Gloria, and she might suspect why Justine wanted such a book. It would be a terrible betrayal to reveal Gloria's illness to her.

But was Gloria ill? Justine had seen her crushingly sad, but she was inclined to think that a person with Gloria's history would be unbalanced if she *weren't* sometimes sad. She had seemed completely in control of her faculties as she applied logic to the mysteries of the Carbon Division. Justine decided to leave open the question of whether someone was listening at Gloria's windows and bugging her house and depositing unexplained cash into her bank account. Perhaps they really were doing that. It was far more likely, though, that Gloria had been so emotionally crushed by the loss of all three Byrnes that she wasn't thinking clearly, and Justine bore part of the blame for that.

To unlock the secrets of how to help Gloria, she would need to go to another library, perhaps at a medical school, and it would take her some time to figure out how to wangle her way into one of those. In the meantime, she supposed her godmother was safe at home.

Even if she did find another Miss Hopkinton willing to let her plunder through a medical library where she had no privileges, and even if she found a miraculous book there that solved Gloria's problems, Justine knew in her heart that there was no book anywhere titled, *Why Would Anybody Kill My Parents, And If Not, Why Would Gloria Think Somebody Did?* It would take time and courage to face that question, and Justine didn't have enough of either to spare.

Fortunately, the library had held the books she came for. Justine now trudged down Julia Street with two book bags looped over each arm, hoping that they held answers. The hard part was going to be surviving the last few blocks to The Julia while serving as a book camel.

Justine was strong, so she and her books made it up The Julia's front steps, through the front door, and into the front parlor where Georgette sat. Her new friend was surrounded by young women playing records and practicing their dance steps. She sat at an old walnut dining table, hunched over a pad of paper as she worked through the algebra exercises Justine had given her.

At her first sight of Justine, Georgette jumped up. "Whoa, Nelly! You think maybe you got enough books there? Let me carry some of them things upstairs for you."

As soon as they were through the door to Justine's room, Georgette whispered, "I gotta tell you something, but I didn't want the girls downstairs to hear."

"Tell me now. Don't keep me waiting!"

"You know Shirley? The blond-haired machinist who works the night shift?"

Justine wasn't sure. "Does she live on the first floor, down the hall from you?"

"That's the one. You just walked past her in the lobby, showing her roommate how to do a double arm slide. Well, Shirley came home from work this morning with some news that made my jaw drop open. She was telling everybody that would listen." She lowered her voice even further. "You know all those whatsits we been making?"

"You know I do."

"Well, somebody—I guess it was the government—sent an

airplane to pick 'em up this morning. Them gadgets didn't leave the Michaud plant on a truck or a barge or a train, no. They went on a plane, and there wasn't nothing on that plane but Carbon Division products."

Justine tried to make this make sense. "An airplane? Our little black-and-shiny gadgets just don't seem worth that kind of expense. Somebody wants them right away and damn the cost."

Georgette shrugged. "That's what it sounds like to me. And there's gotta be important stuff going on, 'cause Shirley told me that when Mr. Higgins hisself comes to speak to the whole plant next Sunday about poor Cora Becker and them other people that got hurt, he's gonna give another special speech just for the Carbon Division. There's gotta be a reason why we're getting so much attention. And an airplane."

"Shirley must know somebody in shipping. How else would she know that nothing else went on that plane unless somebody told her? Does she know where the plane went?"

Georgette shook her head. "Nope. Flew in. Landed right behind the plant. The folks on it got off the plane and drove a truck up to our loading dock. They went inside that walled-up assembly center—you know, where the machinists take their carbon parts and they get joined up with our steel parts—and they hauled out a buncha crates of boxed-up finished goods. Everything we got made so far, I'm thinking. They loaded them crates on the truck, and the truck drove out to the landing strip where them same folks loaded the crates on the plane. Then they got on it and took off as quick as all the loading was done. That's all I know."

"So we're assembling something that the government thinks is worth significant time, money, and trouble. And somebody's been using a simple little rasp to hack on a few lateral guides, trying to slow us down. You know what I think?"

Georgette said, "You know I don't. I don't even know what to do with an *x* when there's some parentheses and a plus sign behind it."

"I think our saboteur is going to have to try harder to stop us Carbonites from building something that the government wants really bad. And that scares me."

———

As Justine piled the library books on her table, carefully stacking the volumes on carbon science in one pile and the ones on industrial uses of carbon in another, Georgette was reading their titles out loud.

"*Electrochemistry of Organic Compounds.* Brought home a little light reading, did ya?"

"Oh, there's nothing light about them," Justine said, rubbing at the red marks that the book bags had left on her arms.

"*The Manufacture of Chemicals by Electro…lye…*something. What's that word?" Georgette tapped her nail on the lettering stamped on the book's spine.

"Elec-TRAH-luh-sis. Electrolysis. That's when you pass electricity through a substance to get a chemical change."

"Okay. Yeah. Whatever you say. Please don't even try to explain this one—*The Cata…lye…tic…*"

"CAT-uh-LIT-ick."

"You could get on a girl's nerves. You know that? But okay, let's say it that way. Just because you say so. Here goes—*The Catalytic Oxidation of Organic Chemicals in the Vapor Phase.* I said all the other words right, I bet."

"You did."

"You went to see your *marraine* this morning, didn't ya? I thought you went to ask her about the carbon parts we're making. Only one of these books says 'carbon.'"

"Organic chemistry is all about carbon. All organic chemicals have carbon in them. And hydrogen."

"Well, then why don't they say so?"

Justine couldn't say.

"What did your *marraine* think? Did she have any idea 'bout what we're making?"

Justine felt around inside her head for a way to answer this without having to say her fears for Gloria's mental state out loud.

"She had some ideas about what we're not making. To begin with, she doesn't think we're making radio parts. She thought that components for RADAR installations would make more sense, but the machined carbon parts seem wrong."

"But she didn't have any ideas about what those carbon thingies *are*?"

Justine shook her head. "She gave me some ideas about where to look, but that's all she's going to be able to do. She's not...she's not well."

She looked up at Georgette, who towered a full head taller than she did. Sympathy was written on her friend's face, and Justine was so close to letting it all spill out. It would have been so easy to tell her about taking a trip into her past just by walking down a few streets lined with family homes. It would have been a relief to say, *I'm so afraid for Gloria. I'm afraid she's losing her mind*, but saying it would make it real.

Instead, she faked a bright smile and said, "I'm sure Gloria will be fine. She just needs to rest, so I'm not going to bother her. I'm going to read these books and figure out how to solve my own problems. But first, I'm going to open a can of beans for my dinner. Care to join me?"

"I got some rice and the last of them grapes. And some pecans. Papa came to visit me this afternoon and he brought me some."

Justine felt selfish. She'd been so upset over Gloria that she'd never even asked Georgette what she'd done with her day off.

"Did you and your papa have a good time?"

"Oh, yeah. We always do the same thing. He just loves to walk to the cathedral and rest in that pretty garden out back. You know, where the statue of Jesus is. After that, we always go inside and light candles to keep my brothers safe. I save my pocket change for that, because he don't need to put all his money in the donation box after he bought a bus ticket to get here."

Justine wondered what she'd do with her parents if she could have them back for an afternoon.

"We always leave smiling. The cathedral's so pretty inside, so quiet and cool, and the light coming through the colored windows ain't like any other light I ever saw. You been there?"

Justine nodded and said, "Yes. It's a holy place." Saint Louis Cathedral seemed to hold the souls of every last person who had ever said a heartfelt prayer there.

There was something about the expression on Georgette's face that made Justine ask, "Is something wrong at home? Your brother—the one that's wounded—is he okay?"

"Robbie? Papa says he's doing good. Up on his feet and perky enough to take care of the chickens. It's the other four that worry me."

"Are they still writing letters home? All of them?"

"Yeah. Sometimes. They just ain't saying much. Papa says that their letters all changed, all at the same time. Now they're just, 'Hey, how are you? Not much to report here.' They may not still be in the South Pacific or even still on ships. I worry."

With the good news coming in from Europe, Justine knew—and she knew that Georgette knew—that things would have to heat up in the Pacific Theater before the war was over for good. "I'm glad they're still writing," she said, "even if they don't say much."

She turned to put the library books on her shelf, lining their spines up precisely with the front edge of the shelf, because this allowed for air circulation behind them and because she liked the way neat bookshelves looked. The well-worn volumes smelled like dust. When Justine placed her hands on them, they felt like prayers for her parents and for Georgette's brothers. And for Gloria.

"Okay," she said in a tone that sounded brighter than she felt. "We'll have beans and rice, then we'll finish those grapes before they spoil. The pecans will keep, though, so hold on to those. I'll see if I can get a block of cheese to go with them. In the meantime, take a look at this."

She picked up her purse and pulled out the gifts that Gloria had slipped into it while Justine had been self-importantly sloshing coffee between their cups. Justine had only discovered them when she was on the streetcar, too far down the road to take them back.

Ever the scientist, Gloria had calculated how much she could hide in the purse without increasing its weight enough to make Justine suspicious, and she'd gathered her gifts in the time it had taken two scrambled eggs to set. Justine pulled each small and nearly weightless treat out, one at a time, and listened to Georgette squeal.

Six tea bags.

An envelope full of sugar, sealed and taped shut.

A tiny bag of coffee, also taped shut.

A pocket-sized box of raisins.

A pack of chewing gum.

The pack of gum was still sealed, but Justine was sure that she could smell the spearmint. Her mouth watered at the thought.

"Holy cow," Georgette whispered. "I'm gonna need some help with them algebra problems, so we might be up late again. Do you think—" She swallowed, and Justine thought Georgette's mouth was probably watering, too. "D'you think we could make a cup of coffee and split it? Just to keep us awake while you explain to me what it means when there's a *x* outside a set of parentheses that's got a math problem inside it?"

"I do think so," Justine said. "And we're going to put a little sugar in it, too."

———

Justine lay in her hard, narrow bed beneath her acid-green chenille bedspread. She couldn't sleep, and it wasn't the coffee's fault. It had been weak, and hours had passed since she drank it.

She closed her eyes, and it was as if a movie were playing on the inside of her eyelids. Planes were landing behind the Michaud plant, one after another, and people were hustling to load them full of...something. Inside the plant, she, Georgette, and thousands of other people were working feverishly to make more of whatever it was.

Sonny, the plant manager, and everybody up to Andrew Higgins could tell her that she and her friends were making "radio parts," but they couldn't make her believe it. That special plane told Justine that she was working on something secret and important. It was so important that the powers that be couldn't make themselves let the people doing the work know what was going on.

And one of the people inside the Carbon Division was a betrayer. She prayed it was only one of them.

The mysterious plane was proof that the saboteur hadn't slowed production appreciably. It would take something far more destructive than a few small, broken parts to keep more planes from filling with cargo that must be quite precious. The sabotage would be ramping up any minute now. Maybe it already had.

By Justine's guess, the saboteur had been testing the waters, preparing for a strike that might wash away everything that she and her colleagues were trying to do. It might wash them all away, too. In their own way, they were soldiers in the most brutal war the world had ever seen. This thought made Justine wonder how many people had been killed because of the work she did for Higgins. How many more deaths would be on her hands before the war dragged to a close? Did she even want to keep doing this job?

Now her eyes were open and she wouldn't be sleeping soon. Justine loved a good metaphor, but she should never have indulged in the notion of a saboteur testing the waters that might wash away a throng of innocent people. The image put her in mind of tires spinning, powerless to stop their skid as a much-loved driver tried to keep his car on a wet country road.

Maybe Gloria had been wrong about what had happened to her parents. Her thoughts were obviously muddled these days. But what if she'd been right? What if her parents' deaths were no accident?

Justine knew the answer to this question. If someone had murdered her mother and father, then she had no choice. She would hunt down the culprit and get justice for her parents.

Gerard and Isabel Byrne hadn't been soldiers or commanders. They hadn't been factory workers like Justine, manufacturing weapons to win a war. They hadn't been politicians with the power to make decisions that saved or ended lives. They had been scholars.

They had traded in one thing. Knowledge. If they had been killed by an enemy, it could only have been for what they knew. Her heart froze inside her when she realized that Gloria probably still knew it.

Justine was scared that she might know this deadly thing, too.

Chapter 13

"I saw that." Georgette worked beside Justine, her hands busy with her repetitive job while she talked.

"Saw what?" Justine asked, although she knew exactly what Georgette was talking about.

"I saw you eating your lunch with Charles Trahan, like you've been doing for a week now, every single day since he helped me save you from Sonny. Y'all looked real cozy sitting on that stack of empty crates all by yourselves in the corner of the main plant."

"I don't know what you're talking about," Justine said, but her cheeks were as red as her hair.

"And that ain't all. Let me see if I can remember all the things I saw today. And the day ain't over! First thing I saw when the bus stopped was Charles waiting to walk you inside. Then Martin Bevans hurried over to talk your ear off for your whole break. You should have seen him ditch the big ol' satchel he was carrying and hustle to get close to you before Charles did. And did you see what Charles was up to while he was doing that?"

"I did not." Actually, Justine had been watching him out of the corner of her eye, but she wasn't about to admit it.

"He was standing by the security closet door, staring at you like you was the only thing in the world."

"Are you saying that he was watching me in a romantic way? Was he thinking, 'I must duel the dastardly Martin for the hand of the maid Justine?' Or was he watching me like a masher who was planning to follow me home and scare the life out of me? Or worse. I really don't know how to tell the difference."

Georgette gave her wrench a hard whack with the heel of her hand, trying to loosen a bolt that was giving her trouble. "Ain't sure there's much of a difference between a man who's wanting to duel for you and a man who's wanting to follow you around till you give up and love him. If you feel the same as him, you like those things."

This was a disturbing thought, so Justine didn't answer. Her own bolt was giving her trouble, giving her a chance to hide her face while she wrestled with her wrench.

Georgette must have been able to tell that she'd made Justine uncomfortable, so she said, "Or maybe you could find a man with better sense."

Candace, standing on the other side of Georgette, giggled. The blond curls around her face swayed as she laughed and said, "Good luck finding one of those."

Georgette ignored her. "You can keep looking, and I think you should, but right now you got Charles and Martin to keep you company. If you want them to. So which one do you like? Charles or Martin? Both of 'em? Neither of 'em? Somebody else? Ain't no law says you've gotta decide, but they've both been chasing after you for the whole week since Sonny tried to drive us home. One of them's gonna make a move any minute now."

Justine countered the questions with one of her own. "I saw Jerry hand you a grape soda at break time. Again. Higgins must pay its maintenance chiefs well because he's brought you one three days running, ever since he heard you say you like them. Do you like him?"

Georgette laughed. "I might, and I sure do like them cold drinks. But never mind that. You're trying to throw me off the scent, and it won't work. I saw your face when I said 'Charles,' so now I know which one you like. I kinda guessed he was your type. Pale as a bookworm. Glasses like a bookworm, with nice friendly eyes behind them. Friendly smile. Real thin, like maybe he gets to reading and forgets to eat. Maybe he even needs you to feed him."

Justine let out a sharp bark of a laugh. "You've tasted my cooking. Charles shouldn't get his hopes up."

Georgette kept talking as if Justine had never said a word. "On the other hand, Martin looks like he eats a dozen raw eggs for breakfast, and that'll be quite the time-saver for his wife. I bet he picks up cars to kill time when he's bored, but I doubt he's ever picked up a book. Not on purpose. But he's a good-looking thing with that orange buzz cut and that big laugh. If you wound up with him, the two of you would sure have some happy red-haired babies."

Mavis, standing on Justine's other side, tittered and elbowed her hard in the ribs. "Justine's got a boyfriend."

"Or two," Georgette said, and then all the women standing within earshot giggled along with Mavis. "Just think. If Sonny hadn't been such a crumb last week, you might never've caught their notice. Actually, I rounded 'em up for you. Got anything to say to me?"

"Thank you? I think?"

Justine felt her cheeks go pink again, but she had to admit that it was nice to have men act like they liked her. And the women she worked with—they acted like they liked her, too. This felt really good after a childhood spent as the weird smart girl. It helped that Georgette had taken Justine under her wing and made sure she spent time talking with any woman in their vicinity.

"How's Charles to talk to?" Mavis asked. "You know. His ears."

If a man under forty was working at Higgins, and if he wasn't doing essential work like airplane design, then he'd been rejected by the military for some reason. It was widely known that Charles was hard of hearing, and some said that he couldn't hear at all.

"It's just his left ear," Justine said, grateful that her work required her to keep her eyes on it. "He says he can hear me fine when I stand on his right side."

A brown-haired woman who Justine now knew was named Nadine said, "Heck. My husband can't hear a thing I say, unless it's 'Time for dinner!' But the Navy must think he can hear, because he's been on a ship since '42."

Justine's face must have shown what she was thinking, which was that she hoped Nadine didn't resent Charles because the military wouldn't take him. Nadine patted her on the elbow and said, "I'm glad you've found a beau or two. Get a few more. String 'em all along. A pretty young girl like you should have some good times before she settles down, and men are hard to find when there's a war on."

Justine, with her incandescent hair and her freckles and her mud-brown eyes, had never felt pretty before. Not at all. But Charles looked at her as if he liked the way she looked, and he didn't seem to mind that she had no idea how to flirt. She just said what she was thinking, like she was talking to any person. The other women seemed to have different voices when they talked to men, higher and sweeter and more tentative. Different vocabularies. Different ideas, or perhaps it was better to say no ideas. They somehow managed to be completely inoffensive, and Justine was just perverse enough to be offended by that.

"What about you, Georgette?" asked Betty, a middle-aged

bleached blond with a scratchy voice that sounded like cigarette smoke. "I been seeing you walk alongside Jerry's chair all the week, just a-chatting and a-laughing. I like that man's smile. You can tell a lot about a man by the way he smiles."

A high voice from down the line said, "Or whether he smiles at all."

Several women called out "You bet!" and "You said it!" and Justine wondered if it was strange that her father had smiled all the time. Her mother had been more reserved, but a little teasing from her father had been guaranteed to make a smile bloom across her serious face.

Just that morning, Charles had told her a joke and then said, "I can't stop looking at the way you smile." As she remembered that moment, she thought she might understand why her mother had seemed to enjoy Gerard's steady stream of jokes that were honestly pretty silly.

Then Charles had followed up the compliment by saying, "I wouldn't mind looking at that smile all the time. The reason I'm still single is that I never found a woman with a mind like yours and a smile like that."

Justine knew that she would not be telling Georgette this, because she knew what Georgette would say. She'd say, "You better be sure you like that man, because he ain't looking for a girlfriend. He's looking for a wife. And he knows exactly what to say to you to get you to say yes before you know enough about him, *chère*. I wouldn't buy a boat without taking it for a spin, and neither should you. You gotta put that man through his paces before you let him talk to you like that."

Distracted by those memories and by the recalcitrant bolt, she'd missed a bit of conversation, but her attention snapped back when she felt her friend flinch at her elbow. All eyes were on Georgette.

There was a lot of laughter happening, and Nadine was shrieking, "Look at her blush!" Georgette's face wasn't a pretty blushing pink. It was as red as a beefsteak.

Through clenched teeth, Georgette said, "You can keep that kind of talk to yourself, Della."

Candace, who hadn't heard what Della said, or who maybe just wanted her to repeat it and stir up more trouble, called out, "What'd you say, Della? I missed it."

A half dozen women said, "Me, too," so Della must have been keeping her voice down.

Della had a broad face, an ash-brown ponytail, and a snotty expression. Determined to prove that she wasn't scared of Georgette, Della held eye contact with her while she spoke loud and clear.

"I said, 'Jerry might make a crackerjack boyfriend, even in that wheelchair. Even if nothing else works, I bet his hands do.'"

So many women caught their breath at the vulgarity that Justine could hear the noise like a short gust of wind. Nadine followed it with "*Della!*" Some responded with a wordless "Ooh…" Some could only manage a nervous giggle.

Georgette dropped the bolt and wrench in her hands. They hit the concrete floor with a percussive clang, and the voices of the women around Georgette rose as they took sides.

"You got no call to say that kind of thing in front of these people," Georgette said. "He knows them. He sees them every day. He works right here in this room with us, and he's a nice man. There ain't no call to embarrass him that way."

Della slid the words, "I think she likes him, chair and all," into the moment before Sonny came running over to them yelling, "Hold on. Hold on. Settle down, ladies. You got work to do. How else are we gonna get this war over and bring your fellas home?"

Georgette looked at him. She looked at Della. She raked a glare over everyone around her but Justine. Then she stepped over the wrench and bolt that she'd slammed to the floor and walked away.

"I guess she's going to the bathroom," Sonny said. "Is she going to the bathroom?"

Nobody answered him.

"She coming back?"

Still no response, but Sonny's workers were now quiet, with a razor-sharp focus on their work. He barked out, "If you can't talk nice while you work, don't talk. But don't you dare slow down the line." Then he retreated, leaving his subordinates to work out their own differences.

As she stood at her station, everyone that Justine could see was a woman, expressionless and focused on the work at hand. All those averted eyes gave Justine a chance to study their faces. Somebody with access to the Carbon Division's equipment had sabotaged the conveyor belt three times, and God only knew what they'd done elsewhere. Was it one of these women? How would she ever know? She had two thousand coworkers. If one wanted the others to fail, she would have no way to identify who it was.

Justine dropped her eyes to her own work, like everybody else. It felt dangerous to stand out in the crowd.

Nobody spoke for a long time.

———

When it was time for Justine to do her afternoon trash run, she was more than ready to flee. The women around her had gone quiet when Georgette left, and they'd stayed that way. The air had been thick with anger.

Georgette had eventually returned, taking her place without a word and resuming her work. Justine had noticed that Sonny was too chicken to yell at her for taking too long in the bathroom.

She didn't blame him. Georgette was physically imposing, tall and strong, and she was personally imposing as well. Della had guts to take Georgette on in front of a crowd.

An uneasy peace had settled, and the strain of it all had turned Justine's stomach. She was glad to have a big, heavy door between her, Della, and Della's silent, hostile friends, even if her destination was a lowly trash pen. Relieved to leave them behind, she exited through the Carbon Division's double doors into the main plant and passed through the nearest back door to get outside.

Since the Carbon Division was located on the southwest end of the plant, the trash pen that Justine used was the last of several that were spaced out equally along the rear of the long, roughly rectangular building. Each pen sat on the wide strip of pavement that provided truck access to the back of the plant. Each one sat between a door and one of the open loading docks where the trucks brought raw materials and left with finished products.

The trash pens stood far enough from the back of the building to allow an easy flow of truck traffic. Beyond a scattering of sheds and support buildings, wind blew through swamp grasses. An airstrip sliced through all that green, but Justine had never given it a moment's thought before. Now, she knew that the government was sending planes to transport the Carbon Division's products. This made the airstrip seem like a mystery stretching hundreds of feet through the weeds. She felt an illogical need to walk out there and stand on the airstrip, as if it would give her answers, but that was silly. The airplane hauling away their carbon creations had left nothing there, except maybe black marks rubbed off of its tire treads.

Justine took her time walking toward the trash pen, waiting to hear the door open behind her. She hadn't been alone the last five times she did this chore, because Charles knew when he could find her out here. As a security guard, he was able to organize his rambling through the premises, meeting her at the door and taking the crate out of her hands. This was silly, because she had been carrying it perfectly well every afternoon before he came along, but he liked doing it for her. So she let him.

It wasn't a romantic way to be courted by a man. She wore no flattering hairstyle created just for a date with him, just a frizzy red ponytail. She had no makeup on her bare face. She wore no flattering dress or high-heeled shoes, just some shapeless blue coveralls and a pair of work boots. With a pocketknife in her right front pocket and an adjustable wrench in the right rear one, she felt ready for almost anything, but not for love. Maybe she'd watched too many movies, though, because Charles hadn't seemed put off by the way she looked. He didn't even mind the greasy rag spilling out of the pocket where the wrench lived.

But there was no Charles today. It was humiliating to realize how much his absence hurt. She knew that he was probably just busy doing his job, but that didn't stop her from reliving their entire lunchtime conversation in her head while she wondered what she'd said to make him stop liking her. But maybe it wasn't her words at all. Maybe it was her nervous giggle when he looked into her eyes for a moment that was too long for comfort.

The truth was that her experience with men was nil. She had been embarrassingly flattered that Charles had chosen to spend time with her for six days in a row, but six days was nothing. She owed him nothing, and he certainly didn't owe her a stroll to the trash pen. Only now was she realizing that those six days had made her feel so bright and alive because she didn't have very much to look forward to.

Since her parents had died, her life had consisted of work, errands, chores, and a few hours a week spent alone with her books. This week, she'd had the excitement of Charles, and she'd had her new friendship with Georgette, and these things had distracted her from the evenings she'd spent scouring her books for answers about carbon chemistry. She needed to be wary of falling for a man simply because he gave her life a tiny spark of excitement.

She walked slowly, still hoping to see Charles's rangy frame loping out the door. She wished for his intelligent blue eyes under heavy, dark brows. She wanted his quick, crooked smile. She wanted to reach for his hand and know that it would feel the same way it did when he had, just once, held hers for a moment. Even after a rational assessment of how silly it was to crave a man's company after six short days, she still wanted all of these things so badly. She was a fool.

Walking slowly didn't solve her problem because Charles didn't appear. She unlatched the gate and walked into the trash pen, intending to dump her trash and go, but something propped in the corner of the pen beside the gate caught her eye. It was neither in the pile of trash nor the pile of empty crates. It was all by itself in a place where trash did not belong. The workers at the Michaud plant were orderly with their refuse, and this thing was out of place.

It was a rectangular piece of metal screen, maybe two feet tall and a foot and a half wide, and it was framed as if for a house window. Justine had never seen anything like it at the plant, nor at the St. Charles plant when she'd worked there, but it wasn't like she knew everything that went on at either factory. Somebody had obviously decided that it was at the end of its useful life and dumped it at the trash pen, but they hadn't bothered to walk a few extra steps to put it where scrap metal belonged. It bothered her orderly nature to see it misplaced. It also bothered her to see metal wasted, especially when people running scrap metal drives were working so hard to get the raw materials needed for the war effort. She hurried across the pen to get rid of the crate and free up her hands to throw the framed screen in the scrap metal pile.

She dumped the junk in her crate onto the teetering pile in the far corner, as usual, and then stacked the wooden crate with others that would be gathered for reuse. As she went back to the funny little screen, it occurred to her that she might be able to use it. The screen on her window at The Julia was ancient and corroded. She'd gotten some fine wire at the hardware store and sewn its frayed rips closed to keep the hummingbird-sized New Orleans mosquitoes out of her room, but maybe she could replace the whole thing with this scrap screen. Or at least maybe she could make some patches out of it.

As she bent over to pick it up, an odd, bright array of spots on the trash pen's wooden wall behind it caught her eye. Dropping into a deep squat beside the screen, she saw that sunlight shone through its openings, projecting a fine grid pattern onto the pen's wall that looked wrong in a way that she couldn't describe. Looking closer, she saw that the screen looked wrong, too. Some of the openings were larger than others, as if someone had hammered a nail here and there into the screen's fine grid. This irregular pattern, projected onto the wooden fencing, was the thing that had caught her eye. It looked human-made, somehow. It looked intentional.

Justine squinted at the tiny sunlit squares. The scattered dots made her think of Morse code. She wondered whether it would be possible to punch Morse code into a screen. She guessed it would work, as long as the person doing the coding came up with a way to represent dashes, perhaps with two adjacent dots. Still, it wouldn't be a very good code. Nobody who wanted to keep a secret would use an encryption method as easily solved as Morse code. And then reality dawned, as if she were hearing her own thoughts spoken out loud.

Nobody who wanted to keep a secret…

Saboteurs kept secrets. Spies kept secrets. Spies were the kings and queens of secrets. Who had put those deep scratches in three lateral guides, anyway?

Those scratches had haunted her for more than a week now. Someone had made them, and she'd hung on to the possibility that it was a fellow employee angry at Higgins Industries, or maybe someone mad at Mr. Higgins himself, who had intentionally broken the Carbon Division's equipment. The possibility that the enemy was behind the sabotage was just so hard to believe. But this screen looked to Justine like a coded message. Angry employees who were acting alone didn't need to send messages, but enemy spies did.

She heard Gloria's warnings echo in her ears:

If you think your parents' deaths were an accident, then you are a fool.

You must be more careful than they were.

Deep down, she had known that the possibility of enemy sabotage was real, and she'd known it since she saw that crane come down on Cora Becker, but her conscious mind had kept shoving it away as unrealistic. Ridiculous, even.

Still, fear of a spy's secrets had gone with her everywhere since she saw those deep, orderly scratches and ever since Gloria had spoken those terrifying words. It had driven her to search her books for answers. It had cost her nights of constant, sick worry that someone had killed her parents and, thus, their deaths could have been avoided. The fear had stolen her sleep. The books, the worry, the dreams—none of them had come close to answering her questions, but this oddly mutilated screen just might.

Her eyes turned toward the airstrip. She couldn't see it from the spot inside the trash enclosure where she crouched, but she knew where it was. It cut through the shaggy grass between the spot where she stood and the bayou, and its pavement was practically still hot from the wheels of a mysterious government plane.

Her mind had been dulled by fear, but now it was sharply focused on the coded message punched into this screen. She assigned herself a thought problem, since her mother nor her father nor Gloria was there to do it for her. Suppose that the spy *inside* the Carbon Division, the one who was doing the sabotaging, needed to get information to someone *outside* the Carbon Division. Maybe another spy and maybe a boss spy. How would he do that? Or maybe the question was "How would she do that?" because Justine worked with a lot of women.

Camouflaging a secret message as a piece of garbage and leaving it in the trash pen would be an excellent plan. It was even possible that this message was intended for somebody on the next plane that landed on the airstrip. Anybody in the plant could have put their hands on a piece of scrap screen, a frame, and a nail, so it was the simplest possible medium for a code made up of dots.

Justine desperately wanted to take it home with her. But how?

She fumbled in the pockets of her coveralls. She had a wrench and a pocketknife. Could she get this screen out of its frame with those?

Oh, yes. She could. She just needed to do it before somebody else decided that they needed to take out some trash.

Chapter 14

When Justine heard the grinding noise of a heavy factory door opening, she panicked.

Not Charles. Don't let it be Charles on his way out here. Not now.

She almost laughed when she realized that she had been wishing the exact opposite thing just a few moments before.

Justine was crouched on the pavement, her coveralls open to the waist on the very day she'd decided to leave off the blouse she usually wore under them, because she was tired of sweating through two layers of fabric. Today, there was nothing between her torso and the coveralls' blue canvas but her bra. A cool breeze tickled the skin of her chest and belly as she yanked the mysterious screen out of its frame. The pocketknife and wrench she'd used to bust its frame clattered to the ground, forgotten. She had less than a minute before the person who opened the factory door reached the trash pen and opened its gate.

It was imperative that she hide the screen. She bent it in half lengthwise, stopping just short of creasing it, because it would be self-defeating to obliterate its message while she was trying to save it. Then she held it up to the front of her body.

Yep. It would fit.

Steady footsteps grew closer, and she knew that somebody else with a crate full of trash was coming fast. Or maybe it was the person who had punched the holes in this screen. It could even be Charles, looking for her, and she was at grave risk of him finding her squatting on the ground, half-dressed.

Grateful that she was flat-chested enough that nobody would notice a change in her shape, Justine clasped the bent screen flat against her abdomen and started to button.

By the time she reached the third button from the top, she wasn't sure the coveralls were going to close. The clomping sound of boots on pavement grew louder and closer. Mashing the screen harder against her body, she felt its jagged edges gouge her tender skin, but she kept pulling. Turning her back to the gate to gain one more second before an interloper caught her exposing herself in the trash pen, she yanked one more time and got the next button through its buttonhole. The top one was a lost cause, but maybe people would just think she was trying to be alluring.

Straightening up carefully, because every last raw edge of the piece of screening was digging into her flesh, she scooped up her knife and wrench. Hurrying, she shoved them into their respective pockets and faced the gate with a bright smile. Justine hoped the smile said, "Hi! Good to see you among the garbage. I have absolutely no ulterior motive for loitering here!"

A beefy face crowned by a bright red brush of close-cropped hair appeared at the opening gate. "Hey, Justine," Martin said. He stood outside the trash pen holding a wooden crate piled high with scrap metal that easily outweighed the load she'd just dumped by a factor of three.

His voice was several decibels softer than his usual bellow. Martin always spoke to Justine this way, and Georgette said it was because he liked her.

"Hey, Martin," she said. She wished he were Charles, but she was also glad he wasn't, since she was moving like a woman wearing an awkward grid of metal wire pressed against her chest.

Martin didn't seem to notice. He hurried to dump his trash and toss the empty crate on the pile where it belonged. Then he stopped lumbering around like a nervous bear and said, again, "Hey, Justine."

He reached out a hand like a bear paw and cupped her elbow with it, gently. Then they walked together back to the factory door, and they did it slowly, because Martin wanted to tell Justine how pretty she was.

———

Stepping back inside the factory building after being in the cool, quiet outdoors was like being dropped into a steel barrel being pounded by a million hammers. The air around Justine was full of sounds, all of them percussive or grinding or sharp or all three, and it smelled like diesel exhaust and bearing grease. How was it that she stopped noticing the din and the smells every day after a quarter-hour on the job? She spent her workdays breathing fumes and surrounded by jolting noise, having casual conversations at the top of her lungs for hours on end, and this situation was just… normal. Could human beings truly get used to anything?

For the few minutes before adaptation set in, she would hear the racket, so Justine took a second as she and Martin entered the plant to listen to sledgehammers pounding sheet metal into shape. She heard circular saws shrieking their way through plywood. Cranes whined in the background. Overlaying it all was the sound of human voices trying to be heard in the ruckus. The factory was so loud that Martin had stopped trying to talk to Justine the second they stepped through the door, and she was embarrassed to realize that she was relieved.

She found it much easier to talk to Charles. He had interests and he was willing to talk about them. Some of them were the same as hers, books and music. Some of them—football, for instance—weren't, but he was interesting when he talked about them. He also seemed to like movies, and she thought it was altogether possible that he was gearing up to ask her to see one with him. Or she had thought so until he didn't show up to help her with her trash dumping.

Martin, on the other hand, didn't seem to have much to say to Justine other than, "You're pretty." These were words that she hadn't heard a lot, so she wouldn't have thought that it was so easy to get tired of hearing them.

They walked a few steps into the plant in silence, then Martin stopped walking. He looked like a man who had no talent for conversation but who nevertheless still wanted to say something. He grabbed her hand and tugged it, signaling that he'd like to step back outside.

As they passed back through the door, he leaned down and yelled in her ear. "Will you get in trouble if we stay out here for five minutes and just…you know…talk?"

This was a new development. Maybe he really did have things to say to her and he'd just been saving them up. She shook her head and said, "No, I won't get in trouble, as long as I'm just a few minutes late. I'm not sure Sonny can actually tell time." Then she followed him back outside, wondering if maybe she liked this man after all. It was a shock to realize how deeply she desired a man in her life who wanted to talk to her.

Martin closed the door behind him, then leaned up against it and crossed his arms. Justine could be oblivious, but she knew why he'd chosen that spot to lean on. Nobody could come out the door and interrupt them without him having at least a split second of warning.

Without looking at her, Martin started to speak. "I'm glad to be working here because I like being able to eat, but I don't like working here. You know what I'm saying?"

"I do," Justine said, wondering if she was supposed to say more than that.

"I just—I just don't know if this is the way I'm supposed to spend my time. I mean—" Finally, he looked at her and, for the first time, she noticed the fine lines beneath his freckles and wondered how old Martin was. There had to be a reason he wasn't off fighting the war, so maybe he was too old to serve, but how old was that? She had no idea.

The harsh sun lit Martin's lines and creases and golden-red eyelashes, and she used the moment to study his face. She hoped that this would help her understand what he was trying to say. And why he was saying it to her.

He tried again. "We only get seventy years. Eighty, if we're lucky. Maybe ninety, but I've seen ninety-year-olds. I'm not sure I wanna say that living to be ninety is a lucky thing."

Justine still wasn't sure what he wanted her to say, so she said the only thing she could think of. "I wish my parents had gotten more years than they did."

"Exactly," he said, and now she saw a light in his eyes that hadn't been there before. "If your parents could come back, how would they spend their time? Working? Or enjoying life? Mr. Higgins doesn't pay better wages than everybody else because he loves us and wants us to be happy. He pays us what it takes to make himself richer every day, and he doesn't pay us a cent more. That's what you call capitalism, and capitalists stand on the backs of people like you and me."

So Martin had been going to political meetings. Or reading. Justine had underestimated him.

She had some thoughts about her answer to his question

about how her parents would spend their time if they could have more of it, but she could see that he wasn't finished. Martin wasn't a talker, but he was apparently more of a thinker than she'd believed.

The words came out of him like an explosion. "Why should I spend my time on this earth cleaning up after people who are building machines to blow other people up? I don't even know those people. Maybe they're not evil. Maybe the newspaper people and the radio people are just telling me things to make me hate people I don't even know. How could I tell if they were?"

He stopped to breathe and to give her an intense look she didn't understand. Then the torrent of words resumed.

"Why shouldn't I spend my time doing things that make me happy, and to hell with everything else? Don't you think your parents would have rather spent the time they had enjoying it? Instead, I bet your father went off to work every livelong day and then came home to cut the grass. And I bet your mother spent her life cleaning things that just got dirty again. They were dirty again a day after she left this earth. Am I right?"

Her father hadn't come home to mow the grass since she was twelve, because Justine had taken over the job, but this was not pertinent to Martin's question. And she did know the answer to this question.

"My parents loved their work. They would have done it for free. After I was born, my mother did do it for free. They thought the work was important, but they didn't think that it was the only thing that was important. They told me, and I believed them, that they also loved our time together at home, including the housecleaning and the yard work. Even after she lost her sight, my mother took a lot of pride in keeping our home comfortable and clean. Having fun is great, but people who can't enjoy doing the everyday things aren't ever going to be happy."

His glance was sharp as he looked at her, and this made Martin look nothing like the affable lunk that he pretended to be. And his lunkishness was a pretense. Justine was sure of it now, but she didn't know why he would pretend to be something he wasn't. She did know that glimpsing the depths of the man beneath the pretense intrigued her. It attracted her, and this was a surprise to Justine.

"But this job?" he asked. "You're happy being a cog in a wheel? When you're on your deathbed, are you really going to say, 'I never saw the pyramids or a volcano, but I riveted together some bombs and they killed enough people to make somebody else's soldiers stop killing ours?"

Justine wanted to tell him about her cousin Fred in the South Pacific. She wanted to tell him about her parents' friends who had written letters about the rise of the Nazis and then fell silent, leaving her mother weeping over their empty mailbox. She wanted to explain that her job was important, but she was stuck on the words "cog in a wheel." And on the word "bomb."

No. She didn't want to be a cog in a wheel. She certainly didn't want to blow people to bits. And, yes, she wanted to see the pyramids.

All she could say was, "I want...I don't know what I want."

Rather than press his point, he changed the subject and Justine was grateful.

"What did your father do for a living?"

"My *parents* were physicists. If Mama and Papa had lived, maybe their work would have finished the war already."

"But what about this work here? What about the things we do for our paycheck?"

Justine pushed away the image of the laboratory where she'd imagined spending her working life. She shut out thoughts of finishing her workdays with enough energy for...for anything, really. Escaping her life as it was with somebody who wanted to see the pyramids sounded better than she would have expected.

Martin repeated his question. "But what about this work? Is there any way it will ever give you a life that will make you happy?"

Justine was too young to know that she didn't have to answer a question just because someone asked it of her, so she answered him. She gave him an answer that she wasn't sure she believed any longer.

"I guess I'm saying that there will be time for fun when the war is over. Right now, I'm happy to be doing my part to help the world make sense again."

He nodded as if she'd given him the secret answer to everything.

"But is there any rule against fun?" he asked. "I mean, as long as you wait until you've done all the saving-the-world stuff a girl can manage in a day?"

She laughed and shook her head.

"Then come dancing with me tonight," he said.

Justine tried to remember her mother's advice that she shouldn't make herself available to a man on short notice, but it was very hard to say no to Martin, who had suddenly decided that he knew how to talk and that he liked doing it. He told her about the dance club where they could kick up their heels. He told her all about the hot band from somewhere out west that would only be playing one night. He made sure she knew that the bartender had a source for fine liquor, not the harsh stuff that wartime had forced on most drinking establishments.

Justine wasn't sure that she wanted to go alone to a nightclub on the first date with this man she barely knew, but she didn't know how to say so. She wasn't sure if Martin could tell that this was bothering her, or whether he was taking a lucky shot in the dark, but she was ridiculously relieved when he gave her an odd, close look and said, "Would it sound more like fun if I talked to

Jerry? Maybe see if he wants to ask Georgette? We could make it a double date."

The words "Oh, yes, that sounds like a lot of fun," came out all in a rush. "Yes, I'd like that."

"That'll be sweet," he said. "Don't you live somewhere near the St. Charles plant? That's the bus I see you riding. The club opens at ten, but it's a little bit of a walk from there. I'll pick you up at nine thirty. Put your glad rags on, 'cause it's a swanky place. You're so serious, like somebody that needs a real good time. I'm gonna show you one."

Then he looked her up and down, taking in the carbon dust caked on every visible square inch of skin, and said, "I think you're gonna need a little time to get ready. Tell me where you live, and I'll be there to pick you up at ten."

Only when she'd given him her address did he stop leaning on the door that stood between the two of them and every human being for miles around.

———

Martin watched Justine pass through the door that separated the Carbon Division from the rest of the plant, and he thought, "You, my dear, were not made for this place. You're not going to last long here. Not long at all."

Then he went back to the kind of chore that filled his days, moving boxes from one part of the plant to another.

Chapter 15

Justine had begun to believe that Sam-the-Timekeeper would never blow the end-of-shift whistle, but its earsplitting screech finally came. After working three solid hours with a piece of sharp-edged metal screen stuck between her coveralls and her bra, she would be oh-so-glad to get home and rid herself of it.

Unfortunately, Sonny stood between her and the door to sweet freedom. As was his habit, he leaned unpleasantly close to her and put his lips next to her cheek, so that he could holler straight in her ear. Sonny knew that he could get away with this, because they were standing too close to the machinists' whining lathes to be heard any other way. The icky thing about Sonny was that he so obviously enjoyed it.

"I'll be quick, 'cause I don't wanna make you miss your bus. I need you to come in to work tomorrow."

She tried to say, "I've been working for six straight days. I need my day off, Sonny," but he cut her off.

"I know Saturday's your day off, but I'll make it up to you." Sonny's breath was hot on her already sweaty face. "You can take Sunday off. Mavis has Sundays off, and she's been after me to schedule her for more hours. She says them kids need clothes and she's gotta work more hours to pay for 'em. She'll be happy as a pig in mud to cover for you on Sunday, so's you can have your day off."

None of this told Justine what he wanted her to do on a Saturday morning that Mavis couldn't. She dreaded the thought of another long day doing monotonous assembly work.

Sonny's whiny voice kept droning on. "I got another couple of broken parts and nobody wants to spare me one of their full-time welders. I can't wait until the other foremen start feeling generous with their welders' time. Good thing you can weld a little."

Justine could weld more than a little, but she held her tongue about that.

"Just tell me what you need me to do, Sonny. If you want something cut, I'll cut it. If you want something put together, I'll put it together. But please do me a favor and make sure your boss knows I can do those things. I'd dearly love to put my welding skills to work on a full-time basis."

"Because it pays more?"

Yeah. Because it pays more. Why do people usually go to a job like this one every day? To work for free?

The rebellious feelings came to her so quickly and with such heat that she wondered whether she should stay away from Martin and his dreams of escape, because she couldn't afford those dreams. Justine swallowed her words and her anger because it wasn't worth antagonizing Sonny.

"You've got yourself a welder. I'll be here tomorrow morning. What do you need me to do?"

"This place seems to be falling apart at the seams. Another lateral guide broke a minute ago, and I know you know how to fix that. And I need you to do it before the dang replacement part breaks, too, and I'm left with nothing. The line's still running today because Jerry found me a spare part. One. And who knows how long it'll last?"

Justine felt this news in the pit of her stomach. A fourth broken lateral guide was one more fact supporting her fears that a saboteur was at work, breaking things that seemed unimportant but weren't. A lateral guide was just a chunk of metal until it broke and the conveyor belt stopped bringing her parts to bolt together. Just like that, everyone on her line was idle, and whatever they were supposed to be making for the war effort wasn't getting made.

The next thing out of Sonny's mouth really got Justine's heart going. "The other thing I want you to fix is part of a grinder in the machine shop."

The machinists were critical to the Carbon Division's work. Every one of its assembly workers would be idle in an instant if the machinists stopped crafting parts out of nothing but blanks of carbon or steel. The women running those machines—and most of them were women—had the special swagger that came with the knowledge that they had rare and indispensable skills. Interfering with their work would be an excellent way for a spy to gum up the works.

"What's wrong with the grinder?" Justine asked, hoping it was something that she knew how to fix.

"It's just a broken tool rest, and it seems like Nelle oughta be able to keep working without that. Ain't no woman alive needs to make a machinist's pay, but she does, so why can't she hold her own dang tools? You know?"

Justine held her face absolutely still, but it was a good thing that Sonny was looking at her ear instead of her eyes. She wasn't sure her welding skills were valuable enough to force him to overlook her current level of insubordination.

Since he couldn't see her eyes, he kept talking and he kept insulting Nelle, who did something every day that he could never master in a million years. "Seems like I'm wrong about her holding her own dang tools, as it turns out."

His tone turned even more mocking than usual. "'You gotta get it fixed, Sonny,' Nelle says. 'The specs are right there in black-and-white. The tolerances on the slot I'm grinding are in mils.'" He cast an I'm-smarter-than-you look at Justine and said, "A mil's a thousandth of an inch, y'know."

Justine badly wanted to tell Sonny that she knew what a mil was, but he was still talking.

"Anyhow, Nelle had the nerve to say that not even a man can hold something steady enough to grind it to those specs. Without that tool rest, she says she might as well throw everything she does in the trash. Well, maybe that's true and maybe it ain't, but she's got me over a barrel. There's plenty of work for the night shift machinist that don't need a grinder, but I don't have enough of that kind of thing for Nelle to do tomorrow. She's gonna be sitting on her hands if it ain't fixed bright and early."

He turned his mockery and his anger from Nelle to Justine. "So, ya see, honey, if you can't fix that tool rest, Mr. Higgins might as well take all that money he's paying Nelle and light it on fire."

Justine wanted to say, "Why do you care what Nelle gets paid? Is it coming out of your pocket?"

Instead, she said, "So the tool rest is important?"

"Yeah. Fixing that broad's tool rest might win the war. Just like anything you do around here might win the war."

Spare me the patriotic motivation, Sonny. I already agreed to come in on my day off.

"You'll be here first thing tomorrow, ready to weld?"

"Yes."

"Good. Now run on out and catch that bus, 'cause I ain't got time to take you home. The wife and I got places to go on a Friday night."

Justine grabbed her bag and hurried to clock out, jogging along and dodging incoming workers clad in clean coveralls. Workers in dirty coveralls were still moving toward the exits, and that gave her hope that she might make the bus. It hadn't been all that long since the quitting time whistle blew, so she might even be getting ahead of people like Georgette, who had probably stopped in the restroom to clean up.

Apparently, Justine could move fast when she needed to, because the bus was still only half-full when she got there. The driver greeted her with the nickname he used for all the women whose work clothing, blackened by clouds of carbon dust, showed that they worked in the Carbon Division.

"Hey there, Dusty!"

She had flailed around for days to find a suitable nickname for him. She wasn't good at lighthearted banter, but she had settled on a name for the bus driver that must be okay, since it made him smile.

"Hey there, Cabbie! Take me home?"

"You got it, Dusty. For you, cab fare is always free."

He was smiling as she hauled her tired, sweaty body up the steps, dropping into a window seat a few rows behind him. The aisle seat beside it was empty, so she could save it for Georgette, who was still nowhere in sight. Wincing as the screen inside her coveralls jabbed into her armpits and belly, she leaned down awkwardly to tuck her bag between her feet. Pausing there, she reached inside her boots and rubbed her ankles, swollen from six long days in a row on her feet. Those feet needed to hold up one more day before they got some rest.

Something large dropped into the aisle seat while her face was still in the vicinity of her knees. She figured it was Georgette, so she mumbled, "Are you as ready to get home and crawl into bed as I am?"

The voice that said, "Could you repeat that? I want to hear it again," was not Georgette's. It was deep with a masculine edge, yet somehow still soft enough to make her want to lean closer. She didn't have to look up to know that Charles was the person whose butt had hit the seat next to her. Knowing this, she never wanted to sit up straight again—not if it meant having to face Charles—but she couldn't spend the rest of the ride bent double. Slowly, she unfolded herself.

Face burning, she raised her head but couldn't meet his eyes. Instead, she spoke to his cheek and jaw, faintly stippled by the black stubble of a long day. "I was talking to—" She tried again. "You're not—" She gave up and looked him in the face. "I thought you were Georgette."

"I know you did, and I shouldn't have teased you that way. But you're really pretty when you're blushing. You're really pretty all the time."

Charles had never said she was pretty before. He'd kept his chatter light and, frankly, not very romantic, except for the weird moment when he had skipped straight to telling her what he wanted in a wife. Except for that one moment, and except for that one time when he'd taken her hand, Justine had wondered whether he was just looking for somebody who liked to talk about movies and books. She felt a little bit bad for Martin because all of his admiring talk had done nothing to make her feel this way. Charles had accomplished it with six words.

You're really pretty all the time.

Justine wished her younger self could hear those words, the freckle-faced one who didn't get anything close to a woman's figure until she was past seventeen. And she wished her current self knew how to answer Charles with enough enthusiasm that he would know she liked him, but not with so much that he would ever take her for granted.

Because she was a coward, she blushed and giggled, then changed the subject.

"I'm confused," she said, masking her feelings with another giggle. "This isn't your bus."

"You're not glad to see me?"

"Oh, I am, but don't you live somewhere near the lake?"

"I've got some errands downtown, so I thought I'd let Mr. Higgins and his employee bus save me the cost of getting there. I can get myself home on a city bus after I finish shopping."

"Good thinking," she said, then she let the conversational ball drop for an awkward moment. Ahead of her, she saw Georgette slip quietly into the seat behind the driver, carefully setting her brand-new bag, large and navy blue, on the seat beside her. Georgette cast a knowing grin over her shoulder as she did.

Charles waited until the silence was truly uncomfortable, then he leaned over until his lips were almost brushing her ear. Why did it give her a thrill when he did this? When Sonny did it, she wanted to elbow him away and then boil her ear.

"While I'm downtown tonight," Charles whispered, "do you want to see a movie?"

Justine had been waiting—anxiously and almost pathetically—for Charles to ask her out. She was not prepared to be angry when he did so.

Tonight? He wanted her to hustle her sweaty, tired body into a bathtub, so that she could be ready to spend time with him at the drop of a hat? What was wrong with these men? Did they think she sat home alone every evening, waiting for one of them to decide he wanted to show her a good time?

Well, she sort of did. Sit at home alone, that is, so she'd only been mildly upset with Martin for showing that he knew it was true. When Charles did it, though, she was incensed because she actually liked him. Therefore, she forgot her manners. She told him how it was, and then she rubbed it in a little by telling him that tonight's date was a little more grown-up and exciting than a simple movie.

"I'm so sorry," she said, looking at him through her eyelashes the way that she'd seen other women do. "I have a date tonight. Martin's taking me out for drinks and dancing." Then she spoiled her coquettish act with a moment of self-deprecating truth. "Not that I'm much of a Jitterbugger, and I imagine that's what everybody will be doing."

His face fell. Sorry that she'd hurt his feelings, she said, "Another time?" so quickly that she could just imagine what Georgette would say to her.

Chère, you need help with talking to men. They're gonna chew you up and spit you right out. Especially now when the few fellas that aren't out fighting have got their pick of women.

Charles seized the lifeline she'd thrown him. "Tomorrow night? A movie?"

Her face must have said "Yes," because he continued talking without waiting for her answer.

"I'll pick you up in time for the eight o'clock show," he said. "To tell you the truth, I didn't really need to ride this bus all the way downtown just to be makin' groceries. And I certainly don't need Mr. Higgins to cover my bus fare to the grocery store. I just wanted an excuse to sit and talk to you on this long, long trip all the way into town today. Tomorrow, I can ride the city bus on my own dime to pick you up. Come to think of it, I may be able to get there on the streetcar, depending on which line runs close to your house. Where do you live?"

And that's how Justine gave her home address to two men she barely knew in a single afternoon. To do otherwise would have insulted them. It wouldn't have been ladylike to say, "I don't trust you enough to tell you where I live. I'd rather take a walk in the dark on city streets to a movie theater or, worse, a public drinking establishment. Then I'll just sit there, conspicuous and alone, until you show up." Also, it wouldn't have been safe.

Was she safe with Charles and Martin? She had no idea, but the rules of dating were not created to give women an awful lot of control over their safety. She shoved aside her fears because they couldn't be helped, not unless she planned to be alone for the rest of her life. Instead of worrying about whether she was wise to make herself vulnerable to either of them, she chatted with Charles all the way home while she fretted over her date with Martin.

Her lips were chattering about the latest Barbara Stanwyck movie, but her brain was reviewing the contents of her wardrobe. She hadn't bought a party frock since her parents died, so her dresses were several years old, and they had been chosen for a high school girl by a protective mother with old-fashioned taste.

Justine was virtually certain that not a scrap of her clothing would qualify as a glad rag.

About a mile down the road, Justine said, "I've been told that it was almost impossible to build this highway. The land around here is barely above-water at low tide. At high tide, it's a coin flip as to whether we'd be standing on wet or dry ground. If we got off the bus, I mean." Then she kicked herself for sounding like an egghead instead of prattling on about the latest Bing Crosby record.

"So we'd be hip-deep in wet mud or muddy water?"

"Exactly. I heard that the engineers who built Chef Menteur Highway brought in a dredge boat to scoop up the clay for the road bed, which seemed like a great idea until the boat sank. When they finally got all the clay they wanted, they still didn't think the road would stand up under heavy traffic, so they brought in railroad cars full of slag all the way from the steel mills in Birmingham to stabilize it. Now that I think about it, though, I'm not sure how they built railroads that could support all that slag, not on this muck. So maybe they used barges."

Now Justine was kicking herself for taking the conversation to the unromantic topics of steel mill slag, barges, and dredged-up mud, but she was terrible at small talk. Give her an interesting topic, though—and apparently she thought slag and mud were simply fascinating—and she could hold forth for hours. This could be deadly if Charles wasn't interested in slag and mud, but he was leaning past her to look out the window at the unending marshes alongside the highway.

"*Prairie Tremblante,*" he said. "I've heard it called that. I'd hate to try to build a highway on top of land that trembled when I walked on it. Why do you think they needed to bring in slag when they could have used something close to hand like...I don't know...crushed oyster shells?"

"I would've at least given crushed oyster shells a try. There's certainly plenty of them around here, and they're cheap."

He was interested in the same things she was, and he appeared to be interested in her. Justine was trying to make herself believe that this was true when Charles leaned toward her and said, "Do you mind if we swap seats?"

Justine stopped talking and looked at her hands, trying to remember which was the right one and which was the left one. More importantly, she tried to remember which of Charles's ears was the one that was hard of hearing. When she realized that she'd been talking into the wrong ear since he sat down, she wished she could fall through the floorboards of the bus, right onto Chef Menteur Highway and its steel mill slag foundation.

He laughed at the look on her face. "It's okay. I've been keeping my head turned so I can hear you, but it would be easier if I were sitting in the window seat."

"Yes, yes, certainly," she said, trying to stand up and change seats with him while avoiding full body contact.

If she hadn't known better, Justine would have said that Cabbie the Bus Driver was aiming straight for every available pothole during this maneuver. Twice, she was thrown hard into Charles's body, but she twisted herself in mid-air, pressing only her side, shoulder, and hip into his. She would have absolutely fallen through the floorboards if she'd found herself pressed against him, breasts to ribcage and pelvis to pelvis. More than that, though, she couldn't let him feel the hard, sharp springiness of the folded wire screen tucked inside her clothes.

"I hear you've been welding lately," he said, as he settled himself into the window seat.

She searched his face to see whether he thought this was a good thing. Did he like women who stuck to women's activities? He was smiling, but his face was somehow still unreadable.

"Yeah. Papa taught me how. Who knew that it would come in so handy?"

"I think it's impressive that you can weld."

She felt the tensed muscles in her hands relax.

"Does it ever bother you, though, that you're building machines that will kill people? Maybe a lot of people?"

She started to blurt out that he did the same, then she remembered that he didn't. He was a security guard. He protected the people who were building weapons, but he didn't build them himself. Was that really so different?

"But we're defending ourselves. We aren't entitled to do that?"

"Ah, yes. Pearl Harbor. It was a terrible thing. A cowardly sneak attack. But it can't excuse us for everything we do in the name of the people who died there. Maybe it can for now, but not forever."

Justine's brain began an argument with itself, cycling between

"He has a point," and "I'm proud of my work," and "I like this man and I want him to like me." Her pride won.

"I think my work is important. It's not just a paycheck to me. Although I have to admit that the paycheck is pretty important."

"No kidding. Mine, too. And it's big enough to pay my bills—"

He paused, looked at her thoughtfully through eyes that squinted when he smiled, then added with a grin that seemed not quite sincere, "—and buy movie tickets for me and a pretty girl from time to time. I can do those things because of the union's hard work. If we didn't stick together, that wouldn't be true."

Justine didn't know what to say, but she wanted to keep the conversation light.

"You sound a little teensy bit like a Communist," she said with a smile that she hoped lightened a statement that could have been taken as an insult.

"Is that so bad?" She thought he might be about to laugh at her. Instead, he maintained a wide smile while he chose words intended to tweak at her naïveté. "We have nothing to lose but our chains, and we have a world to win."

Now Justine was really flailing. She'd read *The Communist Manifesto* because her mother had been serious about assigning her extracurricular readings. Isabel Byrne's opinion had been that women should be conversant in politics, and it bothered her that the nuns running her daughter's all-girls high school didn't agree. To be fair to the nuns, this was the first moment when a single word of her mother's extracurricular readings in politics had come in handy when Justine was talking to someone whose last name wasn't Byrne.

The time had come to whisper, *You were right*, to her late mother. Or maybe her mother wasn't right, because every other woman in the world would have told Justine that challenging a man intellectually was the death knell for romance. Well, so be it. If she couldn't find a man like her father, who had enjoyed his wife's mind and encouraged the work of the women around him, then she'd be a happy spinster.

Wearing a look that said, *You want to talk politics with little old me?*, she quoted Marx and Engels right back at him, saying, "Where is the party in opposition that has not been decried as Communistic by its opponents in power?" Then she waited for him to reject her because he preferred dating featherbrains. It had happened before.

Instead, Charles sat there for a moment, his face silent and blank, as if as if thinking maybe both ears had stopped working.

Then his face lit up. "I knew I'd enjoy talking to you. You're interesting."

———

Justine held a bright smile that she hoped was slightly coquettish as she exited the bus in front of The Julia, waving goodbye to Charles.

"See you tomorrow night!" she chirped in imitation of young women who were popular with young men. She was doing her best, but she was dead-sure that her filthy coveralls and carbon-caked hair detracted from the effect.

As soon as the bus where Charles sat started rolling, she slipped through The Julia's front door, closed it behind her, and then leaned against it as if she were trying to keep out the Big Bad Wolf. Georgette, who had been a lot quicker to get off the bus, was waiting for her in the parlor.

"Well, look at you," Georgette said, yanking Justine off the door and wiping with her hand at the carbon smears her clothes had left behind. "You look like a woman excited about her date tonight, but you won't be going nowhere if Mrs. Guidry kills you because you got her door dirty. Why on earth was Charles on our bus? Did he ride all this way, just for a chance to ask you out?"

"I think so. And I do have a date tonight. Just not with Charles."

"I know who your date is." Georgette flapped her hands in excitement. "Jerry stopped me right when I walked out of the Carbon Division, wanting to know if I'd go out with him and you and Martin. Said he was sorry for asking at the last minute. He was real sweet about it, so I said yes."

Justine started to wonder what it would be like for Georgette, going out with a man in a wheelchair to a place where everybody else would be dancing, but Georgette looked happy, so her concern went straight back to herself. It occurred to her that Jerry might well be a better dancer in his chair than she was on her feet.

"Holy mackerel."

Georgette laughed in her face. "Them's strong words for you. You're practically cussing."

"I'm going to have to dance, and dancing isn't my best thing. And I don't think any of my dresses will pass muster."

"Have no fear, *chère*. You have come to the right place. I will take care of you, but believe me when I say that you're gonna have to scrub all that carbon off yourself first."

Chapter 16

As he sat on a busy wharf, watching the sun turn the Mississippi River molten orange, Mudcat looked back on a most success-ful day. Later, he could revisit his plan and make sure that all of the moving parts were working as they should be to put Justine Byrne right where he wanted her. Right now, though, a single sentence was bouncing around in his brain.

She took the bait.

————

Not far away from Mudcat, Fritz sat on the levee, watching the same sunset. He had decided to make his move.

He couldn't go on working as a sole agent with no word from the Fatherland. His last message and his last infusion of cash had come shortly before the disaster in Normandy. With Europe fall-ing, one nation at a time, he might well be marooned forever in this country. He didn't relish spending the rest of his life one step ahead of the American operatives who would like to see him in the electric chair or swinging from a noose, so he was mounting an all-out effort to save himself by making contact with what was left of Germany. He had given the effort a grandiose title like the ones so beloved by military men, and he had also named it after himself: Operation Fritz.

Mere weeks had passed since the strange new items had come into production at the Michaud plant. An unexplainable veil of secrecy had surrounded the Carbon Division from the start, and people didn't bother to keep secrets about things that were unimportant. Based on this truism, these mysterious items were the key to Operation Fritz.

The Carbon Division had sprung up from nothingness, fully formed, like Athena from the forehead of Zeus. In wartime, this could only mean that its mission was critical to the war effort. The goal of Operation Fritz was to get word that he had information on that critical mission, whatever it was, to someone who could pull him out of his position behind enemy lines. His superiors in Germany? Their peers in Japan? Someone on Mars? He did not care.

No security detail had been posted to guard the Carbon Division's closed doors. He'd never even seen a security guard pass through them, and this seemed perversely sinister. It meant that the purpose of those carbon parts was so secret that even security guards couldn't be trusted. The Carbon Division workers served as their own security detail. They were sworn to secrecy, they knew who belonged behind the closed doors, and they would tolerate no intruders.

The personnel managers at Higgins were shrewd. The people assigned to work behind those closed doors had no obvious vulnerabilities, and this had complicated Operation Fritz. Fortunately, Fritz knew that everybody's armor had a chink in it. This was good, because he had recruited one agent behind those doors, and he needed another one who wasn't so dimwitted. This thought took him straight to the not-dimwitted Justine Byrne.

His agent inside the Carbon Division had managed to interfere with a key conveyor belt four times, slowing production of whatever it was that the American government wanted Higgins Industries to build. His agent was incapable of finding out what that mysterious thing was, but there was value in slowing down production while Fritz plotted his next steps.

Justine Byrne had foiled these efforts by welding the broken parts back together again and again, and this intrigued Fritz. A woman who could mend broken parts was a woman who could effectively break them and make sure that they stayed broken. She was a woman who could ferret out the reason for the Carbonites' apparent importance.

Was Justine the capable, competent agent that he needed so desperately? He thought she was. Without her, he might never learn the full extent of Higgins Industries' capabilities.

Fritz found Higgins Industries, and Andrew Higgins himself, fascinating. Andrew Higgins had been a one-person geyser of innovation since the war began. He had designed boats that could carry tanks. He had designed a lifeboat that could be dropped from a plane and stay seaworthy. He had designed one shallow-draft vessel after another, culminating with the duck-billed Higgins Boats that had carpeted Omaha Beach with invaders. This meant that the key to avoiding the terrible losses in Normandy had been here in New Orleans all along.

The Higgins Boats had changed everything, but they had never been the real secret weapon. Andrew Higgins was.

Fritz knew, deep down, that the value of a top-flight inventor always lay in the next improbable dream. He knew in his soul that Higgins's next dream was in production at the Michaud plant, right now. It was behind the doors to the Carbon Division. He just needed somebody to tell him what it was.

Fritz would have given his right eye to recruit Andrew Higgins, but the idea was laughable. The man had grown rich by supporting the Allies, and people whose prosperity is tied to their political systems are impossible to turn. He'd considered assassination, but no. It was far better to let Higgins be Higgins, then steal his designs. There were notes and drawings at his house that would help the Fatherland immensely once he was able to get them there. They gave critical details on the construction of Higgins boats, ships, and planes, all of which he'd been able to observe in the main plant throughout the construction process. But he couldn't get through the doors of the Carbon Division, so he had failed to get his hands on those designs. He needed an agent who could bring them to him, and time was running short. Who would have thought that his best hope would be a woman?

Justine Byrne was an extraordinary human being in many ways, and one of them was her capacity to rise above the limitations of her gender. The Michaud plant was chock-full of women who couldn't do that, yet they were earning paychecks that had caused them to forget their place. They strode around with their wide hips crammed into trousers, like poor imitations of men. Blacks moved among them, side by side with Jews. He had no doubt that there were homosexuals on the Higgins payroll, certainly among the rawboned women who looked far too comfortable in their ill-fitting trousers. It was even possible that some of the brown-skinned ones were *Zigeuner*, the ones called Gypsies in this country. If Herr Eichmann could have seen the subhumans employed by Higgins Industries, he would have told Fritz to put a torch to the place at first sight. Instead, Fritz had brushed shoulders with people who disgusted him, and he had waited for just the right agent to help him. He had waited for Justine.

Fritz was good at what he did. If he'd been assigned to work for Andrew Higgins just six months sooner, he would have seen the Higgins Boats for what they were. He would have set all the

Higgins plants aflame, and those damnable amphibious boats with them. Instead, the chunky, unassuming little flat-bottomed boats had wallowed right up onto the beaches of Normandy, lowered their innovative ramps onto the sand and waves, and vomited out enough men to justify the overwrought moniker, Operation Overlord.

He had arrived too late to stop Operation Overlord, and now he was grieving the debacle in Normandy. But maybe it wasn't too late to salvage victory. Maybe Germany could take back the lost European territory and more. The right weapon could still turn the tide.

Up until now, his instructions had been clear. He had been told to let the Michaud plant's mongrels and its mannish women and its womanish men continue to breathe, so that he could steal their secrets. But did those instructions still hold now that he'd been cut off from his superiors?

Self-preservation had driven him to consider other options. Soon, he would have to decide whether to follow his orders or to strike out on his own, preferably with the help of a certain red-haired woman as an operative. If Operation Fritz played out to its ultimate conclusion, his superiors would know that he was alive, and they would know where to come for him. And, he hoped, for her.

Chapter 17

Justine sat in an old claw-foot tub that was big enough to hold all of Lake Pontchartrain, and the water was even warmer than that big brackish Louisiana lake. She wanted to soak the evening away, but every woman on the hall needed time in the bathroom. Taking the time to soak the stiffness from her muscles would have earned her some enemies. Also, she needed to get ready for her date. Regretfully, she got out of the cooling water and drained it, dried off, put on her bathrobe and house shoes, and shuffled down the hall to her room.

Georgette was already there, staring balefully at the clothes hanging in one of the battered walnut chifforobes that Mrs. Guidry provided for each room in lieu of a closet. It was just a narrow, tall, double-doored piece of furniture that didn't hold much, but then Justine didn't own much.

"D'you even know how to dance?"

"Some. My mother taught me the foxtrot. And some other things, like—"

"Can you Jitterbug? Because I don't even want to hear about them other dances."

Deflated, Justine shook her head.

"Where are they taking us?" Georgette asked, still staring into the closet. "Jerry didn't say."

"I think Martin called it the Ticky-Tacky. Something like that."

"Ooh. The TickTock Club. I've heard about that place. The owner goes to New York every year, just to find out how they're doing things in Harlem. The decor, the music, the costumes... they're all the latest. These clothes ain't even a little bit right for The TickTock. Mine ain't great, but they'll do, so let's spend our time on figuring out what to do about you."

She stuck her head in Justine's chifforobe again and considered the dresses inside, one by one. Justine could hear each wooden hanger sliding along its wooden bar and clacking into the next one. "Nope. Nope. Goodness, no. Nope. Um...maybe?" She held up a plain black silk dress with a short bolero jacket and studied it. "I say we ditch the jacket. I hope you got a ruffled slip or two to go under the skirt. With the cute cut of that bodice, your waist'll look so little he'll be worried that you might break in half."

Georgette yanked the bolero off the coat hanger, leaving a full-skirted dress that was very simple, yet with a certain austere elegance. It also had narrow straps that would show all of Justine's collarbones and shoulders. She felt cold looking at it.

"It's a lot better than your coveralls, and that's all these men have ever seen you wear. Anything's a big step up from baggy, dirty coveralls."

"I can't argue with you there." Justine set up a mirror on her table and sat in front of it, ready to set her hair in pin curls. Georgette's hair was already tied up in rags.

"I don't know why I'm doing this," Justine said. "It's not going to dry in time."

"Sally down the hall has a hand dryer. I borrowed it for the both of us."

"I've heard about those. Never seen one."

"I'll go get it while you twist your hair up. And, for goodness sake, eat something. You can't go to a nightclub on an empty stomach." She shuffled through the food on Justine's shelf and found the last piece of a loaf of bread. "This'll do."

Opening a jar of peanut butter, Georgette dipped a case knife deep into the brown goop and spread a thick layer on the crumbly white bread. "Here you go. It'll keep you sober. Well, sober enough."

As Georgette headed for the door, she said, "Get a move on. I gotta have time to teach you to dance."

"I told you I could foxtrot. And my mother taught me how to do the Lindy Hop."

"The Lindy Hop? Is this 1929? You're gonna Jitterbug because I'm gonna teach you. I ain't gonna let you embarrass yourself, and I sure ain't gonna let you embarrass me. Let me go get the hair dryer before you and your foxtrotting give me a conniption."

Georgette was out the door, but Justine could hear her mumbling. "She can do the Lindy Hop. Heavenly mercy. I bet her mother taught her the Charleston, too."

Justine did indeed know how to do the Charleston, but this was a fact that she would not be sharing with Georgette.

She cast a nervous glance at the top shelf of her bookcase. She'd tucked the coded screen securely behind the books on that shelf, and she'd planned her to spend her whole Saturday alone with it, but now she was going to have to work. Maybe she should have turned Martin down and stayed home instead of going dancing, but how could she have known that Sonny was going to make her work on her day off?

Besides, what if there really was a spy watching her? Nothing would set off louder alarm bells than a woman turning down an evening at The TickTock and sitting home alone. This shameless bit of self-justification made Justine laugh at herself.

Nope. She was going to go dancing because she wanted to go dancing. It would be a great big joke on her if she stayed home, only to find out that she was wasting her time on a beat-up piece of window screen that was worth nothing more than any piece of scrap metal. She twisted up another curl and pinned it in place, promising herself that she would at least stay up late enough to transcribe the screen's punched pattern onto a piece of paper before she went to bed. That way, she could carry the paper to the plant and work on it whenever she had a spare minute.

Her pin curls were done when Georgette returned with the hand dryer, a sleek, teardrop-shaped device made of powder-blue sheet metal and fitted with a wooden handle. Justine flipped its switch and pointed the nozzle at a pin curl just in front of her right ear.

Georgette had changed into a burgundy taffeta dress with a swingy skirt that stopped just below the knee, and she was carrying a couple of hemmed scraps of green taffeta that she held out to Justine. "Once you get the dress on, tie this long one around your middle. It'll make a right pretty sash that'll perk up that black dress."

The other scrap of fabric had been twisted into an elegant rosette. Georgette balanced it on her palm, and the light caught its emerald softness. "This one will be real nice in that red hair of yours."

"Oh, thank you! I'll take good care of it for you."

"I made it for you. Keep it. Now get that hair dry. I still need to show you the difference between the Lindy Hop and the Jitterbug. You do pretty much the same thing with your feet, but the Jitterbug's all about what you do with your rear end."

———

Justine quickly learned that holding a machine next to her head while it blew hot air on her wet hair was boring, even while munching on an open-faced peanut butter sandwich. Georgette had gone back downstairs to put makeup on her face and legs, so Justine couldn't pass the time by talking. Moving the blast of hot air to another pin curl, she stretched her arm out and grabbed her mother's copy of *The Theory of Spectra and Atomic Constitution* by Niels Bohr off the bookshelf. She was immediately captivated by the essay on atomic structure and the physical and chemical properties of the elements, so she said only "Hmmm?" when Georgette returned, wearing a head full of brunette ringlets waiting to be brushed and styled. She was carrying a hairbrush and a cloth bag full of hairpins.

"Doing a little light reading again, I see. Care to tell me what that book's about? And do you maybe care to tell me why you're reading something like that when you're supposed to be excited about your date?"

"Is Martin exciting? Sometimes I think he is, but I can't decide."

Georgette shrugged. "He might be a little more of a thrill if the two of you were on the same side of forty, but there's a war on. When it comes to men these days, you take what you can get. Anyway, you're just gonna dance with him. You don't have to marry him."

"You think he's that old? I knew he was older than me, but I wasn't sure."

Justine stopped to consider the men she saw from day to day. It was obvious that Sonny's foot had kept him out of the military. Jerry's wheelchair had done the same, and so had Charles's hearing. How old were any of them? She thought Sonny was in his late twenties, but Charles and Jerry might be past thirty. And maybe Georgette was right that Martin was over forty.

Georgette was still speculating about Martin's age and

physique. "I couldn't tell you how old he is, but there's gotta be some reason he ain't in the Army or on a ship someplace. Or flying a plane. Either he's too old or he's 4F. And if he's 4F, it ain't for any reason you can see with your eyes. He's got quite a body on him."

Justine unpinned one of her curls to see if it was dry. Not yet. She coiled it back up and clipped it to her head. "Well, like you say, I'm just going dancing with him."

A knock sounded, and the door opened before Justine could say, "Come in," or "Who is it?" or even "Go away!" Mrs. Guidry was the one opening it, and Justine was not surprised. The woman had no concept that her tenants' monthly rent gave them any claim to privacy.

"I looked in your room, Georgette, and you weren't there. All the other girls said that this is where I'd probably find you. You've got a phone call from somebody named Sonny," she said, then she waited for Georgette to follow her downstairs as if she had no idea where the telephone was.

As she left Justine's room, Georgette was muttering, "He wants me to come in tomorrow. I just know he does. We're both gonna lose our day off. But does that mean that I'm not gonna kick up my heels tonight? No, it does not."

Justine sighed in solidarity and aimed the hair dryer at the next pin curl. Then she went back to reading what Niels Bohr had to say about the Stark effect.

———

"Still got your nose in that book?" Georgette's shoulders were slumped as she trudged back into the room, so Justine knew that she, too, had lost her day off. "Maybe you should try drying those curls while you're lying in the bed. You're gonna wish you did tomorrow, when you're working all the day after dancing all the night."

Justine patted her head all over with the palm of her hand. "Too late. I'm dry. Time to do my makeup."

She spread the contents of her makeup bag across the table, starting with a shiny metal pot of pancake makeup to cover her freckles and even out any pinkness, plus another pot of cream rouge to put pinkness in the right places. Beside it, she set a smaller compact of cake mascara and her two tubes of lipstick, Pink Champagne for daytime and Red Coral for evening. All of her pots and tubes were encased in the same golden metal. A matching palm-sized compact held face powder to set all the other makeup so that it would hopefully stay on all evening. Another small compact held dark-brown powder for her pale-red brows. The best part of all was the tiny cut-glass bottle full of real perfume that she had so few occasions to wear.

"Holy Mother of God," Georgette said, brushing her fingers over the gleaming tubes and pots. "You go out every day with a bare face when you got all this stuff?"

"Who needs powder in the morning when you're just an hour away from getting dusted with black carbon?"

"You got a point."

"My mother got this set for me for my eighteenth birthday, only a couple of months before Pearl Harbor," Justine said.

She did not go on to say, *Only a couple of weeks before she died.*

"This was her favorite brand. The company stopped packaging makeup like this when the war made metal so hard to get. Fortunately, I don't use it much, so it's going to last me a long time."

"And that's one of her books you're reading?" At Justine's nod, Georgette said, "She must have been quite a lady. D'you think I might be able to understand that book if I read it real slow?"

Justine considered, then shook her head and said, "Someday, but not yet."

Instead, she pulled another volume off her shelf and handed it to Georgette. "This is the book my parents used to start teaching me physics. Simple machines, ballistics, heat and light, thermodynamics. Things like that. You'll need to keep practicing your algebra, but I think you can work on this at the same time."

Georgette flipped through the pages. "Simple machines, you say. 'Simple.' Huh. Well, I'll give it a try. You're gonna be surprised at how friendly I'm getting with them little x's and y's."

Georgette clutched the book so hard that her knuckles were turning white. Justine could see how badly she wanted to understand what was in it, but the book in Justine's hand, the one that lay out of her reach for the time being, drew her like a candle draws a moth. "You're reading this one particular book why? Out of all them books you've got to choose from, I mean. Why this one and why today?"

Justine took a second to answer as she colored her lips with Coral Red lipstick. After pressing them together and blotting them on a handkerchief, she said, "I'm just flailing around. My parents and their friends were doing some interesting work in using spectroscopy for separations. Everybody but Mama, Papa, and Gloria got jobs and moved far away, some of them right before the war started and some of them right after. I thought it was weird that they were so hush-hush about what they were going to be doing. Don't you think most people would be chattering away about a new job that was so much better than their old one that they were willing to move across the country and start their lives over?"

Georgette's big laugh bounced off the walls. "I talked the ears off of everybody in Des Allemands when I got this job. 'I'm goin' to the big city! And they're gonna pay me so much!' Everybody got sick of hearing it."

"Exactly. I remember hearing Gloria say something once about the government scooping everybody up, but Papa elbowed her and she stopped talking. And I've been remembering something else lately. About 1940, there was a big stink about a paper on neptunium written by McMillan and Abelson. *Physical Review* published it, and why shouldn't they? I mean, they'd identified a transuranic element, for goodness' sake. Neptunium."

Georgette's mouth was full of bobby pins, but she managed to say, "I know I always publish my neptuniums."

"Yeah, well, the British government got all upset about that paper giving away what they called 'nuclear secrets.' At the time, I thought, 'Every atom's got a nucleus. What's so secret?' Rumor has it that Seaborg wrote a paper about another transuranic element that got pulled and still hasn't been published."

Georgette was shaking her head. "I ain't even gonna ask what 'transuranic elements' are.'"

"They don't occur in nature, and they're really, really big."

Georgette nodded sagely. "That's what I thought."

"Anyway, the same thing happened to us a couple of months later. Papa was an associate editor for another journal, and Mama helped him with it. When she lost her vision, I helped her. Somebody submitted a paper about using carbon as a neutron modulator in fission piles. Uranium fission, I think. The British didn't like that article, either. We had to pull it just before the journal went to press."

"I only understood one word you just said, and it was 'carbon.' Does that connect this transuranic stuff to what us Carbonites do?"

"Exactly. Well, maybe. So while we're dancing tonight, just imagine me thinking about using carbon for neutron modulation in uranium fission piles."

"You're gonna live alone for the rest of your life. You know that?"

Justine flashed her a brilliant Coral Red smile and batted her blackened eyelashes. "Look at me. He won't be able to tell I have a brain in my head."

"Repeat after me. 'I'm supposed to think about the man I'm dancing with, not about transneuroniums.'"

"What's wrong with thinking about both?"

Using a tiny brush cut to razor sharpness, Justine darkened her eyebrows, one stroke at a time. "Your hair's so dark, I bet you don't have to do this."

"Yeah. Not my eyelashes, neither. Saves me some money on eye makeup. Just like them silk stockings sitting there on the bed save you money on leg makeup, but good lord. Where'd you get 'em?"

"I've had them since before the war," Justine said, knowing full well that she was admitting that she hadn't done any dating since before the war.

Georgette missed the opportunity to tease her about her scintillating social life, because she was still fascinated with the Bohr book on spectra. "You said that people are doing separations with spec-TRAH-scopy. Did I say that right?"

"You did."

"So what's the government wanting to separate?"

Justine was once again impressed by the way Georgette's raw intellect cut straight through to the heart of things. She figured she should get just as quickly to the point.

"Do you know what an atom is?"

"The littlest, tiniest piece of stuff that there is?"

Impressed again, Justine said, "Basically, yes, but atoms are made of even smaller parts. Not long before the war, Niels Bohr announced that he'd broken a uranium atom in two." She waved Bohr's book so that Georgette could see the connection between their conversation and the essay she'd been reading.

"So that's what you mean by 'separation'? Breaking an atom?"

"No, not actually. Breaking an atom is usually called 'fission,' which comes from the Latin word for 'split.' You know...splitting an atom. But before you can get to the fission part, you've got to decide what atom you're going to split, and Bohr used uranium. If I understood everything I heard right, there's a particular isotope—"

Georgette gave a frustrated sigh.

"Just think of two uranium isotopes as different kinds of uranium. One kind doesn't weigh as much as the other one, and it splits better. Because life is hard, the easy-to-split kind is really rare and it's all mixed up with the regular kind. Don't breathe a word of this, because all those scientists probably shouldn't have been talking about top secret stuff in front of their friends' little girl, but I think a bunch of spectroscopists got hired by the government to figure out how to separate uranium isotopes."

"Honestly, Justine. I like hearing about this stuff, but guys can be...limited. Please try to be more interesting in front of the fellas."

Justine dipped her fingers in the pot of rouge. "Splitting an atom releases an incredible amount of energy, way too much energy to be boring."

Her words were met with a blank stare.

Justine tried again. "If you could control that energy, you could do a heckuva lot of things. You could power trains and cars and airplanes and boats. You could heat a city all winter long. You could make electricity. You could—"

Justine had been taught to follow every idea to its logical conclusion, but speech failed her when she reached the end of this train of thought. Slowly, she was able to make her lips frame the words. "Nuclear fission releases so much energy that you could use it to build weapons. You could build a bomb." She tried to say, "You could build the biggest bomb you could ever imagine," but her words failed her again.

Ever reasonable, Georgette said, "But we've already got bombs, and they do a real good job of blowing things up. Or so the newspapers say. What's so special about a bomb that's made out of atoms?"

It was a perfectly reasonable question. Skipping the opportunity to muddy the waters by telling Georgette that all bombs were made out of atoms, Justine said, "You've seen newspaper stories about whole squadrons of planes—lots of squadrons of planes—dropping bombs on a target, one after another after another? Right? Maybe you saw newsreels about it when you went to the movies that time. Every time that happens, hundreds of pilots risk their lives. Hundreds of factories like ours build the planes. And the bombs. Some of those pilots and planes don't come home."

"Well, sure. Everybody knows about all that."

"What if it only took one plane carrying one bomb to do all that damage and more? What if you could wipe out a whole entire city with one bomb, one plane, and one crew? Maybe the enemy's capital city?"

Georgette, who knew only one city that was a fraction of the size of Tokyo and Berlin, could still picture that level of destructive power. She paled.

"If we had a bomb like that, we could drop it on Hitler and on Emperor Hirohito and on everybody around them. This would all be over."

Justine said, "Yes, it would," and then she caught her breath at how easily they were both speaking of uncountable deaths. Then she said, "Or they could wipe out Washington, DC."

"Not to mention our military bases. And every port we got."

Both of their faces turned involuntarily to the Mississippi River not half a mile away. Just a few miles in the opposite direction was Lake Pontchartrain. The two bodies of water floated away everything Higgins could build, all the way out to the Gulf of Mexico and then to the world. The lake and river floated in raw materials to make more.

More, more, more. There was always a need for more materials, more planes, more boats and ships, because the war was a ravenous thing that ate planes and ships and human beings, always asking for more.

"We're a target," Georgette said. "Right here in New Orleans. We're a target."

Justine could see that this was the first time that Georgette had given their peril any real thought. She envied Georgette that innocence, which must have taken some perseverance for her to hold on to, considering that New Orleans had endured blackout drills to prepare its citizens for an enemy attack.

"Yes. We are a target. And that's why we have to be first."

"The first to kill a city with a single bomb," Georgette said, her voice rough.

"If we're not first, then the enemy will be. They'll pick one of our cities and destroy it. Maybe a lot of our cities."

The details weren't clear to Justine, not yet, but her gut said that carbon parts would be very useful in separating the uranium isotopes that an atomic bomb would require. She came home every day and washed carbon dust off her hands, but she wasn't sure she could ever wash off the blood of a pulverized city. She grabbed her compact and brushed blindly, fluffing powder over her whole face as she tried to brush away her horror.

Chapter 18

With Georgette's expert help, Justine's hair had been curled and styled until it had the burnished glow of coiled copper wire. Justine thought that coiled copper wire was beautiful, so she was happy with this result. The somber black of her dress and the gleaming green of the taffeta rosette only made her hair look brighter. Georgette approved, so she switched her focus to her next goal, which was improving Justine's dancing.

Their housemates were already out with their dates, because their jobs hadn't required them to wash off a thick layer of carbon dust, so The Julia's parlor was all theirs. Georgette was a good teacher, so she ran Justine through the basic Jitterbug step and some underarm turns in minutes, before charging right into some real showoff moves. By the time a knock sounded on The Julia's door, Justine was dizzy from doing The Eggbeater, and she wasn't sure she'd ever remember how to transition into Fishtails, but she'd forgotten how nervous she was. The knock brought her nerves right back.

"Upstairs! Upstairs! Shoo!" said Mrs. Guidry, who took it upon herself to ensure that her residents' dates began with decorum. "I'll answer the door. Never forget. A lady must make an entrance."

So they waited in Justine's room until Mrs. Guidry made a slow, sedate walk upstairs to tell them what they already knew. Their dates had arrived.

They followed her decorously down the stairs to the parlor where Martin waited alone.

Mrs. Guidry leaned toward Georgette, and her whisper was loud enough for everyone to hear. To be honest, Jerry likely heard it outside, where he and his wheelchair waited at the bottom of the entry stairs.

"I'm so sorry, dear. If this gets to be a regular thing, I'll have somebody build a ramp."

Martin extended both arms, so that Georgette and Justine could each take him by the elbow. "It's not a problem at all, ma'am. Jerry and me, we'll come over here on our next day off and build you one. Even if this lady shows Jerry the road tomorrow, lots of people do better on a ramp than they do on the stairs. Maybe it'll even help your business if you can rent to ladies who could use a ramp to get in this fine establishment."

Martin suddenly looked much better to Justine. Up close, she could see the clear gray of his eyes and the determined set of his full lips. She had always liked his sunset-orange buzz cut. She slid her hand comfortably into the crook of his elbow as they walked out of The Julia, nestling it between his firm biceps and brachioradialis muscles. She was pretty sure he knew she noticed their size, because he flexed them against her hand.

As they passed through the door, Jerry came into view, sitting relaxed in his wheelchair and wearing a smile brighter than his white-blond hair. Georgette dropped Martin's arm like a bad habit and clattered down the stairs in her black stack-heeled shoes. At the bottom of the steps, she paused for an awkward moment, unsure how to greet him. The option of casually taking the arm of a seated man didn't exist for a woman approaching six feet tall in her heels. Leaning down to kiss him on the cheek was way too intimate for a first date. She might have taken his hand, but they weren't even at the holding hands stage yet.

Jerry didn't let the awkwardness last for even a fraction of a second. He spun his chair with a flourish, bringing himself knee-to-knee with Georgette. Taking her by the hand, he brushed his lips across her knuckles and said, "Greetings, mademoiselle."

Martin said, "Heck. I shoulda done that. Can I have a do-over?"

Too nervous to speak, Justine gave him a little smile and moved her hand a fraction of an inch in his direction. Martin grabbed it and moved in close. With his lips pressed hard against the back of her hand from wrist to knuckles, he kissed it with a resounding smack that seemed to echo all the way to Julia Street. The noise surprised Justine into laughter. This made her worry that she'd insulted Martin, which made her want to run back into The Julia and slam the door behind her. Martin, who didn't seem to insult easily, just laughed right back.

Jerry said, "Shall we make our way to the dancing establishment, ladies? But first, the flowers."

That's when Justine saw that Jerry was holding two corsages in his lap, both of them made of big white chrysanthemums festooned with ribbons. He handed one to Martin, then they both made a big show of presenting them to their dates. She and Georgette helped each other pin the flowers to their dresses, then stood back to check the effect.

"Devastating," Jerry pronounced.

"Yeah," Martin said with a dazzled grin. "What he said." Then he grabbed Justine's hand and took off walking, calling out, "Let's go dancing!"

Justine stumbled over her peep-toed pumps, but she managed to catch up with him without being dragged off her feet.

Jerry gave his chair's wheel an extra-hard spin to catch up with

Justine and Martin, but Georgette didn't have a bit of trouble keeping up with him. She even threw in a rock step and a free turn, both done so quickly and deftly that Justine couldn't have duplicated them on a bet.

"Let go of her hand, Martin," Georgette ordered as she shuffle-stepped down the uneven sidewalk. "I already gave Justine one dance lesson this evening, but there ain't much space in The Julia's parlor. This sidewalk gives us some room to kick up our heels. I'm gonna make a dancer out of her long before The TickTock's bouncer tells us hello."

———

Under the streetlights, Georgette and Justine danced on uneven brick sidewalks all the way to The TickTock Club. True to Georgette's word, Justine's tuck turns and breakaways were really quite passable by the time they got where they were going.

Martin hadn't let Georgette carry the teaching responsibilities alone, stopping her every block or so to show them both a new dance move. Jerry had taken a similar approach to entertaining the ladies, putting his shiny steel wheelchair through its paces in patterns that made Justine think of ice skaters doing figures. She was also now in possession of the knowledge that he could spin his wheelchair on a dime, because he'd done it about six times.

Justine had gone to girls' schools for junior high and high school, so her knowledge of men over twelve was limited, but she was coming to believe that they never stopped behaving like twelve-year-olds. Or maybe they did grow up, but reverting to exuberant adolescence was a human mating ritual along the lines of a peacock spreading his tail feathers. She was surprised to find that she rather liked seeing Martin and Jerry this way, relaxed and happy, with no thoughts of the war that was going on without them. Or perhaps it was more accurate to say that none of the four was harboring thoughts of the war that they were willing to show.

The TickTock's bouncer handed the two couples off to a cocktail waitress who fawned over the men and told the women their dresses were adorable. Then she efficiently conducted them through the crowd of revelers to a table on an aisle that made it possible for Jerry and his chair to get to the bar, the bathroom, and the dance floor with ease. Justine could tell by his relieved grin that he hadn't always gotten this kind of service. The waitress was rewarded with a kiss on the hand from Jerry as he slipped a generous tip into the hand he was kissing.

"Ask the ladies what they're drinking," he said to her. "This guy and me—we'll have Sazeracs. This round's on me."

Martin grinned his thanks and said, "And the next one's on me, so keep 'em coming."

Justine tried to order an Old Fashioned, since it sounded quaint and traditional, but she must have hesitated long enough to signal that Georgette should have coached her on cocktails. Cutting her off after "Old Fash—" Georgette said, "No, honey. You want a Pimm's Cup, but you can taste my Hurricane and see what you think."

The TickTock Club was as loud as Higgins's Michaud plant, but instead of manufacturing boats, The TickTock manufactured fun. In the place of screeching lathes and clanging hammers, The TickTock offered hot jazz, clinking glasses, and a rising tide of human voices. The big, open room was crowded with four-person tables spread with snowy white cloths. The tables surrounded a wooden dance floor on three sides, with a stage for the spotlit band rising above the fourth side. The walls were covered in paper printed in gemstone colors—ruby, emerald, sapphire, and topaz—and lit by wooden sconces crafted out of cuckoo clocks. The TickTock theme extended from the clock-shaped floor lamps that lit the room, but not too much, to the massive spotlights rising above the band on bases that looked like grandfather clocks.

Justine didn't know what the clubs in Harlem looked like, so she was going to have to take Georgette at her word that this was how they did things in New York. She was terrified by the thought of venturing onto the crowded dance floor, but she would have been happy to quietly soak up the room's music and ambiance all night long.

Their drinks had hardly arrived when she saw somebody she knew, several tables away. "Look, Georgette. It's Darlene from work. I want to go say hello."

The women rose together. As they maneuvered through the crowd, faces started to turn their way. By the time they neared Darlene's table, everyone in the vicinity was looking. Justine paused in mid-step, leaning toward Georgette to whisper, "Why's everybody looking at us? Is it because Darlene and her friends are Black? Did I do something wrong?"

"No, sweetie. Look around. The band, the singers, the bartender, the owner, and more than half the audience—they don't look like us. I'd say we're guests here, and we need to show some good manners."

They finally reached Darlene, who squealed as all young women do when they see their friends. They squealed back and everybody admired each other's dresses and hairdos and corsages.

Darlene squeezed their hands and said, "Looks like everybody's out here spending our paychecks tonight. Thank you, Mr. Higgins, for those pretty paychecks! Do you know Nelle and Ralph? And my husband, Kenny? Kenny and Ralph are on the custodial crew with that muscled-up redhead you're with, Justine. Martin's his name, right? And Nelle came to work in the Carbon Division this week. She just got finished training as a machinist."

Georgette looked as impressed as Justine was.

"You keep that up!" Georgette said. "The country needs a lotta machinists these days."

"And welders," Darlene said, smiling at Justine, who wanted to say something like, "Oh, shucks," but just ended up blushing as only a redhead can.

"You two been here before?" Darlene asked.

Justine shook her head. "No, but it's beautiful and so is the music."

"So are the drinks. Trust me," Darlene said. "Have the Planter's Punch. It's the specialty here. If you like pineapples and rum, you'll thank me."

The two women shook hands with the men and hugged the women, then they made their way back toward their dates. Halfway there, Justine stopped to look around the room.

Georgette must have seen how hard she was thinking, because she said, "You got something to say that the men can't hear, doncha? I do, too. Let's go find the ladies' room."

The TickTock's ladies' room featured a lounge with furniture upholstered in pink chintz printed with cartoon clock faces, and nobody was sitting in there. The women dropped into two chairs, and Georgette spoke softly, in case anybody walked in.

"You been wondering for hours why somebody like me has got a dress like this one."

Justine stammered, but nothing sensible came out of her mouth.

"Well, somebody in my family has a fais-dodo every week that rolls. I can't buy me a bunch of dresses to go to all them dance parties, but I can sew. I imagine Darlene and Nelle made their dresses, too. I mean, heck. Nelle can operate a lathe. It's a sure thing she can run a sewing machine. Everybody ain't as well off as your family was, but there's places like this where regular people can have a good time."

Justine had never once thought of her family as "well off." Her hand brushed the green rosette in her hair that Georgette had made for her, and she said, "My parents' idea of a good time was to invite a bunch of their friends over to drink wine and argue about Dr. Einstein's last paper. That means I know that I like red wine, but I wouldn't know a Sazerac if it jumped up and bit me. Speaking of which, it makes me feel...odd...to see our dates spending so much money on us. The drinks, the corsages, the tips. It's a lot. If what Mr. Higgins says is true, he doesn't pay the men any more than he pays the women. I couldn't afford to take Martin out for an evening like this, so unless a custodian makes more than an assembly line worker, he shouldn't be doing it for me."

"Well, he might make more than we do. All the custodians and security guards are men, so paying them more would be a sneaky way to say everything's all equal when it really ain't. But you forgot one thing. You and I both know that we're gonna lose these jobs the second the soldiers come home. Plus, we're just getting started in the world. We ain't had years to put money aside like our dates have. We can't afford to act like a man without a care in the world—no wife, no kids, no mortgage, no nothing, just a nice little savings account. And no worries about getting another good job. Jerry and Martin can."

This was true, and it didn't take into account the money that Georgette was sending to her parents.

"I hope I don't embarrass you because I don't know how to act at a place like this," Justine said. "Or how to talk to men. Or how to dance the Jitterbug. Do you think I embarrassed Darlene by going over there?"

"Goodness, no. And you know what else? Folks pay attention when somebody's nice. After tonight, you'll always have friends here at The TickTock, and your drinks will always be strong. If our dates get fresh, people will look out for us."

"So I didn't do the wrong thing?"

Georgette shook her head. "No. You didn't. Your mama taught you how to behave. You saw your friend, and you said hello. That's what nice people do."

"Do you think I embarrassed our dates?"

"They didn't say nothing, but they didn't come with us, neither. Let's say that they're on trial for now. That's the way it's supposed to be when you're steppin' out with a new man."

"He's on trial and you're the judge and jury deciding whether he gets to continue enjoying your company?"

"You got it, honey."

Chapter 19

Now that Justine had it in her head that Martin was on trial, she felt like she was a teacher giving a student marks for their performance. She knew a lot more about being a good student than she did about dating, so this was helpful.

Martin had been friendly and considerate all evening. She'd be a liar if she said he wasn't good-looking. He was a good dancer, but not so good that Justine felt stupid trying to keep up with him. He made his leads obvious, so she could usually tell when he wanted her to twirl. She could also usually remember the things Georgette said about swinging her backside the Jitterbug way. She was having a really good time, but Jerry was having enough fun for all of them.

The dance floor was crowded, but people made room for the man who could make his wheelchair rock and spin. Jerry danced in his chair, holding Georgette's right hand lightly with his left. Sometimes he leaned forward to lead her back and forth in complicated patterns that made Justine's head swim. Sometimes he tossed her hand in the air as a cue for her to take a double turn on her own. And all the time, Jerry was laughing and smiling.

Justine could see why Georgette liked him.

———

Justine had lost count of how many songs she'd danced to, much less how many Planter's Punches she'd had since Darlene recommended them, but she was starting to worry about sweating through the bodice of her dress. It was a relief when Martin said, "Do you want to get some fresh air?"

Putting a gentle but firm hand on her shoulder, he guided her through the crowd that blocked their way to the door. His hand made Justine acutely aware that her shoulder was bare except for a flimsy silk strap. Every time he steered her left or right, she ended up a little closer to him, so she was snugged right up under his arm by the time she felt the evening breeze on her face.

As they moved away from The TickTock's brightly lit entry, his hand slid to her waist, but slowly, so slowly that she was sure he could have counted every hook and bone in her longline bra. She had no doubt that he was interested in what was under her dress, but it wasn't her bra that he was thinking about. She was glad when his hand, gliding down the smooth silk of her bodice, stopped at her waist. It pressed her flesh in a way that left no question what he was trying to say to her.

Since her experience with the opposite sex was limited to fending off the awkward fumblings of teenagers whom the nuns had imported from a boys' school to make the dances at her girls' school more interesting, the enormity of her ignorance struck her hard. She knew one thing for certain. Martin had been to The TickTock at least once, most likely in the company of a woman, because he knew exactly where he was going. Steering her past a handful of couples pretending that the darkness hid their embraces, he pulled her around a corner of the club's brick façade and into a secluded alcove.

Now both of his hands were on her waist, and he was turning

her to face him. A boy would have already been pawing at her breasts and she would have been reflexively pushing him away. But Martin knew how to let the moment be. He held her just close enough, so that she could feel the heat radiating from the body that had just been dancing with hers. Justine wanted him to kiss her more than she had wanted anything for a long time.

Instead, he gave her what she'd always said she wanted. It was what she did want when she wasn't pinned to a wall by a man she desired far more than she'd realized. He gave her a man who wanted to talk.

"I'm not staying in this town forever," he said, his lips a quarter-inch from her brow. "I want things I can't get here, but I don't want to leave alone. There's a whole world waiting for me. It could be waiting for us, you know."

She tried to speak, but the words kept spilling out of him. "I know we just met. I can give you time, but I can't give you much time, because I'll die inside if I have to stay here much longer. And I'll die inside if I have to leave without somebody to share the world with me. I've been around long enough to know that you're one of a kind, Justine."

She tried to tell him he was out of his mind, but nothing came out.

"I've been watching you for longer than you know, since I started working at the St. Charles plant. From the start, I couldn't take my eyes off you. Don't tell me you didn't know I was there."

She tried to tell him that she knew nothing about him, if only so she could hear the words and remind herself that they were true. Nothing came out.

"Give me a chance to show you what I've been feeling for a long time. Let me take you to dinner tomorrow night. And the next night. I want all your nights."

She tried to tell him that the next night was out of the question because she had a date with Charles, but she couldn't, because his mouth was on hers. Even if it hadn't been, she couldn't have spoken because he had taken her breath away.

———

Justine hoped her hair wasn't rumpled as Martin guided her back to the table where Georgette and Jerry waited. Two full drinks were also waiting, thanks to Jerry. She didn't want any more alcohol to come between her and her good sense, but she took a sip to be polite. The top layer was watery. She knew it wasn't because the bartender was pouring her skimpy drinks, because Georgette had been right. The TickTock's bartender seemed to want to be Justine's friend for life. If this one was watery, then she and Martin had stayed outside long enough for the ice cubes to melt.

To hide her nerves, she took another sip, a deep one. Once she drained the watery top layer, she reached a layer that was more rum than pineapple juice. This was not optimal. She was now permanently dizzy, and it wasn't just from a full night of jitterbugging.

"You two missed some good songs. Let's dance," Georgette said. She reached out to tuck a loose strand of Justine's hair behind her ear, and Justine knew by this that her hair was indeed rumpled. At least Georgette wasn't feeling the need to straighten her dress out for her.

She made it onto the dance floor without staggering, no mean feat when wearing high heels while tipsy, and then muscle memory set in. Martin's strong hands whipped her through turns and patterns that threw the whole room into a blur, but she was keeping up with him and she was still on her feet.

Georgette's voice was calling out, "Look at her go!" It

penetrated the background roar of happy voices, so she was apparently doing better than keeping up. She was dancing well. It was entirely possible that she would dance well until she dropped, and it was entirely possible that this was going to happen soon.

Georgette had been teaching her to make her turns smooth by keeping her eyes on a single spot, and Justine thought that this might save her. Her eyes, darting around in search of an anchor, landed on something that looked stationary, safe, dependable. Only when she had fully focused on her new anchor did she see what it was. As she finished her double turn and her eyes returned to that point, there stood Charles.

There was no doubt that he knew she was there because he was staring straight at her. His eyes were unreadable, but she could see one thing. The vulnerability, the humor, the kindness— everything that she had liked about Charles was gone. He raised a full glass and consumed half the amber liquid in it with a single swallow. Then he slammed the glass so hard on the table in front of him that some of his drink sloshed out, but he didn't see it happen because his eyes never left her face.

What on earth was he doing at The TickTock? She knew that he hadn't had longstanding plans to go dancing, since he'd asked her to go to a movie that very night.

Had he followed her? This was certainly possible. Just hours before, he'd been sitting on the bus that had deposited her at The Julia's front door. It would have been easy to park himself somewhere nearby and wait for her to leave on her date. It seemed romantic when men did things like this in the movies, but the thought of it happening in reality made her queasy.

Justine leaned toward Martin and half-yelled, so that she could be heard over the band playing the intro to the next song. "I'm a little tired. Let's go sit down for a minute."

"Sure. I'll order another round of drinks."

Justine did not want another drink. Charles's unreadable face made her want to gather her wits.

Georgette and Jerry must have seen them leave the dance floor, because they were right behind them. Justine thought that another trip to the ladies' room might be in order, so that Georgette could reassure her that she was fretting over nothing. Then she saw that Charles had positioned himself so that she couldn't get to the bathroom or the main exit without passing him. It had been almost two years since hundreds of people had died in a fire at a nightclub in Boston, the Cocoanut Grove, so surely there was an emergency door or a back door or a service door or something. Surely New Orleans had laws requiring such things by now. Surely her friends at The TickTock, who cared enough about her to pour her drinks that were mostly ethanol, wanted to make sure that she didn't burn to death along with all the other revelers around her.

Justine settled herself in her seat, the same seat where she'd been having so much fun before Martin had so thoroughly confused her and before she'd seen Charles's stare. Unfortunately, this put Charles behind her. If she craned her neck over her right shoulder, she could see him, but then he would see her looking at him. Instead, she busied herself with arranging her rustling black skirt under the snowy tablecloth. She could feel his eyes on the nape of her neck, which was tingling as the skin atop her cervical vertebrae crawled.

Justine's distress apparently didn't show, since Georgette, usually so perceptive, was leaning over with a grin to tell her something funny. Then Georgette's face froze, still grinning as it stared past Justine's shoulder.

"What's he doing here, and why's he looking at us like that?" Georgette's voice was barely audible, but it trembled.

Justine felt the fear of a fox cornered by baying hounds. She felt like prey.

A wood-on-wood groan sounded, obvious even over the ear-splitting band. Justine turned her head and saw Charles dragging a chair up to their table, which was only large enough to seat four. Determined, he shoved Jerry's wheelchair until it rolled far enough forward to let him pass, then he jammed his chair and his body between Justine and Georgette. They both stared as his lean form dropped into the interloping chair. His body no longer looked lanky and harmless. It looked like a spring under tension.

"What's cookin'?"

Charles smacked his drink on the table hard, but there was so little left in the glass that nothing sloshed out. Raising his hand, Charles made eye contact with a waiter, who hurried away to fetch him another drink. Before the waiter had taken three steps, Charles tossed the rest of his drink down his throat.

"You told me you weren't much of a dancer this afternoon, Justine," he said, leaning so close she could smell the bourbon. "You said it in the same breath that you said you were going dancing with another man. I had to come see whether you were just being modest. Turns out that you're quite the hoofer."

"I dance. I never said that I didn't dance at all." Wondering why she felt like she needed to defend her truthfulness, she got specific. "I only said that I didn't Jitterbug much."

The Planter's Punches appeared to have loosened her tongue because she kept prattling on about dancing.

"I can Foxtrot. I can do the Lindy Hop. I can waltz."

"Waltzing sounds like fun. Dancing slow, up close and face-to-face, can't be bad." His hand was flat on the table, but he was sliding it in the direction of hers, the one that wasn't holding her drink. She switched her Planter's Punch to that hand as a way to fend him off.

She was too nervous to make eye contact with Martin. The extra chair, the one that was holding Charles, had smashed the two couples uncomfortably close together, so she could feel Martin's anger. Against her outer thigh, hip to knee, his leg was trembling.

Justine didn't know what to do other than to keep blabbering about dancing. "You're right. Waltzing *is* fun. So's the Foxtrot. And the Polka. My godmother's Polish, and she taught me to do the Polka. And my parents' other friends taught me their dances, like the Der Deutsche and the Zwiefacher and the..."

"Der Deutsche?" Martin said. "That sounds German."

Dizzied by the pent-up hostility around her, and also by the Planter's Punches, Justine didn't connect the word "German" with her country's enemy, only with people she loved who had taught her their native dances. "A lot of my parents' friends were German. A *lot* of them. There were a lot of people doing great physics in Germany back when my parents were alive. Guess they still do. Some of them got out in time, but some of them are still there."

The rum was really talking now. She had admitted that her parents were dead, so she'd lost any protection she might have had from two touchy suitors who both knew where she lived.

"Are those people in Germany...are they Nazis?" Jerry asked. "Maybe they want to still be there."

She felt Charles draw away from her, and her tipsy brain thought, *Maybe this is how I can nip this thing in the bud. Maybe Charles doesn't want to be stepping out with a woman who's friendly with Germans. Of course, Martin may stop liking me, too. Do I care? I don't know.*

"I don't know about most of my parents' German colleagues. They seemed perfectly friendly and warm. But a few? I was pretty young when we were over there, but I heard what a few of them had to say about *die Zigeuner* and *das Judentum*. My parents gave me a talk about how wrong they were, and we never saw those people again. They wrote letters, but my mother threw them away. So yeah. Probably Nazis."

"You've been to Germany?" Martin was silent a moment, then he said, "Do you speak German?"

"My parents started teaching me German when I was just a kid. More and more science is being published in English, but not so much that you can ignore German publications."

And now she was compounding the sin of fraternizing with the enemy with the crime of being an eggheaded woman. Everybody at the table but Georgette looked shocked. Georgette looked like someone who wanted to be shocked but who also would never let down her friend.

Jerry and Martin were literally recoiling, leaning hard against their chairbacks. It seemed that Justine had perfected the art of pushing men away.

Charles, by contrast, had recovered from Justine's revelation. His brushed-back dark hair fell onto his forehead as he leaned over to whisper in Justine's ear, and it took everything in her to resist brushing it away from his brow. When he'd said what he had to say, he let his hand drop onto hers, caressing it in a way that was guaranteed to get a reaction from her date. His touch left Justine utterly shaken. Everything she had felt in Martin's arms—the pounding heartbeat, the quickened breath, the all-over flush of blood suffusing her skin—all of it paled in comparison to the feel of Charles's cool hand on hers and the resonance of his deep voice in her ear.

She turned her head to look at him, and there was a question in his sharp, intelligent eyes. She couldn't have hid her answer if she had tried.

She didn't know if Martin saw. Surely he saw.

Her date leapt to his feet, shouting, "Stop touching her or I'll make you sorry. And you—" His eyes were on Justine, and his glance was as hostile Charles's glare had been when she first saw him lurking across the room.

Standing in a half-crouch, Martin shoved the table hard in Charles's direction, oblivious to yelps from Georgette and Justine, whose legs were battered by the table's legs.

Charles's hands shot up, palms out, and the moving table stopped like it had hit a brick wall. He rose to his feet and sent it back at Martin, harder, banging its legs against the women again. The table caught Martin just at the hinge of his hips. He folded, throwing his center of gravity so far forward that he couldn't stay on his feet. When Martin went down onto the tabletop, sending their glasses to shatter on the polished wood floor, the word "Fight!" rippled through the crowd. Immediately, the groaning sound of a few hundred chairs being pushed back drowned out the band's rendition of "Chattanooga Choo," but the musicians had seen bar fights before. They kept on choo-chooing.

When Martin lifted himself off the table, leaving it clear of everything but the liquor-splashed tablecloth, Justine acted. Fed up with both men, she lifted the edge of the table a quarter-inch. Raising her toes, she set the nearest table leg down on the inner sole of her peep-toe shoes. Keeping her hands flat on the table for stability, it was easy to use her foot to lift her side of the table slightly off the floor and balance it in that precarious position for a moment.

When she saw that the men had fully distracted each other, Justine used the mechanical advantage of her strong thigh muscles to raise her foot three feet off the ground, canting it away from her so far that the table almost flipped onto its side. Then she yanked her shoe out from under the table's leg and let it crash back to the ground.

Georgette must have been watching Justine's every move, because when the table landed, she quickly jammed the toe of her own shoe under the leg nearest her, ready to repeat Justine's trick. Or, judging by the set of her jaw, she was ready to flip it all the way over, if need be.

The three men, flabbergasted, stared at Justine while she smoothed her skirt back down over knees. "Stop it," she said in a quiet, intense voice. "Stop it right now." And they did.

Jerry's voice was saying, "Cut it out, guys. The manager will call the police. Maybe he already did."

Martin wasn't listening. He still looked like he was about to crawl over the table to get to Charles.

Before Justine had drawn another breath, two men had appeared, one at her elbow and one at Georgette's. It was Kenny, Darlene's husband, and Ralph, Nelle's husband. Kenny said, "You two don't worry about these guys. We'll look out for you."

"Not that you need it," Ralph said, aiming a nod of respect in Justine's direction. "That table trick was slick."

Hurrying up behind her husband, Darlene said simply, "Kenny."

Justine saw fear in her friend's eyes. It wasn't safe for Ralph and Kenny to challenge White men. She had to make this stop.

Pasting on a smile, Justine said, "We're fine, Kenny." Locking eyes with Ralph, she said, "Truly, gentlemen. We're fine. But thank you."

Kenny and Ralph returned to their wives, and Justine saw Darlene's hand grab Kenny's arm so hard that it left marks.

Justine raised her eyes to scan the crowd and was shocked to see another familiar face.

Sonny.

He must have been there all evening, but he also must have been avoiding them. Either that, or he had somehow failed to notice them on the dance floor. This was hard to imagine, since they'd been with a man who could make a wheelchair spin.

One thing was clear. Even though he worked beside Justine and Georgette every single day, he was not among the people rushing to their aid. Mrs. Sonny, a dark-haired woman so petite that her head hardly cleared the back of her chair, never even turned her head their way.

With her eyes locked on Sonny, Justine wasn't watching when the table started tilting again. Martin was leaning on it with all his weight because he wasn't finished trying to push Charles around with it. An enormous cracking sound brought her eyes to Jerry as his calm voice said, "I'm not kidding, fellas. That's enough."

He had produced a stout wooden baton from somewhere under the table, presumably from a holster strapped to his lower leg, and its assault on the table had been earsplitting.

"Just because I'm in this chair, it doesn't mean I can't take care of myself or these ladies…although they seem to be doing very well without my help. You gentlemen should presume that I'm always armed with something that lets me defend myself from a permanent sit-down position. Because I am."

Charles and Martin looked like they would happily wring Jerry's neck, if his simple but effective weapon weren't making that unwise.

"The two of you are going to apologize to the ladies and settle up your bills, and then you're going to exit the premises." He paused, as if remembering that Justine might have something to say about him ejecting her date. "Is that okay with you, ma'am?"

She gave Martin a long, searching look, then she gave Charles one that was even longer. "Yes. It's okay with me if they both leave."

"So that's how it is," Jerry said. "I will make sure the women get home safely, but you two need to go now."

Out of the corner of her eye, she could see Charles trying to make eye contact with her as he threw a fistful of cash on the table. She refused to give him the satisfaction of meeting his gaze, but she heard what he was saying as he walked away, and it was "I'm sorry. Forgive me."

In refusing to look at Charles, she turned her head toward Martin, who was apparently too angry to speak. He tossed a wad of cash onto the soiled tablecloth and left her behind without a word.

The owner materialized at Jerry's elbow, flanked by two large men. "Sir, is everything all right? Can I help you or the ladies in any way?"

Jerry was as calm and unflappable as he'd been all evening. "Everything's fine. I hope we can keep the police out of this." He produced a tip that the owner waved away.

"I thank you for this kind gesture," he said, flashing a tight smile that was set off by a close-cut and razor-thin mustache. "And have no worries about the police. It is my policy to settle disputes without their assistance. As you can see, my bouncers are more than capable of helping your excitable friends find the door. And if either of them—or anybody else—thinks that they might want some revenge on people who were just trying to help out two lovely damsels in distress"—his eyes turned to Kenny and Ralph—"then my bouncers will take care of that problem, too."

———

The distance between The TickTock Club and The Julia was substantial, but it had seemed like a mere stretch of the legs when Justine had walked it the first time, strolling and dancing without a care alongside Martin, Jerry, and Georgette. They had laughed. A light breeze had rustled Justine's black silk skirt and the trailing ends of her green sash. Though she hadn't been able to see the festive green rosette tucked into her curls, she had known it was there.

Georgette had glowed in her burgundy taffeta and the black shoes that she saved for dancing. Now, while retracing those carefree steps, loose brunette strands hung from the fashionable rolls of hair framing her face, and her dress was creased across the lap. She walked like her feet hurt her. Justine knew for certain that her own feet were hurting.

Jerry, though, looked just the same. He spoke to them in a quiet voice that somehow made everything better. Wheeling himself along the sidewalk with one hand, he used the other one to hold Georgette's hand. Justine felt like she was barging in on their date, but she didn't miss her own date a bit. She felt like she'd come to this point just in time. Martin was a very handsome and persuasive man, but she was repelled by the repressed violence she'd just seen on his face. His whole body had trembled with it.

Truth be told, she was more upset about Charles. He, too, had seemed drunk with the possibility of violence. He had also seemed drunk, plain and simple, and not in a I-had-one-drink-too-many kind of way. Justine did not need a staggering, mean drunk in her life. There was no way that she would be going to a movie with Charles in less than twenty-four hours, or ever. And she had really liked him.

She could still feel Charles's hand on hers in that last moment before he left The TickTock Club. No man had ever touched her that way, not even Martin with his persistent caresses. Or perhaps it was better to say that no man's touch had ever made her feel that way. His face had brushed hers as he leaned in to whisper in her ear. Even then, even when he was drunk and angry and dangerous, she wanted Charles, and that wasn't good for her.

She could still hear what he had said to her and only to her. Nobody at their table could have understood his words. Even if he'd broadcast them to the entire TickTock Club, few others besides Justine would have known what he was saying, perhaps none. And Charles knew that this was true.

With a perfect accent and an appropriately idiomatic choice of words, he had said, "*Ich bin so froh, dass Sie Deutsch sprechen.*"

Drunk with rum and raging hormones, she'd felt her breath leave her, but not just because a man she wanted so badly was so close to her. Her breath had left her because of what he'd said.

I'm so glad that you speak German.

Chapter 20

It was well past midnight. Justine was still tipsy, and she was groggy with sleep. In a few hours, she would need to put on a clean pair of coveralls and smooth her carefully curled hair into a utilitarian ponytail. It would be hard to weld safely when her mind and body were so shaken, but she would find a way. She would also find a way to keep the promise she'd made to herself to transcribe the pattern embedded in the grid of the strange screen before she went to bed. Once she'd put it on paper, she could carry it with her, using scraps of time on the bus and during her breaks to work on it.

The scene at The TickTock had left her so jittery that she startled at each nighttime noise filtering through her bedroom window as she prepared to transcribe the screen's pattern. She moved around as quietly as she could to avoid waking the women asleep in The Julia's warren of rooms. She only needed three things—a pencil, the finest-gridded graph paper she owned, and the screen itself. No, she needed a fourth thing. Her pencil was dull, so she needed a knife to sharpen it.

Holding the pencil over her wastebasket, Justine methodically opened her pocketknife and scraped its edge over the pencil's tip, fashioning wood and graphite into a point sharp enough to fit within the finely spaced squares of her graph paper. Then she put the knife in the usual pocket of the next day's coveralls and she took the piece of screen from its hiding place behind the books on her top shelf. She laid the screen on her bedspread, where the acid-green cloth would show clearly which squares had been stretched out of shape. Setting her dining table next to the bed and smoothing her graph paper across its surface, she began the task of copying the pattern that someone had poked into the screen.

It wasn't hard work, but it required focus, and her night at The TickTock hadn't left her much. Using her left index finger to count squares, she laboriously transferred the pattern to the graph paper.

When her work was done, Justine surveyed the array of dots that she'd copied. She felt in her bones that this was an encrypted message. It had to be.

Why would someone use this method to communicate with someone else at the Michaud plant? Why not just talk to each other? The answer could only be that the two parties couldn't find a way to be face-to-face or that they didn't want to be seen together.

And why wouldn't they simply communicate by a note written in English? The only reasonable answer to that question was that it was imperative that nobody else be able to read the message if it were found.

Well, then, why couldn't they write on paper like normal people, using a code to keep their message secret? The use of the screen instead of an ordinary piece of paper signaled how critical it was that no one ever knew the message even existed at all.

It had taken her several pieces of graph paper to transcribe every square of the screen. She suspected that the real message was punched into a small area at the center of the screen, and it was surrounded by a frame of nonsense holes, but she'd copied it all, just to be sure.

She forced herself to stay awake a little longer, using scarce cellophane tape to join the pages. By butting the pages edge-to-edge and covering each seam with tape, she was able to fold the finished sheet on those seams, forming a stack the size of a single page. Sighing, because she really didn't want to crease the sheets, she folded the stack two more times to make a packet that could be buttoned into the front left pocket of her coveralls.

It was comforting to secure her work firmly within the canvas of a pocket sealed shut with a wooden button. Her work was done, and she finally could go to bed.

Justine slipped off her dress, its silk discolored by perspiration and drops of spilled alcohol. She hung it on a hook until she could get it to the dry cleaners, then she opened her jewelry box and tucked the green rosette and sash inside. Her loose cotton nightgown felt wonderful after so many hours strapped into a longline bra and a girdle, all of it overlaid with beautiful but bulky slips and a dress with a snug-fitting bodice. Her cool, smooth sheets felt just as good. If only cool, smooth sheets could quiet her mind enough to let her sleep.

Moonlight streamed through her open window, illuminating her neatly folded coveralls, and the sight bothered her. For some reason she couldn't have expressed, she wanted the packet of papers in her coverall pocket to be safer, more secure. She got up, grabbed the coveralls, and stood wavering in the middle of the room. After a moment, she folded the coveralls into a firm, tight rectangle of cotton twill that she slid between her mattress and the wall, completely out of sight.

A sudden wind ruffled her curtains. Footsteps pattered down the sidewalk below her. Justine shut the window and, at last, she fully gave in to her fears. The act of hiding both versions of the screen's code—the transcription behind her mattress and the screen itself behind her books—released something inside her. She finally felt her utter fatigue, and she finally felt enough comfort to sleep.

It wasn't restful sleep. Her dreams were full of men with angry faces who knew where she lived. They wanted something from her, and she didn't want to give it to them. Their voices were loud in her head, echoing and distorted. Threading through each disorienting dream-scene was another voice. It was calm and soothing as it repeated a single sentence.

The sound of Charles's voice pervaded her sleep as he told her over and over how glad he was that she spoke German.

Chapter 21

When Justine opened her eyes, she doubted that she'd slept an hour. Her mind had kept churning while she slept, and she sensed that it had done important work. She just didn't know what it was.

She was out of bed before her mind had fully grasped what the face of her clock said. It was three a.m.

Two thoughts were fighting for space in her brain. One of them was simple.

I need to see Gloria.

The second was tenuous, diffuse, hard to grab, but it was everything. Justine had dreamed a dream, and the answer to… something…was hiding behind her wispy memories of it.

The intuitive leaps made by scientists dreaming dreams are famous and legion.

Mendeleev dreamed of an array of elements arranging themselves by atomic and chemical properties. Awakening, he transcribed the periodic table of the elements.

Kekulé dreamed of a dragon seizing its own tail, an image that led him to the ringlike chemical structure of benzene.

Bohr dreamed his model of the atom into being, electrons

moving around a nucleus in orbits distinguished by their energy levels.

Einstein dreamed of sledding, faster and faster, while looking at the eternal stars shift above him. His theory of relativity was inspired by this dream, and he later said that his entire career flowed from it.

Like them, Justine had found what she needed in a dream. She had seen piles of earth and rock blasted with energy and vaporized. The resulting mixture of earth and gas had rocketed along, uncontrolled, until it encountered a barrier that was blacker than black, with only a narrow opening to pass through. This narrow opening—A slot? A door? A window? A gash? No, a slit!—had brought order to the rocketing vaporous stuff, and this was the key to…something.

The word "slit" took her straight to Thomas Young's famous double-slit experiment, and that's when she knew that she had underestimated Gloria. She had let her concern over her godmother's mental condition make her forget how brilliant she was, but the dream had pointed her at the truth.

What was it that Gloria had said?

"Young. He is young."

Why had she been so quick to believe that her godmother was losing her mind? Gloria had been fully aware of what she was saying, and she'd believed that Justine would understand her. Gloria had believed that spies were watching her—and who was to say that they weren't?—so she had been speaking in code. Justine should have known.

What Gloria had actually said was not "He is young." It was "He is Young."

She'd been speaking of Thomas Young, the polymath who had lived in the late 1700s and early 1800s, during a time when scientists dabbled in everything.

Young's description of elasticity had lived on in physics texts as "Young's Modulus."

He had lectured on the function of the heart and arteries.

He had pioneered the study of the eyes.

He had first used the word "energy" in the modern sense.

He had developed the "Young Temperament" for tuning musical instruments.

He had helped translate the Rosetta Stone.

But it was none of this work that had caused Justine to dream up the beginning of a solution to her own problems. The work of Thomas Young that had startled her awake was his double-slit experiment.

Justine hadn't yet gotten a close look at the work of the Carbon Division's machinists, but she'd heard that they were carefully cutting slots—long, narrow holes that might as well be called "slits"—into thin carbon slabs and that they were doing this to very fine tolerances. She'd told Gloria this. By pointing her to Thomas Young, Gloria had been trying to tell Justine that the slits were important.

What else had Gloria mentioned? She'd said something about electrodes being positive and negative, which was so self-evident that she must have been trying to get Justine to think harder about electrodes and their purpose. She would have to mull that one over.

Justine hadn't figured everything out yet, but an idea was forming. And it was terrifying. There might be nothing she could do. Probably, there was nothing that she could do, but she had to try.

Gloria would be angry at her for coming, but Justine needed to talk to her. Her godmother would yell at Justine for exposing herself to the ominous forces that she believed to be everywhere. And perhaps they were. Perhaps Gloria wasn't delusional at all.

Justine had no other option than to simply go to Gloria. If she called her on the house phone, everyone on the first floor of The Julia would hear everything she said. A pay phone might work, but she didn't like the idea of standing behind the glass door of a phone booth, exposed. Not at this time of the night, and not while suspecting the world-shaking importance of those slits in those closely machined carbon parts.

Justine yanked her nightgown over her head and put on a bra. Pulling a shirtwaist dress off a hanger and slipping her feet into a pair of loafers, she was dressed to leave The Julia in seconds. But how was she going to get to Gloria's house?

She could hear Gloria's voice in her ear. *Don't let them follow you.*

She trembled at the thought of being alone at night on the streets around The Julia, but stepping on a streetcar would be as stupid as stepping into a phone booth. Penning herself up that way would be like the star of a Western movie choosing to ride his horse alone into a box canyon, only worse, because the box canyon would have glass walls.

Besides, she didn't know whether the streetcars ran at all at that time of night. She'd never had any reason to know.

Nevertheless, Justine had grown up in this city. She knew its streets, so she knew a million routes to Gloria's house and she could walk any of them in an hour or so. If her luck held, she could talk to Gloria, grab an hour of sleep, then take the streetcar home in a crush of morning commuter traffic that would make her less of a target. She could do this.

Her dress was black as carbon. Her shoes were black. The purse slung over her shoulder was black. Her orange curls were fairly well fluorescent, so she covered them with a black scarf. She was ready. She opened her window and stepped out onto the fire escape, then she descended into the dark streets of The Crescent City.

Chapter 22

Fritz had made himself a comfortable nest in a vacant lot down the street from The Julia. From this vantage point, he could see the rooming house's front door and a three-block stretch of the street. He had a blanket beneath him and another blanket over him, and his hat, cocked low over his eyes, would have hidden his identity from his own mother. A half-empty bottle in a bag sat six inches from his face, and his left hand curled around it like a buzzard's talon. He was as sober as a judge, but he looked like he was in the process of drinking his life away. The casual observer would think he had come to a place in life where he owned nothing but his hat, his tattered clothes, the two blankets, and the nearly empty bottle of rum. That is, he would have looked like that if the casual observer had paid him a millisecond of attention instead of walking past with averted eyes.

He needed help with this job, but he had none. He couldn't maintain twenty-four-hour surveillance on his target alone. He had to sleep. He had to work, if only to pay the cost of parking his car nearby, so that he could follow Justine wherever she decided to go. Tonight, he had chosen to forego sleep, because he felt that the affair of Justine Byrne was coming to a close. It had to come to a close. He was a day away from complete collapse, two at the most.

He thought he knew how best to sway her. This was a woman who could be tempted by work that valued her capabilities. She was not meant to be ground down in a thankless job and she would not tolerate such treatment forever. This much had become obvious. He had a real chance of recruiting her and, in so doing, seducing her into so much more. Here was a woman who was worth his time.

Fritz imagined coming out of New Orleans, ready to broker both the secrets of the Carbon Division *and* the services of a most capable new spy. Those secrets and that spy would save him even if Germany was no more when he finally escaped this country of vermin, because the Japanese would be just as interested in what he had to sell. The proceeds from that sale would buy him an extremely nice retirement, and he didn't care at all whether it was in Berlin or in Tokyo.

When the time was right, he would tip his hand and ask her to join him. Given her intelligence, he might not need to tip his hand for her to see him for what he was, and this made her dangerous. Very soon, she would either ally herself with Fritz, or she would become his adversary. Living as he did, alone in a country full of adversaries, he needed an ally badly. He was coming to understand that he wanted this particular ally badly.

If he could make her love him, then he would win, because love was weakness. This made his feelings for her dangerous. They made him fear for Justine because he felt certain that powerful forces swirled around her. Powerful forces other than Fritz, that is.

And thus, here he was, lying on the cold, hard ground. It was his mission to make sure that she was safe unless she committed herself against him. A decision like that would render her unsafe indeed.

———

Justine stepped quietly off the fire escape and hesitated in the pool of darkness there. She could turn right and find herself on the street she traveled every day on the bus to work. The Julia faced this street, and its front door opened to it.

Or she could step out of the shadows and move left, toward the less-traveled, shabbier-looking street that hugged The Julia's back wall. Tonight seemed like a night to do the unexpected. She turned left.

———

Fritz, pretending to sleep, kept his half-closed eyes on The Julia's front door. Until the moment hours later when he saw Justine hurrying from the streetcar stop, trying to get home in time to dress and catch the bus for work, he would never know that she'd been gone.

———

Justine didn't dare travel the direct route to Gloria's house. This would have taken her down St. Charles Avenue, lined with sprawling homes separated from the world by ornate iron-work fences. St. Charles was such a major thoroughfare that she would surely be seen by someone, even in the middle of the night. Instead of taking that risk, she cut a path parallel to its well-traveled lanes that took her through residential neighbor-hoods where the streets weren't the best place for a woman at night, alone.

Here, people lay sleeping in their beds, just on the other side of each open window that she passed. From their gardens, the scents of angel's trumpet and ginger blossoms reached out for Justine, one variety toxic and psychoactive, and the other variety merely delicious. The white flowers of both plants glowed in the moonlight.

She moved from shadow to shadow, trying and failing to keep the leather soles of her penny loafers from tapping on the pavement. At last, she leaned down and removed them, carrying her loafers in one hand and padding barefoot down the sidewalk.

Block after block, she moved in silence, only attracting attention once. Two men who were also keeping to the shadows stepped into the middle of the street to catch her attention. The weird light of a quarter-moon illuminated their foreheads, noses, cheekbones, and chins, leaving the hollows of their faces in darkness.

"Hey, sweetheart. Whatchoo doin' out so late? You need us to help you find a bed for the night? C'mon, say yes."

She broke into a run with her very next step. Acorns punched hard into her bare soles. They hurt her, but she ran, and she kept running.

Nothing pursued her but the sound of the men's voices calling after her. Their slurred words and over-sweet tones said that they were far too drunk to chase her. She ran anyway.

"Hey, baby. Ain't no need to run so fast. We don't wanna hurt ya. Maybe just a little squeeze."

She ran. Over the hard acorns and the jagged pavement and the many-pointed pine cones, she ran.

Mudcat gave himself a pat on the back. He had homesteaded the darkest spot on Gloria Mazur's street, because he had guessed that the coded screen would probably send Justine to her godmother for help in deciphering it.

Though she was keeping her path to the sidewalks, weaving out into the empty roadway only to avoid the light cast by streetlamps, he could see her. He drew deeper into a magnolia tree's dense shadow.

She had tied her beautiful hair up in a scarf the color of a crow's wing, but curling tendrils of it had escaped. Even in the low light, her hair glowed like something that burned from within. Her black dress rendered her nearly invisible, except for those tendrils, the pale skin of her face, her hands, her ankles, and her bare feet.

Her shoes dangled from one hand, and she moved like she was tired. Of course, she was tired. She'd worked a long day and danced half the night. And now she'd walked for miles.

This would be the night when she figured out that, together, she and Dr. Gloria Mazur were unstoppable. This could be a problem for Mudcat.

He had told his superiors everything he'd learned about Dr. Mazur at the library, only to find that his organization already knew all about her. They had known all about Justine's late parents, too. His superiors understood Dr. Mazur's potential, and they understood her essential weakness. She was too valuable to lose and too unstable to trust. They had been watching her for years, for the entire war, making sure she was hidden from an enemy that would probably give a lot to get its hands on her, if it knew her true value.

When she'd stopped teaching, they had begun working with the bank to ensure that funds were shifted into her account in a constant flow of tiny errors that were always in her favor. She was too good with numbers to fail to notice this subterfuge, but the bank had been told to pay no attention when she reported the discrepancies. They'd also been told to pay no attention to the fact that the man who had co-owned the account with her, since women weren't allowed to have accounts of their own, was now dead.

When she'd stopped leaving the house, his organization had inserted an agent in a rental house down the street who posed as her delivery boy. He was tasked with making sure no strangers were coming around. He watched her house. He mowed her yard for a quarter of the going rate. He served as an errand boy, returning her change in the bag with each delivery, and each time the groceries were slightly underpriced and the change was slightly excessive. Again, she was too good with numbers to fail to notice, but he routinely walked away when she tried to repay him.

In aggregate, the money that the organization had managed to funnel to Dr. Mazur had kept her solvent, more or less. And that had kept her off the enemy's payroll. The organization was taking good care of Gloria Mazur because it would be tragic if they had to swoop in and remove her from her everyday life, just to keep her secrets safe.

He watched Justine creep barefoot across Gloria's lawn and step into an overgrown flower bed. Her arm brushed a tall shrub as she reached down to lift up a heavy object, probably a brick, that was propping up its leaning trunk. A warm breeze carried a cloyingly sweet smell to his nose. She retrieved something lying on the ground and replaced the brick, and now he knew that Gloria Mazur hid her spare house key at the foot of a sweet olive bush.

He watched Justine enter Gloria's house. After waiting a few moments, he headed down the street in the direction from which she'd come. He had no need to see how long she stayed with Gloria, only that she'd come, which meant that matters were coming to a head. There was no point in following her home. He already knew where she lived.

The most important thing that he'd just learned was where Justine was at this moment in time. Because this also meant that he knew where she wasn't.

Chapter 23

"Gloria. It's Justine."

Justine heard her voice echo in the darkness as it struck the hard surfaces of the interior of Gloria's house—wooden floors, plastered walls and ceilings, plain wooden trim.

"I know who you are. Come in here where I am."

A click sounded and the lamp on the bedside table emitted a dim light. Gloria sat up in her bed, her back supported by pillows. She looked the same as she always had upon waking, except for the sizable carving knife in her hand. When Justine entered, Gloria asked, "Are you alone?"

When the answer was yes, Gloria tucked the knife under her pillow and smiled. "Welcome, my sweet. I told you to stay away, but I had no faith that you would listen to me. At least you've come at a time when we can have some hope that you evaded the eyes that are always on me."

Gloria wore a high-necked embroidered nightgown made of a powdery blue cotton batiste, fine and half-sheer. It flattered her black eyes and graying black hair. Even when she slept, Gloria always had style. She reached out a hand toward an upholstered chair beside her bed where a matching blue batiste bed jacket lay. Justine handed her the bed jacket and sank into the chair. Its tweed felt rough against her legs. After carrying her shoes for miles, she could finally drop them to the floor. They clattered when they struck the polished oak.

"You look like you can barely hold up your head," Gloria said. "Tell me what you came to say and then go to sleep. Your old bed is always waiting here for you."

"You still have my rag doll on it, don't you?"

"And I always shall. So why are you here? I trust that it is important, since I specifically told you not to come."

"Since I saw you, I heard my boss talking about how hard it was for one of our machinists to machine slots into the carbon parts she was making, because she's working to such close tolerances. That had to percolate in my brain for a while, but I woke up tonight thinking of Thomas Young's double-slit experiment. And that made me remember what you said as I was leaving last week. You said, 'Young. He is Young.' I didn't understand you then, but now I know that you were trying to send me a signal. You wanted me to focus on those openings in those slabs of carbon."

"Yes. And I was doing that because I live in constant fear that my enemies are listening, but by all means keep talking. You might humor me by lowering your voice, though."

Justine dragged her chair up to Gloria's bedside and leaned in. She whispered, "You wanted me to pay attention to the design of the machined carbon parts. I'm going to get a chance to do that tomorrow."

Gloria listened silently, nodded once, then picked up the notebook at her bedside and wrote:

You would not believe the pace at which my colleagues are advancing technology. I cannot be sure that they have not built infinitesimal microphones that can detect the faintest whisper. I have slept, so I do not trust that my home is free of such devices. It is not safe to speak outside, but I doubt that they have made such devices weather-safe, so it is safer than here. Follow me.

Gloria donned the delicate bed jacket and slid her narrow feet into a pair of blue satin slippers. Silently, she moved through the darkened house. The only sound came when she clicked the knobs on three dead bolt locks, then eased her back door open.

Gloria's satin soles and Justine's bare feet made no sound on the leaf-strewn brick patio as they crossed it to sit side by side on a wrought-iron settee.

Gloria's voice was barely audible as she murmured into Justine's ear. "So why are you here tonight?"

———

Mudcat had made it around the street corner where Gloria's house sat. It was probably overkill at this time of night to move so carefully and stick so closely to the shadows, but his caution had kept him alive for quite some time. It had become an engrained part of him.

He was moving slowly when he heard the metallic click of a dead bolt lock opening. Then another. And another. The sounds brought him to a halt in the dark space beneath the branches of a live oak. Standing there, he could see something—no, two somethings—moving in the space behind Dr. Gloria Mazur's house. One was wrapped in a garment as light and ethereal as moonlight, and one was wrapped in darkness. He remembered Justine's coal-colored dress and scarf, so he knew which vague form belonged to whom.

They settled themselves on some patio furniture and began a conversation, quiet but intense. He would have given a lot to be able to walk across the street and stand in the shrubbery along Dr. Mazur's backyard fence, but the risk was too great. Even an unusually loud breath would give him away.

Instead, he stood rooted on the concrete sidewalk, listening to voices but not words. He heard intensity. He heard a sudden nervous laugh, just one. He never heard anything he could use, nothing that enlightened him about what Justine Byrne and Gloria Mazur knew and what they were planning. The urgent tone of their voices confirmed what he already knew. Woe would befall anyone who underestimated them. Mudcat could think of no circumstance—outside of a contest of physical strength, perhaps—under which he would want to be the adversary of these two women. They were trying to ferret out war secrets—and possibly succeeding—while sitting on the patio of a nondescript bungalow in a New Orleans residential neighborhood.

When they finished their conversation and moved back inside, he would be able to resume motion in the direction that he needed to go. He reached within himself for the strength to be motionless for as long as it took.

———

"Why did you come?" Justine had never heard Gloria's voice like this. It was urgent, afraid but strong.

"Like I said, I wanted to talk to you about Young's double-slit experiment, and I'm trying to make sense of the other things you said. Also, I came to get a book."

Gloria's face turned sly in the reflected moonlight. She said, "Will you tell me what else I said?" and Justine couldn't tell whether it was the kind of rhetorical question Gloria and her mother had always used when teaching, or whether she was trying to cover for the fact that she didn't remember what she'd said.

Still murmuring, Justine said, "You reminded me that electrodes were both positive and negative. I know that, of course, but it made me think about electrodes. Anodes, actually. I know that some anodes are made of carbon, and that made me wonder about those slits that are being machined into carbon slabs. Maybe the carbon would work as an anode that attracts…something negative. I don't know what. And then the slit in each carbon piece would allow some of the negative particles—"

"Whatever they are."

"Yes, whatever they are. The slot would allow them to pass through, perhaps accelerate them, maybe to a place where they could be collected."

"A separation process."

"Yes, a separation process, and that's why I'm here. Separation is what you do."

"It's what your parents did, too."

Justine's eyes were fixed on Gloria's face. She hadn't forgotten the other thing that her godmother had said.

If you think your parents' deaths were an accident, then you are a fool.

"You also asked, 'Do you know which way?' Of course I know about the thought experiments that build on Young's double-slit work, the 'which-way experiments' that illustrate the dual nature of photons, but I can't connect them to the carbon pieces being machined at Higgins. Were you just trying to call my attention to the slits?"

Gloria nodded and spread her hands as if to say, "How smart you are to notice my clues. Too bad it took you a week."

"So," Justine said, "do you think I'm getting closer to understanding what's going on? And can you lend me some books that will help? I think I need to start with Papa's Thomson book. You know, *Recollections and Reflections.* I saw it here just last week."

"It was one of his treasures. He entrusted me with it years ago, but you should have it now. Come." Gloria rose from the settee like a goddess wrapped in fine linen, instead of a blue cotton nightgown. She glided into the house and paused to triple-click her dead bolts into place. Then she stalked her house from bookshelf to bookshelf, carefully selecting three volumes.

"The Thomson book," she said, placing it gently in Justine's hands as if it were made of eggshells. "It is autographed. Did you know that?"

"Yes." Justine remembered her father taking it off his shelf when she was young and saying very simply, "This is my teacher. Everything I have done that is of worth, other than loving you and your mother, was because of him."

She opened the book and found the autograph on its inside cover, two swooping, stylized "J"'s followed by "*Thomson*" in careful nineteenth-century penmanship. Underneath his name, he'd drawn a bold, straight underline, as if to say, "Pay attention. I discovered the electron, and the Nobel Prize people were very happy about that." Thomson had died shortly before her parents did, but she only heard about it later. When she'd learned that he was gone, it was as if her father had died again.

"You recall that Thomson did far more than just discover the electron?" Gloria asked. "He had to invent the mass spectrometer to be able to do that."

"A separation technology," Justine said.

It was not a question, but Gloria answered it anyway. "Yes."

She handed Justine a second book, *Isotopes,* by F. W. Aston. It was a beautiful thing, bound in black cloth mottled with a colorful abstract pattern, with gilt-lettered red leather protecting its spine.

The third book was less grand. It consisted of hundreds of pages of scientific papers that were amateurishly gathered into a cardboard binding. Justine flipped through its pages and she saw work by Thomson, Aston, Meitner, Prout, Dempster, Einstein, Bohr, and many others. She recognized all of the names from her studies. Some of them she also associated with the kindly faces of people she'd met when her parents took her to Europe when she was very young.

"Your father wanted his most important sources bound into one book that he could keep at hand while he was writing or teaching. He could not be bothered to hire a bookbinder to create this text, because he was convinced that there was nothing that he could not do. This unmitigated arrogance is the physicist's curse. He and your mother passed this trait on to you, unless I miss my guess."

"You're one to talk." Justine looked at the lopsided book in her hand with the unfortunate creases across the spine and laughed. "Well, he could weld."

"He could do a great many things, as could your mother, but nobody does all things equally well. And now it is time for you to sleep."

The crispness of Gloria's features had softened. Her mouth and eyes were more relaxed that Justine had ever seen them, as if she had unloaded her own burdens and placed them on Justine's back. This moment of vulnerability revealed lines etched below her eyes and the slight sag that was forming along her jawline. For a moment, she looked maternal and, for the first time, Justine saw that she was beginning to look old.

Desperate to look away from evidence of the incontrovertible fact that she would eventually lose Gloria, too, Justine looked at her wristwatch. "I can't sleep long. Maybe an hour and a half. I have to get back to my room and get dressed before the bus comes to take me to work."

"Oh, my dear. Surely they can do without you for just one day."

"You don't understand. Tomorrow...today...is the day that I can talk to the carbon machinist without making anybody suspicious."

The softness was gone, and so were the traitorous wrinkles. "I see. Then you will have to finish your sleep tonight, after a long day of questioning some unfortunate machinist. I will wake you in ninety minutes, and you will not be silly about the breakfast I will have ready for you. Today is a day that you should begin with wholesome eggs and strong coffee."

Chapter 24

Fortified by ninety minutes of sleep, two eggs over easy, two slices of toast, and a cup of jet-black coffee, Justine tried to make herself small, even unobtrusive, in her streetcar seat. She felt like an actress in a spy movie who hadn't been given a script.

Would it have been safer to stand, since she would have been able to get to the exit quickly if need be? Or would that have been like pinning a sign to her chest that said, "Here I am!"?

Or maybe nobody was after her at all. Perhaps this was how Gloria's fears had begun. What had it taken to make her see pursuers everywhere?

Justine balanced Gloria's books on her lap, then she sat on her hands to keep herself from obsessively tucking her curls under the scarf. It was a relief when she reached her stop and could step down from the streetcar and run. Now she didn't look insane, running down a city sidewalk in a gray morning drizzle. She merely looked like someone who was trying not to get wet as she rushed to work.

Rushing through The Julia's front door, Justine hurried up the stairs to her room where she could change into her coveralls in time to catch the bus. She got there without seeing a soul, unlocking and slipping through the door with a sigh. Her task list was short—don her coveralls, tie back her hair, and brush her teeth if she had time—but her mind was so rattled that she stood stock-still in the center of the room and tried to remember what she needed to do.

Oh, yeah. Coveralls.

It took her a full minute of frantically pawing through the chifforobe before she remembered that she'd stuffed them between her bed and the wall. The prospect of missing her bus was upsetting, but the prospect of losing the papers she'd buttoned into the pocket was worse. Relieved to find them, she practically jumped through the unbuttoned opening, deftly buttoning herself into the coveralls, then she opened the left front pocket where she'd put her papers.

Yep. The graph paper, covered with her carefully made markings, was still there. She slid her pocketknife into its usual pocket and buttoned everything closed again. Brushing her hair into a ponytail took thirty seconds. Running down the hall and using her toothbrush took maybe a minute more, and she still had time to spare.

Each of the three books that Gloria had lent her was a treasure, with the autographed one and her father's homemade one being irreplaceable. They sat waiting for her on her rickety table. She didn't like seeing them there, so she decided to take a few seconds to shelve them. Putting a hand on the books already sitting on her shelf, Justine knew in a millisecond that something was wrong.

Every once in a while Georgette picked up one of her books to look at it when Justine wasn't around, and it would mortify her to know that Justine knew when she did it, because she never put it back quite right. This was different. Sometime during the night, every one of Justine's books had been shoved to the rear, flush with the back of the shelf. How could this be? It had only been a few hours since she'd left.

The displaced books meant that somebody had either picked her door lock or come through the window that she'd left unlocked so that she could come and go by the fire escape. What were the odds that this intruder had gotten lucky by breaking in on the one night when she was gone among the hundreds when she was not? They were nearly zero unless someone was watching her.

Thus, someone was almost certainly watching her.

She had carefully tucked the encrypted screen behind her books...only there now was no "behind her books." She yanked a few books forward to look behind them, but there was no point in it. She knew what she would find.

The screen was gone.

Somebody had watched her hide it or searched her room, because it beggared belief that anybody could come through the window and walk straight to her hiding place. Nothing else appeared disturbed, so any search had been done by somebody who knew how.

Somebody like that would not make the mistake of displacing her books. Therefore, the intruder wanted her to notice that they'd been disturbed. This action was almost like a code. If she had to guess, the encoded screen had been taken by the person who made it. Otherwise, there were two people sending her encoded messages, and that seemed unlikely.

Her time was up. If she hesitated another instant, she would miss a bus that she couldn't afford to miss. She needed her job, she needed her chance to prove herself as a welder, but most of all, she needed a chance to talk to a machinist. She needed to get an up-close look at the carbon parts being crafted at the request of the government of the United States of America.

———

Fritz had spent a long night with his blankets and his near-empty bottle, pretending to be a man at the absolute end of his luck. He was not pleased to learn that the time had been wasted. He would have done himself exactly as much good by sleeping in his own soft bed, and by "exactly as much good," he meant "none at all."

The image of Justine Byrne swam in his eyes, running headlong down the sidewalk in a black dress and scarf that looked nothing like what she'd been wearing when he had watched her enter The Julia the night before. She had changed clothes, and she had left, and she had come back, and he'd never known any of it. This was a crisis. She was too smart to leave at large, and she was up to something. It was possible that she needed to be neutralized. It was more than possible. He had always known it, but he hadn't wanted to admit it. Because he needed Justine.

Justine was as singular as her parents had been. They had been known associates of people with high-level security credentials. They themselves had worked on projects so critical that Fritz had been aware of them and their work. More than aware, actually.

And now Justine was left to make it on her own, and Fritz was left trapped in a web of entangled cause-and-effect that only a physicist could love. His superiors had told him to force Gerard and Isabel Byrne off a rain-slicked road, and that is what he'd done. The loss of her parents had forced Justine to seek work, and she'd found it at the most logical place during wartime, a busy munitions manufacturer. He had been ordered to seek work at the most logical place for an embedded agent during wartime, the very same busy munitions manufacturer. Then he had been cut off from all support by the very same war that had brought him to the place where Justine was, the same war that had cut her off from the support of her parents.

This mirroring of their lives could be no accident. It was driven by a force like gravity, like the electromagnetic attraction between a positive ion and a negative ion. Justine was meant for Fritz, but she had to choose him, and she had to do it now. His time at Higgins Industries was about to come to an explosive end.

———

Georgette watched Justine limp down the front steps of The Julia like a woman who had danced like there was no tomorrow. Well, tomorrow was here.

She tried not to smile as her friend struggled up the bus steps. She didn't feel very good herself. Her head ached, her feet ached, and she could still feel the grooves carved into her torso by the boning of her dress-up underwear. Nevertheless, none of these small irritations would be keeping her from being back at a dance hall just as soon as Jerry asked her to go. She wished that Justine could look forward to spending time with somebody as nice as Jerry.

Well, maybe she could. Martin and Charles weren't the only fish in the sea.

In the meantime, she saw it as her duty as Justine's friend to distract her from the misbehaving men in her life. Fortunately, there was an algebra book in her bag that she knew would get Justine's attention. Her friend's passion for numbers and knowledge was a little weird by some people's measure, but Georgette admired her for it. Actually, she loved her for it.

She waited while Justine trudged down the center aisle of the bus, ready to distract her with talk of polynomials and simultaneous equations. Those topics would get Justine smiling in no time, or Georgette missed her guess.

———

Justine tried not to be rude to Georgette, but it couldn't be helped. She would have loved to spend the bus ride debriefing their disastrous double date. She would have happily rehashed everything—the weirdness of Charles butting into her date with Martin, Martin's confusing request that she run away with him, the near-fistfight that broke up the evening, everything but the confusing but private moment when Charles spoke to her in German—but she just couldn't. She was exhausted.

She sat, head lolling, on her side of the double bus seat, barely awake enough to be surprised that her friend didn't want to talk about men at all.

Georgette reached into the oversized bag she'd been carrying all week and pulled out Justine's algebra book. "I been using my lunch breaks to practice factoring these polynomials. Did I say that right? PAHL-ee-NOME-ee-uhls?"

Justine gave her a weary nod and hated herself for being too fatigued to show her how impressed she was.

"But you've been eating lunch with Jerry."

"He's pretty good with them polynomials. He's a big help."

Now Justine understood why Georgette had started carrying her big new navy-blue bag. While Justine had been dividing her breaks and lunches between Charles and Martin, Georgette hadn't been spending all her free time flirting over grape sodas with Jerry. She'd been pushing numbers around a blank page, and he'd been helping her. This made Justine want to give Jerry a big hug.

"But me and Jerry—we're stuck on this chapter."

Justine wanted to help Georgette out by checking her work so she could move on to the next chapter, but all she could do was say, "I'm sorry, Georgette. I have to sleep, but tell me one thing before I do. You looked really happy last night, despite the behavior of my date."

"Dates, maybe? I think you had two."

"I don't even know the answer to that question. Anyway, tell me. Do you like Jerry? I mean do you really like Jerry?"

"I really do. Everybody don't treat a girl from the bayou without any money or education as nice as you and Jerry do. I never met a man so smart and kind and funny. You'd think maybe he'd be bitter and mean—after the polio, I mean—but he just...well, he just gets on with life, and he tries hard to help everybody else get on with theirs. He told me that being in that chair taught him that everybody's got big problems. They just don't always show. That's a man worth spending time with, doncha think?"

"Yes. I do think so. I'm really happy for the two of you," Justine said. Then she curled up against the wall of the bus with her head resting on the cool glass window.

Rain pattered on the window and on the metal roof above her. She supposed it was possible that Charles would show up on the bus again, since he seemed to make a habit of being where he wasn't supposed to be. If he did magically appear on the bus, then he would be disappointed. Nothing was going to keep Justine from grabbing a few minutes of sleep while she could, not even the opportunity to yell at a man who had disappointed her by behaving like a complete jackass.

———

Mudcat was once again the proud owner of a nondescript piece of metal screen that he had defaced, over and over again, with a nail. Perhaps it was made more valuable by the fingerprints of Justine Byrne, whom he was coming to admire more by the hour.

Perhaps she'd had the screen in her possession long enough to solve the code through sheer intellectual power. Or perhaps she'd had it long enough to copy it somehow, so that she could take her time and solve it the way a scientist would, with painstaking care and deliberation.

Or perhaps she'd failed to do either of these things and was now regretting that failure, because the coded screen was gone. In any case, she would have learned something important. A good agent makes the most of resources when they're available, because life offers no promises. And she would have learned that the person who left the screen for her to find was not to be trifled with. He had gifted her with a critical clue, and he'd taken it away.

He'd learned some things about Justine Byrne already. She was not immune to making mistakes, but he would be a fool if he presumed that she'd ever make the same mistake twice.

Chapter 25

Justine strode through Higgins Industries' Michaud plant like a woman who wasn't reeling under the aftereffects of no sleep and a heckuva lot of Planter's Punch. She kept her gaze straight ahead, hoping to minimize the odds of making eye contact with Charles or Martin. Their job duties meant that either of them could be wandering loose anywhere in the main plant, but not behind the doors of the Carbon Division. All she had to do was get through those doors. As the Carbon Division's maintenance chief, Jerry did work behind those doors, of course, but Jerry was not the problem. Georgette walked close beside her, and Justine presumed that she, too, had her eyes locked straight ahead.

Shortly before they reached those doors, Justine felt Georgette flinch, but she tried to keep moving. No luck. It seemed that Charles was willing to humiliate himself for her, because now he had sprinted into her path and stopped cold, so close to her that she almost plowed into him.

He didn't say, "Hello," or "How are you?" He got straight to the point.

"I'm so sorry. So very sorry. I don't drink very often and there's a good reason for that. I'm not myself when I drink."

Justine was having trouble making her mouth form words, so Georgette stepped in.

"Oh, yeah? Well, maybe you *are* yourself when you drink. Ever think of that? My friend is waiting for somebody who'll treat her nice, 'cause she can have her pick of men."

Justine was pretty sure that wasn't true, but it was nice of Georgette to say so.

Charles wasn't finished talking. He was acting like a man who wanted to make all his points before she had a chance to make hers, and this was not helping his case. "Maybe Georgette's right. Maybe I'm not as nice as I think I am. But I can be better. I want to be better."

He leaned in, trying to bypass Georgette and talk one-on-one with Justine.

"You're a special woman. I'll work hard to be better for you. Do we still have a date tonight? I think we need some time together to talk, one-on-one."

His gaze was gentle and intense. It said, *Trust me.*

She wanted to trust him, and she hated herself for it. Was she really considering forgiving this man?

Georgette elbowed her in the ribs hard. What did this mean? Was she urging her to accept Charles's apology and go with him to the movies? Somehow, Justine thought not.

She said, "No. I don't want to go to the movies with you," and it was mostly true.

Georgette mumbled, "Attagirl," in a soft voice, as if it were possible to speak to Justine at that moment without Charles overhearing.

Justine didn't want to scuttle around Charles. She had her dignity. She wanted him to move out of her way. She didn't know how to accomplish that, so she just stood silent with her eyes fixed on his face and waited. Unable to face her cool appraisal, Charles took a step back and to the side, opening a path for her.

She'd hardly started moving when Martin came into view, and she could see that he, too, wanted to tell her he was deeply sorry for his behavior. At the sight of his hangdog face and sheepish eyes, she felt indecision again. Was there any possibility that she wanted to forgive him?

As she asked herself that question, she felt something inside of her snap. It didn't tell her how she felt about Martin, deep down, but it did tell her how to handle this moment.

No, she was not going to let him block her path. No, she was not going to stop walking to talk to him. No, she was not even going to give him the time of day. He and Charles needed to talk to each other about how stupidly they had behaved. They also needed to apologize to Jerry and to Georgette. They did not need to bother her with any of it, at least not at that moment.

She charged ahead, putting one foot in front of another with a firm confidence that said, *Don't get in my way, because I'll walk over you.*

Martin could see how it was, so he had to content himself with standing to the side and calling out to her, "Justine. Justine, I just want to talk to you."

The worst thing of all was that part of her was playacting. The rational side of her was angry with Martin and Charles, and with good reason, but part of her heart wanted to forgive. Forgiveness could be weakness and it could be strength, but she was never going to know whether she was weak or strong if she let these men sway her before she even knew her own mind.

The double-door entrance to the Carbon Division was in her sights and those doors were starting to look like the Pearly Gates. As they passed through them, she heard Georgette expel a long pent-up breath, then she heard the pattering of clapping hands. Eight or ten women had seen what was going on and were waiting to applaud her as she came through the doors. One of them was Darlene. The only way the others could know about the way Charles and Martin had acted at The TickTock Club would be if Darlene or Nelle had told them. Or Sonny, she supposed, although that seemed unlikely.

Darlene pounded her on the shoulder and said, "Those two had it coming. They had worse things coming, actually."

A woman Justine didn't know said, "Don't let the knuckleheads spoil your day. There's other fish in the sea."

Mavis hurried up to the group and blurted out, "I heard all about last night," instead of hello. Then she moved in close and said, "So both of your fellas managed to show their asses on the same night? Are you gonna forgive either of 'em? Both of 'em? Neither of 'em? I could understand you cutting them both loose, but it *is* nice to have a fella to dance with, when you're in the mood."

Words burst out of Justine's mouth on their own. "They showed me who they were last night, and I didn't like what I saw." This was true, but it didn't mean that she had felt nothing when Martin and Charles had asked for her forgiveness.

There was sympathy on her friends' faces, and Justine didn't want to look at it.

"Forget about them," she said. "I've got some welding to do."

As the two of them walked away, Georgette gave her a sisterly pat on the elbow, as if to say, *Who needs men, anyway?*

"I'm sorry I dozed off on the bus," Justine said. "Want to work on your polynomials over lunch? I mean, if Jerry doesn't show up to court you with a bottle of something purple and fizzy?"

"That'd be great. Jerry's a nice guy, but that don't mean he gets to decide how I spend all my spare time."

Waving goodbye to Georgette, Justine headed for Jerry's

maintenance shop, which was a freestanding, drop-ceilinged shed in the middle of the factory floor—like Sonny's office, only much bigger. Sonny probably hated that, but Jerry needed a lot more space for his tools and whatsits.

Jerry's shop was a way more pleasant place to be than Sonny's office, and not just because Jerry himself was more fun than Sonny. Justine simply loved being around tools, from small ones like the adjustable wrench in her back pocket to the massive cranes used to hoist aircraft engines in the main plant. She liked the cold, heavy, powerful look and feel of them. They sang of possibility.

A broad workbench, lower than usual to accommodate his chair, took up most of the back wall of Jerry's shop. The space beneath the workbench that another mechanic might have used for storage was cleared to make room for his knees. The bench was fitted with vises to hold his work steady, like any workbench would be, and the wall behind it was lined with drawers for hardware like nuts, bolts, nails, and such.

Pegboards kept his hand tools within reach, and his bench tools were arrayed on either side of the workbench. The beam of a shop crane stretched from wall to wall, with a hoist attached that enabled Jerry to lift objects too heavy or bulky to handle from his chair. Once lifted, he could slide the hoist along the beam and move things where they needed to go. The rest of the shop was devoted to equipment that could be checked out for maintenance work. Jerry's workshop was a shrine to efficiency, and also to ingenuity, since he had built the adapted equipment himself.

It occurred to Justine that the war had been as big an opportunity for Jerry as it had been for her. Before the war, Higgins Industries might not have been willing to pay for the space and equipment that Jerry needed to do his work. Fortunately for the company, the war had opened their eyes to Jerry's talents, and they'd gained a man who could ask machines why they weren't working and make them give him an answer.

Jerry was waiting for Justine with a pair of welding goggles and a bottle of aspirin. Before he even said hello, he said, "Hold out your hand."

He tapped two aspirin into her palm, then he closed the pill bottle and opened his thermos bottle. Holding the bottle's red cap by its handle, he sloshed some still-steaming coffee into it and handed it to her. "Leave it black and down it all in one go—coffee, aspirin, and all. You'll feel better." As he spoke, he screwed the inner cap back onto the thermos bottle's neck to keep the heat in.

Hoping he was right, she obeyed. "Are you a hangover expert?"

"Not particularly, but I've spent a little time in bars, and I've got a feeling that you haven't. Your equipment's all set up for you at that station right out there." He pointed out the front door of his shop.

"Oh, Jerry. That's for me? That's so sweet. No wonder Georgette likes you."

He paused to wipe out the plastic cup, place it over the inner lid, and screw it on. This job seemed to take a lot of focus, because he wasn't looking at her when he said, "You think she likes me?"

Justine blurted out, "I know it," then her voice faded into embarrassed silence. Even awkward Justine knew that telling a girlfriend's secrets just wasn't done.

She tried to fix it by saying, "Not that she's told me. I know it by looking at her," but that just made it worse. She stammered out a thanks for the aspirin and coffee, then she fled his shop.

Justine made her way to the station where Nelle used her machining tools to cut and grind carbon blanks. Every measurement had to precisely duplicate the shapes on Nelle's blueline drawings. Every rough spot had to be ground down. And, according to rumor, every thin slab of carbon had a slit that had to be perfectly cut. Or maybe it was more than one slit. She was about to find out.

"Good morning, Nelle. I'm here to get your equipment all fixed up," Justine said, walking up as the woman was busy doing her morning safety inspection. "Sonny told you I was coming?"

"He would have if he made a habit of doing his job. But Jerry told me."

Nelle spoke without looking at Justine, and she handed Justine the broken part without looking up. Justine would have gotten her feelings hurt, but Nelle followed up by saying, "Real glad to see you. And I'm real glad that you're looking so perky after your two fellas acted like such drips last night."

"Yeah. Well…" Justine didn't know what else to say, so she just let her voice trail off.

Nelle smiled, but she still didn't look up from the lathe she was checking out. "I don't mean to be short with you. Higgins keeps signing contracts for big orders, and it don't leave me enough time to catch my breath, much less mind my manners. I'll be more than ready for that tool rest when you get it finished, and I'm grateful to you for fixing it. I've got some other work to do, but I'm gonna get way behind if I have to go on for long without it."

Justine heard Nelle's message loud and clear, and it was "Go fix my tool rest and stop taking up my time." She decided to push her luck anyway.

"Do they have you doing the same stuff all the time?" she asked. "Or does your work change from day to day?"

Nelle's eyes were still on her work. "Everything I do is carbon, but I make different parts on different days. Today's foot scraper day."

"What scraper day?" Justine asked, looking around Nelle's machinist's tools to see if she saw something that could be called a scraper. Nope. She just saw the usual grinder, lathe, and mill.

Finally, Nelle looked up. Justine knew that people who were good at their jobs liked to talk about them, so she'd done well to push her a little bit. "Foot scraper. That's what we call the gadgets I'm making today. We have to call 'em something, but nobody will tell us what they are. So we just call 'em what they look like. Or sometimes we just call 'em what everybody else calls 'em, and nobody knows why. This one does look like a foot scraper to me. You know? When you've been to the swamp and your mama wants you to clean off your feet before you even step foot on the porch? We used to have a cast-iron foot scraper at the bottom of the porch steps just for that."

She held out a thin slab of carbon, maybe four inches wide and two or three times that long. "Some days, I make a smaller piece that gets fitted to this one. When you put the two pieces together, they kinda look like my mama's foot scraper."

Nelle's foot scraper was interesting but it wasn't what Justine needed. For reasons she only vaguely understood, Gloria was fixated on parts with slits in them.

Still studying the carbon piece, Nelle muttered, "The boss is coming," out of the side of her mouth.

Sonny appeared, pointedly looking at the two broken pieces of metal in Justine's hand. "You gonna be able to fix this thing, Justine?"

"You bet, Sonny. Anything to make your life easier." Justine flashed him a grin so big that she felt a cold breeze on her gums.

He grunted at both of them, then wandered away to find more employees to bother.

"You don't like him, either," Nelle said, and Justine heard laughter in her voice.

Good. Maybe a moment of we're-all-stuck-with-Sonny camaraderie would get Nelle to open up a little more.

"I think it's really interesting what you do," Justine said.

"Then you should put your name in for machinist training. Unless you can get a job welding. You're already real good at that, so you wouldn't have to train. If you ask young Mr. Higgins's secretary, Wanda, for an application, she'll slip it in the right file. Sonny'll never do it for you."

"Don't I know it? Sonny would keep me on the assembly line until the war's over and they kick the women out of this place. It never occurred to me that I could put my own name in the pot."

"Women take care of other women." Nelle flicked a speck of dust off her lathe. "Ain't nobody else gonna do it. Sonny won't never know you done it till it's too late."

"I'd be happy with either welding or machining, honestly. Is most of your work like these pieces, where you cut the blanks into rectangular shapes and then finish them?"

"Not all of it, but a lot of it. Sometimes they have me making these." Nelle held out two more slabs of carbon. One was a thin, plain, rectangular plank, the same width as the foot-scraper.

At first, Justine thought that this might just be the most boring machining job she'd ever seen, then she did a double-take. "Can I hold it?"

Nelle smiled a little and handed it over.

"It's a tiny bit thinner on one side than the other, isn't it? It's just slightly wedge-shaped."

"Good eye. You might have it in you to be a machinist. Yeah, it's wedge-shaped, and you wouldn't believe how tight those specs are. The government really and truly cares how thick that leading edge is, believe you me."

She handed over the other slab of carbon. It was the same width, but about twice as thick, and its leading edge was sharply angled into a more pronounced wedge. If Justine held it with the longer side of that wedge on the bottom, she could feel a series of horizontal grooves extending across the full width of the slab under her fingers.

"You're wondering what those grooves are for," Nelle said. "I got no idea. We call the plain one the 'R-piece.' The one with ridges? We call that the 'Q-piece.' Don't ask me why."

Faced with objects that could have passed for modern sculpture, Justine was fascinated, and she was baffled. She had so hoped to be able to report to Gloria that they'd been right about the slits.

Nelle was warming up to the idea of having an audience. "The other girls and me—we think they make two sides of a box, along with the foot scraper. We think the steel parts that they work on—" She gestured at another line of machinists. "We think they're making the other sides of the box."

"But that's three pieces—R-piece, Q-piece, and foot scraper. Why don't you think we're looking at three sides of a box?"

Nelle handed her the foot scraper. "Here. Hold this one flat."

"Parallel with the floor?"

"Yeah. Think of that as the bottom of the box."

Justine did, and then Nelle took each of the other two pieces, one in each hand. She held them a few inches above Justine's piece, a fraction of an inch apart and also parallel to the floor. "We think these two pieces together make the top of the box, only with a gap between them. See? The gap between the two pieces is the slot, like a piggy bank."

"Oh, a slot," Justine blurted out. "I would have called it a slit."

Justine could hear Gloria's laughter echoing in her head. They were on the right track.

"Slot. Slit. They mean the same thing. They even sound the same. Here's a drawing of another slot. Slit. Whatever you want to call it."

Nelle unrolled a blueline drawing. "Here. Take a gander at this one." She pointed at the dimensions of something shaped like a long, very narrow, square-cornered letter *O*.

Justine wanted to kiss the dusty blue piece of paper.

"Well, wouldja look at that?" Nelle said. "We been calling these things slots all this time, but that ain't what the blueline says." She pointed at the title block beneath the drawing. "It says that this part is called a 'J-slit.' Whattaya know? Let's look at the other one."

She rolled up the drawing of the "J-slit" and unrolled another one. There, beneath a drawing that was almost identical to the other one, was a title block that read "G-slit."

Gloria was going to be ecstatic.

——

Justine stuck her head in Jerry's shop door, but nobody was home. She smiled when she saw the red-capped thermos sitting on the top shelf on the far wall. Thanks to Jerry, his coffee, and his aspirin, she was feeling much better. She didn't need his help to get started on her work, so she didn't hang around and wait for him. She just went to her station and got things under way.

The first order of business was to do a safety check on her equipment. The welding machine was a make and model she'd used before, so there was nothing tricky about the controls. The hoses were brand-new and supple, with no cracks or damaged fittings that could cause dangerous acetylene leaks. The cables, too, were new, unfrayed, and with no exposed wires.

She found the nearest fire extinguishers in a rack bolted to the outside wall of Jerry's shop, next to all the other safety equipment the Carbonites could need, right down to a bucket of water for regular everyday fires. She made sure she knew which extinguisher was rated for electrical fires, slapping her hand on its cold, hard tank, just because. Everything was ready to go.

Justine clamped the pieces of Nelle's tool rest in place, ready to weld, and strapped a magnifier to her head. She dabbed degreaser on the broken pieces, because a solid weld requires a clean surface. Then she took a good hard look at the area right around the break.

There they were. Deep, parallel grooves, just like the ones she'd seen on the broken lateral guides. There was no innocent explanation for seeing them on a tool rest. Nelle wouldn't have banged her equipment up like that. Besides, the grooves were at an angle too awkward for Nelle to easily make while she was working. They only made sense if they'd been made by someone standing to the side.

She pictured someone passing close to the equipment, making a few quick hacks with a metal rasp, and then hurrying away. Yes. That was the obvious way damage like this could have been done.

The reason for the break wasn't routine, but repairing the tool rest was going to be. It would be no trickier than repairing the lateral guides had been. Someone who wasn't Justine might have let her mind wander, but her father had drilled caution into her from the time she first picked up a torch. Everything about a welding apparatus was dangerous and, although danger wasn't to be avoided, it did require focus. Justine took off the magnifier, made sure her safety goggles were securely in place, and got to work.

———

Justine had made quick work of the tool rest, so she was ready for her next welding job. Unfortunately, Sonny wasn't ready for her.

He looked up from a desk covered with payroll records. "You gotta take your break. I can't spend time on you right now."

"It's not even close to time for my break. If you'll just give me the broken piece you want me to fix—"

"I said for you to take your break. I'm the boss. You can't understand that? Where are you gonna be? I'll send somebody to get you."

Justine hated the idea of taking her break so early. When it was over, the rest of the morning would feel interminable. Well, it couldn't be helped.

Nothing could have enticed Justine to take her break in her usual spot, sitting on a stack of boxes near the security office where Charles could often be found. It was a stone's throw from the janitor's closet where Martin kept his mops. She preferred even Sonny's company to theirs, and that was saying something. Where should she go?

An image of grass and sky and a slow-moving bayou popped into her head. She wanted to be somewhere away from the concrete floors and steel girders and echoing noise that surrounded her, but the morning rain shower had turned into a thunderstorm loud enough to penetrate the plant's ever-present din. As much as she might want to spend her break walking through the grass out back behind the trash pen, she didn't have that option. There was only one place inside the plant where she could look outside.

"I think I'll go sit by the loading dock."

Sonny looked at her like he thought that was an exceptionally foolish place to spend her free time, but he didn't say anything. He just waved a hand that said, *Get out of here.*

Justine took a long route to the loading dock, passing Jerry's open door and smiling at him, sitting alone at his workbench. She got a big smile from him as he saluted her with a hand that held a red plastic thermos lid. Ambling slowly, she moved past the machinists to try for another glimpse of the parts they were shaping. She saw nothing new, just modest-sized chunks of something very black that was being shaped to strict tolerances, but being close to the action was tickling her intuition.

Images from her dream bubbled up. Glowing earth and rock, melted and vaporized, spewed a scalding hot vapor that flowed in a great curving arc, then split into two arcs, moving side by side like two rainbow stripes rocketing toward…something. It was something black, with a narrow slit that only let some of the vapor pass into a chamber where it stayed, trapped.

She moved like a sleepwalker toward the back of the plant. The loading dock was a broad, tall opening in the plant wall, something like an open garage, except it was elevated four or five feet off the pavement below. This allowed trucks to back up to the opening and roll cargo directly out of their trailers. The loading dock could be closed with an overhead door designed to be lowered over the opening, but it stayed open most of the time to handle the frequent truck traffic needed to keep the Carbon Division going. A concrete ramp extended from the factory floor to the pavement below, and that was where Justine was headed. The ramp was beneath the overhang of the factory's roof, making that area a quiet, dry place to sit on a rainy day.

As it turned out, a small crate, wooden and stamped with indistinct green lettering, sat in the dry area beside the ramp, and it was way more inviting than the hard, slanted concrete. The crate was tucked into a corner so that she could lean against the wall and look outside, making her think that someone else had thought this would be a nice place to sit. Settling herself on the crate, she could see the trash pen, not too far away. Farther out, black thunderclouds hung over the black pavement and the sheds beyond it and the bright-green grass beyond them.

Behind her, inside the plant, a closed door marked the final assembly room where Nelle's carbon pieces and the metal parts that Justine helped screw together were assembled and made ready. Ahead of her, she knew, an airstrip cut through the grass, and that was where a government plane had whisked away those mysterious gadgets.

Justine leaned against the hard, damp wall and thought about hot rocks.

Chapter 26

Justine was dozing when the crate beneath her rocked hard. Jerry had descended the ramp on silent wheels and tapped the crate with one tire, just enough to startle her. Laughing at her as she cartwheeled her arms to catch her balance, he said, "Aw, I wouldn't let you fall. I came to say that Sonny's looking for you."

Then he thrust a cold bottle of Coke in her direction. "Georgette said you liked Cokes the way she likes grape soda."

She grasped the squatty bottle. The beads of condensation on its ice-green glass were wet on her palm. "Thanks, Jerry. I need this as much as I needed that coffee. My brain is not meant to run on alcohol and no sleep."

"Nobody's is, but that doesn't stop most of us from giving it a try. Besides, your brain runs better than most people's. You can get away with a long night out now and then."

She rose from the crate and said, "Sonny called, so I guess that means I have to go."

"I'll roll slow. Nobody will think you're slacking if it looks like you're waiting for me, and it'll give you time to finish that Coke."

She upended the bottle and sucked down a big slug of fizzy sweetness. It tasted nothing like wartime.

Keeping his voice low so that Justine had to lean down to hear him over the plant's racket, Jerry said, "We need to get you off that line and into a job that won't make you bored and bitter. I like you the way you are."

His words startled her. "Do I seem bored and bitter?"

"Not at all. You're always pleasant, always personable. You do your best, day in and day out, no matter how monotonous the work is. But if you could see how you perk up when you get to do something that interests you. Welding. Learning a new dance step. It almost doesn't matter what it is. I see it even more when somebody says something that interests you. It's like a spotlight shining on your face."

Justine had never noticed that Jerry's speech was different from most of the people in her life since her parents died. Her parents' and their friends' perfect grammar had seemed natural when it came out of their mouths. Their lives had been spent in getting an education and, for most of them, in educating others. Some of them, like Gloria, had learned English from books, and their pride was bound up in speaking it well.

On a factory assembly line, Justine and her way of speaking stuck out like a sore thumb. And so, she was realizing, did Jerry's. She knew he and Charles had grown up together in New York, but that's about all she knew about his past. Her parents had brought her up to believe that it was in poor taste to dwell too much on social class, so she'd never thought much about things like what Jerry's upbringing had been like or what his father had done for a living. It had never occurred to her to wonder about Charles's and Martin's backgrounds, either, not in that way, so she thought about it now. Martin sounded like a man from small-town Mississippi, which was exactly who he said he was. Charles spoke like he'd spent a good bit of time in school, although maybe not as much as Jerry. That was all she knew, and maybe it was all she needed to know.

Jerry was talking about Charles and that brought her back to their conversation. "Charles noticed how bright your eyes get when you're doing something interesting. He told me so. That's one thing he likes about you."

Justine felt a rush of happiness when she heard that Charles liked her. Then she got a bad taste in her mouth when she remembered that she was mad at him, so she took another big swig of Coke.

Jerry must have seen that the thought of Charles upset her, because he said, "Forget him. I'm talking about you. You need work that makes you as happy as mine does, and I'm keeping my eye out for whatever that turns out to be."

She shot him a glance that asked, "Why?"

He answered the question she hadn't asked. "You're Georgette's friend. And mine, I hope. Georgette's going to need something more, too, someday. Right now, she's happy seeing new places and learning new things. Like polynomials." And then he laughed out loud, a big belly laugh.

"You're laughing at us!"

"No, honey. It just makes me happy to see two people so full of life."

They'd reached the front door of his shop, and it made Justine smile to see that Georgette was standing inside waiting for him.

"Go weld," Jerry said, as he wheeled himself through the door.

———

Sonny had left the broken pieces of the lateral guide in Justine's workspace, so she was able to start working without having to speak to him. Giving her equipment a quick check, she clamped the pieces in place, got her torch and rod ready, and turned on the welding machine. Justine figured that this job would go quick and easy like the first one had, and then she supposed that Sonny would put her to work at her usual job for the rest of the day. The boredom she felt when she thought about standing on the line for hours and hours, after standing on it all day for a week, made her know that Jerry was right. She needed more interesting work to do. The problem was that she didn't know if she could get it. She pushed those thoughts aside and focused on her welding.

As always, she heard her father's voice when she welded, which was partly why she loved doing it. *"Watch the puddle, Justine,"* he was saying. The memory of his voice was so sweet, and it took her so far away from the here and now, that a moment passed before she felt the pain.

Jolted back to reality, she felt something scalding-hot on her lower arm, at the narrow gap between her rolled-up sleeve and the top of her welding gloves. At the same time, she heard someone scream, "Fire!"

Justine was surrounded by heat and light, and there was too much of it for her to assess the situation and act rationally. Fear bubbled up and she pictured herself on fire, with her hair alight and her skin aflame. In a heartbeat, she would be consumed. If she panicked, all was lost.

Her rational mind had switched off when she felt the flames lick her arm. All she could do was to act on instinct, and instinct was speaking in her father's voice. His words were urgent but calm, and they were correct.

Cut the gas.

Cut the power.

Then—and only then—put out the fire.

Her welding goggles were doing their job, protecting her vision while she got to the shutoff valve for the acetylene. As she moved, she pressed her flaming right sleeve hard against the leg of her coveralls, trying to smother the fire.

Jerry always made sure that a wrench stayed clamped to the acetylene valve so that it would be easy to shut off in an emergency, just as her father had taught her to do. Justine slammed the valve into the closed position and was pivoting toward the electrical switch when Georgette barreled out of Jerry's shop.

"I'm coming, Justine," she yelled as she headed toward the safety equipment bolted to the wall of Jerry's shed. Justine's heart stopped when she saw Georgette pass up the correct fire extinguisher, the one rated for electrical fires, as she headed straight for the bucket of water.

Georgette was strong, so she hefted the bucket as if it were nothing. She was bold, so she didn't hesitate in running headlong toward the smoldering hoses and the burned cables with their exposed wires, ready to end any chance of the fire spreading. She was a good friend, so nothing was going to keep her from saving Justine, not even Justine's own voice crying out, "Stop! Georgette, stop!"

Justine turned away from the electrical switch toward Georgette. Her father's voice was yelling for her to cut the power, but love for her friend overrode his words of caution. It overrode her safety training and even her knowledge of the physics of electricity. Leaving the electrical switch behind, she threw herself at Georgette so hard that, had their sizes been reversed, she would have thrown the other woman to the floor in an easy tackle.

Unfortunately Georgette was a lot heavier and her moving body had momentum that Justine's body—also fast-moving, but light—couldn't overpower. All Justine could do was hang on with one hand and let the larger woman drag her while she used her other hand to wrestle the bucket of water away from Georgette's strong grip.

Justine was accomplishing nothing, other than to slosh water out of the bucket as she trailed behind the hard-charging

Georgette. The cool water splashing on her burned arm eased the pain, but just for an instant. It quenched her smoldering sleeve, but it created another big problem. When Justine went to cut the electrical power, she would be standing in a puddle of water that amplified the electrocution risk.

All the while, the whole time she was being dragged across the wet floor, Justine was bellowing at Georgette, "Stop STOP you have to stop or we'll be electrocuted. STOP! Georgette, we could die."

When the word "die" registered, Georgette turned her head, meeting Justine's gaze from just inches away. Her face was set, determined to eliminate the danger for her friend—for all of her friends, some of whom were fleeing and some of whom were rooted to the floor, horrified.

Justine spoke again, trying to reach her one more time. "Stop. We could die."

Georgette faltered. She stumbled to a halt just as Jerry was able to wheel himself in his rubber-wheeled chair to the emergency electrical shutoff, only feet from the spreading puddle of water. He cut the power, grabbed the proper extinguisher, and covered Justine's whole station with chemicals designed to make sure the fire stayed out.

Justine let go of Georgette and dropped flat on the wet floor, shaking all over and too breathless to speak.

"What?" Georgette wanted to know. "Why couldn't you people just let me put the fire out?"

Words were spewing out of Justine. They were directed at Georgette, at herself, at the blackened hose, at the empty air. "My fault. It's my fault. You could have died, and it's my fault."

She scuttled backward like a crab, trying to put space between her body and Georgette's. She wanted to say more, so much more, but it wasn't safe. What she was thinking, though, was that there were only two possible reasons for the fire. Either she'd been inexcusably sloppy with incredibly dangerous equipment, and she really didn't believe that she had, or the saboteur had escalated from destroying things to destroying people. Or maybe it was no escalation. Maybe Cora Becker had died at the hands of the same person who had tampered with Justine's equipment. So, perhaps, had her parents if Gloria's hypothesis was correct. These possibilities put Justine at the very center of a danger that could engulf all the people around her. It wasn't safe to be close to her. She wanted to run away, but where could she go?

Jerry wheeled over and reached down a hand to help Justine to a seated position. He gestured for her to stay on the floor, probably because he knew she needed to gather her wits.

Then he cupped Georgette's chin and turned her face toward him. Looking straight into her eyes, he said, "You didn't know, honey. Now that I've seen you in action and I know you've got a hero's heart, I feel a lot safer around here. You just didn't know that it's not safe to mix water and electricity."

Seeing the blank look on her face, he tried again, explaining things in a way that a woman who'd lived her life outside could understand. "It would be a lot like getting hit by lightning while you're standing in the bayou."

Georgette looked around. A crowd had gathered and all eyes were on her.

"Stupid." She shook her head as she spoke, like she was trying to shake some sense into it. "I'm too stupid to be around you people. I'm so stupid that I'm gonna get somebody killed."

The metal bucket clanged to the concrete. Georgette didn't cry or run. She just walked, expressionless, away from all those eyes. She pushed her way through the doors to the main plant and out of their sight.

Justine wanted to go after her. But her arms and legs weren't working too well, and neither was her mind, so she just sat sprawled on the wet concrete and watched her go.

———

"This doesn't look too bad," Jerry said as he applied ointment to Justine's burn. "It might leave a little scar, but maybe not, if you keep some of this on it."

Justine looked at the swath of pink skin encircling her arm below the elbow, just above where her protective gloves had stopped. It fascinated her, but in a distant way, as if the mark were on somebody else's body. It probably hurt, but she couldn't feel it. She didn't feel scared. She didn't feel relieved. She didn't feel anything.

"I've got lots more in the first aid kit, so take this home with you." He handed her the jar of ointment and wrapped a bandage around her arm. "Right now, go sit by the loading dock. Go hide in the ladies' room. Go walk it off. Just don't sit here and dwell on what could have happened, because it didn't. Nobody's hurt. Everybody's okay."

"I'm fine," she said, even though she wasn't sure whether she'd know if she wasn't fine.

"You're in shock, the same as if you'd just walked off a battle-field. You need to be easy on yourself."

She walked toward the mess left behind by the fire extinguisher, pretending that Jerry wasn't speaking. The fire had been put out quickly and there hadn't been much flammable material in the area to feed the flames, so there wasn't much to see.

"Do you have a mop in that shed, Jerry? I need to clean up my mess."

"I'll get somebody to mop up the water and get rid of the burnt hose, and I'll check out the welding machine myself. You don't need to push yourself to do it."

She stood over what was left of the hose, but there wasn't enough of it to tell her what she needed to know. She hadn't had the time or the composure to be able to see and remember everything that had happened during the fire, but it must have been started by a leak in that hose. She wasn't stupid enough to keep flammable material at her station. The hose. Her clothes. Her. That was about it, in terms of things that could catch fire. What else, other than a leak in the acetylene hose, could have caused it?

Now her arm was starting to sting. The scorched patch of skin on it was evidence for her leak theory because the hose had been snaking past her lower arm when the fire started. But how could the brand-new hose have developed a leak when she'd checked it that morning?

It had operated just fine before she took her break. She'd looked at it again before resuming her work, but had she really checked it thoroughly? How much scrutiny does a brand-new hose need, just a half hour after functioning perfectly well?

Had she come a millimeter from killing Georgette and herself, and who knew who else, because she'd been careless? She almost wished that this was true, because the alternative was worse.

She knew that a saboteur had been sawing on the lateral guides. There wasn't enough left of the burnt section of hose to confirm her suspicions that the same person had been at work on it, but she couldn't see any other explanation for the fire.

A quick jab with a sharp implement would have opened a barely noticeable pinhole in the hose. An awl, a tool punch, even a stout needle would have been enough. Even the most thorough visual inspection might not have uncovered the damage. Maybe Sonny sent her away so that somebody—perhaps even Sonny himself—would have a chance to ease up to her station while she was gone, damage the hose, and then move on unseen.

As she worried over this problem, a voice sounded near her ear, but she heard only fragments.

"...coulda got us all killed...oughta fire your ass...listen to me when I talk to you, Justine...are you listening..."

Sonny was suddenly inches away from her face, spewing angry words, but she couldn't focus on him. She didn't see anything but the burnt hose.

Mavis, too, had materialized out of nowhere. Justine couldn't see her, either, but she could feel the terrified hands grasping at the remnants of her scorched sleeve.

Justine stayed standing, wobbly but erect, because she didn't want to be at Sonny's feet while he bawled her out. She looked over at Nelle and remembered her husband, Ralph. How would he have felt if she'd killed Nelle with her negligence? She thought of Sonny's wife and, oh God, Mavis's children.

She could hear their little voices, and they drowned out Sonny's tirade. Then even their voices were swamped by the roar of the fire that might have swept through the whole Michaud plant before anyone could get out. And it would all have been her fault. Her legs went weak under her and she fell.

———

Justine woke up to the feel of Mavis's hands rubbing hers. There were tears streaming down her friend's face.

Sonny was talking, and Justine had the feeling that he had never stopped talking. "You gotta take her home, Mavis. People are standing around talking. Crying. I just caught some of 'em smoking cigarettes while they watched the goings-on, like they're at a circus or a zoo or something. It's like they *want* to set the place on fire. Nothing's gonna settle down until she's outta here."

Mavis put a hand on Justine's cheek, index finger to her cheekbone and pinkie under her jaw. With the practiced air of a mother who had tended to children's sicknesses and injuries for years, she used the hand to raise Justine's chin. Looking her straight in the eye, she said, "Can you hear me, Justine? Nod your head if you understand what I'm sayin'."

Justine managed a tiny nod. It was more of a twitch of her neck muscles, actually, but it satisfied Mavis. Maintaining eye contact, Mavis said, "I'm taking you home. You got food there? I'm gonna make sure you get a hot meal and some rest. And some coffee or tea, if you got it, but only after you lay down and rest."

Jerry said, "I'm not sure she understands you," and Justine wanted to tell him that she did, but it was just too much effort to open her mouth.

"I'll keep tellin' her all the way home, then I'll go inside and get the food warm. Where's Georgette?"

Sonny said, "Just take this one to the car. I'll send somebody to look for Georgette and you can take her if she shows up before you leave. If she don't, just go. I want this one outta here. Now."

But Georgette didn't show up while Mavis was ushering Justine to her car. Justine just let herself be loaded into the back seat, unable to say, "Wait for her," and that cut her to the heart.

Mavis closed the car door for her like she was a child. "Stretch out back there and don't try to talk. Don't think. You didn't do nothing wrong, and everything turned out okay."

Justine did a very good job of obeying Mavis's order to stretch out, and she definitely didn't try to talk. She utterly failed at obeying the "Don't think," instruction, though.

Telling Justine not to think was like telling her not to breathe.

———

Georgette had walked out of the Carbon Division and through the main plant. She had walked past Martin as if she'd never seen him before in her life, and Charles, too. Something inside her blamed them for the fire, for her humiliation, for everything. This was not logical, but she had just shown the world how stupid she was, so she figured she wasn't required to be logical.

She'd always been embarrassed about the things that she didn't know. Other people had gotten more schooling or they'd learned things just by living someplace that wasn't Des Allemands. None of that was her fault, but she knew they judged her for it. She'd learned to plunge ahead in the world and figure things out as she went along. It had never occurred to her that her ignorance could kill somebody.

She couldn't face the people she might have hurt. She wasn't even sure she'd be able to face Justine, who was fast becoming the best friend she'd ever had. She needed some time to lick her wounds like an injured bird dog. Eyes straight ahead and head high, she strode out the back of the plant like she was headed for the trash pen, despite her empty hands. Then she kept walking across the pavement, into the grass, and across the airstrip. She didn't stop until she reached the brushy cane and tall grass at the edge of the bayou.

It was raining, but Georgette didn't care. The air and the water were as warm as her skin. She didn't even mind the occasional flash and crack of thunder and lightning. She sank to the muddy ground and let the wet weeds hide her. She'd spent her whole life on bayou banks, aboard boats, on an open-air sleeping porch, and in a house where the windows were always open to a swamp-scented breeze.

She was more at home here in the mud and rain than she'd ever be in a loud, airless factory. It would take no effort at all for

Georgette to sit here until the whistle blew, telling her it was time to take the bus home and face Justine.

———

Lying on the back seat of Mavis's car, Justine's body was at rest but her mind was not. Her thoughts turned inward and they focused on machined slabs of carbon and intricately shaped pieces of stainless steel.

In her mind's eye, she could see them formed into the cube-like box that Nelle had described. No, that wasn't right. She mentally adjusted the box, slanting one side a bit.

There. That was right.

Some distance away, she visualized a mass of hot rock— uranium, surely—emitting ions, ready for the G-slits and J-slits to focus them into a stream and accelerate them.

A magnetic field would bend the stream of uranium ions into an arc-shaped path. No, make that two arcs, one made of Uranium-235 and one made of Uranium-238, because the path of the heavier U-238 ions would bend less. Their mass determined their path, just as Justine's lack of mass had kept her from changing the more massive Georgette's path. Behind her closed eyes, Justine could see the two hot, glowing arcs bending like a rainbow.

And that was the key. There could be no atomic bomb without a source of U-235, which was far less stable than U-238. Once the magnetic field had separated them, all that remained was to capture the U-235. The U-238 atoms could fly to hell, for all the scientists doing the separation cared.

And Nelle had shown her how the U-235 would be captured. The boot scraper and the two pieces that made the slit above it—they were pieces of the collector that would gather up the hard-won stream of U-235. The carbon parts would be durable when battered by the relentless kinetic energy of the uranium streams. They could even be burned to capture every last bit of precious U-235.

This was the Carbon Division's reason for being. It had to be. Justine and her friends were cogs in a wheel, but it was a very important wheel. Without their carbon-and-steel gewgaws, there could be no fuel for a giant explosion that would surely end the war. To Justine's way of thinking, once people knew that such a thing existed, war would be unimaginable. The bomb would never need to be dropped at all, and that was something to work for. It was something to pray for.

This explained the secrecy. It explained the mysterious plane that had rushed their unimportant-looking parts away to... somewhere. It explained the constant drive to produce, produce, produce, before the enemy had time to build the same bomb and drop it on the Allies.

Unable to wrap her mind around that thought, she let herself relax. She let her mind go someplace comforting. She conjured up her parents' faces in her mind's eye, and the love in their eyes made her believe that everything was going to be okay.

Justine slept. When the car stopped, she woke and dragged herself out of it. She was vehement about refusing Mavis's offer to help her climb upstairs and put together a meal. She could do it herself. She wanted to do it herself. She wanted to be far away from Mavis and her maternal ways and her tears. She needed to capture her thoughts on paper before they flew away at the speed of an ionized uranium stream.

———

Mavis wept as she drove. Her heart broke for the poor child who had spent the long ride home from the Michaud plant flat on her back. The sight of Justine, silhouetted by flame, would never leave her. Nor would she forget Georgette charging gamely toward danger with Jerry not far behind.

And all of these things were her fault.

She'd never understood her instructions, but she'd always followed them. In the first days after the Carbon Division had started work, she'd sawed with a rasp at the little parts underneath the conveyor belt, just like she'd been told. Then she'd watched them break, one by one, as mechanical stresses and strains took their toll on the metal she'd damaged.

She'd sawed at some other things, too, when Sonny wasn't paying attention because he was trying to find yet another woman to help him cheat on his wife. Some of the things she'd damaged had already broken, and some of them were ticking time bombs waiting to break, but none of this had affected Mavis. Nothing had affected her but the extra money in her purse.

Nobody had been hurt, and she'd pocketed some sorely needed cash. The only result of her actions, as far as she could tell, was that the Carbon Division's work had been slowed down a bit. That didn't sound like a bad thing to Mavis. Maybe Higgins Industries would schedule some extra hours to make up for the time it took to fix the things she broke, and maybe she'd get some of those hours. Feeding and housing three children felt like shoveling cash money into the maw of an always-hungry monster, and the Navy didn't pay Denny nearly enough to make up for the cost of having him gone.

And they had debts. House. Car. Department store. Grocery store. Overdue doctor bills for the kids and her mother and her grandparents. If her mother got too sick to take care of her kids and her grandparents, then where would Mavis and her family be? There was never a moment when the need for money didn't drive her.

Mavis had answered her contact's questions as best she could, although he interested her only to the extent that he paid her money. She sensed that more money would come if she could tell him something about the Carbon Division's work, but she didn't understand the Carbon Division's work. Mavis was a woman who had squeaked through high school with C's. Her contact had been clear that he found her help inadequate.

After all those failures, she'd presumed that there would be no more work for her and, thus, no more cash...until that morning, when he'd told her to use the fine point of a punch tool to stab a barely visible hole in Justine's hose. She'd felt very shrewd as she'd watched Justine walk to the back of the plant for her break. Mavis had taken her chance right then, and she'd punched the hole.

But Mavis hadn't realized what that hole would do. She'd thought this was just another task intended to slow the Carbonites' work down. She'd thought it would make Justine's welding equipment useless, not dangerous. Panic and flames had been the furthest thing from her mind, but this wasn't true for the man who had ordered her to punch the hole. He'd known exactly what he was asking her to do.

Mavis cast a glance at her purse, sitting next to her on the big car's bench seat. There was a tidy bundle of cash inside, and the thought of it made her weep even harder.

Chapter 27

Justine drifted through the lobby of The Julia, nodding at the women who sat there enjoying their Saturday. A feeling of urgency took her to the stairs, and the thumping of her work boots on the wooden treads accelerated as she rose. Her hand shook as she fitted the old key into its keyhole, which made her think of slots and slits, but she managed to get the door open.

Slamming it behind her, she crossed the room in two steps, opened her folder of graph paper, and laid it on the table. She retrieved the books she'd fetched from Gloria's house—the Thomson book, the Aston book on isotopes, and the lopsided little book that her father had made out of his friends' papers— and she spread them across her bed. She grabbed a pencil, paper, and a straightedge and, as if in a dream, she drew firm, sure lines.

The ion source.

The G-slit and J-slit, made by Nelle and her friends and positioned to focus the ions.

The rainbow-like double-arc of uranium ions, U-235 and U-238.

And the wedge-shaped carbon-and-steel box, made of parts

crafted by the entire Carbon Division, with its slitted opening positioned to capture the priceless and unstable U-235.

As she set that drawing aside, she glanced down at her carbon-stained coveralls, now dried stiff. She needed a bath, and she needed the hot meal that she'd promised Mavis she'd eat, because her work had only begun. She had more drawings to make, and she had an encrypted message to decode.

As she gathered her clothes, towel, soap, and washrag, she also gathered two precious documents—the graph paper bearing the transcription of the dots punched into a window screen and her drawing of the uranium arcs. She rolled them into a tube, secured them with a rubber band, and wrapped them with her spare towel for camouflage. She wasn't leaving these documents alone, not even for the time it took her to take a quick bath. As she planned her attack on the window screen code, she harbored one wordless and happy thought.

She couldn't wait to tell Gloria what she'd learned.

———

Fritz was pleased. He had created the kind of mayhem that would shake Justine to her core. It was just one step from there to the question that could turn her to him.

Why should someone with her gifts labor for people who couldn't hold a candle to her?

Fritz had turned men into traitors, but he had never before recruited a woman. This gave him two extra tools in his arsenal. Sexual manipulation was the obvious one, but he was learning the power of his other tool, the desire of someone like Justine to strike back at a system that smothered women alive. There had to be a deep well of bitterness in the soul of a woman with Justine's unusual capabilities. It must gall her to know that she would be forced to kowtow to men like Sonny for every day of her natural life. It was right and proper that a woman should do so, even to men like Sonny, but Justine would fight her destiny every step of the way.

This had been the fate of Justine's mother. Most women, when faced with the necessarily limited opportunities offered for their limited capabilities, did the wise thing and settled down to a life of motherhood and only motherhood. Isabel Byrne might have been the rare woman who was capable of doing physics at some level, but she had not been wise.

Fritz was beginning to understand women like Isabel. Cursed with a finer mind than any woman needed to fulfill her rightful functions of consort and mother, a woman like Isabel would spend her life contorting herself into a shape that let her pursue her interests. She would try to serve child, husband, and science, giving none of them what they deserved. She would allow herself to be subordinate to a man who was willing to throw her the dregs of what she wanted.

Isabel had lived her life in a gilded cage. Her husband had built it for her with love, but it had still been a cage. Justine must see that her own future led to this destiny or to a desiccated spinsterhood. If he could offer her a better one, she would be his, body and soul.

He must plan his next step carefully. The time had come, as it always did, when he must state flatly what he wanted her to do. This required him to reveal himself. In that moment, Justine Byrne's fate narrowed to two possibilities.

Either she would join him or she would die.

———

A hot bath left Justine feeling fresh, as if she'd slept for a full night. Dressed in a crisply pressed gingham blouse and a pair of dungarees, with her wet hair wrapped in a towel, she resharpened her pencil and grabbed her scale ruler. Taping down a plain sheet of paper and picking up her straightedge, she drew a horizon line near the top of the page and marked two vanishing points on it. Now she was ready to make a scale drawing of the carbon-and-steel collector. For such a little gadget, it sure was causing a lot of trouble for a lot of people.

As she worked, she heard a knock. Georgette's voice sounded through the cracks around her crooked old door.

"I'm so sorry," her friend said. "I'm so sorry I didn't listen to you. I didn't know it was dangerous to put water on electricity. I didn't know. I feel so ignorant, but I never meant to hurt you."

Justine had never meant to hurt Georgette, either, but she had come so close to killing her. It wasn't Georgette's fault somebody had sabotaged Justine's welding equipment, but that didn't stop her from coming just inches from death. Justine wasn't willing for her friend to die because she couldn't solve her own problems. The only way to avoid that was to push her away.

Maybe Justine would need to go away altogether, rather than bring danger to the whole plant. She was heading into her day off, so she had some time to decide whether she was ever going back, but her time at Higgins Industries might well be over.

Maybe if Georgette wasn't sure she was home, she would go away. Justine worked silently, hoping a creak of her chair or a squeak of her pencil didn't give her away.

———

Georgette's voice sounded again. "Justine."

She had sat outside Justine's door for…well, Justine wasn't sure how long she'd been there. She had winced every time she heard her name, but she'd maintained her silence, and she'd distracted herself with her work. During the time Georgette had spent sitting on the hallway floor, Justine had produced a scale drawing of an assembled Uranium-235 collector in two-point perspective. Now she was making orthographic projections of key parts of the assembled whole.

Each time she finished a drawing, she folded it carefully, wincing as she made irrevocable creases through her careful work. The only way to keep these papers safe was to wear them on her person, and that meant folding them. She'd bought these dungarees for their large patch pockets, cute and practical, with buttons to hold them closed. Now those cute pockets were coming in handy.

"Justine. I was hoping that you'd still want to be my friend if you knew how sorry I was."

She paused, but Justine didn't speak.

"I'm sorry you can't forgive me. I'll go away now and leave you alone. But I'll miss you."

She heard Georgette's work boots striking the floor. Right foot. Left foot. Right foot, left foot. The sound of her friend's steps faded as she moved away, changing in timbre as she descended the stairs.

"I'll miss you, too," Justine murmured. "But I'd rather keep you alive."

Then she opened the folded pieces of graph paper where she'd transcribed the coded message, preparing herself to match wits with a spy who was sniffing around an operation that was critical to the separation of uranium isotopes. This person presumably had a lot more experience with wartime encryption than she did, but Justine had no choice but to break the code. Failure to do so could have explosive results.

———

Georgette opened the introductory physics book, the one she was going to have to give back. Through her ignorance, she had destroyed her friendship with Justine, and she couldn't be beholden to someone who wasn't her friend any longer. Before she took the book back, though, there was just one thing that she wanted to learn. If water and electricity didn't mix, and apparently they did not, then Georgette was determined to find out why.

Chapter 28

Justine had been staring at the encrypted message for hours. She was recording her ideas in a clothbound notebook, and there were depressingly few coherent thoughts written in it. Nevertheless, the notebook made her feel strong—hopeful, even. Identical to her godmother's signature notebooks, it made Justine feel as if Gloria were there, using her favorite teaching tool, incessant questions, to guide her to the answers she needed. The questions sounded in her ear in Gloria's beloved voice, one after another.

There are a lot of dots. Could you try a variant of Morse code?

Maybe Morse code would work, but Justine couldn't really see a consistent way to identify dashes. If she counted two dots that were right next to each other as a dash, then she saw something that looked like a recognizable *D*, but the next cluster of dots made no sense unless she counted three dots as a dash. She labored over dots and dashes for longer than she probably should have, then she gave up.

The area at the center is different from the area framing it. The frame looks truly random, but there are blank areas in the centers. Can you do anything with that?

If Justine had to guess, those blank areas were spaces between words. They were all two spaces wide, but they weren't all the same height. Many of them were three spaces tall, but three of them were six spaces tall.

Six and nine were both multiples of three, and this made Justine's heart skip a beat. She was very familiar with a code consisting of letters that were three spaces high and two spaces wide. She quickly counted the width of the dot patterns that she was calling "words."

Bingo. The width of each word was divisible by two. This made Justine want to kiss her graph paper.

Her imaginary Gloria must have thought she was on the right track because the voice in her head stopped asking questions and let her get to work.

Justine had learned a code constructed of letters that were two spaces wide and three spaces tall at her mother's knee. On the very day that her mother was told that she would go blind, she'd bought a book called *Learning Braille*. Isabel, her husband, and their little red-haired daughter had sat at the dinner table, night after night, and learned a communication system built on dots. When the time came that Isabel couldn't read with her eyes, she could read with her fingers, and so could Gerard and Justine.

It was just possible that Justine was looking at words constructed of braille letters that were all mashed together, with single spaces separating words. It was better than possible. It seemed likely. Justine copied the pattern of the words, just to get a sense of the shape of the message:

XXXXXX
XXXX XXXX XX XXX
XXXXXX XXX XXXXX
XXXXXX XXXX XXXX
XXXX XXXX XXXXXXX
XXXXXXX
XXX XXX XXXXXX
XXXXXX XXX XXXXX
XXXX XX XXXX XX
XXXX XX XXXXXXXX
XXXXXXX

It made her happy to see the message laid out this way. Seeing the pattern of letters and spaces was a first step to discovering how it was encrypted. Still, the pattern made her want to curse because there were no one-letter words. Presuming she was working with a substitution code, one-letter words were the quickest route to learning to recognize the letters *a* and *i*, and vowels were the key to everything.

Well, at least she had now learned that the message didn't seem to use the word *a* or the word *I*, not even once. This was probably by design.

It was time to exercise her braille skills. She had no doubt that she could translate the holes punched in the screen into letters. She might even have been able to read them by brushing her fingers over the back of the screen. She simply doubted that anybody would use an encryption system so simple as mashing braille letters together.

And she was right. As she transcribed each two-by-three block of six squares, she found that every single one of them could be read as a braille letter, but the letters didn't form recognizable words.

One important thing was obvious. Some of the words were repeated. Here was evidence that this was not a random bunch of holes punched in a screen. It was an intelligible message. It had to be.

But now what? If she needed a decryption device with nested disks that a spy would twirl until it spit out the right letter, then she was sunk. And if the code was based on a printed text key—say, she needed to open a particular Bible to the book of Joshua and use the letters on its first page as a decryption device—then, again, she was sunk. But if this scrambled message was based on a simple substitution code, then she could crack it. Therefore, she was going to bet all her chips on a substitution cipher.

Justine leaned back in her chair and looked at the message as a whole.

```
DBSCPO
DPNF XJUI NF BOE
DIBOHF UIF XPSME
DIBOHF ZPVS MJGF
GJOE ZPVS QVSQPTF
KVTUJOF
ZPV BSF OFFEFE
TFF UIF XPSME
NFFU NF IFSF BU
OPPO TVOEBZ
KVTUJOF
```

As she sat pondering the nonsense words, she heard sounds outside her door. She heard bare feet on wood planks and soft breaths. And she heard someone set something gently on the floor.

The footsteps sounded like Georgette's. Then she turned her

eyes to her bedroom window and remembered that someone had come through it to steal something that she'd hidden. Who was outside her door, really?

The thought of someone, perhaps a man, intruding in the female space of The Julia Ladies' Residence made her feel violated. She shivered and wished for a cardigan to keep her warm, but she didn't want the mysterious person to hear her moving around. Instead, she sat quietly, goose bumps on her arms, and waited for the sound of quiet footsteps to recede.

———

When Justine felt that she'd heard enough silence, she quietly eased her door open. No one was in the hallway, and there were no lights on that she could see. All she heard were the soft sounds of women sighing in their sleep. Something sat on the floor outside the door, but it was too dark to see what it was.

Without stopping to think that it could be dangerous, she dropped to her knees to get a better look. What she saw on the floor brought tears to her eyes.

In a neat pile sat her algebra book, her introductory physics book, and a battered school notebook. She brought them inside her room and eased the door shut. The books belonged on her shelf with the other books her parents had given her, so she put them there. The notebook was unfamiliar, so she opened it. Inside, she saw pages and pages of lined paper covered with neatly worked-out algebra problems.

Georgette had done everything Justine had told her to do. She had worked through the algebra book, chapter by chapter, showing her work and double-checking her answers. She'd finished a third of the book in a week. There was so much desire in the painstakingly solved problems that Justine couldn't bear to look at them. She closed the notebook, rested her forehead on it, and let herself cry for a while. Then she set Georgette's algebra homework carefully on her bookshelf and went back to work.

———

The problem, Justine decided, was that she wasn't sure where to start.

She could focus on the two-letter words. There were only so many commonly used two-letter words in English, and one of the two letters would be a vowel. But not both. Or at least she hoped she wasn't dealing with two-letter words made entirely of vowels, because they were a bit specialized. If she was looking at a message about "Io," the satellite of Jupiter, or "oi," the British interjection, then she was probably sunk.

There were multiple three-letter words. Presuming that the message was in English, one of those three-letter words was probably "the" and one of them was probably "and." Either of these would give her three very common letters. Attacking three-letter words would be another reasonable strategy for breaking the cipher.

Justine bent to her work, never once considering that this puzzle, designed just for her, might not be simply a message. It might well be a test.

———

Mudcat lay awake, trying to rationalize away his nerves.

This was not the first time he had recruited an agent. He had always slept well the night before the encounter, despite the fact that every one of the other recruits had been more dangerous than Justine Byrne. For one thing, she was unarmed, to the best of his knowledge. There was no reasonable chance that she would put a bullet in his heart, although he supposed that she might be able to swing that wrench she carried in her back pocket pretty hard. She was at her most dangerous, physically speaking, when she held a torch and a hot rod, but these were poor weapons because they tied her to a single spot. He would not be encountering her when she was anywhere near her welding equipment, so he didn't need to worry about the torch and rod.

He felt a pang when he realized that he'd never seen her weld, and this was when he knew that he had lost the objectivity that had kept him alive. He imagined her face lit by the reflections of an eye-searing flame and white-hot sparks. Her coppery hair, pulled away from her face into a waterfall of ringlets and fluff, would reflect the torch with its own warm light. This was an image that made his heart constrict, but it wasn't what he really wanted to see. He wanted her to turn her eyes away from the burning light and pull the protective goggles away from her face. He wanted her to face him, backlit by the glowing torch. He wanted her eyes on him, because they showed her for what she was, pure intelligence and love.

Suddenly, life was very simple. He wanted Justine.

———

Fritz should have been able to sleep, since he'd passed his last night lying awake on the ground outside Justine Byrne's rooming house, but he couldn't. He was wracked by adrenaline, because he had decided that it was time to put the final stage of Operation Fritz into motion. If he stayed in America any longer, he would be marooned there, possibly for life. But surely there was someone in Germany who still had the ability to get him out. He just had to reestablish contact with the Fatherland.

His superiors knew where he had been before he lost contact. If a great conflagration were to consume the Michaud plant, the German government—what remained of it—would know that he was alive and that he had accomplished a tremendous disruption. If his organization still existed in any form at all, destruction of the Michaud plant would prompt them to do their best to get him out of America, along with the classified information concerning the construction of Higgins's planes, ships, and boats that he'd amassed. Information on the Carbon Division would have been the pièce de résistance, but it was not to be. The things he'd been able to learn should be quite enough to earn him a hero's welcome.

Fritz had been sent to America with a tremendous pack full of fuses and timers and explosives and incendiaries. He'd been trained to assemble these materials into bombs, and he'd been trained in how to use them. He'd even been trained to build devices of destruction from such prosaic items as dried peas, razor blades, and lumps of sugar. He'd spent his entire time at Higgins Industries assembling what he needed to take aim at the Michaud plant. Over the past weeks, he had put his bombs in place, one by one, while he developed a plan for deploying them when the time came.

The Michaud plant was a vast place, so perhaps he couldn't bring the whole thing down, but he could certainly make a holy mess of it. And if Justine was on the premises when this happened, he could make her choice crystal clear.

She could walk out the doors of the Michaud plant with him, ready for travel and adventure. Or she could be blown to hell right along with it.

Chapter 29

Justine studied the encrypted message, ignoring the unidentified letters themselves and, instead, studying their patterns.

```
DBSCPO
DPNF XJUI NF BOE
DIBOHF UIF XPSME
DIBOHF ZPVS MJGF
GJOE ZPVS QVSQPTF
KVTUJOF
ZPV BSF OFFEFE
TFF UIF XPSME
NFFU NF IFSF BU
OPPO TVOEBZ
KVTUJOF
```

"OPPO" was an interesting word. It would represent words like "peep" that only had two unique letters in them, with one of them being a vowel. "OPPO" might be the weak point in the cypher that would let her crack it open. She made a list of words that fit this pattern, reflexively using the rule that ciphers were spelled with capital letters and the deciphered parts of the message were spelled with lowercase letters.

```
anna
boob
deed
kook
noon
otto
peep
poop
toot
```

She didn't know anyone named "Anna" or "Otto," and she could think of no reason to go to the trouble of encrypting childish words like "boob," "kook," "peep," "poop," or "toot." "Deed" and "noon," however, were important words that grown-ups used in matters of money and time. She decided to work with "noon." If a specific time was important enough to communicate in this roundabout way, it meant that she was working against a ticking clock.

Okay, then. If "OPPO" equaled "noon," then O equaled n and P equaled o. What could she do with that?

```
DBSCon
DoNF XJUI NF BnE
DIBnHF UIF XoSME
DIBnHF ZoVS MJGF
GJnE ZoVS QVSQoTF
KVTUJnF
ZoV BSF nFFEFE
TFF UIF XoSME
NFFU NF IFSF BU
noon TVnEBZ
KVTUJnF
```

What else could she use to break this puzzle open?

Well, "DIBnHF," "ZoVS," "KVTUJnF," "XoSME," and "NF" were used more than once. That could be helpful.

Her eye kept returning to the first, sixth, and last lines. Each of them consisted of a single word, and two of those three words were identical. The first one, "DBSCon," had six letters. The repeated word, "KVTUJnF," had seven letters. Together, these two words included thirteen letters and only one of those letters was repeated.

If she deciphered these two words and twelve letters fell into her lap, she'd have almost half the alphabet, including two vowels. She thought it was no accident that they were highlighted by being segregated into single-word lines.

It was as if those two words were lit up and flashing. If this message was meant for Justine, then the encrypter would aim those two words directly at her. She certainly had reason to believe that this cipher was meant for her. The screen had been left in a place where she went every day and at the specific time she went there.

The stronger evidence that the code was meant for her lay in its very specific construction. There couldn't be many people walking the floor of the Michaud plant who knew braille. She didn't like it that this unknown person knew that her dead mother had been blind. She didn't like it that this person knew anything about her mother at all.

She heard Gloria's words in her head. They made her want to beat her head against the table until the coded message solved itself.

If you think your parents' deaths were an accident, then you are a fool.

———

When Justine saw the truth, it got her attention as quickly as if someone had been calling her name. Because someone had.

There was indeed a word with deep meaning for Justine that had seven letters, all of them different. And the "n" was even in the right place. Her hand shook as she wrote her guess at that key word into her notes.

```
KVTUJnF = justine
```

Seeing the encrypted word and her name side by side solved everything. It told her what cipher to use. She tried that cipher on the other keyword and there it was, a second word that was deeply important to Justine and, apparently, to the federal government. And, also apparently, it was important to the person sabotaging the work of the Carbon Division.

```
DBSCon = carbon
```

Now she saw that she was working with one of the simplest encryption systems around, the Caesar Cipher, which had supposedly been used by Julius Caesar. To use the Caesar Cipher, the message-sender simply pushed each letter farther into the alphabet by a specific number of letters. This message used the simplest Caesar Cipher of all. Each letter was pushed only one letter forward—*a* became *B*, *b* became *C*, and so on down the line.

The message-sender had really wanted her to read this message, thinking that if she didn't recognize her own name, perhaps she would recognize "carbon." And if she missed both of those easy clues, surely she would try the easiest ciphers and hope to get lucky. Even a child could decrypt the Caesar Cipher.

If only she understood what the person had meant by writing these words:

```
carbon
come with me and
change the world
change your life
find your purpose
justine
you are needed
see the world
meet me here at
noon sunday
justine
```

The cynical part of her thought that it read like an Army recruitment letter. The dreamer in her felt a hard knot of anger at her core loosen. She'd never even known the anger existed until this message soothed it.

Nestled in that core of bitterness was the sound of all the voices that had said she would never amount to anything because she was a girl. This was where she had tucked the pain of seeing Gloria and her research shunted aside. It was where she had hid the sight of her mother toiling at home in support of work that would always put her father's name first.

Justine would never have dreamed that she could be so moved by a handful of words of just one or two syllables.

```
change the world
find your purpose
you are needed
```

Someone wanted her to come with them…to run away with them.

Martin had as much as said that he wanted to see the world,

and he wanted a woman to see it with him. Martin was attractive, and he was exciting, but there was something unsafe about him. Well, hell. Maybe she was ready for something unsafe.

Charles had been hinting at radical politics, and radicals were all about changing the world. He had hinted at marriage, or at least something long-term. He seemed to have plans that did not involve working at a factory in New Orleans for the rest of his life, but did he really think he could change the world? And that she could somehow help him? How? By ending the war?

That idea smacked of full-on megalomania, but there were strange doings afoot at the Michaud plant. Maybe the message was from the saboteur who had tried to set her afire, but maybe it was from someone trying to stop the sabotage. That could be a world-changing effort, and maybe she could be part of it.

Who sent the message? It would be a mistake to presume that it came from Charles or Martin, just because they were the ones who wanted to date her. Neither of them could possibly be the person who did the actual sabotage, because they had never darkened the door of the Carbon Division. Higgins Industries had rules, and those rules barred the door to Charles and Martin.

Sonny was in a position of authority, but the idea of him constructing a coded message was laughable. Unless he was a terrifically talented actor, that is. She supposed that spies usually were.

Jerry had full access to the Carbon Division, and he was certainly smart enough to craft this message and leave it for her, but he'd shown no signs of wanting her to run away with him. The image of Georgette's face flashed into her mind. She'd already caused her friend enormous pain. She had no interest in making it worse by running away with her new boyfriend.

She supposed one of the women might want her to run away with them. If so, then she'd been keeping that desire to herself.

Or maybe it was someone she didn't know at all, someone

who truly had the ability to change the world and mysteriously wanted her to help them do it. The plant manager, young Mr. Higgins? Andrew Higgins himself?

None of these thoughts made any sense, and this was probably because she had barely slept in two days. She needed to sleep, and she needed to think about this invitation to be…somewhere…by noon.

Hmmm. The message said "here." She'd found it at the trash pen, so she was going to presume that was where she was supposed to meet the person who sent her a secret message. If she kept that meeting, it meant that she couldn't obey her instincts to walk away from the Michaud plant for everyone's safety. Not yet. She would have to go the plant one more time, but she had hours to decide if she was going to do that, because she had the day off.

How would she get there without taking the early morning bus, which would require her to lurk suspiciously for hours? Taking a cab that far was out of the question, but she could take a streetcar to Gloria's and borrow her car. This gave her a workable plan, but only if she decided to go.

At the moment, Justine could do nothing. She couldn't even gather her thoughts well enough to decide whether showing up at the trash pen at noon made any sense at all. She needed to sleep.

She pulled off her clothes and put on a fresh nightgown. Just a few feet away from her right arm was the window where somebody had entered and stolen the screen with its original message. How could she keep that from happening again?

Swiftly, she stripped the bed, laid her notes and all her drawings on the mattress, and made the bed again. Then she crawled under the covers, put her cheek on the pillow, and slept the sleep of the dead.

———

Mudcat rarely panicked, but he was coming near that state. He needed to talk to Justine, but he was being blocked by random events. It should mean nothing that a twenty-one-year-old factory worker was ordered by her boss to shift her day off from Saturday to Sunday. This event should be significant to no one but the annoyed twenty-one-year-old.

In this case, he was losing his chance to speak to her, and this meant that he might lose her. But this was worse than simply losing the chance to recruit her as an agent. Somebody was working against him. If the day went poorly, she might become his adversary.

Justine Byrne would be a formidable adversary indeed. He wasn't sure he could best her.

But there was another problem here, and it was close to his heart. If she became his formidable adversary, he was altogether unsure that he would survive having to kill her.

He sat down at his desk and jotted a note for Justine.

Chapter 30

Fritz loaded the freshly assembled devices into the satchel he took to work on a daily basis. Run-of-the-mill factory workers didn't need to carry much more than a lunchbox, but he had carried empty satchels for a long time. His coworkers were now accustomed to seeing him with them. Over the past few weeks, he had begun filling the big bag every morning with one or more explosive devices. They were crafted from the materials he'd brought from Germany, augmented with odds and ends from the hardware store that would be blasted by his bombs into stupendous shrapnel.

His job took him all over the plant every day. Nobody kept track of him from minute to minute, so he could be anywhere. Or he could be nowhere if he had something offsite he needed to do.

It had been no small trick to plant boxes loaded with explosive death in the plant's quieter corners, but he'd done it. They might well remain undisturbed right where they were until the war was over—but not if he set the timing devices he had carefully attached to the explosives hidden inside. He would spend the coming morning doing this. Once he had begun, there would be no turning back.

The wooden boxes were completely unobtrusive, marked only with a subdued green stamp that looked like an inventory code but actually served to mark the boxes for Fritz. To Fritz and only to Fritz, those green stamps said, "Beware! High Explosives!"

Most of the bombs were small, capable of dealing out significant damage to perhaps a fifty-foot radius. Bits of shrapnel might fly much farther, depending on air currents and physical distances and the whims of God. Only the incendiary devices had the potential to bring the whole factory down, so he had tucked most of them into the shadows of fuel tanks, which had their own potential for throwing flames. And then he had hoped for the best. This, too, was in the hands of God. Or of the devil, because he didn't have to burn the whole plant down to put thousands of people into an ear-blasting hell.

Absent an all-out conflagration, the Carbon Division was harder to reach with his instruments of destruction, but he had managed. One of the incendiary devices was in the hands of someone else, the witless mole who had given him the only access to the Carbon Division that he was ever likely to get without the help of Justine Byrne. He'd explained her mission as that of a simple courier, taking a classified message to another spy behind those double doors. Then he'd packed a device in her lunchbox, telling her that he'd make her rich if she set it on the shelf where everybody kept their lunchboxes and then walked away. He also told her that he'd know if she looked inside and he would kill her if she did.

She would likely die, either way. The bomb would be going off just at noon. It had to. He could not let anyone wonder why his mole had no lunch.

He'd retained two of the incendiary devices for the most important placement of all. Tucked among the wooden boxes that always sat outside the Carbon Division's loading dock, their flames would destroy the mysterious room where the black-and-silver devices acquired their final form. Those flames would also block an important escape route for the people inside, as would the devices he had placed on either side of the big double-door entry.

His goal was to make enough heat and light and noise to generate press coverage that would be seen in Germany, thus attracting someone willing to rescue him from this hellhole country. If he destroyed the mysteriously important Carbon Division, his superiors would be too grateful to leave him in the Louisiana swamps to rot. And if his superiors had been consumed by the war in Europe, then there was always the Japanese. Somebody would want to rescue the hero who had pulled off such a tremendous act of spycraft.

———

Justine awoke to a slight scraping sound. Rolling over in bed, she saw three notes being slid under her door. Two of them were in envelopes, and the other was just a torn sheet of scratch paper folded in half. It was barely daylight, so somebody was really intent on getting a message to her. Or three.

Ordering her body to wake up and be vigilant because weirdness was afoot, she went to the door and picked up the notes. She guessed that the folded scratch paper was from Mrs. Guidry, since she didn't believe in wasting good paper to communicate with her tenants.

The envelopes, though, were different. Unfamiliar. One of them was clearly marked with Justine's full name and The Julia's street address, written in black with a fountain pen by someone who had gotten good grades in penmanship. Below the formality of these lines was a note written with a blue ballpoint pen in Mrs.

Guidry's more hen-scratchy handwriting. It said, "Somebody put this through the mail slot sometime during the night."

The second envelope was plain and white, just like the first one, although it was made of cheaper paper. It lacked a full address, being marked only with "Justine Byrne" printed with a black ballpoint pen. The handwriting was perfectly legible, although less elegant than the other envelope's beautiful penmanship. This one, too, bore a note from Mrs. Guidry saying that it had come through the mail slot.

These envelopes were interesting and unexpected, so she set them aside for more scrutiny and unfolded the note from Mrs. Guidry first. She'd gotten notes on these ragged-edged sheets of scratch paper before and their messages were always simple and straightforward. They were also usually infuriating, like the time she'd gotten a complaint that her light had been on until the wee hours of the night. And it had, but who had it bothered, really? She'd just finished committing the same infraction again, which was probably the topic of this scrawled note.

She plopped down on her bed and spread the note from Mrs. Guidry on her lap. Immediately, she wished that it had been a complaint about her late-night habits.

Your boss called. He wants you to come in to work today.

The paper might be raggedy, but the message was crisp and clear, and it dictated how Justine was going to respond to the coded invitation to a mysterious meeting. It would be problematic to say she was too sick to work and then show up a few hours later at the trash pen, healthy as a horse. People would ask questions she didn't want to answer. It looked like she needed to work at least one more day before deciding whether to walk away from Higgins forever.

This meant that she was going to have to find a way to make

her weary self stand on an assembly line for yet another ten hours. And she wasn't even going to get a real lunch break, because this was the day that Mr. Higgins was speaking at the plant.

The scorched skin of her right arm burned and ached, as if to remind her of how important the events of this day were going to be. She needed to reapply the ointment that Jerry had given her.

She was in the midst of mulling over the best way to execute an incomplete plan—take the bus, work till noon, take a lunch-time meeting with someone who might have tried to burn her to death…and then what?—when she remembered that she'd gone to bed without deciding whether she was actually going to keep the meeting. It seemed that she'd decided in her sleep.

She turned her attention to the cheaper envelope, the one marked with just her name by a ballpoint pen. Sliding her finger under its sealed flap, she pulled out a one-page note hand-printed on plain, inexpensive paper.

DEAR JUSTINE,

I NEED TO TALK TO YOU. I NEED TO EXPLAIN MYSELF AND I NEED TO APOLOGIZE. PLEASE MEET ME FOR LUNCH DOWN BY THE LOADING DOCK. IT'S SUPPOSED TO BE A BEAUTIFUL DAY AND THAT WILL BE A NICE PLACE TO SIT IN THE SUN AND EAT AND JUST TALK IN PRIVATE. EVERYBODY ELSE WILL BE WATCHING MR. HIGGINS SPEAK, SO WE'LL HAVE TIME TO OURSELVES AND I WANT THAT VERY MUCH.

PLEASE COME.

I'LL BE WAITING FOR YOU.

SINCERELY,

MARTIN

Justine had been doing a very good job of blocking the memory of Martin's lips on hers, and now it came roaring back. She closed her eyes, hoping to blot out memories of the sight of him, but all this did was focus her mind on the scent of his cologne and the sound of his voice asking her to go away with him.

She wanted to be someplace else. She had been slow to realize this, but she knew it now. But did she want to run away with Martin? Her feelings for him were a confusing morass of anger, attraction, and curiosity about a man who pretended to be simply affable while harboring thoughts of political ferment and travel to faraway lands.

Martin was an interesting question, but her answer to the problem of Martin didn't matter, and neither did her desire to be somewhere else. Not today. Today, she needed to figure out who was sabotaging a key part in the manufacture of an atomic bomb, and she needed to get that information to somebody who knew what to do with it. Until then, her own desires could wait.

Having clarified her thoughts, Justine was able to recognize the most important thing that Martin's note told her. If he wanted to meet her at noon at the loading dock, then he couldn't be the person who had left the coded message, because it had asked her to meet at the trash pen at noon.

Opening the second envelope, she could see two things immediately.

First, the note came from the same person who had sent her a message encoded on a screen. And second, the person was in a hurry. Or the person wanted Justine to read it in a hurry. Or both.

Like the encrypted message, this one was written in a facsimile of braille, but it was written in flat dots of ink that only a sighted person could read, and quickly, because the writer had removed all elements of confusion. The letters were not smashed together, and they were not garbled by the Caesar Cypher. They said what they meant.

Most importantly, the message was meant to be read only by her, because the message was in German, and Justine was pretty sure that there weren't many people in her general vicinity who read both German and braille. Someone who wasn't Justine would probably have needed a trip to the library to read the two-line note:

Es gab unerwartete Probleme.
Ruf mich an. Galvez 1869.

Someone wanted her to know that there had been unforeseen problems. That same someone also wanted her to call Galvez 1869.

Justine was coming to understand that she didn't have to do something just because somebody told her to do it. Was she going to dial this number?

What did she have to lose? Even if the person could somehow tell that she was calling from The Julia, this was not news for someone who had left a note for her there. And, if the voice that answered the phone was one she recognized, there was an excellent chance that this would tell her who the saboteur was.

Absolutely, she was going to dial the number. But first, she had to deal with an idea that had come to her in her sleep. It was so exciting that she had to take a moment to think it through. After due consideration, she whispered out loud, "I think this could work." Then she spread out a sheet of stationery and wrote a note that began with these words:

Dear Mr. Higgins,

I have reason to believe that the secret operations of Higgins Industries' Carbon Division are in jeopardy.

She seriously doubted that Mr. Higgins was a traitor, considering how thoroughly his inventions had trounced, and were still trouncing, the Allies' enemies. If it was safe to tell anybody her suspicions, it was safe to tell Andrew Higgins. And, finally, she knew how to get this message to him.

————

Justine stood alone in The Julia's parlor, lit only by early morning light seeping through its old windows. She held a receiver to her ear and listened to a phone ring. The next sound she heard would be the voice of the person who had sent her the encrypted message asking her to come away and change the world. Did she want somebody to answer or not?

The sound of a genial "Hello" knocked the wind from her lungs. The urge to answer "Hello, this is Justine" was strong. That was the normal way one conducted telephone calls with people one knew, so it was a good thing that she couldn't draw a breath. She needed to think.

Justine had expected to hear Charles's voice. He had been the one whispering German words in her ear. Wasn't it reasonable to expect him to be the one writing her messages in German?

She'd been hiding her own truth from herself. She knew now that she had wanted Charles to be the one waiting for her at the trash pen at noon, asking her to join him on impractical voyages that were somehow supposed to change the world. If she had found him there, asking her to do that, she would have warned him that she'd discovered his sabotage, knowing that this meant he must go or face prosecution as a traitor. And, just possibly, she would have gone with him if he had asked.

She hoped she would have had the strength to say no, but now she would never know, because he was not the person speaking to her. What was she supposed to say to the words, "Is someone there? Hello?" She didn't know. She just knew that they weren't being spoken in Charles's voice.

How was she supposed to answer Jerry, kind and jovial Jerry, as he said again, "Hello?"

Justine might have run away with Charles. She might even have run away with Martin. Until the encrypted message had dangled the possibility of escape in front of her eyes, she hadn't even known how badly she wanted to flee the drudgery of her life. She was shocked to realize how trapped she felt. She would do almost anything to stop being a nameless gear in the vast machinery that was keeping a world at war.

But she wouldn't run away with Jerry. She had already hurt Georgette enough.

She replaced the receiver on its cradle so gently that Jerry probably never heard it happen. Then she went upstairs to her room, so that she could choke down a can of beans and get ready for yet another grueling and mindless day. She would be doing this job for the rest of the war and a similarly mindless one for the rest of her life. She might as well eat something so that she didn't have to do her stupid job for ten hours on a stupid Sunday on a stupid empty stomach.

Chapter 31

The car that took Fritz back and forth to work every day was a rust bucket. He had no choice. Cut off from the financial support of the Fatherland, he was forced to make do on the salary that Higgins Industries paid him. A rust bucket was all he could afford because every spare cent had gone to fulfilling his mission.

It had taken time and cunning to assemble the timers and fuses and sundries that he had carried on his cross-country trip from the Florida beach where the U-boat had put him ashore. It had taken time and cunning to assemble the makings of a small constellation of bombs on a factory salary.

When the bombs went off just as Andrew Higgins's speech was really getting rolling, the remaining leadership of the Fatherland would hear his message loud and clear. Fritz was alive. He was still dedicated to halting the Allies' apparently unavoidable victory. He was a hero. And he deserved a hero's rescue.

By noon, it would be safe to let Justine Byrne know what was coming, because it would be too late to stop the blasts. If she wanted to leave with him, she would be quite the trophy to present to his superiors when he was rescued. And, given the coal of passion for her that burned inside him, she would be his own trophy as she worked beside him to resurrect Germany's hopes.

But if she refused to leave with him, he would walk away and leave her to the fire.

Come noon, he would know where she stood.

———

Mudcat's grip on the steering wheel was firm. Events were hurtling to some kind of conclusion. A fiery attempt had been made on Justine. Had it been an attempt on her life or merely an attempt to get her attention? He didn't know.

His guess was that the other side saw the same potential in her that he did. If she chose to be cooperative, she could be the most valuable agent within a hundred miles, and he was counting himself in that radius. Thus, the only rational thing for either side to do would be to recruit her. And if the recruitment effort went poorly, the only rational thing for either side to do would be to kill her. He knew these things to be true, but the odds that his aim would be steady if he were called upon to eliminate her were infinitesimal.

This left him only one option. He had to get her to talk to him, and he had to do it without attracting the attention of his adversary. He had tried, and he'd failed. Time was running out.

The most straightforward thing to do would be to get her alone under the guise of romantic attraction. This strategy had the added benefit of being true.

Come noon, he would know where she stood.

———

After folding each stack of documents neatly into a small package, Justine loaded her pockets. Originals of all the important documents—her drawings, the encrypted and decrypted message punched into the screen, the letter to Mr. Higgins—were buttoned into her coveralls' front left pocket. Copies of each of these documents were buttoned in her front right pocket. This left her rear pockets free for tools and weapons, so she slid her pocket knife into the left one. When she got to work, her adjustable wrench and rag would go in the right one.

She needed to get all those papers to Andrew Higgins, and she'd woken up with an idea of how to do it. Ordinarily, she would have had to wade through assistants and secretaries, none of whom would be inclined to waste his time with her suspicions, and any of whom could be untrustworthy. Ordinarily, she probably couldn't even have found him, since he had seven plants to run and he often jetted off to talk business with the president or the secretary of the Navy. Today, he would be on her home ground, and she was going to grab that chance.

She'd seen Higgins speak before, twice. If she'd wanted to get close to him either of those times, it would never have happened. Higgins had stood on a raised stage far above his workers, before rushing away to his waiting convertible while attended by a coterie of underlings. But this time would be different. It had to be different, because she just had to get those papers into the hands of the big man.

This time, Higgins was giving his regular speech to all the assembled workers, but he was also giving a special pep talk to the workers of the Carbon Division. Here, Justine had a fighting chance of reaching him. There was no room on the production floor for a big stage. There was really only one place for a crowd to gather, and that was in the open area between the manufacturing floor and the loading dock.

This setup was ideal. She could leave her station a little before noon, when everybody else would be going to hear Mr. Higgins speak in the main plant. Instead, Justine would take a detour to the loading dock where there was a ramp to give her access to the outdoors. Martin would be waiting for her there, probably to make a romantic declaration of some kind, and their tryst would provide cover for her real goal, which was to eyeball the trash pen.

Everything she knew said that Jerry would be wheeling his way out there to be ready for their noon appointment, but she needed to be sure. The note she'd written to Mr. Higgins had incriminated Jerry, but part of her would never believe in his guilt unless she saw it for herself. If somebody else was standing at the garbage pen, she could strike Jerry's name from the note and incriminate that person instead.

Even if it was Jerry out there waiting for her, she still needed to hear what he had to say for himself with her own ears. She would need to brush Martin off and make the walk to where Jerry sat, just so she could hear him spout treason. If she heard from his lips that he was a spy for Germany, then she'd have the strength to give her note to Mr. Higgins, knowing that it would mean a death sentence for this man whom she liked very much.

A simple question remained. Why?

Why would Jerry send her a hidden and coded message asking her to meet him? If he wanted to talk to Justine, he could simply talk to her.

If the thing that he wanted to say to her was "Come away with me to see the world," then he was going to have to do some explaining. Why would he pay Georgette so much attention and then ask Justine to run away with him? That made no sense at all. But it also didn't make any sense that this morning's message and the message in the screen could have come from two different people. How many people could possibly want to play stupid spy games with her? And how many people had been snooping around in her past enough to know that she could read braille and German?

She didn't know what Jerry was up to, but she was going to find out.

———

Georgette already missed Justine's physics book. And her algebra book, but mostly the physics book. She missed Justine, too.

After work the day before, she'd delved into the introductory physics text, trying to figure out what she'd done with the bucket of water that had been so very wrong. A lot of the words in the electricity chapter were strange to her, so it had taken her a while to read it, but she'd slogged through. By the time she got to the end, she understood how close she'd come to committing murder and suicide, all at the same time. She made the sign of the cross every time she thought of it.

No wonder Justine wouldn't even answer the door when Georgette knocked. No wonder Justine had let her sit alone outside her door with her apologies all bottled up inside her.

She'd been right to return Justine's books, but she missed them and she missed her friend.

———

Justine sat on the fire escape, watching for the bus to roll past. When it did, she'd have a matter of seconds to crawl through her window, lock it, pass through her door, lock it, run down the stairs, hurry through The Julia's front door, clatter down the front steps, and get to the bus before it rolled away without her.

She'd gone downstairs, planning to wait on the sidewalk with the other women, but the sight of Georgette standing among them had stopped her in her tracks. Sonny must have called her to come in, too. Of course he had. He was bringing in all hands so he could look good in the eyes of the big boss.

The sight of Georgette had made Justine retreat to her perch on the fire escape. She couldn't look at her friend. Georgette was going to get hurt when Justine implicated Jerry in industrial espionage, no doubt, but she'd almost been physically hurt—maybe killed—and all because of Justine.

Justine couldn't have that, but she couldn't stand an arm's-length away from Georgette and not speak to her, either.

When the bus rolled into view, she executed her plan. After unaccountably making it down the stairs at top speed without breaking her neck, she burst through The Julia's front door. The driver must have been lifting his foot from the brake because she could see that the bus was starting to roll, but then his head whipped toward her and he mouthed, "Dusty!" The bus stopped its forward roll abruptly, as if his sturdy leg had jammed the brake back down so he could wait for her.

"Cutting it close, Dusty," he said as she flung herself onto the bus.

Her words came between gasps. "I know, Cabbie. I'm sorry."

She dropped into the seat right behind him, the one that was always empty because it was reserved for social pariahs. She'd caught a glimpse of Georgette, five seats back, but she couldn't see her once she was settled in the seat. Good.

She rested her head on the window. As she pretended to sleep, Justine thought through her day. Her morning would be spent working and watching Jerry's every move, and all the time the papers would be burning holes in her pockets. Her brain would be furiously working through what she knew and trying to understand why. Why would Jerry sabotage everything they were all working for?

When the time came, she would have her conversation with Martin and, most likely, she would ask Martin to keep an eye on her while she spoke with Jerry. Surely she would be safe enough if she did that.

And then she would decide. She would decide whether to rewrite her letter to Andrew Higgins, leaving Jerry out of it. More likely, she would turn him in. If he'd sabotaged the work of the Carbon Division while in the employ of the enemy, he would die.

What then? What would she do after she'd sold out her friend?

She would work all afternoon. She would endure another bus ride while avoiding Georgette. She would get herself to Gloria's house as fast as the streetcar would take her. There, she would dump copies of the papers she'd given Higgins on her dining room table. If Gloria looked at all the evidence and thought she'd done the wrong thing, if she thought that Jerry was innocent after all, then maybe Justine could still undo what she'd done.

Gloria would know what to do next. Surely, Gloria would know what to do next.

Justine sat hunkered behind the bus driver, making eye contact with no one. The bus was driving down a stretch of the Chef Menteur Highway where the *Prairie Tremblante* and its swampy greenness stretched along both sides of the road. When the vast flat-topped buildings of the Michaud plant rose ahead of her, she felt a flash of grief, as if she'd never see them again. The papers were heavy in her pockets.

As she felt the wheels beneath her roll to a stop, she sat up straight and uncrossed her legs. It was imperative that she be ready to hop off the bus as soon as it stopped moving. She couldn't face

Georgette. She was only now admitting to herself that she might never see Georgette again.

———

Every morning, Jerry rode shotgun as Charles drove them both to work. And every morning, he watched Charles steer the old car into a parking place with an empty spot on its passenger side, so there would be room for Jerry's chair. Every morning, Charles walked around the rear bumper, grabbed the chair out of the back, and set it in just the right spot. And then he grabbed Jerry by both arms and helped him get himself into the chair.

Jerry could stand on his own for short periods, and he was steady enough to get his wheelchair in and out of the car. He could shift his weight enough to get himself into the car via a sort of controlled fall, and his arms were strong enough to pull himself back out of it. He'd built special controls that enabled him to drive the car with only his hands. When he needed to be someplace, he could get there, but it helped a lot to have a housemate who didn't mind helping him out. There were few things worse than arriving for a ten-hour shift, knowing that you'd worn yourself out just by coming to work.

Jerry settled himself into the wheelchair, lifting each leg by the thigh to put it where it needed to go. As he did every morning, Jerry shook Charles's hand and said, "Thank you, friend."

Then Charles, as he did every morning, clapped him on the shoulder and said, "You're welcome, friend."

Today, his friend looked troubled, and Jerry didn't blame him. He was troubled, too.

———

Justine stumbled as she got off the bus because she was doing it in such a tearing hurry. A busload of people was behind her, and one of those people was Georgette, so she needed to move. She wrenched her knee pretty hard as she tried to stay upright, but she managed it. Her burned arm was hurting, so her knee might as well hurt, too. She hustled for the factory entrance as soon as her arms stopped flailing.

She was almost running but not quite as her eyes raked across someone else she was avoiding. There, in a far corner of the parking lot, were two familiar faces.

Jerry saw her first. He was sitting in his chair on the passenger side of the car. He'd just finished using his hands to lift his feet into the wheelchair's foot supports, and his eyes caught hers as he lifted them from that task. Charles, standing over him, was reaching out a hand to meet Jerry's for a handshake. As their palms met, Charles jerked his hand in Justine's direction. Dark hair swung into his eyes as he turned her way.

She could see by the way he drew breath that he was about to call out to her, but she just couldn't stand it. She didn't want to hear his voice, and she certainly didn't want to hear Jerry's. She should have known that they would be together, the man who had sent her his phone number in an encoded German message and the man who had whispered German words into her ear.

They looked very chummy for two men who had been on the verge of a fistfight two nights before. Were they working together? Were they both German spies? Had their big argument at The TickTock been faked for her benefit?

Justine tried not to think about what it would mean if she implicated both Charles and Jerry for espionage, but she failed. It could mean the death penalty for both of them. They looked so gentle and so manly as they shook hands after working together to get Jerry in his chair, like two friends dealing with the troubles life sent. The morning sun reflected off Charles's spectacles and Jerry's bright white hair. They looked so alive.

Justine broke into a run, just to avoid their faces. Maybe people would think she was late for work. Maybe they would think she had a disastrous case of diarrhea. She no longer cared what anyone thought. She had a job to do.

———

When Justine stepped through the entrance to the Carbon Division, the sound of voices was deafening. They bounced around the big open factory, as if someone had moved a tremendous flock of chickens into the cavernous space. The chattering roar made her want to run screaming.

As she had guessed, Sonny had brought every last Carbon Division employee in to work the day shift, even people who worked other shifts under other foremen. Obviously, he wanted Andrew Higgins to be duly impressed with the magnitude of his managerial responsibilities. Unfortunately, he hadn't thought ahead, so there was hardly room enough for them all on the factory floor. There certainly wasn't enough room for them all to work comfortably.

Sonny was pretending that he hadn't made that tactical error as he bellowed across the crowd of workers. "You've got room for somebody to stand next to you, Georgette. See there? Scooch over a little bit."

Georgette looked around for a place to scooch. It wasn't there.

Sonny bellowed, "I said, 'Scooch,'" and everybody in Georgette's vicinity sucked in their stomachs and tried to make room.

Justine scuttled away from Sonny, from Georgette, from all of them, looking for a place where she could at least look busy for a few hours. She gave Jerry's shed a wide berth. Though he had just arrived, he was already surrounded by workers that Sonny must have assigned to him, saying something like, "Just keep 'em busy, Jerry." Two of them were working on a pile of rusty fittings with a wire brush, and two of them were carefully wiping down Jerry's hand tools with mineral oil.

Justine took a hard left and cruised through the machinists' stations. Nelle caught her eye and said, "C'mere." She crooked a finger at her, beckoning. "You don't need to get all mixed up in Sonny's cluster of craziness. I don't really need a helper, but you can be my helper today. Just keep your head down. And when I give you something to do, take a real long time to do it."

For the next few hours, Justine did that. When Nelle handed her a finished piece, she fondled its smooth carbon surface, studied its angles, and tested its grooves with her fingertips, imagining how it would fit into a finished Uranium-235 collector. She carefully wiped every speck of dust off each piece. Then, after taking three times as long as the job required, she carefully packed each one in a crate with the other pieces that Nelle had finished.

While Justine perfected the art of working really, really slow, she kept an eye on the back of the Carbon Division's long factory space. As she had expected, some of Sonny's surplus workers had been assigned to prepare that area for a VIP event. A small dais had been set up, low enough for someone to easily mount with a single step, even a stocky older man like Andrew Higgins. A podium was waiting for him. A handful of chairs surrounded it, so that VIPs could watch him speak.

Her plan was going to work. If she lurked just outside the loading dock, she'd have easy access to Mr. Higgins after he finished speaking. She could rush up the ramp to the stage from the rear. He traveled with an entourage to keep pesky employees at bay, but they would be focused on what was in front of them.

She knew she could get close enough for Mr. Higgins to hear her. If she could just get the word "Espionage!" to him, he would talk to her. He would look at her drawings. He would know what to do.

Chapter 32

Justine was watching the big clock on the factory wall, the one that ruled the lives and paychecks of hourly workers. As its minute hand cruised toward twelve, she timed her work so that the crate of carbon parts filled at just the right moment. When the time came, she closed the crate, hefted it, and said, "Be right back," to Nelle, knowing that she wasn't coming back. Then she hauled the crate where it needed to go, which was near the assembly area just inside the loading dock. And that was exactly where she needed to be.

When Sam-the-Timekeeper blew the whistle, she was in place. Its shrill sound wasn't marking lunchtime or going-home time. It was calling Mr. Higgins's employees to walk in an orderly fashion through the main plant and line themselves up with the other workers for his speech. There wasn't a ghost of a chance that anyone would notice Justine wasn't with them.

Instead, she was hiding behind the temporary stage. Behind her was the open maw of the loading dock. As her coworkers filed out into the main plant, she crept to the ramp leading down to the pavement and, from there, outdoors.

It wasn't noon yet, so she felt confident that she would be alone when she reached the bottom of that ramp. She would be in place to watch Martin as he walked her way. More critical to her plan, she would be in place so that she could watch the German-speaker she presumed was the saboteur as he strolled—or rolled—out to the trash pen.

Justine waited beside the ramp. The green-stamped crate where she'd been sitting when Jerry brought her a Coke was still there. Now, another just like it sat on the other side of the loading dock. She stepped into the shadows beside the nearest crate and waited.

———

Georgette didn't mind watching Andrew Higgins speak once, but she was not excited about hearing him speak twice. Especially today, when she really just wanted to find a quiet place to be sad in peace.

When the whistle blew, she'd taken a few steps in the same direction as everybody else, then she'd given up. She couldn't do it. She couldn't clap her hands and cheer over a rah-rah speech, and she certainly couldn't come back into the Carbon Division in a little while and do it all over again.

A moving hank of orange frizz caught her eye. It was Justine's ponytail, and it swayed with her determined stride. Justine and her ponytail were headed in the wrong direction.

Georgette turned around and followed the ponytail before she even gave the matter any thought. There was nothing to think about. She needed to patch things up with Justine. Even if Justine thought she was too stupid to breathe, Georgette valued her friendship. Justine was generous, she was funny, and she was kind. Georgette had known those things about her since they'd cobbled together a meal out of two cans, a bag of macaroni, and a tea bag, and they hadn't changed. If she needed to humble her-self to make amends for the water bucket incident, then so be it.

————

Jerry sat in his assigned position, hidden behind the trash pen. His role was to be the lookout, only stepping in if needed. He hoped he wasn't needed, because he cared about Justine, and he didn't want anything to happen to her.

————

Martin saw Justine before she saw him. She was loitering in the shadow of the loading dock, looking away from him. He could see that she had presumed he'd be approaching from the back door of the plant nearest to the trash pen, so her eyes were fas-tened on that door. He liked to subvert expectations, so he'd exited early and waited on the far side of the loading dock.

He gave her a moment to get nervous, then began walking her way. He hoped this encounter went according to plan. He would soon be walking away from the Michaud plant forever, and he hoped that Justine was at his side when he went.

————

Charles executed his part of the plan, exiting the factory build-ing through the same door that he'd walked through with Justine when he was courting her by carrying her trash. Or when he'd been pretending to court her. Even he wasn't sure what he'd really been doing.

And he wasn't sure what he was doing now. He had no reason to believe that Justine would be meeting him today, because he had no reason to believe that she'd decoded his message. But surely she had been able to read the note he'd left at her house. It had been encoded, because that was protocol and he followed protocol, but its content should have been crystal clear for a woman who knew both German and braille.

And yet she hadn't called, so he hadn't been able to warn her that he was being pulled off this assignment, despite the fact that he was sure an enemy agent was at work. And despite the fact that he was sure she was on the trail of that agent. Why else had she taken the coded screen home with her? Why else would she have made that midnight trip to consult Gloria Mazur, the only person left in New Orleans who could make sense of the goings-on in the Carbon Division?

Charles knew in his gut that the acetylene leak that could have killed Justine was no accident. And he couldn't even warn her, because she hadn't called. Or perhaps she had called. Jerry had told him about the hang-up call he'd taken that morning, and for this he kicked himself. He hadn't told his housemate not to pick up the phone, because why wouldn't Justine speak to kind, friendly Jerry?

It was mistakes like this that cost lives. It was mistakes like this that lost wars.

———

Justine didn't know how able she'd be to rise to a crisis, and she wouldn't know until the moment came. When Martin came into view, carrying a box and emerging unexpectedly from her blind side, she felt herself losing control of the situation.

Still a dozen feet away, he said, "Hey, Justine," and there was nothing in his voice to make her trust him or doubt him.

The surprise of seeing him in the wrong place caused her

to give herself away by letting her head whip back in the other direction. Now he knew that she was looking for someone else. His eyes followed hers, and Jerry's position was given away by the light glinting off his chair. They both saw him hiding behind the trash pen at the same instant, out of view of anyone coming toward him from the factory door.

In that instant, that door opened, and Charles passed through it. He made his way toward the trash pen and took his position at its gate, presumably so Justine would see him waiting for her. Now she knew who had sent her the message in the screen, and probably the message in German that morning, and it wasn't Jerry. But did Charles know that Jerry was behind him? Was Jerry hiding from Charles or from her?

Remembering the two men exiting the same car that morning, she thought that she understood one thing. She'd always known that they were friends, but it had never occurred to her that they were also roommates. This did not, however, mean that they were both spies or even on the same side. Maybe Jerry had sent the message, but it was just as possible that Jerry had merely picked up a call not meant for him.

Did this mean that Jerry was innocent of the sabotage? Her letter to Mr. Higgins would probably get him executed, so she had to know the truth before she delivered it.

Jerry certainly looked guilty as he lurked in a spot where Justine assuredly wouldn't have seen him if she'd been where Charles expected her to be. A woman might ask another woman to wait out of sight nearby when she met a man, just for safety, but she was no danger to Charles. Why would he post Jerry as a lookout?

Martin shot her a look that she couldn't read, but she guessed that it was jealousy. He did have cause to be jealous, and it was surely obvious by the way she was staring at Charles.

At least one of these three men had to be the saboteur who

was threatening the work of the Carbon Division. Maybe two of them were in on it. And perhaps even all three of them had been working to cover their tracks by confusing her.

What did she know for certain? Random facts struck her like thunderbolts.

Fact One: She'd just seen Charles and Jerry getting out of a van. Jerry had been sitting on the passenger side, so it was presumably Charles's car. Whoever owned the car, Charles had been dishonest when he suggested that he was dependent on buses to get around.

Fact Two: She remembered Jerry's red-capped thermos sitting on the top shelf in his shed just a few minutes after he'd poured her a cup of coffee. A few minutes later, he'd held that cap in his hands, and there was nobody nearby to fetch it for him. He could never have reached that shelf while sitting in his wheelchair. Now she knew that Jerry was lying about his physical condition.

Fact Three: Jerry or somebody who lived with him had sent her an emergency message asking her to call. Seeing the two of them get out of the same car suggested that they might be roommates, so the message-sender wasn't necessarily Jerry. It could have been Charles. There was no way to know.

Fact Four: The saboteur would likely be working for an enemy nation. Charles spoke German, and that made him a strong candidate. One or more of them could be a Japanese spy, but the German language was cropping up too often to make this likely.

Fact Five: Gloria had believed that Justine would be in danger if the saboteur learned of her suspicions. Gloria had emphasized the danger by saying, "If you think your parents' deaths were an accident, then you are a fool." Justine believed that she was in the presence of the saboteur. If Gloria was right, then she might be in the presence of her parents' murderer. Or murderers.

Based on these facts, her thoughts focused on a single goal:

How would you go about identifying a German spy? An idea for answering it burst out of her subconscious, a shot-in-the-dark idea that might just show her who she was dealing with.

Loud and clear, she shouted, *"Proletarier aller Länder vereinigt Euch!"*

Charles's head whipped her way, as she had known it would. She knew he spoke German, and she knew that he knew the Communist Manifesto. He would absolutely react when she shouted, "Workers of the world, unite!" She half expected him to respond, "You have nothing to lose but your chains!" but he was just staring at her, slack-jawed.

Jerry's reaction, however, was different. His head turned a fraction of a second slower than Charles's had, and his expression was not shock. It was confusion.

Jerry didn't speak German. Justine was sure of it. He had not been shipped over from Germany to sabotage the war effort, despite the stereotypical Aryan whiteness of his hair, but that didn't mean he wasn't an American collaborator.

Charles spoke German and Jerry didn't, so Charles was likely the one who sent the coded messages. If so, he was also the person who wanted her to run away with him…who wanted her to change the world with him. Did spies think of themselves as world-changers? Justine supposed that they did. Was he trying to recruit her to work for the enemy?

But she couldn't waste time on these questions because Martin's reaction to her German rally cry was the real revelation. He was stalled in his tracks, staring at her.

"I heard you say that you spoke German," he said, "but I dismissed it as a butchered schoolgirl thing. What can't you do?"

She watched Martin as, slowly and gently, he lowered the box in his hands to the ground. She didn't like the way he was lowering it. He was taking too long.

Martin had consistently presented himself to her as a man consumed by sexual passion. That man would have dropped the box with a thunk by now and hurried to her. Now, at this moment, that box was the most important thing in Martin's life, not Justine. This man was not what he wanted her to think he was.

And, she was thinking, neither was that box.

She stole a glance at Charles and Jerry, both of them moving her way at top speed. They had both lied to her. They weren't the men they pretended to be, either. She had no one to count on but herself.

She took a careful step back and then another.

Martin said, "You're not afraid of me, are you? You didn't seem afraid of me the other night. It seemed like you liked me a lot."

He reached out a hand, one of the hands that had held her so tight, roaming so freely over her body. It was aimed at her shoulder, but it missed, because her shoulder was no longer there. She had taken another step backward and dropped to a squat beside the box that had appeared since she last stood in this spot, a box with the same green stamp she now saw on the one he'd just put down.

Without thought, Martin yelled, "No!" This told her that she was in the right place, doing the right thing. She opened the box that he very much wanted her to leave closed.

Lifting its lid, she saw a mechanical device and the unmistakable shape of a stick of dynamite. Worse, she smelled some kind of petroleum-based fuel. Gasoline? Kerosene?

It hardly mattered. The person who built this bomb had known what to use.

Justine was a soft-spoken woman who had grown up with soft-spoken parents. She hadn't let out an untrammeled shriek since she was a toddler. If asked, she wouldn't have been sure she still knew how. But she did know how, and the sight of a timed explosive device gave her voice all of its power.

"Bomb!" she cried out. "Bomb! Firebomb!"

She had no idea if anybody inside the plant could hear her. They were all on their way to Mr. Higgins's speech. Charles and Jerry could hear her, but she didn't even know whose side they were on. All she knew was that the man in front of her had set bombs that threatened her friends Georgette and Nelle and Nadine and Mavis and Candace and Darlene and Betty and Shirley and, yes, even Della and Sonny. His bombs threatened Andrew Higgins and his son. They threatened thousands of other people filling the Michaud plant. Right now, at this moment, she was looking at her enemy.

Not the Germans. Not the Japanese. Martin. Or whatever his name really was.

Martin was her enemy.

As for Charles and Jerry, the jury was still out.

———

Georgette peered over the edge of the loading dock. She'd gone looking for Justine, hoping to patch things up with her, but she couldn't do that when her friend was in the middle of a romantic tryst. There she stood with Martin, who was not Georgette's favorite individual. As far as Georgette was concerned, he wasn't even her favorite man trying to get Justine's attention, but that was Justine's decision to make.

She didn't like leaving Justine alone with a man who had Martin's temper, but Justine had chosen to slip out of the plant with him. She was going to have to take care of herself.

As Georgette backed away from the loading dock's open bay toward the temporary stage waiting for Andrew Higgins, she heard Justine's voice, and she wasn't whispering sweet nothings in Martin's ear. First, she called out something in a language

Georgette didn't know. Then she started screaming that there was a bomb. Specifically, a firebomb.

Georgette spun and ran for the door where a huge crowd of her coworkers waited for Sonny to tell them it was time to go. Georgette dodged them as easily as she'd once dodged alligators in her pirogue. When people refused to get out of her path, she stuck out a stiff arm and shoved them out of her way like her brothers had done when they'd played on their school's football team back home.

Being strong, long-legged, and determined, she made it to the door ahead of most of the crowd, where she paused just long enough to break her stride. Standing in the entranceway where she could be heard both inside and outside the Carbon Division, she yelled, "Get out, all of you! Get out! There's a bomb. A fire-bomb!" She knew that this was true because her friend said so.

And then she was running again, but not for the doors. The Carbon Division workers were stampeding for the front entrance nearest them, but Georgette had someplace else to be.

———

Justine flung herself toward the ramp, trying to put distance between her body and the man who had planted the bomb at her feet. Probably he had planted more of them, including some in the other green-stamped boxes she could see. Others could be anywhere in the plant, which was stuffed as full of people as it could possibly be.

The small-time sabotage of the Carbon Division—the broken lateral guides, the broken tool rest, the punctured acetylene hose—had been leading up to this. It made sense for a spy to try to slow down production until everything was in place for a full attack. Timing the explosions for the day that Andrew Higgins was onsite was a stroke of genius. Higgins had designed the boats that made the landing at Normandy possible. Killing him would be a true act of revenge.

Justine stumbled as she tried to climb the ramp, bloodying both palms on the rough concrete, but she didn't stop moving away from Martin—or whatever his name was. She reached up with both hands, crawling on all fours, and she was doing it. She was nearing the top. But then her whole body jerked to a stop. Martin's big hand was wrapped around her ankle, and it was all she could do to hold her ground as he pulled her down toward him. She had nothing to hold on to—no banister, no ledge, no handhold at all—and she knew she only had seconds before his strength overpowered hers. She cut that time in half by letting go with one hand to fumble with her pocket buttons.

The worn, often-washed twill of her coveralls' buttonholes yielded easily, allowing her to unbutton the front right pocket and reach for her pocketknife. Papers flew. The wind took some of them skittering across the pavement toward the grassy marshland. Others were ground under Martin's feet as he struggled for purchase against the smooth blacktop at the bottom of the ramp. Justine couldn't be bothered about the loss of all that work, and it didn't matter anyway. The information was in her head. To preserve it, all she had to do was survive. Maybe she would, if she could only find that knife, but there was nothing at the bottom of her pocket.

Giving up on the knife, she reached for her right rear pocket, drawing her adjustable wrench out and raising it high in her right hand. She didn't have physical strength on her side, but the wrench was heavy, it extended her lever arm by six inches, and she had the high ground. Gravity was working in her favor. Surely, she could bring the wrench down on Martin's head hard enough to stun him, at least.

She let go with her other hand, knowing that she would immediately go into downward motion from the force he was exerting on her ankle. This downward motion would be added to the downward force when she swung the wrench, so she let it happen. As she started to slide, a flying piece of graph paper reminded her that she'd moved the pocketknife to a rear pocket, the left one, to make room for papers in both front pockets. She reached her left arm behind her back, yanked the pocket's button clean off, thrust in her hand, and grasped the knife.

The hand holding the wrench was beginning its downswing when Martin said, "Don't be stupid."

It was only then that she felt the muzzle of his handgun pressing into her abdomen.

Chapter 33

Cries of "Bomb!" and "Fire!" rose up all around Georgette. The Carbon Division was emptying behind her as she ran, which was a great relief, but the people in the main part of the plant were in danger, too. She continued to scream her warning as she ran to them beneath tremendous boats and airplanes, partially assembled, one after another after another. The war machines loomed over her head, incomplete, like whales and condors ravaged by scavengers.

She'd seen the box that Justine opened and she'd seen Martin moving boxes all week. Maybe longer. He could have put bombs anywhere. Everywhere.

Throngs of people were leaving the plant. Georgette rejoiced for every one of them, but she couldn't go with them. She had two things to do.

———

Justine's pelvis and elbows and skull banged against the concrete as Martin dragged her down the ramp with one hand, using the other one to press a gun to her belly. She could see Charles and Jerry, quite near now.

Their guns were drawn, and Charles was yelling, "Let her go, Martin. This is between us."

Her body was rigid with fear, which was helpful in a way, since her stiff fingers were managing to hang on to the wrench and to the pocketknife concealed in her palm, but her mind had never felt quicker. Her thoughts were sharp. They cut through everything and found inarguable facts. Using those facts as building blocks, they made intuitive leaps that couldn't feel more true.

The guns that Charles and Jerry were training on Martin gave her one fact she could trust. Until she saw them take him on, she couldn't be sure that they weren't all three working together. Clearly, they were not.

What else had she learned? She had already known that Charles spoke German. Now she was certain that Martin did, too. Were they both German spies who were somehow in conflict? Maybe, but the better scenario for Justine was that Jerry and Charles were American spies embedded among Higgins's employees to protect against things like industrial sabotage.

Logic said that the saboteur was Martin, the one who was strewing bombs hither and yon. Logic also said that he had an agent among the Carbonites, because she knew of no way for him to get onto their factory floor to commit sabotage. She tucked that nugget away for later. It was going to be important to find out who his agent was, but first she had to survive the next few minutes.

———

Georgette took the stairs to Sam-the-Timekeeper's office two at a time. He was standing in his open door, peering at the melee below.

She felt disoriented, dizzied by the vertiginous view through the stairs' metal grating. A vast sea of people was moving directly beneath her, emptying one end of the plant, but she could see that word was spreading too slowly. Farther away, the crowd of workers who had already lined up in front of the podium for Higgins's speech stood and waited, oblivious.

Sam-the-Timekeeper's puzzled face was focused on hers. "What's happening?"

Georgette's chest was about to burst and her heartbeat was deafening in her ears, but she needed to find a way to speak. She stepped onto the landing outside his office and bent over, hands on her knees, to catch her breath. Gasping, she got out the words that had to be said.

"Bomb." She dragged in a long breath. "Blow the—" She stopped to cough.

He was already in motion. "We need to blow the whistle and get people out of here."

———

"Drop your guns," Martin said. "She's going with me."

He dragged Justine to her feet, holding her in front of him like a human shield. Locking eyes with Charles and Jerry, he said, "I said to drop your guns."

Crouching slowly, Charles laid his weapon at his feet and stood back up. Equally slowly, Jerry leaned hard forward, eased the gun to the ground, and used his arms to pull himself back upright.

Martin should have taken Justine's wrench, but Charles and Jerry and their guns had distracted him. Her right hand hung at her side, still holding the wrench. In her left palm, she hid a pocketknife that he knew nothing about. Her weapons made her feel a small stir of hope.

Justine was right-handed. It wasn't easy to manipulate the pocketknife, but she was doing her best to slide her thumbnail into the crescent-shaped nick that should give her enough purchase to lever it open. Working in her favor was the fact that the knife was old and well-used.

Hoping that Martin wouldn't feel her brachioradialis muscle flex and ease, she worked to open the blade. Since his attention was still on Charles and Jerry, he never noticed the slight movements of her lower arm, and he didn't notice the involuntary thrill that shook her body, oh so slightly, when the blade swung open on its loose and aged pivot. She let her arms dangle and waited for an opportunity.

Martin leaned down to speak in her ear. "You're going with me because they're fools. All they have to do to stop me is shoot through you, but Americans are too weak for that. We have five minutes before those bombs blow, so we're going to walk to my car, get in it, and get the hell out of here. When this place is far enough in my rearview mirror, I'm going to ask you a question, so start thinking about your answer."

Justine thought she knew what the question was.

"I'm going to give you a choice. You can come with me and leave this mind-killing job behind. I think I can promise you a good life. I know I can promise you an exciting one."

She said nothing, but she let her eyes suggest that her answer might be one that he'd like.

His voice lowered even further to the point where she knew that neither Charles nor Jerry could hear. "Or you can end this day dead and under ten feet of swamp water."

Just like her parents.

Her arm muscles wanted to tense, ready to slam him with the wrench or stab him with the knife, because she was so sure that he was the one who had put them in that bayou to drown. Justine was ready to let Martin shoot her, just for the joy of striking out at the man who took her parents away, even if she only felt it for an instant before the bullet hit her. But she didn't, because she could hear the voices of Gerard and Isabel telling her to relax and wait for the right opportunity. She could hear them telling her to live.

His arm tightened around her. "I was told not to leave anyone alive and on the loose who might help the enemy's nuclear program, but I have plenty of justification to spare you if I present you as someone useful to our goals. Imagine the laboratory they would give you. Imagine the time and the raw materials and the laboratory assistants. Imagine what you could do if somebody believed in you."

He knew what would tempt her, because a beautiful laboratory could certainly do it, but he didn't understand her at all. If he believed that she would run away with a man preparing to firebomb thousands of people, then his mind was truly diseased.

But how could she escape him? Despair tried to take her, but she shook it off. This man had been ordered to kill anyone who might be useful in developing a nuclear program. If he knew about Gloria, then he had just threatened to kill her. Nothing was more important to Justine than protecting her godmother. Nothing was more important than the selfless love that Gloria had always shown her. Surely that kind of love could win the day.

As she felt herself wrapped in the love of Gloria and of her parents, a familiar noise rose over the frantic beating of her heart. Somebody was blowing the factory whistle, over and over.

———

At the word "bomb," Sam-the-Timekeeper had pointed at the dangling cable and told Georgette to pull it, offering her the special thrill of sounding the factory whistle, but she'd held up a hand because she had more to say. It came out with a wheeze.

"Firebomb."

Sam had frozen in place, still pointing at the cable that would blow the factory whistle. All Georgette needed to do to get more people moving toward the exits was to pull it, but the whistle wouldn't be enough. She needed to stop a fire before it started.

Still gasping for breath, she choked out, "Turn on the sprinklers," over the noise wafting up to them from the factory floor. Sam had paused, silent, and Georgette had thought for a heartbeat that he was going to refuse to activate them, and she didn't know how to do it.

She knew it was an odd request that she was making, asking Sam to douse the whole plant and everything in it with water when there was no fire. Still, he had listened when she said, "The person I'd most trust to recognize a firebomb just hollered that there was one. So it must be true."

He'd kept listening when she said, "I think the man standing beside her set the firebomb, and I bet he planted them everywhere. I just know he did. He's been moving boxes around this place all week. Longer, probably."

Sam-the-Timekeeper had a quiet, wise air about him, so he'd merely nodded to acknowledge that he'd heard her. Then he'd asked, "Why do you think it will help if we douse the place with water?"

"I spent a lot of time with my friend's physics book last night."

Sam-the-Timekeeper hadn't even given her a funny look when she'd said that, like she was too stupid to be reading books about fancy things like physics, and she loved him for it. Then she'd explained to him what she'd learned from Justine's physics book, while she was trying to figure out where she'd gone wrong during the welding fire.

"I found out that it's a big mistake to put water on electrical fires, but water cools flammable materials like wood down below their ignition temperature, so that they can't burn. So if the whole plant is being doused with water when the bombs go off, don't that mean that it'll put out the firebombs before they even start burning?"

Using only logic, Georgette had made Sam-the-Timekeeper believe that drastic action was called for. It was necessary. So he had activated the sprinklers while she pulled the whistle cable again and again. She didn't know how to use it to signal an emergency, but she thought maybe people would figure things out if she just kept tooting.

———

Water was everywhere. It fell from the ceiling onto the bellies of boats destined for the South Pacific. It collected in the cockpits of half-built planes that would be flying to points unknown. It dripped onto duckbilled boats like those that had disgorged a winning army onto the beaches of Normandy. It drenched the finely tailored suit of Andrew Higgins, the man who had designed them all. It drenched the throngs of people hurrying away from the rumors of bombs and from the sound of a whistle blasting again and again.

Georgette watched them go. When she was satisfied that every corner of the plant had heard the whistle, she ran back down the stairs as water poured on her head and collected in her work boots. Her instincts said to run and hide, but she had one more thing to do.

She had to make sure that Justine was safe.

The crowd outside the Carbon Division had thinned enough to let her through, so she ran back through the double doors and into the familiar space. Water rained onto the floor, rinsing black dust off the concrete. The floor was slick, but her boot soles gripped it. She could see daylight at the loading dock and that was her destination, but first she needed to stop at Jerry's shed and grab something to help her with the problem of Justine's safety.

———

When Mavis had heard Georgette scream the word "bomb," her eyes had turned toward the innocuous shelves where the Carbonites stored their lunchboxes. She had been uneasy about her instructions to carry a strange lunchbox into the plant without looking inside, but she'd done it. The money didn't motivate her any longer, not since she'd seen Justine come so close to fire and death. Now, she was motivated by fear. She didn't know what her contact would do to her if she said no.

All along, she had believed that she was valuable to him, so it had never occurred to her that he might give her a suicide mission. As she considered this possibility, Mavis had lingered at the back of the crowd leaving the Carbon Division, trying to decide what to do. Georgette was calling out "Justine! Justine, are you still here?" As Mavis watched Georgette squeezing through the throng, running upstream, she knew what had to be done.

Breaking free of the crowd, Mavis had fought through bodies, moving slowly as she dodged one coworker and then another. She needed to reach her lunchbox as fast as her short legs would take her, but there were so many people in her way. The Carbon Division was almost empty of its workers before she reached the lunchbox.

Snatching it up, she ran for the only safe place she could think of. If she could get to the loading dock and hurl it out onto the pavement, away from the plant building, surely that would be a safer place for it to explode.

———

The plant whistle had gone silent. There was no sound but water gushing out of overhead pipes and slapping onto the floor far below. Justine stood with a gun's muzzle pressed to her belly and listened to the sound. The man holding the gun was restless, and Justine knew why. The more the water flowed, the greater the chance that it was neutralizing his bombs.

Dynamite would certainly explode underwater, so the water wasn't going to prevent Martin's bombs from detonating. Some people fished that way, throwing in the explosive and waiting for the fish it killed to float to the top.

A fire fueled by gasoline or kerosene wouldn't necessarily be immediately snuffed out by water, either, since those fuels floated. A nightmare situation of burning fuel floating atop flowing water, being carried hither and yon, was possible, but a whole lot of water should spread out the floating fuel, cooling the flames and snuffing them out eventually. Having the sprinklers on when the bombs detonated was probably a better option than not.

Neither of these ideas were the thing that gave her the most hope. No, the weak point in Martin's bomb design was likely the design of the timers. They probably resembled a watch in the way that they worked, and Justine had never known a watch that tolerated much water. The timers might even be electrical devices that could be shorted out. She cheered on the spewing sprinklers. They might not keep all the bombs from detonating, but every bomb that was ruined by the water was a step in the right direction.

Martin glanced at the boxes at their feet and began backing away from them. The time when all his bombs would detonate must be approaching, because his steps were coming faster. He dragged her back...back...back. He was gaining speed, and she could tell that he was afraid he'd waited too long.

Water was flowing over the lip of the loading dock like a

waterfall, and now it was splashing onto those deadly boxes. Maybe it would defang the bombs. Maybe she wouldn't die from flying debris or flames or a compression wave. This didn't solve the problem of how she would escape a man with a gun.

A motion at the top of the loading dock caught her eye. It was Georgette, kneeling in the water as it flowed over the edge. In her hand was a long-handled sledgehammer, and she looked like a woman trying to decide how best to use it to take her one and only shot.

Justine was hanging onto hope, but Georgette couldn't have saved Justine by beating Martin into submission with her sledgehammer, not any more than Charles and Jerry could have managed it by shooting their guns before Martin made them drop them. There was no way to do those things without the risk of hitting Justine.

A muffled boom sounded from inside the plant and Justine knew that the time had come. Martin was dragging her away from the bombs at the base of the loading dock, but there was no path to getting far enough away. Either the water pouring onto the boxes would stop the detonations, or else they would die. All of them: Georgette, Charles, Jerry, Martin, and Justine. The question of whether the bombs would blow could only be answered by physics, and she didn't have enough information to do the math.

———

Georgette let the water flow around her, watched, and waited for her chance.

———

Mavis heard a bomb blow inside the main plant, then another, then a third one. The time had come. She had to do the right thing, but first she had to decide what it was.

She saw Georgette kneeling in her path, so she changed course. Her plan was to run past the makeshift stage, all the way up to the lip of the loading dock. From there, she would hurl the lunchbox as far as she could. Then she would tackle Georgette and cover her with her own body, hoping that they were far enough away to survive the blast.

But then she neared the edge and saw that this would never work. There were people standing on the pavement below the loading dock. If she threw the lunchbox and its bomb out onto the asphalt, she would be throwing it at Justine, Charles, and Jerry. She would have been happy to throw it at Martin, who had given her the lunchbox and who must have set the bombs she was hearing, but she couldn't risk hurting the others.

Mavis didn't hesitate. Her courage would have failed her if she had. She ran hard toward Georgette and used all the momentum she could gain to shove her off the loading dock to the pavement below. Then she turned away from all of those people and fell on the bomb.

The well-built lunchbox had kept the omnipresent water out, and so the bomb and its timer had stayed dry and functional. An instant after she flung her body over the metal case holding it, the timer ticked down to zero.

Mavis thought of her children, and then she was gone.

———

Justine's heart stopped as she saw Georgette fall and lie still on the pavement. The blast of a nearby bomb rattled the ground under Justine's feet, and she felt a shiver of panic pass through

Martin's body. She felt him obey his reflexes, which told him to release her and run hard, but for just a second. It only took that second for him to regain control and reach out to grab her again, but the second was too long. She used it to wheel away from him, slashing upward with her knife at the hand holding the gun. He dropped it and it slid away from him on the wet pavement.

Unfortunately, it also slid away from Justine, but she still had a weapon in each hand. She swung the wrench at his head and connected, but this succeeded only in bringing him to his knees.

Still conscious, he went for the gun, and this motion took him far enough from Justine for a trained agent to see his opening. Charles dropped to his knees and grabbed his gun. Then he put a bullet neatly in Martin's chest.

Justine fell, stunned but determined to crawl away from Martin's bleeding body and toward Georgette's crumpled form. Georgette lay between two green-stamped crates holding Martin's bombs, and Justine hadn't seen her move since she fell off the loading dock.

"Georgette. Say something. Georgette, tell me you're okay."

Jerry wheeled past her, coming to a halt beside Georgette. He reached down to put a hand flat on Georgette's back. Leaning further, he rested his fingers on her throat, beneath her jaw.

He said something, but the gunshot was still ringing in Justine's ears. She was crawling toward Georgette, hoping for a breath, even a twitch. Anything.

Georgette gasped and her legs stirred. Justine felt hope stir, too.

Jerry looked beyond Justine and spoke to Charles. Her hearing was coming back, so she caught most of it. "...going to have to risk moving her."

She turned to face Charles, hoping she'd be able to hear better if she could see his face. He was kneeling beside Martin, checking his pulse. He stood and shook his head.

"Let's get out of here," Charles said, lifting Georgette and draping her gently over Jerry's lap.

Grasping the handles of Jerry's wheelchair, he turned to Justine, who was already on her feet. He asked, "Can you run?" but the question was pointless. They were both already running.

Some of Martin's bombs had survived the flood of water spewing out of the plant's sprinkler system. Justine knew this, because she felt the ground shake under her feet as she ran, and shake again, but she saw no flames. Charles, in the lead, had chosen the only possible route that would get them away from the building quickly.

Going straight back toward the bayou was out of the question. They would have run out of pavement before they were safely away from a plant building that still might explode in flames, and a wheelchair carrying two adults would not get far in the *Prairie Tremblante* without sinking. Going left would have forced them to run parallel to the time bomb that was the Michaud plant for its entire vast length. But going right gave them a chance of getting well away from danger. The Carbon Division was located at the southwesternmost end of the plant, so they were within striking distance of the end of the building. Charles pushed Jerry, Jerry cradled Georgette in his lap, and Justine sprinted close on their heels.

As she ran, her ears continued to wake up, and they were picking up a soft roar ahead of her. The sound was a cross between a wildfire and music, but Justine only realized what it was when they rounded the corner of the plant and she could see everything that lay beyond it. It was the combined voices of a huge crowd of people. Ahead of them, at the end of a diagonal road taking them to the airstrip, a crowd milled on the pavement. The sight of them made her want to weep. These were the people who had gotten out alive, and there were so many of them. Maybe it was everybody.

Still running, Justine followed Charles and Jerry toward the crowd. Two people broke away from the others, a tall man and a petite woman. The man pointed at Georgette and cried out, "That's her! The one who told me to blow the whistle. She got out!" A cheer erupted.

The woman ran toward them, calling out, "Justine! Georgette! You're okay!" and Justine saw that she was Darlene. As she neared them, Darlene skidded to a halt in front of the wheelchair where Georgette sat on Jerry's lap, head lolling against his shoulder. She reached an uncertain hand out to touch the brunette hair escaping from its chignon, and Georgette whispered something that sounded like, "Hey."

"Jerry?" Darlene asked. "Is she okay?"

"She will be. I'll make sure."

Sam-the-Timekeeper sidled up and said, "That one's got nerve, and she's got heart. She'll be back to herself soon enough."

Then Darlene threw her arms around Justine and started to cry. "We were looking for you."

Candace stepped out of the crowd, with Sonny behind her. Nelle, Nadine, Della, Betty, and Shirley followed. More and more carbon-dusted people approached, and the sight of them put a lump in Justine's throat.

Scanning their faces, she caught Darlene's eye and murmured, "Mavis?"

"Not yet. We're still hoping."

A stocky man hustled toward the wheelchair, saying, "This is the one? The woman in the wheelchair? She's the one who raised the alarm and got us out before the bombs blew?"

He wore a light gray business suit, double-breasted with wide lapels, and Justine would have known him anywhere. This was Andrew Higgins, the man whose boats won D-Day.

He nodded pleasantly at Justine, but his eyes were on Georgette. "Somebody here must know first aid. This woman is injured."

Justine heard Georgette mumble, "...just fine...I'm fine..."

From beneath Georgette, Jerry said, "Actually, sir, I know first aid. She's conscious and lucid. Her pulse and respiration are good. I saw her fall and she hit her head pretty hard, but her shoulder took most of the blow."

"That's a lot of medical information to gather while you're being wheeled at top speed away from a disaster. Well done." Higgins shook Jerry's hand.

Raising her head, Georgette said, "Don't forget Justine. She…" And her voice drifted away again.

Realizing that Justine and Charles were standing there, he shook their hands, too. Then he clasped one of Georgette's hands in both of his and said, "We all owe you a great deal."

Georgette opened her eyes and focused them on his face. This time, her words came more clearly. "…the least I could do. Sir."

Justine watched it all. She did her best to store up every detail of Georgette's big moment, so that she could describe it to her and, perhaps someday, describe it to Georgette's parents and to her brothers.

———

Justine sat in the back seat of Jerry's car, and Georgette lay stretched out with her head in Justine's lap. Every time the car hit a rough patch on the Chef Menteur Highway, Georgette groaned. She cradled her left arm tight against her side, and Justine couldn't tell if it was her ribs, her arm, her head, or her shoulder hurting her. She was glad they were headed for the nearest emergency room.

"We'll be at the hospital soon, and the doctors'll fix you right up."

"I see you're talkin' to me now." Georgette looked up at Justine with an unreadable expression.

"I'm sorry. I'm so sorry. I didn't want to hurt you, but I was afraid that I was dangerous to be around. I was afraid of...of this." Justine gestured at the blood in Georgette's hair and the bruised shoulder peeking through the torn shoulder of her sodden coveralls.

"It sure does take a lot to get your attention, *chère*. Blood. Bruises. Bombs. Guns. Factory whistles. A whole heckuva lot of water. I gotta remember that."

"I don't know why you'd want my attention, after the way I behaved. I'm a terrible friend."

"I wouldn't say that. You're real good at talking about uraniums for hours and hours. And spec-TRAH-scopy. You made sure I knew how to say that. I bet there's women waiting in line to be your friend, just so's they can brush up on their algebra."

Jerry looked over his shoulder and his white teeth flashed. Charles kept his eyes on the road, but she heard a short laugh before he managed to smother it.

Georgette cut her eyes in their direction. "I guess I need to be careful what I say in front of a couple of spies."

Now there was dead silence in the front seat. Justine felt her eyebrows reach for her hairline.

"How ignorant do you people think I am? Somebody tries to blow up a plant full of military secrets, and them two just happen to be standing there with their guns. And you right there with 'em? And the three of you standing there, as quiet as my old corncob baby dolls, while Mr. Higgins gives me all the credit for saving everybody? It's a good thing I was too beat up to talk right then, or I would've given away the whole show."

Nobody answered her.

"That's okay. Y'all take me to the hospital and get me patched up, and make sure you get me some painkilling happy pills, because I'm gonna make Justine explain everything that just happened. I'll probably need them pills to get through all her talk about 'uranium isotopes' and 'nuclear fissions.'"

The car kept rolling down Chef Menteur Highway and the silence held.

Georgette sighed and said, "The less y'all talk, the more I know I'm right."

Chapter 34

"How's your arm? It should be healing up by now. It's been a week."

Charles—or whatever his name really was—reached for Justine's right arm. They stopped their stroll along the riverfront wharves as he examined the pink blotch that Martin's sabotage had burned into her forearm.

"It's fine. Why are you so worried about my arm? I'm still bruised from the back of my head to my heels. Martin banged me around pretty good before you got around to shooting him."

"Bruises heal. Even broken bones heal. But if that little burn leaves a scar, it'll be a problem for undercover assignments."

"Because spies can't afford to have identifying marks?"

He shrugged and said, "Yes, but I prefer to call myself an agent."

"Do you prefer to call yourself Charles? Is that your secret agent name?"

He laughed and shook his head. "It's just a name I use. My secret agent name, if you must know, is Mudcat."

"Mudcat? Is that code for something that I don't understand? And are you supposed to tell me that?"

"I'm gambling that you're going to decide to join us. Mudcat?

I gave myself that name when I moved"—he gestured at everything around them as they strolled along the wharves that lined the Mississippi River—"when I moved here."

The waterfront was like a beehive with workers running in all directions, carrying loads of fruit and wheelbarrows full of iced-down oysters, but Charles didn't seem interested. He was looking at the river. "The fisherman around here tell me that there are tremendous catfish at the bottom of the river, very old. And carnivorous, or so they say. They make their way in the world by foraging on the muddy bottom. My job makes me feel like a mudcat, so I took that as a code name when I moved here."

Justine noticed that he had said a lot of words, but none of them was his real name. She studied the fading pink blotch on her arm. "So would an identifying scar disqualify me from this job you want me to take? The one that I haven't accepted yet?"

"No, but you would spend your whole career trying to hide it. So keep some ointment on it and keep it out of the sun."

He took her arm, rolled her blouse sleeve down, and focused on buttoning the cuff. She wondered if he had any idea how long it had taken her to decide what to wear for a casual walk with a man she wished she knew better. In the end, she'd borrowed the celery green blouse he was buttoning from Georgette, tucking it into a pair of wide-legged black pants that billowed in the river breeze.

The necklace she was wearing, an intricately carved circle of forest-green malachite hanging from a fine gold chain, came out of Gloria's jewelry box. Her godmother had tenderly clasped it around her neck and told her to keep it as a souvenir of her adventure. With her next breath, she had told her that a silly necklace was nothing to cry about, even as she wiped away Justine's tears.

All told, Justine thought that Georgette's blouse and Gloria's necklace looked quite nice with her billowy trousers, but Charles gave no sign of noticing. She guessed that his diffident courtship and his jealous rage over her date with Martin had all been an act.

Never fall for a spy, she told herself.

She wasn't ready to talk about this career he wanted her to have, so she deflected.

"What do we know about how Martin came to be here, trying to blow us all up?"

"The Germans have been using U-boats to drop off agents on our shores for years. We know this because we picked up two groups of them in 1942 in New York and Florida. The government told the newspapers that we'd caught them all, but that wasn't quite true. Even before Pearl Harbor, we knew that the Germans were working to put agents here and they never stopped. Logic says that they haven't all been caught. We heard in early 1941 that Martin had come ashore in Florida, and we've been on his trail ever since. Jerry and I are here because our organization's intelligence said that the missing spy—the one we know as Martin—was assigned to infiltrate the Higgins plants. Unfortunately, we were missing important information like who he was or what he looked like or even which plant he was targeting. We might have figured out that Martin was the man eventually, but he wasn't even our top suspect until we saw the way he went after you. He wanted you as an agent the same way that we did. And he needed you bad, since he was working alone."

"Is that why you behaved so terribly at The TickTock?"

"He was getting too close to you. I needed time to gain your trust."

"By trying to start a fight with my date? I never wanted to see you again after that night."

He chuckled. "Unscrupulous men use tactics like that to attract women all the time. They do something that scares their target, then they make a big apology and say that they can't help themselves when they're so much in love. If you alternate affection, anger, and lies long enough, you can confuse someone until they don't even know what they feel."

Justine had no doubt that she'd been confused by both of her volatile suitors, and this had left her off-balance and vulnerable to seductive dreams of romance and escape. Apparently, alternating affection, anger, and lies was a winning strategy. When she realized how perturbed this made her, she said, "You're doing it now, aren't you?"

"Maybe. But it's harder with you. You see through me. Which brings me back to the topic of this conversation—you'd make a great agent. I knew it for sure when you stopped a bar fight with one foot and a table leg, unarmed."

She brushed away his attempt to flatter her and change the subject, simultaneously. "You didn't think it was possible that Martin just wanted me…you know…as a woman, instead of as a super-secret espionage agent?"

There was the crooked grin that had first drawn her to him. "The two things are not mutually exclusive."

He looked away from her, which deprived her of the chance to read his face.

Now he was looking at her again, and the disarming grin was back. This was a man who didn't say everything he was thinking. And he said none of what he was feeling.

"Jerry and I were sure that there was something about Martin that just wasn't right. We were hearing about Carbonites who were suspicious about all the equipment failures and missing tools around them. You only knew about the ones you were called to fix, but there were more."

"I heard those rumors, too."

"Yep. There were lots more. Something wasn't right, and everywhere we turned we saw Martin. And you. I had identified you as someone who could be very useful, but who would be very dangerous under the enemy's control. So had he. Once I realized that, I knew I had to move fast, but it was as if I were competing with my own reflection. When I trailed you, there he was. When I tried to get your attention…um… romantically, there he was. Sometimes, an agent's instincts are the only tool he's got left in his bag, and those instincts said that the muscle-bound, not-real-smart custodian wasn't what he seemed to be."

"Then maybe you're right that I would make a great agent. There was something about all three of you that just wasn't right, but I couldn't figure out which one of you was the spy. As it turned out, all three of you were."

He shot her an appraising look. "We would be interested in you just for that. Your instincts are impeccable."

"How did you know I read braille?"

"Once I knew who your parents were, it took me one chat with the secretary of the Tulane physics department to learn about your mother's eyes. The hardest part was finding a way to get over there. We have an agent at the City Park plant who's in charge of custodial services. Whenever I needed to do some legwork, like go to Tulane, he called my supervisor here and asked him to send me over there to help out. You'd be amazed at how much freedom that's given me to do spy stuff."

"Like talking to gossipy department secretaries? Miss McCann knows all and sees all. And she likes handsome men."

"She misses nothing. And thank you." He stopped, picked up a pebble, and overhanded it into the water.

Shoving his hands in his pockets, he jingled his change. Was this because he was nervous? Or was it a secret agent trick to make her think he was nervous? Justine could see that taking this job would mean being surrounded by people who never let anybody know where they stood. She let him jingle for a moment before asking her next question.

"Was the message poked into that window screen a test?"

"You got it. If you solved it in time to meet me at the appointed time and place, then I'd know you had crackerjack skills. And I'd also know that you were properly cautious. Suspicious, even."

"Because I wouldn't have had time to do that unless I copied the message before you stole it."

He chuckled and changed the subject without admitting to breaking into her room. "Sniffing out three agents hidden among thousands of people—that's a real achievement. If it weren't for you, those bombs would have caught us flatfooted."

"And Georgette."

"Yes, Georgette saved a lot of people with her quick thinking. But without you, the German spy among us would have gotten away."

"Was he really German?"

"Born and bred."

"Then he was quite brilliant with languages. I never heard a word out of him that wasn't unaccented and perfectly idiomatic English."

"He was quite brilliant in a lot of ways."

"Is your German unaccented and perfectly idiomatic, too?"

"My mother was German. My father brought her home from the last war and married her. It wasn't a match made in heaven. I saw my pop often enough to get my fill of his drinking, and that's it. Most of the time, it was just my mother and me. We spoke German at home until I went to school."

"You miss her."

"Yes, but I'm glad she didn't live to see this war. She was so proud to be an American citizen. Seeing her new country at war with Germany again would have killed her."

He launched another rock into the river and changed the subject again.

"We learned a lot when we searched Martin's house. You wouldn't believe the skill and ingenuity that he put into those bombs. If Georgette hadn't set off the sprinkler system that ruined most of his timing devices, things would have been so much worse. People would have died."

We would have died.

"Mavis did die."

Justine had to believe that Mavis had never intended to put her many, many coworkers in danger, because why then would she have given up her life for just five of them? Mavis had done the things she did based on Martin's lies, and Justine was well aware what a consummate liar he had been. She grieved for her friend.

His eyes were sad. "I would give anything to go back and find a way to save Mavis. She was in over her head. Jerry and I should have seen it. Mr. Higgins is torn up over what happened to her. He's put money in an account to help Mavis's mother take care of the kids, so they'll always have the things they need. They'll never know that her death was anything but an accident. But they won't have their mother, and that tears me up."

And then he maneuvered the conversation back toward a discussion of what a spiffy spy he thought she'd make. "Without you, Mavis wouldn't have been the only one who died. The plant would have been badly damaged, maybe beyond repair. It might have burned down completely. Thanks to you, it mostly just got wet. I'm sure you know how much the Allies need those boats and planes."

And apparently they need some oddly shaped contraptions made out of metal and carbon, but nobody wants to talk about those.

"But I don't think he was targeting the boats and planes," she said. "They were there and he was happy to blow them up, but the sabotage I knew about was all focused on the Carbon Division. Was I right? Are we building parts for some kind of atomic device that will—"

He held up a hand. "I don't think you should tell me about that. My clearance doesn't cover it. There are going to be some very high-level people investigating how Martin knew the importance of the Carbonites' work."

"We were locked behind closed doors. We took oaths of silence. They flew our products out by airplane. It wasn't hard to figure out."

"Not for you. The Carbon Division will barely miss a beat, thanks to you—"

"And Georgette and Mavis."

"Thanks to all of you, the Carbon Division—the whole factory, really—was barely touched by Martin's sabotage. It'll take a little effort to put everything back in shape after the sprinklers wet it all down, but the plant will be back online in days."

Charles/Mudcat cleared his throat and added, "We've also got people with higher clearances than mine poring over every one of the many, many papers Martin left behind in his house. They're encrypted, of course, but my superiors believe that Martin lost touch with Germany shortly after the Normandy invasion last June. After that, he kept gathering information on Higgins's operations, and he continued with the sabotage he originally was sent to do while he decided what to do next. We think that sabotage included the incident that killed Cora Becker and wounded Al Haskins and Yolanda Bergeron. In the end, I think he was doing exactly what I'd do if I were ever marooned behind enemy lines. I'd try to stay alive and undetected. I'd find a way to communicate with people who might be able to help me, even if it meant blowing up a prime target to let them know I was alive. And I'd try to create a life I could live with if I never got to go home again.

My guess is that Martin saw you as someone who could help him make that life worth living."

She could see that he'd given thought to the unimaginable. What would it be like to be trapped behind enemy lines forever?

"I'm authorized to tell you that we found paperwork dated 1941 ordering him to…" His voice grew softer. "The Germans had identified your parents' research as particularly dangerous. Eliminating them gave the Axis scientists more time to catch up with what our research program was doing. We have to presume that he did something—sabotaged their brakes or, more likely, crowded them off the road—to cause their deaths. I'm very sorry."

Justine knew that it was wrong to be happy that someone was dead, but she was going to choose to be wrong about this one thing.

"We found more than bombs at his house, you know. Maybe I shouldn't tell you, because it changes nothing, but his passion for you was real. He had one of these"—Charles slipped a tiny camera out of his sleeve, just for a moment, then slid it back where it had come from—"and he used it. He had folders full of photographs of the spots where he planned to place his bombs, but a lot of his other photographs were of you. In the plant. Getting on the bus. Walking down the street. Just you."

The thought of someone unseen watching her move through the world left Justine chilled.

"They were beautiful photos, really." Charles's voice was kind. He took a close look at her face and said, "You look pale. Let's sit."

She didn't need to sit, but she let him lead her to a quiet wooden dock where they could dangle their feet over the water.

Settling herself on the old boards, she said, "I'm fine. I'm just… disturbed…by the idea of somebody following me around with a camera." She whipped her head around to face him. "Wait. Did you follow me around with a camera?"

"No, of course not." He looked down at her, blue eyes smiling through his wire-rimmed spectacles. "Well, okay, I did a little following, and I took a picture or two, but I didn't need to do much of that. I knew who you were. I knew who your parents were. By the time I'd spent five minutes with you, I knew that we needed someone like you." He stopped himself. "No, not someone like you. We need *you*. The combination of your science knowledge and your initiative and your curiosity and…heck…you even speak German. And you weld. We need you, Justine."

"For what? Sniffing around munitions factories and hoping it will be obvious if there are any spies hanging around?"

"No, not factories this time. We get a constant flow of encrypted messages from both the European and Pacific theaters, and it seems like our enemies change their codes on a daily basis, just to keep us on our toes. You'd fit right in as a codebreaker. We've got a job already lined up for you."

"Don't you people believe in training? You're planning to just drop me into an assignment and see if I survive?"

"In wartime, we do what we have to do. Somebody will be looking out for you."

"You?"

"Maybe."

His refusal to be pinned down on anything was infuriating, so she just pressed her lips together and stared at him. If he wasn't going to say anything useful to her, then she'd be damned if she'd do more than that for him.

After a few breaths, he broke the silence. "Jerry said you were cooler under fire than anyone he'd ever seen. And Jerry's seen a lot."

"The wheelchair's a fake, isn't it?"

He shook his head. "No. Why do you say that?"

"He keeps his lunchbox and thermos on the top shelf in his shed. There's no way he can reach it sitting down."

"You have the eye of an agent. No, Jerry's not faking it. If he was, there'd have been two bullets in Martin's heart, but his gun was on the ground when the moment came and he couldn't get to it. He can stand when he needs to, but that's about it. And not for long. He has braces and crutches he uses now and then to get around, but mostly he's in that chair. Do you remember the long metal beam hanging across his shed?"

"The shop crane?"

"Yes. Jerry uses it as a chin-up bar. You know, to keep his upper body in shape. He puts things like that Thermos bottle on the top shelf because it gives him an excuse to do one-armed chin-ups when he needs to get them back down."

She made him wait for another few breaths while she thought about what she wanted him to tell her. The breeze brought scents from cargo that had been shipped in from all over the world and other cargo that was on its way out. Bananas. Fish. Cinnamon.

"What about your ear? Can you hear out of it or was that a lie?"

"Nope. It wasn't a lie. Can't you tell?"

She looked at the way his head was canted in her direction. The asymmetry carried all the way through his body, starting with his crooked smile. One shoulder was lower than the other. He stood with his weight on his left leg. And all of it was so that he could hold his right ear closer to her lips.

"I do see it now."

"I had a bad ear infection when I was a kid. It perforated my eardrum and I can't hear a thing on that side. I tried to bluff my way into the Army, but they caught it and sent me home. The next day, there was a man on my doorstep who said, 'Son, we're very interested in your scores on those tests you took at the enrollment center. We think you're smart. We think you're sneaky. We think you'd be a helluva codebreaker. We think we can use you.' I had to make the same decision I'm asking you to make. I said yes. I also told them about my friend Jerry, a mechanical genius whose legs had kept him out of the Army. The rest is history."

"Do you get a commission when you recruit an agent?"

He laughed. "No, but I gain a colleague who just might keep me alive. And I gain somebody who can help make our efforts successful. I do believe in what I do. Will you join us?"

"I have another option, you know. Mr. Higgins has promised me a job as an apprentice with the engineering group that designs airplanes. He's already got Georgette set up with a job in book-keeping, where she can learn what she needs to know before she starts a management training program."

"I—we, that is—can offer you so much more."

"That may well be, but I've given the matter a lot of thought and I have some conditions." At his surprised look, she said, "You're pushing me pretty hard to do this. I must be worth something. Why should I sell myself short?"

He acknowledged her question with a nod and said, "So tell me your conditions."

"Georgette comes, too."

He had the composure not to sputter, but it took him a moment to speak. "Georgette doesn't have...she's not...you have the potential to..."

"She only has an eighth-grade education. So what? I dropped out of twelfth grade when my parents died. Neither of us have any pieces of paper to say that we've learned things. You just have to take us for who we are. Maybe you could give Georgette some of those tests the Army gave you. I think she would surprise you."

"Your German is amazingly useful, and she can't offer that."

"She speaks French."

He looked like he hadn't expected as much from an unedu-cated country girl, but said, "That's not quite the same."

"And she speaks Choctaw."

This time his mouth fell open. "Say that in my right ear? Choctaw speakers are worth more than gold."

"Because there's an extra layer of encryption to a message sent in a language only spoken by a few people, pretty much all of them living in this country?"

"That's supposed to be a secret."

"When she told me how hard the military recruited her brothers and how hush-hush their work had suddenly become, I knew they had something special that the military wanted. I thought their language skills might be what it was. I guess I was right."

"We've been using people who speak languages indigenous to the Americas since the last war and we can use more. But maybe Georgette would rather take the management job at Higgins and stay here, so she can be near her family."

"That may be, but it's her decision to make. And I think you underestimate how much my friend craves adventure."

He shrugged and held out his hands, as if to say, "I give up."

"Okay. Georgette has a job if she wants it. Will you say yes now?"

The wind was bringing her the scent of some unnameable spice. It smelled faraway. It smelled secret. It smelled like something she'd sail a thousand miles to taste.

"I said 'conditions.' I have one more."

"I'm afraid to ask."

"I'm not going anywhere unless Gloria gets a job."

Again, his mouth fell open.

"Wait a minute. You have to know that our agents must be rock-solid stable. We can't have…Gloria could never get the clearances she needs."

"There's nothing wrong with Gloria that your people didn't cause. Yes, she's had times in the past when she was sad. Lots of people get sad. If you'd left your family at fifteen, knowing you'd never see them again, you'd be sad, too. But her grip on reality was solid until you people started fooling around in her life. Assigning a neighbor to snoop on her. Tapping her phone. Putting money in her bank account. Sneaking extra change into her grocery bags. Anybody would start looking over their shoulder for the people who were out to get them."

His tone grew defensive. "We had to make sure she was taken care of, financially. She knew too much about that weapons program nobody wants to tell me about, and her teaching job wasn't reliable. She would have been an easy target for an enemy agent trying to learn our secrets."

"She had just lost the two people closest to her in the world. Her friends had moved away." Justine swallowed. "I ran away. Who wouldn't be a little erratic after that? The fact that she didn't utterly collapse is an argument for her strength as a human being."

His voice was gentle. "I never questioned her strength, nor her value as a human being."

"Gloria doesn't need a job where she infiltrates enemy bases and carries a gun. Her life is all about learning things and teaching them to other people." She paused, taken aback. "Will I carry a gun?"

"Maybe. Probably."

This was disconcerting, but Justine knew that she could handle deadly weapons. When she welded, she held one in each hand.

She resumed badgering an agent of the United States government. "Gloria's a researcher and a teacher. Put her to work training your agents in all the new science they're going to be protecting. Give her a laboratory and she'll work wonders for you. Give her a security clearance and a secure phone line, so I can call her when I need help with a job."

She took a breath, but went right back to talking. This was too important to let him interrupt her. "Gloria loves this country the same way your mother loved it. It took her in when she was hungry. Let her serve it. Leaving her to rot alone in her house would be a terrible waste."

"I think I can pull some strings. If you say yes, Gloria gets a job."

Years later, Justine would realize that this was the moment when she should have known that this man was more than he seemed, but she had no knowledge of the Byzantine hierarchies in a secretive federal agency. On that afternoon by the Mississippi River, she was just very glad that she could get Gloria back in a lab of her own. And she couldn't wait to tell Georgette about the places they would go and the people they would see. They were going to have more adventures than a little girl from Des Allemands could have ever dreamed.

"So is it a yes?"

Justine's negotiations were complete, but there was one more thing she wanted before she committed herself.

"Until I say yes, you're not my colleague or my boss, right? You're just...well, you're not Charles. You're just Mudcat."

"Right."

Without another word, she put her hand on his cheek, turned his face fully toward hers, and kissed him. Slowly, his arms encircled her as he returned her kiss. Never again would Justine smell bananas or pineapples or fresh fish or the musical scent of allspice without remembering that moment.

She drew her face away from his and said, "Okay. I'll serve. We'll be coworkers. Fellow agents. I think we'll work well together, Mudcat."

Leaning close, so that the fishers and the dockworkers and the birds and the fish couldn't hear, he whispered in her ear.

"My name is Paul."

AUTHOR'S NOTE

HISTORICAL BACKGROUND: THE HOME FRONT

Novelists and filmmakers began telling stories about World War II before the war was over and before anybody even knew how it would end. These movies and films have often focused on the experiences of the people on the battlefield, as most war stories do. The experiences of the people left behind are less often told, and some of them are in danger of being lost to time. While writing *The Physicists' Daughter*, I listened to oral histories and read the stories of people on the American home front, many of them women, who did far more than wait by the mailbox for word of their faraway, endangered loved ones.

These women built airplanes, cracked military codes, separated uranium for the first atomic bombs, managed households single-handedly while necessities were rationed, and much more, and they did it at a time when many could not even own a bank account. They did it in a world shadowed by a war that touched everyday lives in the United States in ways that aren't always depicted in novels and films about World War II. People on North Carolina beaches watched and listened as submarines sunk American ships. German spies came ashore in Florida and New York. A Japanese submarine bombarded coastal targets near Santa Barbara. Blackouts and air raid drills across the nation drove home the notion that the oceans weren't a fail-safe protection against attack.

Through it all, women held down the home front. The familiar image of Rosie the Riveter reminds us that they built the war machines that won the war, but what was Rosie's life like? The legend of Rosie the Riveter begins and ends with the image of her flexing the muscles she used to get her job done. In *The Physicists' Daughter*, I have tried to give readers more of Rosie in the form of the protagonist, Justine Byrne. Justine, the orphaned daughter of two physicists, brings a specialized expertise to her work that nobody expects a woman to have, and this is very bad news for the Nazis.

PUTTING JUSTINE INTO CONTEXT: FROM WOMEN IN WAR WORK TO LADIES IN THE LAB

Even before World War II, women were pioneering the twentieth-century science that changed the world. Marie Curie is justifiably famous for her pioneering research in radioactivity, but the contributions of other women are too little-known. Curie's daughter Irène Joliot-Curie was a co-discoverer of artificial radioactivity. Lise Meitner was a co-discoverer of nuclear fission. Their work paved the way for the nuclear bombs that ended the war.

My protagonist, Justine Byrne, is literally the descendant of this generation of female scientists. Her parents, like Marie and Pierre Curie and Irène and Frédéric Joliot-Curie, were scientists, colleagues, and life partners, and Justine has been raised to see her future in the laboratory with them. Her parents taught her physics from the time she could talk. They taught her to weld and to blow glass so that she could craft her own laboratory equipment. They made sure that she could speak German so that she could communicate with important thinkers in the field and read their work, but her dreams of college and then a lifetime in science are dashed when they die in a car accident before she even finishes high school.

Resilient and determined, Justine takes work in a munitions factory, where the war means that she can hold a job normally reserved for men and collect a man's paycheck. What her employer—and her unseen adversary—don't realize is that her knowledge of physics means that there are secrets that they can't keep from Justine. She knows that she is not building what her boss says she's building, and she can tell that someone is trying to sabotage her work.

It doesn't pay to underestimate a woman like Justine. The Nazis are no match for the physicists' daughter.

READING GROUP GUIDE

1. What do you think it would be like to love a spy? What complications would that kind of relationship endure?

2. In the 1940s, intelligence wasn't always considered an attractive trait in a woman. Men could find intelligence off-putting, and women's social groups might reject a girl seen as smart. Did that part of Justine's story feel realistic to you? Do you think this situation has changed today?

3. Did you solve Paul's message to Justine?

4. Have you ever really thought about what it meant to be unable to open a bank account because of your sex? Have you experienced that? If so, how did you manage?

5. Do you know or remember women who would have been adults during WWII? (Or perhaps you remember those years, in which case I think you should lead your group's discussion.) Did those women ever talk about their experiences? How do you think it affected them to be competently running a

welding machine and/or a household and/or a family budget, only to be told to step back and hand over those responsibilities when the men came home?

6. Did the descriptions of the physics underpinning the events in *The Physicists' Daughter* make sense to you? Did the story leave you interested in learning more about real-life twentieth-century science?

A CONVERSATION WITH THE AUTHOR

How did you come up with the idea to write *The Physicists' Daughter*? **What most excited you as a writer about telling Justine's story?**

When I heard that World War II was called "The Physicists' War," my first thought was "Of course, it was!" So much science was being done during those years, with radar, sonar, rockets, the atomic bomb, and more being developed literally as the war was happening. It made me think that there must be fascinating stories to tell about that period of time from the point of view of the scientists behind the scenes. I have also always been interested in the lives of women during that time as they were thrust into roles that had been denied to them. They had to step up under enormous pressure, while continuing to meet their responsibilities at home, and all the while they knew that they would be pushed aside when the war was over. When I imagined one of those Rosie-the-Riveter women as a scientist whose specialized knowledge of the secret work that she was doing told her that she was being lied to, I knew I had my story.

How did your scientific background inform the content of the novel?

I had so much fun delving into the workings of the real-life top-secret project that was the model for *The Physicists' Daughter*. The drawings for that project are, astonishingly enough, now available on the internet for anybody to read. I have always believed that science is for everybody, so it's important to me to interpret it in a way that is accurate yet also entertaining and understandable to the lay reader. I can describe to you the path of two ion streams in a magnetic field, or I can compare it to a rainbow. The rainbow immediately puts the image that I want in the reader's mind, so that's how I have Justine perceive it.

Who was your favorite character to write? Why?

I love Justine. She's a truth-seeker, completely without guile, and she is capable of absolute love. Still, it's hard for me to use the word "favorite." I'm always fascinated by characters who say things I don't know they're going to say, and in this book, that's Georgette. And then there are the spies. When I'm writing in their point of view, they reveal their depths, but when I'm writing from the point of view of the person they're manipulating, they button everything down. It's a very special challenge to write about a chameleon because the person still has to be a consistent human being. There are some lies that even a spy won't tell.

What are you reading now?

Sisterhood of Spies by Elizabeth P. McIntosh, who was a spy for the OSS during World War II. I'm reading it as research for Justine's next adventure.

What's next for you in your writing?

I'm sending Justine to Washington, DC, where the government desperately needs her skills as a code cracker.

ACKNOWLEDGMENTS

I'd like to thank all the people who helped make *The Physicists' Daughter* happen. Tony Ain, Erin Garmon, Michael Garmon, Amanda Evans, Rachel Broughten, Anne Hawkins, Moses Cardona, Barbara Peters, Paolo Amoroso, and Adam Hyland read it in manuscript, and their comments were incredibly enlightening. Paolo and Adam, in particular, were hugely helpful in helping me contextualize this fictional narrative with the real-life history of science and technology. My sister Suzanne Quin, who earned her PhD in chemistry with a dissertation on separation methods, helped me with the history of mass spectroscopy and listened to me burble when I found an affordable first edition of J. J. Thomson's *Recollections and Reflections* on eBay. Kali Martin, a research historian at the National WWII Museum in New Orleans, provided valuable assistance to my efforts to learn about the activities of Higgins Industries' Carbon Division. The National WWII Museum's collection of oral histories let me hear the voices of women working on the home front during World War II, and its wartime photographs of the Michaud plant helped me visualize Justine's workplace. The WPA's 1938 *New Orleans City Guide* gave me a roughly contemporaneous glimpse of Justine's hometown, including the nightlife depicted in my imaginary TickTock Club. Jerry Strahan's book, *Andrew Jackson Higgins and the Boats that Won World War II*, gave me insight into Andrew Higgins's innovative designs and into the hard work of the people who made them real. These people helped me avoid many errors, and any that slipped through the process are all mine.

As always, I am grateful for the people who help me get my work ready to go out into the world, the people who send it out into the world, and the people who help readers find it. Many thanks go to my agent, Anne Hawkins, and to the wonderful people at Sourcebooks and Poisoned Pen Press who do such a good job for us, their writers. Because I can trust that my editors, Anna Michels and Diane DiBiase, and my copy editor, Beth Deveny, will help me make my work shine, I can stretch myself creatively and try new things. That's a wonderful place for a writer to be, especially when writing something as different from my previous books as this one is. Molly Waxman, Mandy Chahal, and Anna Venckus do an amazing job marketing my work and helping it find new readers. I'm also grateful to the University of Oklahoma for providing the opportunity for me to teach a new generation of authors while continuing to write books of my own.

And, of course, I am always (always!) grateful for you, my readers.

ABOUT THE AUTHOR

© Nadia Lombardero

In addition to holding a Master of Fine Arts in creative writing, Mary Anna Evans holds a bachelor of science in engineering physics and a master of science in chemical engineering, and she is a licensed professional engineer. All of these things came in quite handy while writing *The Physicists' Daughter*. She is also the author of the Faye Longchamp Archaeological Mysteries, which have received awards including the Oklahoma Book Award, the Benjamin Franklin Award, and a Will Rogers Medallion Awards Gold Medal. Her essays on science and the environment have appeared in publications including the *Atlantic*'s Technology Channel, *EarthLines*, and *Flyway*. She is an associate professor at the University of Oklahoma, where she teaches fiction and nonfiction writing, and she studies the work of Agatha Christie. She is the coeditor of *Bloomsbury Handbook to Agatha Christie*, to be released in late 2022.